Senior Sleuths:
A Large Print Anthology of
Mysteries and Puzzlers

Senior Sleuths:
A Large Print Anthology of
Mysteries and Puzzlers

EDITED BY

Isaac Asimov, Martin H. Greenberg and Carol-Lynn Rössel Waugh

G.K.HALL &CO.
Boston, Massachusetts
1989

G.K. Hall Large Print Book Series.

Set in 18 pt Plantin.

Library of Congress Cataloging in Publication Data

Senior sleuths : a large print anthology of mysteries and puzzlers /
  edited by Isaac Asimov, Martin H. Greenberg, and Carol-Lynn Rössel
  Waugh.
        p.   cm. -- (G.K. Hall large print book series)
    ISBN 0-8161-4854-6
    1. Detective and mystery stories, American. 2. Detective and mystery
stories, English. 3. Large type books. I. Asimov, Isaac, 1920– .
II. Greenberg, Martin Harry. III. Waugh, Carol-Lynn Rössel.
[PS648.D4S4 1989]
823'.087208--dc20   89-36505

Contents

Introduction

SHARPNESS AT THE END

ISAAC ASIMOV

FICTIONAL DETECTIVES come in all varieties. Either sex. Any occupation—from policeman and private detective down to bookseller, or academician. They can also come in any age.

For instance, I have written three series of murder mysteries. In one of them, my sleuth is Larry, who goes to junior high school and is, perhaps, fourteen years old. In another, my sleuth is Henry, who is a waiter and about sixty years old. In a third, my sleuth is Griswold, who is a retired intelligence agent and is at least seventy years old.

What's more, the age of the sleuth in my series doesn't change. Larry has been going to junior high school for about ten years now, despite the fact that he's a very bright kid. Henry has been at it for twenty years and I specifically described him as "sixtyish" to begin with. Now, I still describe him as "sixtyish" and, in fact, I am aggressive about it. I frequently write brief commentaries on my stories and in one of them I stated flatly that I did not intend to have Henry *ever* grow older. The result is that when I started the series about him, he was some ten years older than I was, and now he's about ten years younger than I am. He was a venerable figure at the start, and now I view him as a kid. I am rapidly closing in on Griswold's age, too.

I'm not the only one with problems about my sleuths' ages, either. Consider Nero Wolfe. My guess is that he was about fifty when he started his career with *Fer-de-Lance* in (I believe) 1934. Forty years later, he was still about fifty. What's more, he weighed a seventh of a ton (286 pounds) and in all those four decades of fifty-ness, he never suffered from heart trouble or diabetes or, if I remember correctly, even as much as had a cold or indigestion. I don't think that's fair.

Archie Goodwin is even worse. He was perhaps twenty-five when he first went to work for Nero Wolfe and forty years later, I should think he was pushing thirty, and he was still a devil with the women.

Or consider Hercule Poirot. In his first effort, *The Mysterious Affair at Styles*, published in 1920, he was already retired and commenting in a rueful way about his age. He was perhaps sixty-five. By the time of his last appearance, he must have been 115, but you'd never guess it. In fact, he kept speaking less about his age, as though trying not to draw attention to it.

Of course, time doesn't always stand still for sleuths. Ellery Queen definitely grew older with time, and so, I think, did Lord Peter Wimsey.

But the question is not whether time stands still or gallops. The question is: why do sleuths come in a wide variety of ages?

There are practical answers to this. If you want a detective who has to engage in feats of derring-do, plunge into fisticuffs, imitate a circus performer in the course of a pursuit of a criminal, then you need someone who's in the prime of life.

On the other hand, if you're trying to appeal to an audience of children, you would want your detective to be as young as you can reasonably make him. Youngsters will feel a greater kinship with him, can more easily daydream of being sleuths themselves, and so on.

But where's the advantage of an elderly sleuth? Why on earth should we want an old guy pottering about?

Actually, I think there's something extremely important about age. In the first place, we can eliminate certain things. First, we don't have to get the sleuth involved in strenuous activities. Hercule Poirot exemplified this best. He always laughed rather contemptuously at Sherlockian detectives who studied cigarette ends through their magnifying glasses, or searched the shrubbery for footprints. For himself, it was just the "little gray cells" and, you know, that's *so* impressive.

Secondly, we don't have to worry about love interest for the sleuth. You can still have it as a secondary plot, involving secondary characters, but your sleuth can remain fancy-free. The reader doesn't have to waste emotion but can concentrate on the puzzle, on the suspense, on the mentality of it all.

But do we really want to eliminate action and romance? Yes, in mysteries, we sometimes do, and I will explain why.

We are all of us going to die someday and we know it. We may prefer not to think of it. We may prefer to live each day on the assumption that we'll live forever, but back us up against the wall and say, "All right. Are you going to die someday?" The answer has to be "Yes."

There are, however, different ways of dying. You can die suddenly, while still capable of leading a thoroughly normal life. You can have a heart attack or a stroke and within minutes it may be all over. (In fact, when Julius Caesar was asked, "What is the best death?" he answered, "A sudden one." And, of course, that's the kind he got.)

Such a sudden death may come at 40 or at 90, but you don't have time to feel dismay at having been cheated of fifty years, or glee at having been handed it. It's over before you have time to sort out your emotions.

But deaths don't have to be sudden. They can be slow, too, and in either of two different ways. You can be immobilized physically, by arthritis, by a feeble heart, by a wide variety of degenerative ailments. You may be in a wheelchair, as a result, or bedridden. This is certainly an unpleasant fate, but one can well imagine that, as long as the brain is alive, alert, and functioning efficiently, the essential *you* is still there even if the carrier we call the body has broken down.

Suppose, though, it is the brain that goes. Perhaps your body is still in reasonably good shape, but the memory vanishes, the reasoning faculty slips away, the *you* disappears and the body is vacant and untenanted for perhaps years. It may come on slowly, so that we know that it is happening. And even if we don't know, or we gradually cease knowing as the situation deteriorates, it is something we must look forward to as a possibility with a certain uneasiness.

Especially if one makes one's living or attains one's happiness through mental agility, the advance of age makes every bit of forgetfulness, every lapse of memory, every grope for a word that's on the "tip of your tongue," every loss of a name you ought to know, serve as a frightening and unwelcome reminder of how horrible the result might be.

To read of elderly sleuths, then, of the Hercule Poirots, the Father Browns, or even the aging Sherlock Holmes, and to realize that they are still as sharp as ever, still as impossible to fool, still capable of forging that inexorable chain of logic, is inexpressibly comforting.

It's what we want out of life, the assurance that there is at least *some* reasonable chance of living into old age with a neatly functioning brain. To have sharpness at the end is to rob death of much of its terror, and that is what the "senior sleuths" in the collection of stories you are now holding in your hand are assuring you is possible.

Relax and enjoy, and tell yourself that there are good years up ahead.

The Case of the Perfect Maid[*]

AGATHA CHRISTIE

"Oh, if you please, madam, could I speak to you a moment?"

It might be thought that this request was in the nature of an absurdity, since Edna, Miss Marple's little maid, was actually speaking to her mistress at the moment.

Recognizing the idiom, however, Miss Marple said promptly, "Certainly, Edna. Come in and shut the door. What is it?"

Obediently shutting the door, Edna advanced into the room, pleated the corner of her apron between her fingers, and swallowed once or twice.

"Yes, Edna?" said Miss Marple encouragingly.

"Oh, please, ma'am, it's my cousin Gladdie. You see, she's lost her place."

"Dear me, I am sorry to hear that. She

[*]Note: This story has also been published under the title "The Perfect Maid."

1

was at Old Hall, wasn't she, with the Miss—Misses—Skinner?"

"Yes, ma'am, that's right, ma'am. And Gladdie's very upset about it—very upset indeed."

"Gladys has changed places rather often before, though, hasn't she?"

"Oh yes, ma'am. She's always one for a change, Gladdie is. She never seems to get really settled, if you know what I mean. But she's always been the one to give the notice, you see!"

"And this time it's the other way round?" asked Miss Marple dryly.

"Yes, ma'am, and it's upset Gladdie something awful."

Miss Marple looked slightly surprised. Her recollection of Gladys, who had occasionally come to drink tea in the kitchen on her "days out," was a stout, giggling girl of unshakably equable temperament.

Edna went on: "You see, ma'am, it's the way it happened—the way Miss Skinner looked."

"How," inquired Miss Marple patiently, "did Miss Skinner look?"

This time Edna got well away with her news bulletin.

"Oh, ma'am, it was ever such a shock to

Gladdie. You see, one of Miss Emily's brooches was missing, and such a hue and cry for it as never was, and of course, nobody likes a thing like that to happen; it's upsetting, ma'am. If you know what I mean. And Gladdie's helped search everywhere, and there was Miss Lavinia saying she was going to the police about it, and then it turned up again, pushed right to the back of a drawer in the dressing-table, and very thankful Gladdie was.

"And the very next day as ever was a plate got broken, and Miss Lavinia, she bounced out right away and told Gladdie to take a month's notice. And what Gladdie feels is it couldn't have been the plate and that Miss Lavinia was just making an excuse of that, and that it must be because of the brooch and they think as she took it and put it back when the police was mentioned, and Gladdie wouldn't do such a thing, not never she wouldn't, and what she feels is as it will get round and tell against her, and it's a very serious thing for a girl as you know, ma'am."

Miss Marple nodded. Though having no particular liking for the bouncing, self-opinioned Gladys, she was quite sure of the girl's intrinsic honesty and could well imagine that the affair must have upset her.

Edna said wistfully, "I suppose, ma'am, there isn't anything you could do about it?"

"Tell her not to be silly," said Miss Marple crisply. "If she didn't take the brooch—which I'm sure she didn't—then she has no cause to be upset."

"It'll get about," said Edna dismally.

Miss Marple said, "I—er—am going up that way this afternoon. I'll have word with the Misses Skinner."

"Oh, thank you, madam," said Edna.

Old Hall was a big Victorian house surrounded by woods and park land. Since it had been proved unlettable and unsalable as it was, an enterprising speculator had divided it into four flats with a central hot-water system, and the use of "the grounds" to be held in common by the tenants. The experiment had been satisfactory. A rich and eccentric old lady and her maid occupied one flat. The old lady had a passion for birds and entertained a feathered gathering to meals every day. A retired Indian judge and his wife rented a second. A very young couple, recently married, occupied the third, and the fourth had been taken only two months ago by two maiden ladies of the name of Skinner. The four sets of tenants were only on the most distant terms with each other, since none of them had anything in common. The landlord had been heard to say that this was an excellent thing. What he dreaded were friendships followed by estrangements and subsequent complaints to him.

Miss Marple was acquainted with all the tenants, though she knew none of them well. The elder Miss Skinner, Miss Lavinia, was what might be termed the working member of the firm. Miss Emily, the younger, spent most of her time in bed, suffering from various complaints which, in the opinion of St. Mary Mead, were largely imaginary. Only Miss Lavinia believed devoutly in her sister's martyrdom and patience under affliction and willingly ran errands and trotted up and down to the village for things that "my sister had suddenly fancied."

It was the view of St. Mary Mead that if Miss Emily suffered half as much as she said she did, she would have sent for Dr. Haydock long ago. But Miss Emily, when this was hinted to her, shut her eyes in a superior way and murmured that her case was not a simple one—the best specialists in London had been baffled by it—and that a wonderful new man had put her on a most revolutionary course of treatment and that she really hoped her health would improve under it. No humdrum G.P. could possibly understand her case.

"And it's my opinion," said the outspoken Miss Hartnell, "that she's very wise not to send for him. Dear Dr. Haydock, in that breezy manner of his, would tell her that there was nothing the matter with her and to get up and not make a fuss! Do her a lot of good!"

Failing such arbitrary treatment, however, Miss Emily continued to lie on sofas, to surround herself with strange little pillboxes, and to reject nearly everything that had been cooked for her and ask for something else— usually something difficult and inconvenient to get.

The door was opened to Miss Marple by "Gladdie," looking more depressed than Miss Marple had ever thought possible. In the sitting-room (a quarter of the late drawing-room, which had been partitioned into a dining-room, drawing-room, bathroom, and housemaid's cupboard), Miss Lavinia rose to greet Miss Marple.

Lavinia Skinner was a tall, gaunt, bony female of fifty. She had a gruff voice and an abrupt manner.

"Nice to see you," she said. "Emily's lying down—feeling low today, poor dear. Hope she'll see you—it would cheer her up—but there are times when she doesn't feel up to seeing anybody. Poor dear, she's wonderfully patient."

Miss Marple responded politely. Servants were the main topic of conversation in St. Mary Mead, so it was not difficult to lead the conversation in that direction. Miss Marple said she had heard that that nice girl, Gladys Holmes, was leaving.

Miss Lavinia nodded.

"Wednesday week. Broke things, you know. Can't have that."

Miss Marple sighed and said we all had to put up with things nowadays. It was so difficult to get girls to come to the country. Did Miss Skinner really think it was wise to part with Gladys?

"Know it's difficult to get servants," admitted Miss Lavinia. "The Devereuxs haven't got anybody—but then I don't wonder—always quarrelling, jazz on all night—meals any time—that girl knows nothing of housekeeping. I pity her husband! Then the Larkins have just lost their maid. Of course, what with the judge's temper and his wanting Chota Hazri, as he calls it, at six in the

7

morning, and Mrs. Larkin always fussing, I don't wonder at that, either. Mrs. Carmichael's Janet is a fixture, of course—though in my opinion she's the most disagreeable woman and absolutely bullies the old lady."

"Then don't you think you might reconsider your decision about Gladys. She really is a nice girl. I know all her family; very honest and superior."

Miss Lavinia shook her head.

"I've got my reasons," she said importantly.

Miss Marple murmured: "You missed a brooch, I understand—"

"Now who has been talking? I suppose the girl has. Quite frankly, I'm almost certain she took it. And then got frightened and put it back—but of course one can't say anything unless one is sure." She changed the subject. "Do come and see Miss Emily, Miss Marple. I'm sure it would do her good."

Miss Marple followed meekly to where Miss Lavinia knocked on a door, was bidden enter, and ushered her guest into the best room in the flat, most of the light of which was excluded by half-drawn blinds. Miss Emily was lying in bed, apparently enjoying the half gloom and her own indefinite sufferings.

The dim light showed her to be a thin, indecisive-looking creature, with a good deal of greyish yellow hair untidily wound around her head and erupting into curls, the whole thing looking like a bird's nest of which no self-respecting bird could be proud. There was a smell in the room of eau de cologne, stale biscuits, and camphor.

With half-closed eyes and in a thin, weak voice, Emily Skinner explained that this was "one of her bad days."

"The worst of ill-health is," said Miss Emily in a melancholy tone, "that one knows what a burden one is to everyone around one.

"Lavinia is very good to me. Lavvie dear, I do so hate giving trouble, but if my hot water bottle could only be filled in the way I like it—too full it weighs on me so; on the other hand, if it is not sufficiently filled, it gets cold immediately!"

"I'm sorry, dear. Give it to me. I will empty a little out."

"Perhaps, if you're doing that, it might be refilled. There are no rusks in the house, I suppose—no, no, it doesn't matter. I can do without. Some weak tea and a slice of lemon—no lemons? No, really, I couldn't drink tea without lemon. I think the milk

9

was slightly turned this morning. It has put me right against milk in my tea. It doesn't matter. I can do without my tea. Only I do feel so weak. Oysters, they say, are nourishing. I wonder if I could fancy a few. No, no, too much bother to get hold of them so late in the day. I can fast until tomorrow."

Lavinia left the room murmuring something incoherent about bicycling down to the village.

Miss Emily smiled feebly at her guest and remarked that she did hate giving anyone any trouble.

Miss Marple told Edna that evening that she was afraid her mission had met with no success.

She was rather troubled to find that rumours as to Gladys's dishonesty were already going around the village.

In the post office Miss Wetherby tackled her: "My dear Jane, they gave her a written reference saying she was willing and sober and respectable, but saying nothing about honesty. That seems to me most significant! I hear there was some trouble about a brooch. I think there must be something in it, you know, because one doesn't let a servant go nowadays unless it's something rather grave.

They'll find it most difficult to get anyone else. Girls simply will not go to Old Hall. They're nervous coming home on their days out. You'll see, the Skinners won't find anyone else, and then perhaps that dreadful hypochondriac sister will have to get up and do something!"

Great was the chagrin of the village when it was made known that the Misses Skinner had engaged, from an agency, a new maid who, by all accounts, was a perfect paragon.

"A three years' reference recommending her most warmly, she prefers the country and actually asks less wages than Gladys. I really feel we have been most fortunate."

"Well, really," said Miss Marple, to whom these details were imparted by Miss Lavinia in the fishmonger's shop. "It does seem too good to be true."

It then became the opinion of St. Mary Mead that the paragon would cry off at the last minute and fail to arrive.

None of the prognostications came true, however, and the village was able to observe the domestic treasure, by name, Mary Higgins, driving through the village in Reed's taxi to Old Hall. It had to be admitted that her appearance was good. A most respectable-looking woman, very neatly dressed.

When Miss Marple next visited Old Hall, on the occasion of recruiting stall holders for the Vicarage Fete, Mary Higgins opened the door. She was certainly a most superior-looking maid, at a guess forty years of age, with neat black hair, rosy cheeks, a plump figure discreetly arrayed in black with a white apron and cap—"quite the good, old-fashioned type of servant," as Miss Marple explained afterward, and with the proper, inaudible, respectful voice, so different from the loud but adenoidal accents of Gladys.

Miss Lavinia was looking far less harassed than usual and, although she regretted that she could not take a stall, owing to her preoccupation with her sister, she nevertheless tendered a handsome monetary contribution and promised to produce a consignment of penwipers and babies' socks.

Miss Marple commented on her air of well-being.

"I really feel I owe a great deal to Mary. I am so thankful I had the resolution to get rid of that other girl. Mary is really invaluable. Cooks nicely and waits beautifully and keeps our little flat scrupulously clean—mattresses turned over every day. And she is really wonderful with Emily!"

Miss Marple hastily inquired after Emily.

"Oh, poor dear, she has been very much under the weather lately. She can't help it, of course, but it really makes things a little difficult sometimes. Wanting certain things cooked and then, when they come, saying she can't eat now—and then wanting them again half an hour later and everything spoiled and having to be done again. It makes, of course, a lot of work—but fortunately Mary does not seem to mind at all. She's used to waiting on invalids, she says, and understands them. It is such a comfort."

"Dear me," said Miss Marple. "You are fortunate."

"Yes, indeed. I really feel Mary has been sent to us as an answer to prayer."

"She sounds to me," said Miss Marple, "almost too good to be true. I should—well, I should be a little careful if I were you."

Lavinia Skinner failed to perceive the point of this remark. She said, "Oh, I assure you I do all I can to make her comfortable. I don't know what I should do if she left."

"I don't expect she'll leave until she's ready to leave," said Miss Marple and stared very hard at her hostess.

Miss Lavinia said, "If one has no domestic worries, it takes such a load off one's mind, doesn't it? How is your little Edna shaping?"

13

"She's doing quite nicely. Not like your Mary. Still I do know all about Edna, because she's a village girl."

As she went out into the hall she heard the invalid's voice fretfully raised: "This compress has been allowed to get quite dry—Dr. Allerton particularly said moisture continually renewed. There, there, leave it. I want a cup of tea and a boiled egg—boiled only three minutes and a half, remember, and send Miss Lavinia to me."

The efficient Mary emerged from the bedroom and, saying to Lavinia, "Miss Emily is asking for you, madam," proceeded to open the door for Miss Marple, helping her into her coat and handing her her umbrella in the most irreproachable fashion.

Miss Marple took the umbrella, dropped it, tried to pick it up, and dropped her bag which flew open. Mary politely retrieved various odds and ends—a handkerchief, an engagement book, an old-fashioned leather purse, two shillings, three pennies, and a striped piece of peppermint rock.

Miss Marple received the last with some signs of confusion.

"Oh dear, that must have been Mrs. Clement's little boy. He was sucking it, I remember, and he took my bag to play with.

He must have put it inside. It's terribly sticky, isn't it?"

"Shall I take it, madam?"

"Oh, would you? Thank you so much."

Mary stooped to retrieve the last item, a small mirror, upon recovering which Miss Marple exclaimed fervently, "How lucky now that that isn't broken."

She thereupon departed, Mary standing politely by the door holding a piece of striped rock with a completely expressionless face.

For ten days longer St. Mary Mead had to endure hearing of the excellencies of Miss Lavinia's and Miss Emily's treasure.

On the eleventh day the village awoke to its big thrill.

Mary, the paragon, was missing! Her bed had not been slept in and the front door was found ajar. She had slipped out quietly during the night.

And not Mary alone was missing! Two brooches and five rings of Miss Lavinia's, three rings, a pendant, a bracelet, and four brooches of Miss Emily's were missing also!

It was the beginning of a chapter of catastrophe.

Young Mrs. Devereux had lost her diamonds which she kept in an unlocked drawer and also some valuable furs given to her as a wedding present. The judge and his wife also had had jewelry taken and a certain amount of money. Mrs. Carmichael was the greatest sufferer. Not only had she some very valuable jewels, but she also kept a large sum of money in the flat which had gone. It had been Janet's evening out and her mistress was in the habit of walking round the gardens at dusk, calling to the birds and scattering crumbs. It seemed clear that Mary, the perfect maid, had had keys to fit all the flats!

There was, it must be confessed, a certain amount of ill-natured pleasure in St. Mary Mead. Miss Lavinia had boasted so much of her marvellous Mary.

"And all the time, my dear, just a common thief!"

Interesting revelation followed. Not only had Mary disappeared into the blue, but the agency which had provided her and vouched for her credentials was alarmed to find that the Mary Higgins who had applied to them and whose references they had taken up had, to all intents and purposes, never existed. It was the name of a bona fide servant who had lived with the bona fide sister of a dean, but the real Mary Higgins was existing peacefully in a place in Cornwall.

"Clever, the whole thing," Inspector Slack was forced to admit. "And, if you ask me, that woman works in with a gang. There was a case of much the same kind in Northumberland a year ago. Stuff was never traced and they never caught her. However, we'll do better than that in Much Benham!"

Inspector Slack was always a confident man.

Nevertheless, weeks passed and Mary Higgins remained triumphantly at large. In vain Inspector Slack redoubled that energy that so belied his name.

Miss Lavinia remained tearful. Miss Emily was so upset and felt so alarmed by her condition that she actually sent for Dr. Haydock.

The whole of the village was terribly anxious to know what he thought of Miss Emily's claims to ill-health but naturally could not ask him. Satisfactory data came to hand on the subject, however, through Mr. Meek, the chemist's assistant, who was walking out with Clara, Mrs. Price-Ridley's maid. It was then known that Dr. Haydock had prescribed a mixture of asafoetida and valerian which, according to Mr. Meek, was the stock remedy for malingerers in the army!

Soon afterward it was learned that Miss Emily, not relishing the medical attention she had had, was declaring that in the state of her health she felt it her duty to be near the specialist in London who understood her case. It was, she said, only fair to Lavinia.

The flat was put up for subletting.

It was a few days after that that Miss Marple, rather pink and flustered, called at the police station in Much Benham and asked for Inspector Slack.

Inspector Slack did not like Miss Marple. But he was aware that the chief constable, Colonel Melchett, did not share that opinion. Rather grudgingly, therefore, he received her.

"Good afternoon, Miss Marple. What can I do for you?"

"Oh, dear," said Miss Marple, "I'm afraid you're in a hurry."

"Lot of work on," said Inspector Slack, "but I can spare a few moments."

"Oh, dear," said Miss Marple, "I hope I shall be able to put what I say properly. So difficult, you know, to explain oneself, don't you think? No, perhaps you don't. But you see, not having been educated in the modern style—just a governess, you know, who taught one the dates of the Kings of England and General Knowledge—and how needles are made and all that. Discursive, you know, but not teaching one to keep to the point. Which is what I want to do. It's about Miss Skinner's maid, Gladys, you know."

"Mary Higgins," said Inspector Slack.

"Oh yes, the second maid. But it's Gladys Holmes I mean—rather an impertinent girl and far too pleased with herself, but really strictly honest, and it's so important that that should be recognized."

"No charge against her so far as I know," said the inspector.

"No, I know there isn't a charge—but that makes it worse. Because, you see, people go on thinking things. Oh, dear—I knew I should explain badly. What I really mean is that the important thing is to find Mary Higgins."

"Certainly," said Inspector Slack. "Have you any ideas on the subject?"

"Well, as a matter of fact, I have," said Miss Marple. "May I ask you a question? Are fingerprints of no use to you?"

"Ah," said Inspector Slack, "that's where she was a bit too artful for us. Did most of her work in rubber gloves or housemaid's gloves, it seems. And she'd been careful—wiped off everything in her bedroom and on the sink. Couldn't find a single fingerprint in the place!"

"If you did have her fingerprints, would it help?"

"It might, madam. They may be known at the Yard. This isn't her first job, I'd say!"

Miss Marple nodded brightly. She opened her bag and extracted a small cardboard box. Inside it, wedged in cotton wool, was a small mirror.

"From my handbag," said Miss Marple. "The maid's prints are on it. I think they should be satisfactory—she touched an extremely sticky substance a moment previously."

Inspector Slack stared.

"Did you get her fingerprints on purpose?"

"Of course."

"You suspected her then?"

"Well, you know it did strike me that she was a little too good to be true. I practically told Miss Lavinia so. But she simply wouldn't take the hint! I'm afraid, you know, Inspector, that I don't believe in paragons. Most of us have our faults—and domestic service shows them up very quickly!"

"Well," said Inspector Slack, recovering

his balance, "I'm obliged to you, I'm sure. We'll send these up to the Yard and see what they have to say."

He stopped. Miss Marple had put her head a little on one side and was regarding him with a good deal of meaning.

"You wouldn't consider, I suppose, Inspector, looking a little nearer home?"

"What do you mean, Miss Marple?"

"It's very difficult to explain, but when you come across a peculiar thing you notice it. Although, often, peculiar things may be the merest trifles. I've felt that all along, you know; I mean about Gladys and the brooch. She's an honest girl; she didn't take that brooch. Then why did Miss Skinner think she did? Miss Skinner's not a fool, far from it! Why was she so anxious to let a girl go who was a good servant when servants are hard to get? It was peculiar, you know. So I wondered. I wondered a good deal. And I noticed another peculiar thing! Miss Emily's a hypochondriac, but she's the first hypochondriac who hasn't sent for some doctor or other at once. Hypochondriacs love doctors. Miss Emily didn't!"

"What are you suggesting, Miss Marple?"

"Well, I'm suggesting, you know, that Miss Lavinia and Miss Emily are peculiar

21

people. Miss Emily spends nearly all her time in a dark room. And if that hair of hers isn't a wig, I—I'll eat my own back switch! And what I say is this—it's perfectly possible for a thin, pale, grey-haired, whining woman to be the same as a black-haired, rosy-cheeked, plump woman. And nobody that I can find ever saw Miss Emily and Mary Higgins at one and the same time.

"Plenty of time to get impressions of all the keys, plenty of time to find out all about the other tenants, and then—get rid of the local girl. Miss Emily takes a brisk walk across country one night and arrives at the station as Mary Higgins next day. And then, at the right moment, Mary Higgins disappears, and off goes the hue and cry after her. I'll tell you where you'll find her, Inspector. On Miss Emily Skinner's sofa! Get her fingerprints if you don't believe me, but you'll find I'm right! A couple of clever thieves, that's what the Skinners are—and no doubt in league with a clever post and rails or fence or whatever you call it. But they won't get away with it this time! I'm not going to have one of our village girl's character for honesty taken away like that! Gladys Holmes is as honest as the day and everybody's going to know it! Good afternoon!"

Miss Marple had stalked out before Inspector Slack had recovered.

"Whew!" he muttered. "I wonder if she's right."

He soon found out that Miss Marple was right again.

Colonel Melchett congratulated Slack on his efficiency, and Miss Marple had Gladys come to tea with Edna and spoke to her seriously on settling down in a good situation when she got one.

Never Shake a Family Tree

DONALD E. WESTLAKE

ACTUALLY, I have never been so shocked in all my born days, and I seventy-three my last birthday and eleven times a grandmother and twice a great-grandmother. But never in all my born days did I see the like, and that's the truth.

Actually, it all began with my interest in genealogy, which I got from Mrs. Ernestine Simpson, a lady I met at Bay Arbor, in Florida, when I went there three summers ago. I certainly didn't like Florida—far too expensive, if you ask me, and far too bright, and with just too many mosquitoes and other insects to be believed—but I wouldn't say the trip was a total loss, since it did interest me in genealogical research, which is certainly a wonderful hobby, as well as being very valuable, what with one thing and another.

Actually, my genealogical researches had been valuable in more ways than one, since they have also been instrumental in my meeting some very pleasant ladies and gentlemen, although some of them only by postal, and of course it was through this hobby that I met Mr. Gerald Fowlkes in the first place.

But I'm getting far ahead of my story, and ought to begin at the beginning, except that I'm blessed if I know where the beginning actually is. In one way of looking at things, the beginning is my introduction to genealogy through Mrs. Ernestine Simpson, who has since passed on, but in another way the beginning is really almost two hundred years ago, and in still another way the story doesn't really begin until the first time I came across the name of Euphemia Barber.

Well. Actually, I suppose, I really ought to begin by explaining just what genealogical research is. It is the study of one's family tree. One checks marriage and birth and death records, searches old family Bibles and talks to various members of one's family, and one gradually builds up a family tree, showing who fathered whom and what year, and when so-and-so died, and so on. It's really a fascinating work, and there are any number of amateur genealogical societies throughout the country, and when one has one's family tree built up for as far as one wants—seven generations, or nine generations, or however long one wants—then it is possible to write this all up in a folder and bequeath it to the local library, and then there is a *record* of one's family for all time to come, and I for one think that's important and valuable to have even if my youngest boy Tom does laugh at it and say it's just a silly hobby. Well, it *isn't* a silly hobby. After all, I found evidence of murder that way, didn't I?

So, actually, I suppose the whole thing really begins when I first came across the name of Euphemia Barber. Euphemia Barber was John Anderson's second wife. John Anderson was born in Goochland County, Virginia, in 1754. He married Ethel Rita Mary Rayborn in 1777, just around the time of the Revolution, and they had seven children, which wasn't at all strange for that time, though large families have, I notice, gone out of style today, and I for one think it's a shame.

At any rate, it was John and Ethel Anderson's third child, a girl named Prudence, who is in my direct line on my mother's father's side, so of course I had them in my family tree. But then, in going through Appomattox County records—Goochland

County being now a part of Appomattox, and no longer a separate county of its own— I came across the name of Euphemia Barber. It seems that Ethel Anderson died in 1793, in giving birth to her eighth child—who also died—and three years later, 1796, John Anderson remarried, this time marrying a widow named Euphemia Barber. At that time, he was forty-two years of age, and her age was given as thirty-nine.

Of course, Euphemia Barber was not at all in my direct line, being John Anderson's second wife, but I was interested to some extent in her pedigree as well, wanting to add her parents' names and her place of birth to my family chart, and also because there were some Barbers fairly distantly related on my father's mother's side, and I was wondering if this Euphemia might be kin to them. But the records were very incomplete, and all I could learn was that Euphemia Barber was not a native of Virginia, and had apparently only been in the area for a year or two when she had married John Anderson. Shortly after John's death in 1798, two years after their marriage, she had sold the Anderson farm, which was apparently a somewhat prosperous location, and had moved away again. So that I had neither birth nor death records on her, nor any record of her first husband, whose last name had apparently been Barber, but only the one lone record of her marriage to my great-great-great-great-great-grandfather on my mother's father's side.

Actually, there was no reason for me to pursue the question further, since Euphemia Barber wasn't in my direct line anyway, but I had worked diligently and, I think, well, on my family tree, and had it almost complete back nine generations, and there was really very little left to do with it, so I was glad to do some tracking down.

Which is why I included Euphemia Barber in my next entry in the Genealogical Exchange. Now, I suppose I ought to explain what the Genealogical Exchange is. There are any number of people throughout the country who are amateur genealogists, concerned primarily with their own family trees, but of course family trees do interlock, and any one of these people is liable to know about just the one record which has been eluding some other searcher for months. And so there are magazines devoted to the exchanging of some information, for nominal fees. In the last few years, I had picked up all sorts of valuable leads in this way. And so my entry in the summer issue of the Genealogical Exchange read:

BUCKLEY, Mrs. Henrietta Rhodes, 119A Newbury St., Boston, Mass. Xch data on *Rhodes, Anderson, Richards, Pryor, Marshall, Lord*. Want any info Euphemia *Barber*, m. John Anderson, Va. 1796.

Well. The Genealogical Exchange had been helpful to me in the past, but I never received anywhere near the response caused by Euphemia Barber. And the first response of all came from Mr. Gerald Fowlkes.

It was a scant two days after I received my own copy of the summer issue of the Exchange. I was still poring over it myself, looking for people who might be linked to various branches of my family tree, when the telephone rang. Actually, I suppose I was somewhat irked at being taken from my studies, and perhaps I sounded a bit impatient when I answered.

If so, the gentleman at the other end gave no sign of it. His voice was most pleasant, quite deep and masculine, and he said, "May I speak, please, with Mrs. Henrietta Buckley?"

"This is Mrs. Buckley," I told him.

"Ah," he said. "Forgive my telephoning, please, Mrs. Buckley. We have never met. But I noticed your entry in the current issue of the Genealogical Exchange—"

"Oh?"

I was immediately excited, all thought of impatience gone. This was surely the fastest reply I'd ever had to date!

"Yes," he said. "I noticed the reference to Euphemia Barber. I do believe that may be the Euphemia Stover who married Jason Barber in Savannah, Georgia, in 1791. Jason Barber is in my direct line, on my mother's side. Jason and Euphemia had only the one child, Abner, and I am descended from him."

"Well," I said. "You certainly do seem to have complete information."

"Oh, yes," he said. "My own family chart is almost complete. For twelve generations, that is. I'm not sure whether I'll try to go back farther than that or not. The English records before 1600 are so incomplete, you know."

"Yes, of course," I said. I was, I admit, taken aback. Twelve generations! Surely that was the most ambitious family tree I had ever heard of, though I had read sometimes of people who had carried particular branches back as many as fifteen generations. But to actually be speaking to a person who had traced his entire family back twelve generations!

"Perhaps," he said, "it would be possible for us to meet, and I could give you the information I have on Euphemia Barber. There are also some Marshalls in one branch of my family; perhaps I can be of help to you there, as well." He laughed, a deep and pleasant sound, which reminded me of my late husband, Edward, when he was most particularly pleased. "And, of course," he said, "there is always the chance that you may have some information on the Marshalls which can help me."

"I think that would be very nice," I said, and so I invited him to come to the apartment the very next afternoon.

At one point the next day, perhaps half an hour before Gerald Fowlkes was to arrive, I stopped my fluttering around to take stock of myself and to realize that if ever there were an indication of second childhood taking over, my thoughts and actions preparatory to Mr. Fowlkes' arrival were certainly it. I had been rushing hither and thither, dusting, rearranging, polishing, pausing incessantly to look in the mirror and touch my hair with fluttering fingers, all as though I were a flighty teen-ager before her very first date. "Henrietta," I told myself sharply, "you are seventy-three years old, and all that nonsense is well behind you now. Eleven times a grandmother, and just look at how you carry on!"

But poor Edward had been dead and gone these past nine years, my brothers and sisters were all in their graves, and as for my children, all but Tom, the youngest, were thousands of miles away, living their own lives—as of course they should—and only occasionally remembering to write a duty letter to Mother. And I am much too aware of the dangers of the clinging mother to force my presence too often upon Tom and his family. So I am very much alone, except of course for my friends in the various church activities and for those I have met, albeit only by postal, through my genealogical research.

So it *was* pleasant to be visited by a charming gentleman caller, and particularly so when that gentleman shared my own particular interests.

And Mr. Gerald Fowlkes, on his arrival, was surely no disappointment. He looked to be no more than fifty-five years of age, though he swore to sixty-two, and had a fine shock of gray hair above a strong and kindly face. He dressed very well, with that combination of expense and breeding so little found these days, when the well-bred seem invariably to be poor and the well-to-do seem invariably to be horribly plebeian. His manner was refined and gentlemanly, what we used to call courtly, and he had some very nice things to say about the appearance of my living room.

Actually, I make no unusual claims as a housekeeper. Living alone, and with quite a comfortable income having been left me by Edward, it is no problem at all to choose tasteful furnishings and keep them neat. (Besides, I had scrubbed the apartment from top to bottom in preparation for Mr. Fowlkes' visit.)

He had brought his pedigree along, and what a really beautiful job he had done. Pedigree charts, photostats of all sorts of records, a running history typed very neatly on bond paper and inserted in a loose-leaf notebook—all in all, the kind of careful, planned, well-thought-out perfection so unsuccessfully striven for by all amateur genealogists.

From Mr. Fowlkes, I got the missing information on Euphemia Barber. She was born in 1765, in Salem, Massachusetts, the fourth child of seven born to John and Alicia Stover. She married Jason Barber in Savannah in 1791. Jason, a well-to-do merchant, passed on in 1794, shortly after the birth of their first child, Abner. Abner was brought up by his paternal grandparents, and Euphemia moved away from Savannah. As I already knew, she had then gone to Virginia, where she had married John Anderson. After that Mr. Fowlkes had no record of her, until her death in Cincinnati, Ohio, in 1852. She was buried as Euphemia Stover Barber, apparently not having used the Anderson name after John Anderson's death.

This done, we went on to compare family histories and discover an Alan Marshall of Liverpool, England, around 1680, common to both trees. I was able to give Mr. Fowlkes Alan Marshall's birth date. And then the specific purpose of our meeting was finished. I offered tea and cakes, it then being four-thirty in the afternoon, and Mr. Fowlkes graciously accepted my offering.

And so began the strangest three months of my entire life. Before leaving, Mr. Fowlkes asked me to accompany him to a concert on Friday evening, and I very readily agreed. Then, and afterward, he was a perfect gentleman.

It didn't take me long to realize that I was being courted. Actually, I couldn't believe it at first. After all, at *my* age! But I myself did know some very nice couples who had married late in life—a widow and a widower, both lonely, sharing interests, and deciding to lighten their remaining years together— and looked at in that light it wasn't at all as ridiculous as it might appear at first.

Actually, I had expected my son Tom to laugh at the idea, and to dislike Mr. Fowlkes instantly upon meeting him. I suppose various fictional works that I have read had given me this expectation. So I was most pleasantly surprised when Tom and Mr. Fowlkes got along famously together from their very first meeting, and even more surprised when Tom came to me and told me Mr. Fowlkes had asked him if he would have any objection to his, Mr. Fowlkes', asking for my hand in matrimony. Tom said he had no objection at all, but actually thought it a wonderful idea, for he knew that both Mr. Fowlkes and myself were rather lonely, with nothing but our genealogical hobbies to occupy our minds.

As to Mr. Fowlkes' background, he very early gave me his entire history. He came from a fairly well-to-do family in upstate New

York, and was himself now retired from his business, which had been a stock brokerage in Albany. He was a widower these last six years, and his first marriage had not been blessed with any children, so that he was completely alone in the world.

The next three months were certainly active ones. Mr. Fowlkes—Gerald—squired me everywhere, to concerts and to museums and even, after we had come to know one another well enough, to the theater. He was at all times most polite and thoughtful, and there was scarcely a day went by but what we were together.

During this entire time, of course, my own genealogical researches came to an absolute standstill. I was much too busy, and my mind was much too full of Gerald, for me to concern myself with family members who were long since gone to their rewards. Promising leads from the Genealogical Exchange were not followed up, for I didn't write a single letter. And though I did receive many in the Exchange, they all went unopened into a cubbyhole in my desk. And so the matter stayed, while the courtship progressed.

After three months, Gerald at last proposed. "I am not a young man, Henrietta," he said. "Nor a particularly handsome man"

—though he most certainly was very handsome, indeed—"nor even a very rich man, although I do have sufficient for my declining years. And I have little to offer you, Henrietta, save my own self, whatever poor companionship I can give you, and the assurance that I will be ever at your side."

What a beautiful proposal! After being nine years a widow, and never expecting even in fanciful daydreams to be once more a wife, what a beautiful proposal and from what a charming gentleman!

I agreed at once, of course, and telephoned Tom the good news that very minute. Tom and his wife, Estelle, had a dinner party for us, and then we made our plans. We would be married three weeks hence. A short time? Yes, of course, it was, but there was really no reason to wait. And we would honeymoon in Washington, D.C., where my oldest boy, Roger, has quite a responsible position with the State Department. After which, we would return to Boston and take up our residence in a lovely old home on Beacon Hill, which was then for sale and which we would jointly purchase.

Ah, the plans! The preparations! How newly filled were my so-recently empty days!

I spent most of the last week closing my

apartment on Newbury Street. The furnishings would be moved to our new home by Tom, while Gerald and I were in Washington. But, of course, there was ever so much packing to be done, and I got at it with a will.

And so at last I came to my desk, and my genealogical researches lying as I had left them. I sat down at the desk, somewhat weary, for it was late afternoon and I had been hard at work since sun-up, and I decided to spend a short while getting my papers into order before packing them away. And so I opened the mail which had accumulated over the last three months.

There were twenty-three letters. Twelve asked for information on various family names mentioned in my entry in the Exchange, five offered to give me information, and six concerned Euphemia Barber. It was, after all, Euphemia Barber who had brought Gerald and me together in the first place, and so I took time out to read these letters.

And so came the shock. I read the six letters, and then I simply sat limp at the desk, staring into space, and watched the monstrous pattern as it grew in my mind. For there was no question of the truth, no question at all.

Consider: Before starting the letters, this is what I knew of Euphemia Barber: She had been born Euphemia Stover in Salem, Massachusetts, in 1765. In 1791, she married Jason Barber, a widower of Savannah, Georgia. Jason died two years later, in 1793, of a stomach upset. Three years later, Euphemia appeared in Virginia and married John Anderson, also a widower. John died two years thereafter, in 1798, of stomach upset. In both cases, Euphemia sold her late husband's property and moved on.

And here is what the letters added to that, in chronological order:

From Mrs. Winnie Mae Cuthbert, Dallas, Texas: Euphemia Barber, in 1800, two years after John Anderson's death, appeared in Harrisburg, Pennsylvania, and married one Andrew Cuthbert, a widower and a prosperous feed merchant. Andrew died in 1801, of a stomach upset. The widow sold his store, and moved on.

From Miss Ethel Sutton, Louisville, Kentucky: Euphemia Barber, in 1804, married Samuel Nicholson of Louisville, a widower and a well-to-do tobacco farmer. Samuel Nicholson passed on in 1807, of a stomach upset. The widow sold his farm, and moved on.

From Mrs. Isabelle Padgett, Concord, California: in 1808, Euphemia Barber married Thomas Norton, then Mayor of Dover, New Jersey, and a widower. In 1809, Thomas Norton died of a stomach upset.

From Mrs. Luella Miller, Bicknell, Utah: Euphemia Barber married Jonas Miller, a wealthy shipowner of Portsmouth, New Hampshire, a widower, in 1811. The same year, Jonas Miller died of a stomach upset. The widow sold his property and moved on.

From Mrs. Lola Hopkins, Vancouver, Washington: In 1813, in southern Indiana, Euphemia Barber married Edward Hopkins, a widower and a farmer. Edward Hopkins died in 1816, of a stomach upset. The widow sold the farm, and moved on.

From Mr. Roy Cumbie, Kansas City, Missouri: In 1819, Euphemia Barber married Stanley Thatcher of Kansas City, Missouri, a river barge owner and a widower. Stanley Thatcher died, of a stomach upset, in 1821. The widow sold his property, and moved on.

The evidence was clear, and complete. The intervals of time without dates could mean that there had been other widowers who had succumbed to Euphemia Barber's fatal charms, and whose descendants did not number among themselves an amateur genealogist. Who could tell just how many husbands Euphemia had murdered? For murder it quite clearly was, brutal murder, for profit. I had evidence of eight murders, and who knew but what there were eight more, or eighteen more? Who could tell, at this late date, just how many times Euphemia Barber had murdered for profit, and had never been caught?

Such a woman is inconceivable. Her husbands were always widowers, sure to be lonely, sure to be susceptible to a wily woman. She preyed on widowers, and left them all a widow.

Gerald.

The thought came to me, and I pushed it firmly away. It couldn't possibly be true; it couldn't possibly have a single grain of truth.

But what did I know of Gerald Fowlkes, other than what he had told me? And wasn't I a widow, lonely and susceptible? And wasn't I financially well off?

Like father, like son, they say. Could it be also, like great-great-great-great-great-grandmother, like great-great-great-great-great-grandson?

What a thought! It came to me that there must be any number of widows in the country, like myself, who were interested in tracing their family trees. Women who had a bit of money and leisure, whose children were grown and gone out into the world to live their own lives, and who filled some of the empty hours with the hobby of genealogy. An unscrupulous man, preying on well-to-do widows, could find no better introduction than a common interest in genealogy.

What a terrible thought to have about Gerald! And yet, I couldn't push it from my mind, and at last I decided that the only thing I could possibly do was try to substantiate the autobiography he had given me, for if he had told the truth about himself, then he could surely not be a beast of the type I was imagining.

A stockbroker, he had claimed to have been, in Albany, New York. I at once telephoned an old friend of my first husband's, who was himself a Boston stockbroker, and asked him if it would be possible for him to find out if there had been, at any time in the last fifteen or twenty years, an Albany stockbroker named Gerald Fowlkes. He said he could do so with ease, using some sort of directory he had, and would call me back. He did so, with the shattering news that no such individual was listed!

Still I refused to believe. Donning my coat and hat, I left the apartment at once and went directly to the telephone company, where, after an incredible number of white lies concerning genealogical research, I at last persuaded someone to search for an old Albany, New York telephone book. I knew that the main office of the company kept books for other major cities, as a convenience for the public, but I wasn't sure they would have any from past years. Nor was the clerk I talked to, but at last she did go and search, and came back finally with the 1946 telephone book from Albany, dusty and somewhat ripped, but still intact, with both the normal listings and the yellow pages.

No Gerald Fowlkes was listed in the white pages, or in the yellow pages under Stocks & Bonds.

So. It was true. And I could see exactly what Gerald's method was. Whenever he was ready to find another victim, he searched one or another of the genealogical magazines until he found someone who shared one of his own past relations. He then proceeded to effect a meeting with that person, found out quickly enough whether or not the intended victim was a widow, of the proper age range, and with the properly large bank account, and then the courtship began.

I imagined that this was the first time he had made the mistake of using Euphemia Barber as the go-between. And I doubted that he even realized he was following in Euphemia's footsteps. Certainly, none of the six people who had written to me about Euphemia could possibly guess, knowing only of one marriage and death, what Euphemia's role in life had actually been.

And what was I to do now? In the taxi, on the way back to my apartment, I sat huddled in a corner, and tried to think.

For this *was* a severe shock, and a terrible disappointment. And could I face Tom, or my other children, or any one of my friends, to whom I had already written the glad news of my impending marriage? And how could I return to the drabness of my days before Gerald had come to bring gaiety and companionship and courtly grace to my days?

Could I even call the police? I was sufficiently convinced myself, but could I possibly convince anyone else?

All at once, I made my decision. And, having made it, I immediately felt ten years younger, ten pounds lighter, and quite a bit less foolish. For, I might as well admit, in

44

addition to everything else, this had been a terrible blow to my pride.

But the decision was made, and I returned to my apartment cheerful and happy.

And so we were married.

Married? Of course. Why not?

Because he will try to murder me? Well, of course he *will* try to murder me. As a matter of fact, he has already tried, half a dozen times.

But Gerald is working at a terrible disadvantage. For he cannot murder me in any way that looks like murder. It must appear to be a natural death, or, at the very worst, an accident. Which means that he must be devious, and he must plot and plan, and never come at me openly to do me in.

And there is the source of his disadvantage. For I am forewarned, and forewarned is forearmed.

But what, really, do I have to lose? At seventy-three, how many days on this earth do I have left? And how *rich* life is these days! How rich compared to my life before Gerald came into it! Spiced with the thrill of danger, the excitement of cat and mouse, the intricate moves and countermoves of the most fascinating game of all.

And, of course, a pleasant and charming husband. Gerald *has* to be pleasant and charming. He can never disagree with me, at least not very forcefully, for he can't afford the danger of my leaving him. Nor can he afford to believe that I suspect him. I have never spoken of the matter to him, and so far as he is concerned I know nothing. We go to concerts and museums and the theater together. Gerald is attentive and gentlemanly, quite the best sort of companion at all times.

Of course, I can't allow him to feed me breakfast in bed, as he would so love to do. No, I told him I was an old-fashioned woman, and believed that cooking was a woman's job, and so I won't let him near the kitchen. Poor Gerald!

And we don't take trips, no matter how much he suggests them.

And we've closed off the second story of our home, since I pointed out that the first floor was certainly spacious enough for just the two of us, and I felt I was getting a little old for climbing stairs. He could do nothing, of course, but agree.

And, in the meantime, I have found another hobby, though of course Gerald knows nothing of it. Through discreet inquiries, and careful perusal of past issues of the various genealogical magazines, the use of the family names in Gerald's family tree, I am gradually compiling another sort of tree. Not a family tree, no. One might facetiously call it a hanging tree. It is a list of Gerald's wives. It is in with my genealogical files, which I have willed to the Boston library. Should Gerald manage to catch me after all, what a surprise is in store for the librarian who sorts out those files of mine! Not as big a surprise as the one in store for Gerald, of course.

Ah, here comes Gerald now, in the automobile he bought last week. He's going to ask me again to go for a ride with him.

But I shan't go.

The Man Who Explained Miracles

CARTER DICKSON[*]

WHEN TOM LOCKWOOD first saw her, she was running down the stairs in terror. Behind her stretched the great sweep of stairs up to the portico of St. Paul's; above, Paul's Dome almost shut out the gray spring sky. A pigeon fluttered its wings. But there were very few people to see what happened.

The girl glanced over her shoulder. She was still so badly frightened that Tom's first thought was instinctive: she might stumble and pitch headlong. So he ran towards her.

His next thought, born of his journalistic work, was the grotesqueness of this whole scene, as the bell boomed out the stroke of four: a very pretty girl, with dark hair and wide-spaced eyes, fleeing in blind panic from the House of God.

Then she did stumble.

[*]John Dickson Carr.

Tom caught her before she fell, and lifted her up gently by the elbows.

"Steady does it, you know," he said, and smiled down at her. "There's nothing to be afraid of, really."

Instantly she recoiled; then she saw his expression, and hesitated. Tom Lockwood's own mother could not have called him handsome. But he had such an engaging and easy-going expression, especially in his smile, that almost any woman would have trusted him on sight—and would have been right.

"*Nothing* to be afraid of," he repeated.

"Isn't there?" the girl blurted out. "When last night, by some miracle no one can understand, they try to kill me? And now, just now, a voice speaks where no voice could have spoken? And tells me again I am going to die?"

Taxis hooted up Ludgate Hill. A rather sinister-looking policeman stood at the left-hand side of St. Paul's churchyard. Tom had a topsy-turvy sense that he did not really hear the words she was speaking.

She spoke with passion, in a beautiful voice with—was it?—some very faint tinge accent. Her hair really was black and shining, worn in a long bob; the gray eyes, their pupils dilated with fear, had long black lashes. Tom

49

was so conscious of her physical presence that he hastily let go her elbows.

"You don't believe me!" she cried. "Very well! I must go."

"No! Wait!"

The girl hesitated, looking at the pavement.

And Tom Lockwood was inspired almost to eloquence.

"You're alone," he said. "Oh, there may have been people with you in the Cathedral! But you're alone in yourself; you feel lost; you don't trust anybody. Will you trust a perfect stranger, if I tell you I only want to help you?"

To his intense embarrassment, tears came into her eyes.

"What you need—" he began. It was on the tip of his tongue to say "a couple of whiskies," but, in his present exalted mood, he decided this was unromantic. "Across the road," he said, "there's a tea shop of sorts. What you need is to drink tea and tell me your troubles. After all, hang it, I'm a reasonably respectable bloke! You see that policeman over there?"

"Yes?"

"*He* knows me," said Tom. "No, no, not because I'm an old lag just out of jail! As a matter of fact, I'm a crime reporter for the *Daily Record*. Here's my press-card."

"You are journalist?"

Her eyes flashed up; she pronounced the word almost as *journaliste*.

"Not where you are concerned. Please believe that! And you—are you by any chance French?"

"I am English," she retorted proudly, and drew herself up to her full height of five feet one. "Ah, bah! I am named Jenny. Jenny Holden. That is English enough, surely?"

"Of course. And I'm Tom Lockwood."

"But, you see," Jenny continued, "I have lived most of my life in France. When they brought me here for a visit, things seemed all funny but very nice, until—"

Jenny glanced back over her shoulder. Fear struck again, as though some terrifying presence lurked inside the Cathedral.

"Mr. Lockwood," she said, "of course I will go with you. And we need not be introduced by a policeman." Then her passionate voice rose. "But let us hurry, hurry, hurry!"

They dodged across through the skittish traffic to the tea shop at the corner of Paternoster Row. They passed the policeman in question, who seemed to fascinate Jenny. He was one of the Old Brigade: bulky and almost seven feet tall, just what any foreign visitor would expect to see.

Tom waved at him by way of greeting. The law saluted gravely but, when Jenny's head turned away, gave her companion a wink of such outrageous knowingness that Tom's ears went red.

At the door of the tea shop, however, Tom hesitated and turned round.

"Stop a bit! Was there somebody with you at St. Paul's?"

"Yes, yes! My Aunt Hester and my Cousin Margot."

"*They* didn't frighten you?"

"No, of course not!" Jenny's lips became mutinous. "I do not like my Aunt Hester. She behaves like a duchess, with a lorgnette, and you can hear her talking all over a restaurant. You know what I mean?"

"Bitterly well."

"My Cousin Margot, she is young and I like her. But I wish to get away from them. Please!"

"Right," said Tom, opening the door. "In you go."

He allowed the door to close very briefly behind her so that she should not hear him when his voice carried clearly across to the policeman.

52

"Dawson! You haven't seen us. Understand?"

The law did. His wink was more portentous than ever.

In the tea shop, more properly a tea bar, two girls chattered and banged tins behind the counter. But the place was deserted, including the two booths at the back. When the newcomers sat opposite each other in the farther booth, over thick mugs of a beverage which was at least hot, Jenny's terror was decreasing. She accepted a cigarette, had it lighted for her, and hesitated. Then she burst out: "You see, it is so difficult to say! I don't wish you to think I am silly, or have fancies, or am off my head. That is what *they* think."

" 'They'?"

"Aunt Hester. And others."

"Aunt Hester," said Tom, "shall be hung out on the clothes-line, preferably upside down, at the first opportunity. Meanwhile . . ."

He broke off, because Jenny bubbled with that laughter he came to know so well.

"You are nice!" she declared, like a magistrate imposing sentence. "Oh, how it is pleasant to meet people who make you laugh! Instead of—"

Jenny stopped, and disquiet settled on her again.

"It is silly," she insisted, "but I must say it. Can you explain miracles?"

"No. But I know a man who can. Did you ever hear of Sir Henry Merrivale?"

"Sir Henry *Merrivale?*"

"Yes."

"But he is awful!" cried Jenny. "He is fat and bald, and he swear and carry on and throw people out of windows."

"He is not, perhaps," Tom admitted, "quite the ladies' man he thinks he is. But he can explain miracles, Jenny. That's his purpose in life nowadays."

"You mean this?"

"Yes, I mean it."

"Then I had better explain from the beginning. My name—"

"I know your name," said Tom, looking at the table. "I am likely to remember it for a very long time."

There was a pause, while both of them hastily swallowed tea.

"Well!" said Jenny. "My father and mother went to live in France, at Cannes, before I was born. What with the war, and everything else, I had never been to England. My mother died during the war. My

54

father died two years ago. My guardian is my father's old friend Général de Senneville. And I am now twenty-five: in France, I am what you would call in England an old maid."

"Are you, now?" breathed Tom, almost with awe. "Oh, crikey! Have you ever seen yourself in a mirror?"

Jenny looked at him, and then went on very quickly.

"It was always my father's wish I should come to England. I should see all the sights like any tourist: Westminster Abbey, the Tower of London, St. Paul's—"

"Steady, now!"

"Yes, I am steady. Général de Senneville, my guardian, said this plan was a good one, and did much honor to everyone. So he sent me, in charge of my Aunt Hester, just before I get married."

"Before you—!" Tom blurted out, and then stopped.

Jenny's face went pink. Tom, in the act of lighting a cigarette for himself, held the match for so long that it burned his fingers. He cursed, dropped both match and cigarette into the mug of tea; then, to hide his expression, he shoved the mug of tea down on the floor under the seat.

"But what else could I do?" Jenny asked

defensively. "It was arranged many years ago, between my father and the général. At twenty-five, and an old maid, surely that was best?"

The damage had been done. They could not look at each other's eyes.

"And who's the bloke you're marrying?" he asked casually.

"Armand de Senneville. The général's son."

"Do you love him?"

All Jenny's English feelings warred with her strict French upbringing.

"But you are not practical!" she exclaimed, the more vehemently because her feelings won every time. "An arranged marriage always turns out best, as the général says. It is understood that I do not love Armand, and Armand does not love me. I marry him because—well! it must be done, at twenty-five. He marries me because he wishes to obtain my dowry, which is very large."

"Does he, by God!"

"How dare you!"

"These old French customs." Tom folded his arms moodily. "You hear about 'em, you know they exist, but they're still hard to believe. What about this Armand de

Senneville? He has oily black hair, I suppose, and side-whiskers down his cheeks?"

"You must not speak so of my fiancé, and you know it!"

"All right, all right!"

"He has dark hair, yes, but none of the rest of it. He is charming. Also, he is one of the best businessmen in France. Armand is only thirty-five, but already he owns three newspapers, two in Paris and one in Bordeaux."

"Whereas I . . ."

"You said?"

"Nothing. He's with you, I suppose?"

"No, no! He was bitterly opposed to this holiday. He could not get away from business; he speaks no English and does not like the English. He has to consent, because his father wishes it. But he warns Aunt Hester to keep a sharp eye on me, in case I should be silly and fall in love with some dull, stupid Englishman—"

Abruptly Jenny paused. Her own cigarette, unnoticed, was burning her fingers; she threw it on the floor.

Tom looked straight at her.

"Which you might do, mightn't you?"

"No! Never! Besides, Aunt Hester and the de Sennevilles would never let me."

While Stella and Dolly clattered tins and banged cups behind the counter of a prosaic tea bar, Tom Lockwood took a great and secret and mighty resolve. But he did not show it in his brisk tone.

"Now, then! Let's get down to cases. What has frightened you so much?"

"Last night," answered Jenny, "someone tried to kill me. Someone turned on the tap of the gas heater in my bedroom. It was impossible for this to be done, because all the doors and windows were locked on the inside. But it *was* done. Already I had a note saying I was going to die."

Jenny's eyes seemed to turn inwards.

"By good luck, they save me. But I don't wish to speak of last night! This morning I am very—sick is not a nice word, is it?—no! I am ill. But Aunt Hester said this was nonsense, and it would revive me to go sightseeing again. That is why we went to St. Paul's. Do you know St. Paul's?"

"I'm afraid I haven't even been inside the place for a long time."

"It happened," said Jenny, "in the whispering gallery."

Whispering gallery.

The eerie sibilance tapped against the

58

nerves even in this commonplace tea bar, with traffic rushing outside.

"You climb up stairs," said Jenny. "Spiral stairs. Stairs and stairs, until you are breathless and think you will never get to the top. Then there is a tiny little door, and you go out into the gallery."

Then Tom remembered—how vividly this whispering gallery had impressed him. It was dizzily high up, just under the curve of the dome: circular, some two hundred feet across, and with only an iron railing to keep you from pitching down interminably to the acres of folding chairs on the ground floor below.

Noises struck in with brittle sharpness. Gray light filtered in on the tall marble statues of saints round the vast circle. It was solemn, and it was lonely. Only one verger, black-clad, stood guard there.

More than ever Tom was conscious of Jenny's presence, of her parted lips and quick breathing.

"I am not a coward," she insisted. "But I did not like this place. If you sit on the stone bench round the wall, and someone—even two hundred feet away—whispers near the wall, that whisper comes round in a soft little gurgly voice out of nowhere.

"Please attend to me!" Jenny added, with deep sincerity. "I was not well—I admit it. But I was not unbalanced either. Ever since I have received that first note saying I would die, I have watch everyone. I trust nobody—you were right. But I trust you. And, on my oath, this happened as I tell it.

"There were only five persons in all that dusky gallery. You could see. My Aunt Hester and my Cousin Margot. A fat red-faced countryman who is come to see the sights with a packet of sandwiches and a thermos flask of tea. The verger, in a dark robe, who tells you about the gallery.

"That is all!

"First the verger showed us how the whispering gallery is worked. He leans against the wall to the left—you do not even have to be against the wall. He says something that we, on the right of the door, hardly hear at all. But it goes slipping and sliding and horrible round the dome. Something about 'This Cathedral, begun by Sir Christopher Wren—' and it jumps up in your ear from the other side.

"After that we separated, but only a little. I was nervous—yes, I admit that too! I sat down on the stone bench, all prim. Aunt Hester and Margot went to the railing round the open space, and looked over. Margot giggles and says, 'Mama, would it not be dreadful if I jumped over?'

"Meanwhile, the fat countryman has sat down fifty feet away from me. Calmly he opens the grease-proof paper and takes out a sandwich. He pours out tea from the thermos into the cup; he is taking a deep drink when the verger, who is outraged at sandwiches in St. Paul's, rushes toward him from ten feet away.

"Mr. Lockwood, I know what I saw! The countryman could not have spoken; he is really and truly gulping down tea. The verger could not have spoken—I could see his mouth—and anyway he is too far away from the wall. As for Aunt Hester or Margot, that is nonsense! And, anyway, they are much too far away from the wall, and leaning over the railing.

"But someone spoke in my ear just then.

"It was in English, and horrible. It said: 'I failed the first time, Jennifer. But I shall not fail the second time.' And it gloated. *And there was nobody there!*"

Jenny paused.

With all the nervousness of the past days, there were shadows under her eyes, and she

61

was more than pale. But a passion of appeal met Tom across the table.

"No, I did not say anything!" she told him. "If I had, Aunt Hester would only say I was imagining things. Just as she said I was imagining things last night, and must have turned on the gas-tap myself, because the room was all locked up inside.

"No, no, no! I jumped up and ran out. I ran down those stairs so fast no one could have caught me. I did not know where I was going or what I should do. If I prayed anything, I think I prayed to meet . . ."

"To meet whom?" prompted Tom.

"Well! To meet someone like you."

After saying this, defiantly, Jenny drank stone-cold tea.

"But what am I to do?" she demanded, with tears on her eyelashes. "I know Aunt Hester means me no harm—how could she? But I can't face her—I won't! Where am I to go?"

"I will tell you exactly," said Tom, reaching across and taking her hands. "You are going with me to see old H.M., otherwise Sir Henry Merrivale, at an office which nowadays is humorously called The Ministry of Miracles. Afterwards—"

Bang!

The door of the tea bar flew open with a crash which half shattered its glass panel. Tom, sitting with his back to the door, first craned round and then leaped to his feet.

Outside the door, but not yet looking into the tea bar, stood an imperious and stately lady who was addressing someone beyond her.

"I am well acquainted, constable," she was saying, "with Sir Richard Tringham, the Commissioner of Police. Your deliberate falsehoods will not help you when I report you to him personally. You have denied you saw any young lady run down the steps of the Cathedral. You have denied she met a young man in sports coat and gray flannels. Finally, you have denied they went into any of the shops or other disgusting places along here. Is this so, or is it not?"

" 'S right, marm," stolidly answered Police-Constable Dawson.

Whereupon Aunt Hester made her entrance like Lady Macbeth.

"I am Mrs. Hester Harpenden," she announced to the walls at large. "And I have *distinctly* different information from a newspaper seller. I have—"

Here she saw Tom, who was standing in the middle of the floor.

"That's the man," she said.

Up to this time Stella (rather bucktoothed) and Dolly (distinctly pretty) had remained stupefied and silent behind the counter. Now both of them gave tongue.

"Disgusting place, eh?" cried Dolly. "I like that!"

"Busted the door, officer," screamed Stella. "Busted the door, that's what she done!"

"Busted the door, did she?" repeated Police-Constable Dawson, in a sinister voice. "Oh, ah. I see." And he reached for his notebook.

Meanwhile, as Aunt Hester calmly advanced, Tom glanced back towards Jenny.

But Jenny was not there. She was gone; she was not anywhere in the place.

The sharp pang this gave him was not his only feeling. For an instant he believed he had strayed from St. Paul's churchyard into a world of monsters and twilight, where anything might happen; and, in a sense, he was not far wrong.

"Young man," Aunt Hester asked quietly, "where is my niece?"

"Do you see her here, madam?"

"No. But that does not mean . . . A back

entrance! Ah, yes! Where is the back entrance here?"

"Just a moment," said Tom, stepping in front of her. "Have you a warrant to search these premises?"

"Do I need a warrant to find my own niece?"

"Yes, yer do and all!" screamed Stella. "Either yer orders tea and cakes, which is wot we're 'ere for, or out yer go straight-away. 'S right, officer?"

" 'S right, miss," agreed the law.

Aunt Hester was not fooled for a moment.

Seen close at hand, she was—or seemed—less formidable than bitter and bony, with a high-bridged nose and washed-out blue eyes, as though she had suffered some disappointment in youth and never forgotten it. Tom could tell her clothes were fashionable, as Jenny's were fashionable, without knowing why he knew.

"Then you are all against me, it seems," she smiled. "Well! This will indeed make a budget of news for my friend the Commissioner of Police!"

"By the way," Tom said casually, "*who* did you say is the Commissioner of Police?"

"But Sir Richard Tringham, of course!"

"Oh, put a sock in it," said Tom. "Sir

Richard Tringham has been dead for seven years. The present Commissioner is Colonel Thomas Lockwood. And I ought to know—he's my father."

"Cor!" whispered Dolly.

" 'S right, marm," agreed Police-Constable Dawson.

Aunt Hester, not in the least impressed, merely raised her shoulders.

"Ah, well!" she smiled. "If police-officers are bribed to tell untruths, then I had better be off."

Majestically she strolled towards the front of the shop. With a gesture of contempt she opened her purse, took out a couple of pound-notes, and murmured something about paying for the glass door as she tossed the notes towards Stella.

Then, when she was within a step of the door, she whirled round and screamed at Tom like a harpy.

"Where is my niece?"

And Tom's temper crashed over too, like the glass platform of cakes which Dolly had been nervously handling.

"In a place where you'll never find her," he yelled back, only hoping he was telling the truth.

"If I prefer charges of abduction—"

"When she goes away of her own free will? Don't talk rot! And shall I tell you something else, Mrs. Harpenden?"

"By all means. If you can."

"That girl is of age," said Tom, advancing towards her. "Even under French law, her guardian no longer has any authority over her. But she doesn't seem to know that. She's being pushed and bullied and hounded into a marriage she doesn't want, by a lot of ghouls who are only interested in her money. And I tell you straight: I mean to stop it."

"Ah, I see. *You* want her money."

The steamy room was dead quiet, with fragments of shattered glass and colored cakes all over the counter and floor. Both Stella and Dolly had cowered back.

"Yes, that hurt," said Tom. "You knew it would hurt. All right: if you want open war, it's war from this time on. Agreed?"

"Oh, agreed," replied Aunt Hester, her head high. "And I have a feeling, dear Mr. Lockwood, that you are not going to win. *Good* day."

With all the honors she marched out, closed the door, and turned right toward Paternoster Row. They had time to see a brown-haired girl of seventeen or eighteen, with slanting eyes and a mischievous look, run after her. It could only have been Jenny's cousin Margot.

Tom, exasperated to see those two pound-notes lying on the counter, flung down another two to match them.

"That's for the smashed container and the cakes," he said.

"But, reolly, now!" protested Dolly, in an ultra-refined voice. "This is too much money. And is the Commissioner of Police reolly your father?"

" 'S right, miss," said Police-Constable Dawson, and stolidly marched out.

"Ducks, ducks, ducks!" cried Stella, addressing Tom. Being not very pretty, she was more inclined to sympathize with his bedevilments. "You needn't worry about your young lady. 'Course there's another way out of 'ere!"

"There is?"

" 'Course there is. At the back, and turn sideways. I saw your young lady run out as soon as we heard the old witch's voice outside. Either the young lady's still hiding in the passage past the washroom, or she's gorn out into Paternoster Row."

"My deepest thanks!" said Tom.

He turned and plunged towards the back—

only to be stopped short by another figure materializing in this extraordinary tea shop.

This was a shortish, wiry man with his light-brown hair cropped close to the head after a prevailing American fashion. He was perhaps in his middle thirties; he wore loose-fitting clothes, and his tie could be seen at sixty paces in any crowd.

"Now hold it, brother!" he urged. "Don't go busting out of there or you'll louse up the whole deal."

Tom blinked at him.

"The old lady," continued the stranger, evidently referring to Aunt Hester, "left her car—it would be a limousine—parked in Paternoster Row. It's not there now. She'll be screaming for the cops again, and you'll run smack into her. Besides, the kid is safe now."

"The kid? You mean Jenny? Where is she?"

Something like a self-satisfied smile crept across the newcomer's face.

"I told the chauffeur," he said, "to drive her straight to a guy named Sir Henry Merrivale, at an address he seemed to know. Sit down for a minute, until the old dame stops yelling about her stolen car."

Tom Lockwood extended his hand.

"Maybe you won't want to shake hands,"

retorted the newcomer almost evilly, and put his hands behind his back, "when you hear what I am."

There was about him something distinctly foreign, in a way that no American is ever foreign. Though Tom could not analyze it, his companion enlightened him.

"Get it?" he asked. "I'm a Canadian. Lamoreux's the name—Steve Lamoreux. I was born in Montreal; I can speak French as well as I speak English. In Paris they say my accent is terrible; but they understand me. I'm a newsman for *L'Oeil*. Been in France for six months. Don't you get it *now?*"

"Well! I . . ."

Steve Lamoreux's shrewd brown eyes, in the hard yet sympathetic face, were almost glaring at him. And Lamoreux spoke bitterly.

"I'm the stooge," he said. "I'm the tail. In other words, I'm Armand de Senneville's hired spy to keep out of the way, never let the girl see me, but make sure she doesn't meet any boy friends. If she does . . ."

Tom, aware that both Stella and Dolly were listening with all their ears raised his voice.

"Could we have two more teas, please?"

he called. Then, to Lamoreux: "Into the booth here. And keep your voice low."

They sat down opposite each other.

"What the hell?" said Lamoreux. "I'm only human. That girl's too innocent; I won't see her pushed around. What's more, I can't take this miracle stuff any longer—not for a hundred bucks a week or anything else. Do you realize that, but for a thousand-to-one chance, she'd be lying dead at the mortuary this very minute?"

It was a cold and ugly statement, just as the great bell of St. Paul's boomed out the hour of five.

"She didn't tell you how bad it was last night, did she?" asked Lamoreux

"Not the details, no."

"No, you bet she didn't! The girl has guts—I'll say that for her."

"But how do you know she didn't tell me?"

"Because I overheard every word you two said in here! Look!" persisted Lamoreux, tapping a finger into his palm. "When they started out today, in their grand limousine, I followed in a taxi. Aunt Hester knows me, and knows all about me. Her husband, Uncle Fred, and young Margot—well, they've seen me once, here in England. I couldn't

71

help that, but they'd never seen me before, and it doesn't matter. Jenny doesn't, and mustn't, even suspect.

"Those were my orders from young de Senneville. He didn't dare send a Frenchman as a tail—it might be too conspicuous. But Jenny's seen this map of mine more than once at the newspaper office; if she spotted me, it might shake her faith in good old Armand."

"Quiet!" Tom warned softly.

It was Dolly who appeared, demurely, setting down two mugs of tea already sugared. Though she seemed inclined to linger, Lamoreux's glance sent her away miffed.

"Armand de Senneville," Tom said between his teeth. "What I should like to do to that . . . !"

"Easy, now, brother! You're talking about my boss."

"He may not be your boss much longer. You may get a better one."

"How's that? Say it again."

"Never mind; get on with the story."

"Well! Aunt Hester and Margot and Jenny had the car parked in Paternoster Row. They told the chauffer to wait there. I ditched my taxi, and sat in the car with the chauffeur.

We could see the whole front of St. Paul's. We knew we could see 'em come out."

"And then?"

"You know what happened. About thirty-five minutes later, she comes tearing down the steps. You grab her. I think to myself, 'Steve, this is your job; this is where the balloon goes up.' Over you come to this place. I sneak in the back way, and I'm practically against a matchboard partition behind you. When I heard about a voice speaking in the whispering gallery, when no voice could have spoken, I damn near fainted. And there's another thing."

"Yes?"

Uneasily Lamoreux drew out a packet of Yellow French cigarettes. He struck an old-fashioned sulphur match; he brooded while holding the match until the sulphur burned away. Then, still lost in thought, he lit the cigarette and flicked away the match.

"When I first got a gander at you, see—" Lamoreux stopped.

"Well? What is it?"

"I thought it was an ordinary pick-up. Then, when I heard you two talking, I thought you were a right guy. And I still think so."

They glared at each other, because no man

pays a compliment to another's face. Then, after an embarrassed pause:

"That's why I stuck my neck out. I could see Aunt Hester charging for this joint before either of you two did. I knew Jenny would duck for a way out. And *she* knew the car was parked just beside here. So I rushed out and told Pearson—that's the chauffeur—to drive her straight to this guy H.M. I'd heard of the old—the old gentleman; and I knew *he* was all right."

Lamoreux pointed his cigarette at Tom with grimacing emphasis.

"But get this!" he added. "I'm no guardian angel or *preux chevalier*. The hell with that stuff. Somebody in dead earnest tried to bump off that kid. Somebody'll try again, and I want no part of it. All I'd like to know, for the sweet suffering Moses's sake, is who's doing this and why?"

Lamoreux's voice rose up piercingly until he remembered they were in public.

Then it sank to a whisper. They sat and thought and worried.

"Armand de Senneville—" Tom began.

"Look," the other said wearily. "You've got that guy on the brain. De Senneville wants to marry her for her money. What

74

good is it to him if she's knocked off here in England?"

"Yes. I suppose that's true."

"But take it the other way round!" argued Lamoreux. "Take that gang in their country house near Hampton Court. I don't doubt Aunt Hester, at least, will get a large slice of dough when this marriage comes off. She's been in France dozens of times—she's cheering for matrimony like nobody's business. All right! Then what motive has she, or any of 'em, to kill Jenny and lose the money themselves?"

Steve Lamoreux at last took a sip of tea, which so disgusted him he did not speak for thirty seconds.

"It's nuts!" he said. "It makes no sense however you look at it."

"On the contrary," said Tom, "it's got to make sense! That's why you and I are going to see H.M. as fast as a taxi can take us."

"But I can't go there!"

"Why not?"

"Because Jenny's there, and she might spot me. All the same, if you want to reach me at any time before seven this evening, call me up at this number. If you want me any time after that, here's the number of my hotel near their house."

With a little gold pencil he scribbled two telephone numbers on a sheet torn from a notebook, and handed it to Tom.

"Locked rooms!" said Lamoreux. "Whispering voices! No motives! Brother, I'd give my last dime to go with you! What's the old—what's Sir Henry going to say about this one?"

In little more than twenty minutes, Tom Lockwood found out.

"Y'see," said Sir Henry Merrivale, with surprising meekness, "I'm sort of in trouble with the government."

"How do you mean?" asked Tom.

"Well, sort of," said H.M.

The old sinner, all sixteen stone of him, sat behind the desk in the familiar office, twiddling his thumbs over his corporation. His shell-rimmed spectacles were pulled down on his broad nose, and light from the windows behind him glistened on his bald head. On his face was the look of such martyrdom that it had won Jenny's complete sympathy and only enraged Tom.

"Well, y'see," H.M. pursued, "I've been abroad for maybe two or three years . . ."

"Ah, yes!" said Tom. "It was in New York, wasn't it, that you wrecked the sub-

76

way at Grand Central Station and nabbed the right murderer on the wrong evidence?"

"Oh, son! I dunno what you're talkin' about," said H.M., giving him an austere look.

"And in Tangier, I think, you blew up a ship and let the real criminal escape just because you happened to like him?"

"Y'see how they treat me?" H.M. demanded, his powerful voice rising as he addressed Jenny. "They've got no respect for me, not a bit."

"Poor man!" Jenny said warmly.

"Oh, Lord," moaned Tom. Like most people, he could never resist the temptation to make fun of the great man; and then, to his astonishment, he found women sympathizing with H.M.'s most outrageous exploits.

"But why," he persisted, "are you in trouble with the government?"

"It seems I spent more money than I should have, or burn me, than I can account for. It also seems—would you believe it?—I shouldn't have had banking accounts in New York, Paris, Tangier, and Milan."

"You didn't know, of course, you weren't allowed to have those banking accounts?"

"*Me?*"

"Never mind," said Tom, smiting his forehead. "What happened to you?"

"Oh, Lord love a duck!" said H.M. "When I got back to England, you'd have thought I was Guy Fawkes and the Cato Street conspirators all rolled into one. They hoicked me up on the carpet before an old friend of mine. I won't say who this louse is, except to tell you he's the Attorney-General."

"No," said Tom. "By all means don't breathe a word."

" 'Henry,' he says to me, 'I've got you over a barrel.' "

"Did the Attorney-General actually use those words?"

"Well . . . now!" said the great man, making a broad gesture and giving Tom a withering look. "I'm tellin' you the gist of it, that's all. 'Henry,' he said, 'on the evidence I have here I could have you fined a hundred thousand pounds or stuck in jail for practically a century.' " Here H.M. broke off and appealed to Jenny. "Was this just?" he demanded.

"Of course it wasn't!" cried Jenny.

" 'However,' he says, 'you pay up in full, with a fine, and we'll forget it. *Provided*,' he says—"

"Provided what?"

"I'm to go back to my own office here, d'ye see? It used to be part of the War Office, before they messed everything about in the war. And I'm to be in charge of Central Office Eight of the Metropolitan Police."

"Please," said Jenny in her soft voice, "but what is Central Office Eight?"

"It's me," H.M. replied simply. "Anybody who calls it The Ministry of Miracles is going to get a thick ear. They had enough fun, curse 'em, with the late Ministry of Information. If anything rummy turns up at Scotland Yard—any loony case that doesn't make sense—they chuck it at my head."

Here H.M.'s expression changed.

"Y'know," he said, "strictly among ourselves, I don't mind so much. I'm gettin' old and mellow now—"

"I'll bet you are," Tom muttered sardonically under his breath.

"—and it's comfortable here, sort of. Well!" said H.M., sitting up briskly and rubbing his hands together. "The old man's in business again. You got any miracles you want explained?"

"Have we!" said Tom. "Jenny! Haven't you told him?"

He himself had just arrived, hurrying in to

79

find H.M. pouring out his woes and tribulations. In the old dusty office, high above Whitehall, Tom and Jenny looked at each other.

That office, as H.M. had said, was comfortable. Above the fireplace still hung the Satanic portrait of Fouché, Minister of Police under Napoleon. There was a very impressive-looking safe, inscribed IMPORTANT STATE DOCUMENTS: *DO NOT TOUCH!*—but containing only a bottle of whiskey. The office had seen many strange things happen—it would see many more.

"I told him about what happened in the whispering gallery, yes!" said Jenny. "But I do not even know how I have come here at all! I hated to leave you in the tea shop, but Aunt Hester was so furious I could only run. Then, at the car, the chauffeur says that some Canadian gentleman—"

"That's all right. I can explain later."

"Some Canadian gentleman, who has been sitting with him in the car when we went into St. Paul's, told him to drive me straight to this H.M. of yours. You have said so too, so I go." Jenny's brow wrinkled. "And I was so, so wrong about your H.M.!"

"Oh?" enquired Tom.

"Yes, yes! He does not swear or carry on

or throw people out of windows. He is what you call a poppet."

"Hem!" said the great man modestly.

"Frankly," said Tom, eyeing the stuffed owl across the desk, "I shouldn't call it a well-chosen word to apply to him. You'll find out. However! When I'd chucked out Aunt Hester, with the aid of two counter-girls and a friendly cop, I thought I'd never get here. I was afraid some infernal thing or other had happened to you, and I might never see you again."

"You may see me," said Jenny, and stretched out her hands, "whenever you wish."

"*Oi!*" interposed a thunderous voice.

The alleged poppet was now glaring at them with a malignancy which raised Jenny's hair.

"There's not goin' to be any canoodling in this office, is there?" he demanded. "All my life I've tripped over young people with no idea except to canoodle.—Now listen to me, my dolly."

His big voice altered and sharpened. The whole atmosphere of the office changed as his small eyes narrowed behind the spectacles. He might be irascible, unreasonable, and childish, but he was still the Old Maestro—and you trifled with him at your own risk.

So H.M. spoke gently.

"You understand, my dolly, what I've already told you? That neither Général de Senneville nor Armand de Senneville has any hold over you? And neither have Aunt Hester and Company? That you're a perfectly free woman?"

Jenny pressed her hands against her cheeks.

"Yes," she said. "I suppose I always knew that, really. But . . ."

"But what?"

"People are so *determined*. They don't yield a bit. And it's always gone on like that. So you say to yourself, 'Oh, what's the use?' "

"Yes, I know," nodded H.M. "But that's what causes so much unhappiness in this world, especially for gals. Well, what's your feeling now? Do you want to fight 'em and beat 'em hands down?"

"Yes!"

"Do you still want to go on staying at your Aunt Hester's house? What's-its-name? Near Hampton Court?"

"It's called Broadacres, on the river. Tomorrow, they tell me, they will save the best of the sights for last—they say they will take

82

me to see Hampton Court Palace in the afternoon."

"They say that, hey?" H.M. muttered thoughtfully. Something flickered behind his glasses and was gone. "Never mind! Do you still want to stay at your Aunt Hester's?"

"No. But what else can I do, except return to Paris?"

"Well," glowered H.M. scratching the back of his neck, "I've got a house, and a wife, and two daughters, and two good-for-nothing sons-in-law I've had to support for eighteen years. So I expect you'd better move in too."

"You mean this?" cried Jenny, and sprang to her feet. "You would really want me?" she asked incredulously.

"Bah," said H.M.

"Sir H.M.! How to thank you I do not know . . . !"

"Shut up," said the great man austerely.

Jenny sat down again.

"Then there's your clothes," he mused. "That's a very fetchin' outfit you've got on now, and I expect you brought a whole trunkful?"

"Yes, my clothes! I forget!"

"Don't worry," said H.M. with a suggestion of ghoulish mirth. "I'll send a police-officer to fetch 'em. If that doesn't put the breeze up Aunt Hester to a howlin' gale, I don't know her kind. But understand this, my dolly!"

Again his tone sharpened and struck.

"Aunt Hester'll hit back. Don't think she won't. Also, you're likely to have the whole de Senneville tribe here and on your neck." H.M. blinked at Tom. "I say, son. Shall you and I handle 'em?"

"With pleasure!" said Tom. "And definitely without gloves."

"In the meantime," H.M. went on, looking very hard at Jenny, "I've heard about this rummy business in the whispering gallery, yes. But there's something else you've got to tell me, and very clearly, before I can help you at all."

"Just a minute!" interrupted Tom.

"Oh, for the love of Esau," howled H.M. "What's wrong now?"

"A voice spoke where no voice could possibly have spoken," said Tom. "Do you believe that?"

"Certainly."

"Then how was it done?"

"Oh, my son!" groaned H.M., with a pitying glance. "You don't mean to say that trick fooled you?"

"Do you know how it was done?"

"Sure I do."

"Then what's the explanation?"

"I'm not goin' to tell you."

Tom got up and did a little dance round his chair. H.M. sternly ordered him back into it.

"I'm not goin' to tell you," he went on with dignity, "because very shortly I'm goin' to *show* you. You can see with your own eyes. That's fair enough, hey?"

Whereupon his own eyes narrowed as he looked at Jenny.

"Stop a bit! We don't want Aunt Hester to pick up the trail too soon. You said you came here in a car, with a chauffeur. Is the car still waiting? Or did you send it back?"

"I have sent it back," retorted Jenny. "But I *know* I can trust Pearson—he is the chauffeur. I have told him to say I have gone off on my own, alone, to have tea at Lyons'."

"Which Lyons'?"

Jenny's gray eyes opened wide.

"I am English, I keep telling you!" she insisted. "But how can I know much of England if I am never here? Is there more than one Lyons'? The only London restaurants of which I have heard are Lyons and the Caprice and the Ivy."

"Those three grand old restaurants!" exclaimed Tom, and resisted an impulse to put his arms round her. "H.M., Aunt Hester will think Jenny is giving her the raspberry, which is exactly what you'd do yourself."

"Uh-huh. That'll do. Now then: about this first miracle—of a gas-tap being turned on in a locked room."

When H.M. produced his ancient black pipe, and began to load it with tobacco looking (and tasting) like the steel wool used on kitchen sinks, Tom knew he must brace himself for more trouble.

"My dolly," said H.M., "a lot of bits and pieces have come flyin' out of your story. I can *see* this aunt of yours. I can see her daughter, Margot, who's eighteen years old and up to mischief. I can see your Uncle Fred, who's tall and red-faced and looks like a retired major. I can see this white Georgian house, with long windows, set back from the river. But burn me if I can see the details!"

"How do you mean?"

"For instance. D'ye usually sleep with the windows closed, to say nothin' of being locked? Is that an old French custom?"

"No, no, of course not!"

"Well, then?"

"It is the details," said Jenny, biting her

lip, "I have not wished to talk about. They are—bad. I feel the gas strangle me again. But never mind! First, Aunt Hester put me into a bedroom on the ground floor."

"Why?"

"And why not?" Jenny exclaimed reasonably. "It is a very nice room. But it has two windows stretching to the ground. Aunt Hester is frightened of burglars, and asks me please to keep the windows tight-locked. By the time I am ready for bed, *I* am so scared that I put both bolts on the door as well—on the inside. You see, it was at dinner I received the note."

"What note?"

"It was a little note, folded up in my napkin at the table. I thought—"

"Yes, my dolly?"

"At first," Jenny explained, peeping sideways at Tom, "I thought it was from a young man I met at a tea party they gave. He has made what you call the eyes at me. So—"

"*That's* an old French custom, if you like," Tom said politely. "You thought the note was from him, and you didn't want anybody else to know?"

Jenny turned on him flaming.

"I do not like this young man at the tea party! I do not wish to see him again! But if he has written a note to me, can I give the poor man away?"

"No. Sorry, Jenny. Shouldn't have said that."

"But it is not from him at all, or anything like that. I read it under the table. It was only one line, in a handwriting I never saw before. It said, *'You will die tonight, Jennifer.'* "

Jenny moistened her lips. H.M. had lighted the pipe, and an oily cloud of smoke crept over the desk.

"At first I thought it was a joke. What else can I think? Then I looked at the rest of them, all so normal, with the candles burning on the dinner table. And I know I am alone. I am a stranger, even if I am in my own country—and I am frightened!

"I did not even dare ask if the note was a joke. So I hid it, and afterwards I lost it. At eleven o'clock, when it was time to go to bed . . ."

"Yes, my dolly? Go on!"

"I sleep badly," said Jenny. "Always I have. No matter how late I go to bed, I always wake up at 5 or 5:30 in the morning. There was a custom I had in France, first when I lived with my parents and afterwards at the house of Général de Senneville. A maid brought me a cup of chocolate at six in the morning.

"When Aunt Hester asked if she could do anything more, I asked if I might have the chocolate, or else tea, at that time. I had been there several days, but it was the first time I venture to ask. Aunt Hester lifts her eyebrows and says, 'Do you think, Jennifer my dear, that is quite fair to the servants?'

"I said no, no, please to forget it. But Margot, who has green eyes and is nice, she is always up before six, she says, and will be glad to bring me a cup of tea then. Very well! I go to my room. I turn on the light. I fasten the bolts both at the top and bottom of the door. Then I turn round. And one of the windows, which I have left locked, is wide open."

Jenny paused.

H.M., wrapped in his cloud of nauseous smoke, was as expressionless as an idol.

"I rush across," continued Jenny, her voice rising. "I close and lock the window again. Then I think, 'Suppose someone is hiding in the room?' But I must not be stupid and rouse the whole house. And so—well! I search the room myself. Nobody is hiding there. I think perhaps some servant has opened the window to air the room, and I feel better.

"It is a warm night—very warm, they tell me, for an English spring. So I do not need to turn on the gas heater in the fireplace when I undress. I close the window curtains almost shut. But I smoke a cigarette or two, you can bet, before I have the nerve to turn out the light. But I do turn out the light, finally. And soon I am asleep. Then—"

"Hold on!" interposed H.M. softly, and took the pipe out of his mouth.

"Y-yes?"

"What time did you turn in? Do you remember?"

"Yes. I see my wrist watch. It is ten minutes past twelve."

"Did any of this family know beforehand about your habit of takin' chocolate at six in the morning?"

"N-no, I do not think so. How could they? I—"

Again Jenny was trembling; and, worst sign of all, she was again glancing over her shoulder. Tom got up and put his hands on her shoulders.

"Hadn't we better stop this, H.M.?" he demanded.

"We can't stop it, son, and you know we

90

can't. That gal really *was* in a locked room. It's practically impossible to tamper with bolts when they're at the top and bottom of the door. Those Georgian window-locks are dead sure for safety. Unless I can get a hint about this, the old man's dished."

"I am very well, thank you," said Jenny. "I can go on, if you wish."

"Well?" said H.M., putting the pipe back in his mouth.

"First there was a dream. It was horrible, but I don't remember it now. Then I knew I was awake, and being strangled so I could not breathe. This part is hard to describe. But—when you are dying, or even losing consciousness, you can still hear sounds clearly even though you can barely see?"

"Yes, my dolly. That's right."

"I could tell it was just growing daylight, no more. But somebody was pounding on the outside of the door. And I hear Margot's voice crying my name. I tried to scream back, but there is no breath, and already— this is not pretty—I had been sick.

"Next, which is all confused, I heard a man's voice outside with Margot. It was an American voice I have never heard before. It said, 'What's wrong, kid? Isn't she okay?' Margot screams that the room is full of gas, and can't he smell it from under the door? He says, 'You won't break down that door. Where's the window?'

"Still I am just conscious. I can hear everything, though it must be like being hanged. I hear them run away, and someone else join them. Then I see—all blurry, because my eyes have nearly gone—I see someone's fist, wrapped in a coat, punch through the glass of the far window.

"This is my Uncle Fred, who has been roused too. He unlocks the window and pushes it all the way up. Someone runs to turn off the gas-tap at the heater. I think this is the American. I cannot see, but I hear him say a wicked word, and say, 'So-and-so, but it's turned full on!' He turns it off. Margot rushes towards me, spilling a tea tray on the carpet. That is all I remember, until the doctor is there."

Jenny lifted her hands, and let them fall on the handbag in her lap. As the oily smoke from H.M.'s pipe reached her at last, she began to cough.

H.M. put down the pipe and knocked it out.

"The doctor, hey?" he repeated. "And what did the doctor say?"

"It was not the doctor who spoke to me.

It was Aunt Hester. She said, 'This is not very considerate of you, Jennifer. To try to kill yourself because you are not happy about your future husband.' "

Tom Lockwood's grip tightened on her shoulders. "Your Aunt Hester said that?"

"Yes! And it is not true! But they ask how anyone could have tried to kill me, when the room is all locked up inside?"

"Anything else, Jenny?"

"I say, 'Where is the American?' They say, 'What American?' and claim he is a delusion of mine. They stand round my bed, all big-eyed—Aunt Hester and Cousin Margot and even poor old Uncle Fred—and look down at me. They say it is a mercy the doctor is their family doctor, and will not report this to the police. Dear God, do you wonder I am afraid of them?"

"H.M.!" Tom said sharply, after a pause.

"Well?"

"You may have been wondering about this mysterious American . . ."

"Frankly, son, I have. I don't see where he fits in."

"He isn't an American," said Tom, "but he isn't a delusion either. That gang made a bad slip when they claimed he was. I'll tell you all about him at the proper time. Meanwhile, do you see any clue at all?"

H.M., who had been sitting with his eyes closed and a very mulish look on his face, now opened his eyes slowly and inspected Jenny.

"My dolly," he said, "I've got only one more question to ask now. But I want you to be awful careful how you answer it. You could hear all these voices clearly when you were nearly unconscious. You could hear the pounding on the door, the footsteps running away, and the rest of it. *Did you hear any other sound besides that?*"

"What—what kind of sound?"

"Any kind!"

"No, I don't think so."

"You're sure of that, now?"

"Yes, positive!"

"Oh, Lord love a duck," observed Sir Henry Merrivale, with his mouth falling open. "So *that's* how the locked room was worked!"

"How?" shouted Tom.

"I'm the old man," said H.M., tapping himself impressively on the chest. "You let me deal with this in my own way. I'm goin' into action at once."

H.M. reached for the telephone at his el-

94

bow. He dialed for an outside exchange, and then dialed the number. During a long pause, while they could hear the ringing tone go on interminably, Tom Lockwood listened to an air-vent which hummed and hummed in the ceiling, and at intervals he studied H.M.'s face, now as malignant as the Evil One's.

The ringing tone broke off. There ensued, from H.M.'s side, the following weird and wonderful conversation.

"Looky here, my wench. I want to speak to Sam. . . . Oh, yes, I can! This is the old man. You just tell him I squared it when he was givin' a beautiful party for sixteen beautiful gals without any clothes on, and the silly-ass coppers broke in. Yes, the old man! . . ."

A gratified note crept into H.M.'s big voice.

"That you, Sam? How are you . . . ? Never better, Sam! There's a question I want to ask you. . . . Thank'ee Sam. How many vents are working now? . . ."

Tom Lockwood looked up wildly at the air-ventilator humming and whacking above his head. He looked at an equally bewildered Jenny.

"Only three? You're sure of that? Right, Sam. Gimme their names and descriptions.

95

Yes, I said descriptions! Uh-huh. . . . No, the first one's no good. Try the second. . . . Lord love a duck, that sounds like the one we want! But try the third, just for luck. . . . No, he's no good either. It's Charley Johnson. Gimme the address. It's nearly six o'clock—he's bound to be at home now. . . . Thanks a million, Sam. And try to keep to one woman next time, hey?—All right, all right!"

Ringing off with the handsome air of one who has made all things clear, Sir Henry Merrivale spun the dial once again.

"Sergeant? I want a squad car, to hold three people and a driver, as quick as kiss-your-hand. Two minutes? Outside the Horse Guards Avenue entrance? Right!"

Lumbering to his feet, H.M. took down from a rack an ancient Panama hat and thrust it on. This hat, which had a band of startling colors and whose brim was turned down all round like a bowl, gave an even more sinister look to the great man's unmentionable face.

"Sir!" protested Tom. "What in the name of sense is all this business of air-vents, and how can it help us?"

"You wanted a miracle explained, didn't you?" demanded the great man. "All right. Are you comin' with me, or not?"

Within the promised two minutes, and in the police car—Jenny and Tom sitting in the back seat, H.M. piled in front with the chauffeur—they whipped out of Horse Guards Avenue, turned left, and shot down Whitehall. H.M., who himself has never driven a car without landing through a shop window or against a lamp-post, made caustic comments about driving skill to a red-eared police driver.

Far beyond the towers of Westminster, behind its stately terraces and flats, lies a region of dingy, almost unknown, streets. The red-brick houses in these streets, by a show of brass knobs and letter-slots, try to keep up a brave pretense that they are private homes and not lodging houses.

But gritty winds make discarded newspapers dance along their gutters; children scream; there is an over-riding clatter of dustbins. Before one such dingy house, which did look like a private home and really was, the car stopped.

"Come on, you two," grunted H.M.

He impelled Jenny and Tom out of the car, and up a flight of stone steps to the front door. There he jabbed his finger at the bell.

"For the last time," said the desperate

Tom, "will you tell what an air-vent—"
H.M. pulled down the brim of his hat even
harder.

"Who said anything about an air-vent?"
he howled. "*I* didn't. I said 'vent.' That's
the theatrical and professional term for a ventriloquist.—Didn't you ever hear a ventriloquist?"

Jenny's hands flew to her open mouth.

"According to your story," pursued H.M.,
"there were only four persons in the whispering gallery with you. This time we can
acquit both your Aunt Hester and your
Cousin Margot—they were leaning over the
railing, much too far away from the wall.

"We can acquit the outraged verger in
charge of the place. But who else was there?
According to you, a fat and red-faced countryman—a little too thoroughly dressed up
as a countryman, wasn't he?—who carried a
packet of sandwiches and a thermos flask.

"When you heard the words, he was sitting against the walls and plainly drinking
tea. All right, my fatheads! Who's the only
man alive who can make his dummy speak
clearly while he himself is walloping down a
full glass of water? You know the answer.

"I rang up the king of all impresarios and
found out the names and descriptions of the

only three vents working in London. This Charley Johnson won't know much about the case. Somebody handed him a fiver to play what he thought, and probably still thinks, was a joke. But *he,* when we see him, can tell us who bribed him to—"

The front door was hurled open.

There is no other word for it—the door crashed against the wall and all but rebounded.

In the doorway there stood, swaying slightly, that same fat man Jenny recognized from the whispering gallery. His face was now less professionally red; he was bald, and wore no wig. Instead of his countryman's clothes, he was wrapped round in a somewhat grubby dressing gown of black and orange stripes. In one hand he held a whiskey-and-soda, in the other a half-eaten sandwich.

But what held them was the expression of his face. His eyes were so horribly wide open that a ring of white showed all the way round the iris.

"Look out, you two!" snapped H.M.

Tom dragged Jenny back just in time.

Charles Johnson, making a bubbling noise, took one step forward. Then he pitched headlong down the stone steps, turning over twice before he lay face down on the pavement.

The smashed glass, the half-eaten sandwich, had flown wide and fallen. Because of the man's tiger-striped dressing gown, it was a moment or two before any of them saw the black handle of the knife driven into his back just under the left shoulder blade.

Nobody moved until the police driver sprang out of the car. It did not need the driver's nod, looking up, to tell them Johnson was dead.

Children's roller skates crashed past on the opposite side of the street, amid shouting. A few windows banged up; a few women's heads were thrust out. That was all.

H.M.'s face was white.

"Easy, my dolly," he said, putting his hand on Jenny's arm and speaking with surprising gentleness. "Is that the man you saw at the whispering gallery?"

The shock was too great. Jenny could only nod.

"Then that means," said H.M., "this is no straight business of frightening a gal out of her wits. It means there's somebody who's dead-determined, crazy-mad, to get what he or she wants. Somebody got here before us and shut Johnson's mouth. Murder with a knife is all in the day's work. And that means . . ."

He brooded so long, ruffling his fingers at his temples, that Tom could not remain quiet.

"H.M.!" he said. "What is it?"

"It means there's been a slight change of plans," he answered.

"How?"

"You, my dolly," said H.M., "aren't going to spend the night at my house after all. If you've got the nerve, you're goin' straight back to spend the night at Aunt Hester's."

A golden sky was becoming tinged with purple over the thin Tudor chimneys of Hampton Court Palace.

Sir Henry Merrivale, in his most maddening mood, sat on an upended wheelbarrow, in one of the few remaining Tudor quadrangles: of dark red brick, with its white stone lions uprearing from the walls beside sly little windows. H.M. was again smoking his black pipe, and looked up at Tom without favor.

"Well," he asked querulously, "where's the whole party *now?*"

"As far as I know, they're still tramping through miles and miles of picture galleries."

"But looky here, son!" protested the great man. "According to my watch, and the notices posted up, this place should have been closed for a long time. Shouldn't they all have been flung out of here hours ago?"

"Yes. But it seems Uncle Fred has a lot of influence with the director or the curator or whatever they call him. They're being taken over the whole show at their leisure, particularly since Jenny's keen to see the maze; and that's a long way from here."

"Maze, hey?" H.M. repeated thoughtfully.

"Now listen to me!" roared Tom, assuming an oratorical posture. "Since a few minutes past six yesterday afternoon, when you got rid of us all, until half an hour ago, when I set eyes on your ugly dial again, you've asked questions by the bucket. But you won't answer a single question yourself. Why?"

" 'Cause I'm the old man."

"And you think that's a good enough reason?"

"Sure it is. I say, son. How is . . . I mean, how is . . . ?"

Tom regarded him bitterly.

"How is Jenny taking this?" he asked. "What the devil do you expect, after that asinine order she was to go back to Aunt Hester's last night? She's taking it badly, of

102

course! But she won't let any of 'em see for a minute she's afraid."

Here the old sinner had at least the grace to look discomfited.

"Well . . . now!" he growled. "I had my reasons, hadn't I? Burn me," and H.M.'s voice rose up passionately, "people are always sayin', 'What an old cloth-head he is; stick him upside down in the dustbin.' Then they see what I mean. And they yell, 'Why, Henry; pull him out and dust him off; we should never have guessed it.' And of course they wouldn't have guessed it, the star-gazin' goops! Only—"

H.M.'s eloquence was interrupted only by a back-wash taste from his own black pipe. Then he simply sat and looked evil.

"All right, all right!" he said. "What did you do last night?"

"Steve Lamoreux and I stood guard outside Jenny's windows all night—"

"Stop a bit, son. Does the gal know who Lamoreux is?"

"She doesn't know he's Armand de Senneville's spy, naturally! And she can't meet him. But, for all practical purposes, he *isn't* a spy. He won't stand for violence—"

"Uh-huh. I know. I talked to him in my office today. You were sayin'?"

"Well, while the rest of 'em were at dinner, Steve and I sneaked into her bedroom and dismantled the gas heater . . ."

Tom paused in even more exasperation. H.M., with a silent and ghoulish mirth, was rocking in ecstasy.

"Oh, son! You didn't think the murderer would try *that* simple little trick again?"

"*Simple* little trick?"

"Easy as shellin' peas."

"Will you acknowledge to me," demanded Tom, after a hard-breathing pause, "that the door of the room really was tightly bolted on the inside and couldn't have been tampered with?"

"Sure."

"Will you acknowledge that both windows were securely locked on the inside and that they weren't tampered with in any way?"

"Agreed without a struggle."

"Will you finally acknowledge that, with no funny business about outside gas meters or the like, somebody—*somebody actually in that room*—turned on the gas-tap?"

"That's right, son."

"*Then how in hell did the murderer get in and out of that room?*"

"I'm not goin' to tell you. Now wait!" said H.M., and pointed with the stem of his pipe. "Yesterday you raved and danced about the 'miracle' of the ventriloquist, didn't you? But that was easy. And this is just as easy, maybe easier, if you think about it. I want you to think about it. Meanwhile, you'd better think of something and somebody you've rather neglected."

"Oh? Who's that?"

"Armand de Senneville himself. You hated him from instinct and from jealousy. But maybe your instincts were right. *I* had him investigated today."

"Well?"

"He's tough, son," H.M. said somberly. "He's tougher than you think. He's an outstanding businessman, a first-class journalist, a mechanical expert, and he was liaison officer with the Yanks for four years during the war. Finally, he's as conceited as the devil; he swears, in private, there's *nothing* he ever wanted that he hasn't got."

"But Armand de Senneville's in Paris!"

"He doesn't have to be here, don't you see?" H.M. asked patiently. "Now listen. You, and the gal Jenny, and even Steve Lamoreux, have all thought there was a whole conspiracy of the Harpenden family—Uncle Fred, young Margot, and Aunt Hester—against Jenny Holden."

"And isn't there?"

"No! Coincidence has mixed you up. There's only *one*, one of those three, who has any knowledge of it. One of them, bribed by Armand de Senneville, would pay any price to have Jenny Holden frightened out of her wits. I give you three: which one?"

It was growing darker in the ancient quadrangle. Tom paced up and down the paving stones, his footfalls stirring back ghostly echoes from the walls.

H.M. knocked out his pipe and replaced it.

"Burn me," he said in a worried voice, "where's that whole family now? You were supposed to be keepin' track of 'em, weren't you?"

"I couldn't! Aunt Hester knows me too well, from that bang-up row in the tea shop! But Steve is trailing 'em, and giving me signals from windows whenever he can."

"But they can't stay in there forever! It'll be pitch dark! I'd give my ears to know where they've gone!"

It was unnecessary to sacrifice H.M.'s ears.

From under the archway to a second quadrangle the sound of *"S-s-t!"* hissed at them in a way which made H.M. leap up from the overturned wheelbarrow.

106

Steve Lamoreux approached as warily as a red Indian. Tom, not without difficulty, had persuaded him to put on a dark suit and an inconspicuous necktie. But his short brown hair stood up as wirily as ever, and he infuriated H.M. by addressing the great man as Pop.

"They're outside," he said, "at the back of the joint. They're going along that broad path, at the back of the palace, that runs a long way to the left between the palace and the gardens. They've got the oldest guide here, who's deaf and practically blind.—And for the love of Pete, Pop, get a wiggle on or they'll close the inner gates and *we'll* be locked in!"

H.M., not without much ruffling of his dignity, was hauled and impelled through the archway, across another quadrangle, and then through a very long archway at whose end they could see the last gleam of daylight.

They stopped at the outer edge of the arch. Just ahead lay the immense gardens, their straight-ruled lines of flower beds draining of color in twilight. Peering round the edge of the arch to the left, Tom saw the very broad, sanded path beside ancient walls.

Five persons, their backs to the conspirators in the archway, strolled along this path about a hundred yards ahead. Though it was too dark to discern faces at that distance, Tom knew who they were as they walked abreast.

First, on the extreme left, doddered an old guide in uniform. Next, marching briskly, strode Aunt Hester. Jenny walked nervously between the giggling Margot, who danced with short steps, and the firm military stride of Uncle Fred on the extreme right.

"All right," whispered Tom. "What do we do now?"

"I know what we *could* do," said Lamoreux.

"You do, hey?" sneered H.M.

"Yes! They can't recognize us in this light. If we just strolled after 'em, three abreast but keeping back, they'd take us for another privileged tourist party like themselves. That is, if somebody could do a little spiel like a guide."

The role of guide caught Sir Henry Merrivale's fancy at once.

"Hem!" he said, tapping himself on the chest. "Me."

Lamoreux looked doubtful.

"Okay, Pop, you're the boss. But are you sure you know enough about the history of this joint?"

"*Me?*" said the outraged H.M. "The palace of Hampton Court," he bellowed, "begun by Cardinal Wolsey in the year 1515, was in 1526 pinched from this worthy prelate by that howlin' old ram King Henry the Eighth, whose wives I shall now proceed to—"

"Pop! Quiet!"

"Am I a guide," H.M. asked loftily, "or ain't I?"

"You are," snapped Tom. "And if the balloon goes up, it goes up. Anyway, I can *see* Jenny. They can't hurt her now. Let's go."

Out they marched, trying to tread softly, with Lamoreux on the inner side, Tom in the middle, and H.M. on the outer side.

It was quiet, so intense that they could hear the footsteps of those far ahead of them as well as their own. Peace lay in the hollow of a warm spring night, with the fragrance of grass and trees. You would never have guessed that death was walking with them along the broad white path—and moving closer at every pace.

Tom Lockwood did not know this, of course. But he sensed danger-fangs everywhere. He kept his eyes fixed on Jenny as though she might disappear, and his nerves were twitching like a landed fish.

So he quite literally jumped as a mighty voice smote through his thoughts.

"On our right," it thundered, "we got the famous Hampton Court gardens, forty-four acres of elegant spinach, first laid out by King William the Third and completed in 1734."

"For God's sake be careful," whispered Tom. "William the Third died in 1702."

H.M. swung round, fists on hips.

"And d'ye think I don't know that?" he bellowed. "I didn't say the old sour-puss finished 'em, did I? I just said he laid 'em out—which is what I'm goin' to do to you, young man, if you don't shut up and stop interruptin' my lecture."

"Pop! The soft pedal! Give it the old soft pedal! Holy cats, they'll hear you as far as Thames Ditton!"

But, whatever devilment H.M. had meditated—and Tom knew he had planned it in advance—the damage was done. Five persons, mere shapes in the twilight, turned round and looked back.

Out from the group, head high, marched Aunt Hester. She strode along the full distance that separated them, and looked straight at H.M.

"You, I fancy," she said coolly, "must be the man Merrivale?"

"On our left," bellowed H.M., "we see the celebrated tennis court. The game of tennis, originally played with a wooden ball, was designed with the laudable purpose of knockin' somebody's eye out—which it generally did. One famous match—"

"Answer me, please!" said Aunt Hester. "On whose authority, may I ask, are you in these grounds after official visiting hours."

H.M. gave her a wicked look.

"On Sir Hugh Rossiter's," he said. "The same as yours. Want to ring him and find out?"

Since H.M. knew everybody, this might possibly be true. Aunt Hester did not dare risk the challenge. Besides, she was more interested in someone else.

"One of you, I believe," she stated crisply, "I have already met. Indeed, Mr. Lockwood, I wish to have a word with you."

"Fire away," said Tom.

"Ever since you abducted my niece yesterday, and afterwards returned her in—I *hope*—a condition suitable to a bride, poor Jennifer has been talking nonsense which I propose to stamp out here and now."

"Oh?"

111

"Yes. Absurdly enough, the girl believes she is in love with you . . ."

"Is she, by God!" exclaimed Tom.

Whereupon he completely lost his head. Raising his voice, he shouted clearly and loudly through the twilight.

"Jenny!" he called. *"Jenny! Do you love me?"*

Jenny spun round in the broad white path.

"Yes!" she shouted back.

"Will you marry me?"

"Yes!"

Dead silence.

"Well . . . now!" observed Sir Henry Merrivale, with much complacence. "Since that's all settled and finished—"

"Oh, cripes!" breathed Steve Lamoreux, in a voice Tom had never heard him use. "If that's how people propose to each other in England, maybe it's true you're kind of casual. Do you just get married on the telephone, or what?"

But Aunt Hester was not amused. The paint stood out against her pale face; she was alert, smiling—and dangerous.

"How interesting!" she laughed. "It surely will interest her dear guardian and," Aunt Hester's eyes slid sideways, "the *fiancé* to

112

whom she is pledged. Tell me, Mr. Lockwood, what is your yearly income?"

Tom stared at the ground.

"Well! I didn't want to . . ."

"Come, Mr. Lockwood!" said Aunt Hester, with honeyed sweetness. "You are a reporter on the *Record*, we know. Just what *is* your yearly income?"

"Tell her, son," growled H.M.

"All right!" said Tom, raising his head. "When death duties are subtracted, it'll be about twelve thousand pounds a year."

"*Twelve—thou—*"

"I didn't earn it," snapped Tom. "My mother left it to me. I've published just one unsuccessful novel. When I walked up Ludgate Hill yesterday, I was thinking about chucking my job and trying full-time writing. That's what I'll do, when Jenny marries me. It's why I told you, Steve, you might get a better boss; you can have my job, and they'll hand it to you on a plate. But I've never given two hoots about Jenny's money, and I'd rather prefer it if she didn't have a penny to her name."

"This is the most fantastic—" Aunt Hester was beginning, when she stopped dead.

H.M. slowly extended his neck, and gave

her such a look as could not have been matched by Satan himself.

"Madam," he said, "you've got no business with us. Sling your hook."

"I absolutely refuse—"

H.M. extended his finger until it almost touched Aunt Hester's nose.

"Madam," he said, "are you goin' to hop it? Or do you prefer to find yourself, sittin' down, in the middle of King William's spinach?"

Aunt Hester hopped it. Before that glare, which would have caused the Angels of Light themselves to retire to prepared positions, she could have done nothing else.

She ran hard towards the group ahead, and appeared to be talking rapidly. The whole group faced round and began hurrying, at a faster pace, in their original direction. Jenny seemed violently to object, but Margot gripped her arm and hastened her on.

Tom Lockwood, a powerfully built young man, was all for charging forward and starting a fight at once. His companions held him back.

"Easy, son!" said H.M. "Not just yet, I tell you! We've got 'em in sight. They can't get away."

"Pop," declared Lamoreux, whose face was pale and pinched, "you're a so-and-so. You're a so-and-so and a this-and-that. You deliberately yelled all that guff about spinach and tennis balls, just so the old dame would come tearing back here. Why did you do it?"

"Well . . . now!" said H.M. with a modest look. "I rather wanted to know, d'ye see, if some person would meet some other person. Am I making myself clear?"

"No. You're not."

"Never mind, son," soothed H.M. "I haven't been so much worried about that gal as about another person. Besides, I repeat, they can't get away. We've got 'em in sight."

Lamoreux stopped in his tracks.

"Oh, no, we haven't!" he said in a high voice. "Where are they now? They've disappeared!"

It was true.

Once past the gardens and the long line of the palace, the road was closed in by tall trees, dusty and spectral against a windless night, with an occasional bench on either side. Five persons had vanished from the road.

"H.M.," said Tom, seizing his companion's arm, "you seem to be the expert on Hampton Court. Where does this road lead?"

"Steady, son! It leads to one of the main entrances—the Lion Gate. But, if you turn to the left before you reach the gate, you'll soon get to the open space where they've got the maze—"

"The maze!" said Tom, and every nameless fear boiled up inside him. "Run, you blighters! *Run!*"

That H.M. himself did run, despite his large corporation and his dislike of any pedestrian exercise, can only be stated as a fact. Lifting his chin so as to cleave the air, he belted along that road as fast as his younger companions.

Some hundred and twenty yards farther on, they saw the dim gleam of a light past an avenue of trees branching to the left. Into this they flew abreast, found themselves in a large open space, and stopped.

For the first time they heard the wheezing, rusty voice of the old guide.

"Now, miss," he was pleading, "you don't really want to go into the maze, do you? 'Tisn't very difficult, not what we like to pretend it is. But that's in the daytime. You don't want to go in at night, miss."

"But I do!" Jenny insisted firmly. "All

my life I've been reading about the Hampton Court maze, and I'll die if I don't explore it. Won't you lend me your electric torch?"

In the clearing, a hut or small pavilion had been set well back, evidently used as somebody's living quarters; on a pole against the side of the hut burned a sickly electric bulb.

The famous maze was set well out from the hut. It was roughly oval in shape, a little higher than a man's head, of green hedge raggedly trimmed. Illumined in bright green and dead shadow by the sickly light, it loomed up less as a place of comedy than as a secret, malicious trap.

The entrance must be at the far side, because the entire party was assembled there. Slant-eyed Margot was jumping up and down with joy.

"May I go in too, Mama?" she shrilled. "*May* I go?"

"No, you may not," said Aunt Hester sharply. "Afterwards, perhaps, if dear Jennifer—"

"Lot of nonsense, *I* call it," grumbled Uncle Fred from under his gray military mustache.

"*Please* may I have the electric torch?" said Jenny in a voice no man could resist.

"Ah, well," mumbled the guide. " 'Ere's

the torch, I s'pose I can always climb up on top of the stepladder by the entrance, and give you directions if you get lost. Be nippy, now."

"I will! I will!"

"Jenny!" called Tom. "Jenny, wait! I'm going with you!"

His words did not carry to her. Faintly he heard the creak of a small gate, and the brushing of Jenny's body against the narrow sides of the maze.

Tom sprang forward. Instantly Sir Henry Merrivale locked both his arms from behind, and held him back.

"No, son," said H.M., in so soft and deadly a voice that Tom was startled. "You're not goin' into that maze."

"Why not?"

"Whose life," asked H.M., glancing round him, "d'ye think I've been worried about, as much or more than the little gal's herself. *Yours.*"

"Are you crazy?"

"No. But you're not goin' inside that maze."

Tom, with one sudden heave and jerk, tore loose even from H.M.'s powerful grip.

"I'm sorry, sir. But that's where I'm going, and neither you nor anybody else is going to stop me."

He ran across the sanded space, and round the side to the entrance. He saw the startled face of Uncle Fred, who was swinging a heavy yellow cane. He saw Aunt Hester, with rigid mouth. He saw the pretty, mischievous face of Margot, who was slipping away in another direction.

The guide had already shakily mounted to the top of the stepladder beside the entrance. Tom swung open the little gate, twisted sideways as he plunged into the maze, and attempted to run.

It was impossible.

The hedge-walls were so narrow that tendrils stung his face. Though it was not pitch-dark, just enough light filtered down from the dim bulb outside to distort the eyesight and turn dark shapes into illusions. He might run slap into a hedge-wall at any second, and just saved himself from doing so.

Gently, now!

Stopping at a turn, Tom felt down on his left and found the thin wall, of hard and curved wire, built a little below waist height. In this maze, he remembered it had been said, you must always turn to the left. He did so, and presently turned left again.

119

That was when he saw, deeper inside these thinnish walls, the firefly glimmer of Jenny's torch. It vanished again—but it was there.

"Jenny!" he called. "Wait for me! It's Tom!"

"Tom! Darling!" Her voice slipped through the walls rather than above them. "Where are you?"

"I don't know. Where are *you?*"

"Very near the center of the maze, I think."

"Then stop where you are! Wait until I catch up with you!"

"Oh, no!" Jenny retorted demurely. "I'll get to the center and turn off the torch. Then you can find me and tell me how much you love me."

"Jenny, wait!"

But the firefly glimmer danced away. He could hear her brushing and hurrying on. In a moment or two there was a cry of pleasure, as evidently she found the center of the maze. The light of her torch went out.

Tom moved forward, more slowly and carefully. The electric bulb at the hut was now so distant and so dim that it gave scarcely any light. Tom didn't know where he was. Walls loomed up and closed round him. It wasn't pleasant, being shut into a twisting maze where . . .

Then he stopped, listening.

Somebody was following him stealthily through the maze.

Somebody, not much lighter than his own weight, was stalking him—with what intent? Tom ran forward and stopped. The footsteps behind him ran forward and stopped. Tom ran again. But he was not left in doubt long.

A closer footfall, a looming of a shape in near-darkness, made him glance over his shoulder. He saw the upsurge of someone's silhouette. A distant gleam flashed on the blade of the knife as it lifted high—and struck.

All that saved Tom from being stabbed in the back, as Johnson the ventriloquist had been stabbed, was the dim light and the attacker's misjudgment. The blade of the knife ripped through the cloth of the coat over Tom's shoulder. The attacker, plunging forward so hard that he collided with Tom, sent his victim sprawling one way and drove his own head and shoulders, grotesquely, straight into the hedge on the other side.

Somebody screamed one word, nothing more.

With a crackling of branches, the attacker

wrenched out his left arm and then withdrew his head. Before he could disengage his knife-hand, Tom landed a vicious right-hander that opened his assailant's cheekbone and drew first blood.

Then they faced each other, two dim shapes, between the narrow walls.

There were no Queensbury Rules here. Neither man was a boxer. But both were enraged and both meant murder.

The attacker held his knife blade out, to leap forward and rip up. Just as he lunged, Tom kicked him in the groin. The attacker, in intense agony, began to double up; his knife fell and tinkled. Tom hit him again.

The attacker, straightening up, flew in with both fists. Tom hit him twice, left and right, in the belly. Then he put all his strength into a right cross to the man's jaw—which, if it had landed, would have broken Tom's hand.

But it did not land on the jaw. Instead it landed, with just as murderous effect, in the soft flesh under the man's left ear. The attacker, brain paralyzed and legs suddenly gone to water, reeled backwards and fell.

"Now where the devil," Tom was thinking, "did we get so much space?"

Then he realized they had been fighting

very near the entrance to the center of the maze. For the first time he heard voices, and bodies thrashing about in the maze.

Behind him loomed up the blaze of an electric torch. Above it showed the malignant countenance of Sir Henry Merrivale. Next, cowering away in one side of the maze's center, Jenny switched on her own torch.

Both beams converged on the man who lay on his back in the center of the maze. His eyes were closed; he breathed stertorously; sluggish blood flowed from a cut in his cheek.

Jenny's face grew so white, and she turned her head away so abruptly, that Tom thought she was going to be sick.

But his own feelings were swallowed up in incredulity.

"This is impossible!" he said, pointing to the man on the ground. "That's Steve Lamoreux, the reporter!"

"Oh, no, it's not," said Sir Henry Merrivale. *"That's Armand de Senneville himself."*

"Explanations?" demanded H.M., in a tone of dismal surprise. "You don't mean to tell me you *need* explanations?"

Jenny and Tom, both seated beside the desk in H.M.'s office at the end of the following day, instantly and vehemently said they did need explanations.

H.M. sighed.

"Y'know, my dolly," he said, "you ought to have seen through your *fiancé*, Armand de Senneville, sooner than you did. He tried to prevent your trip to England. He couldn't prevent it—his father's word was law. But he knew how much you'd been repressed and kept under the thumb in France. He knew, as he casually warned Aunt Hester, you'd probably fall bang for the first presentable, easy-going Englishman who made you laugh and didn't think correct behavior was everything in life. Which is what you did."

"I did not!" Jenny cried indignantly. "I have fall bang for Tom, yes. But that is a different thing!"

Tom hastily intervened in order to evade the devastating question, "How is it different?"

"Then de Senneville," he said, "had only to crop his hair, have it dyed brown, wear very loud clothes, and pose as a French Canadian reporter from one of his own papers?"

"But Armand," insisted Jenny, "speaks no English!"

"No?" said H.M. "That's what he told

124

you, my dolly. But as I explained to Tom here, the bloke was attached for four years to the American Army as a liaison officer. So surely he could speak English. In fact, his ear was perfect; his American was perfect. But he had to play the part of a French Canadian to explain how he spoke both languages."

"And yet," exclaimed Jenny, her eyes clouding, "I still do not understand this Armand! If he wished to keep men away from me, why did he not say he spoke English and go with the whole party of us?"

"You don't understand that, my dolly? Though it's the key to his whole character?"

"No! Why is it the key?"

"Because he was too proud," said H.M., "and he was far too conceited. He wouldn't demean himself in public by showin' he was concerned. He wouldn't admit that any man alive could take you away from the great Armand.

"Listen, my dolly, he never wanted to kill *you!* Neither did Aunt Hester. All they wanted to do was scare you so much that you'd run straight back to France. Don't you remember what you said yourself, in this office? I asked, 'Do you still want to stay at your Aunt Hester's?' And you cried out, 'No, but what else can I do except return to Paris?'—Got it now?"

"Then," Jenny blurted out, "just to get my dowry, this Armand has . . ."

"Oh, he wanted your money," said H.M. somberly. "But, towards the end, I don't think that was all. That murderous fight in the maze wasn't done altogether for money. I expect, in his own queer way, he was a little bit in love with you."

Again, since Jenny's eyes were clouding worse than ever, Tom intervened.

"But the locked room!" he said. "Where the gas-tap was turned on even while windows and door were both locked on the inside!"

"Well . . . now," H.M. sighed wearily. "I'd better tell you about it, because that locked room told me the whole ruddy truth before I even knew who was behind it.

"On the famous Night of Terrors," he added, pointing at Jenny, "you found, in your napkin at dinner, a note readin', 'You will die tonight, Jennifer.' Eh?"

"But who wrote the note?" interrupted Tom.

"Aunt Hester wrote it," snapped H.M. "There's never been much mystery about her. Her words and actions were too plain.

She was the dominatin' character of her family, the only one, as I more than hinted, whom de Senneville bribed and prompted.

"After dinner," H.M. continued, still pointing at Jenny, "you went to your room at a little past eleven o'clock. One of the long windows, which you'd left closed, was now wide open. Correct?"

"Yes," said Jenny, and shuddered.

"You closed and locked the window again. You didn't need to touch or go near the gas fire. At shortly past twelve you went to bed, and soon fell asleep. The next thing you knew, Margot was bangin' on the door at six o'clock. A mysterious 'American' voice is asking what's wrong. They ran round to the window, pickin' up Uncle Fred on the way. Uncle Fred smashes the window. The mysterious 'American,' whom you can't see because you're too far gone, rushes over to the gas fire. He says, 'So-and-so, but it's turned full on!' And, apparently, he turns it off. Correct again?"

"Yes, yes."

"Not to me it isn't," said H.M., shaking his head. "Whoever this mysterious American was, he was the joker behind the trick. He told a flat lie. That gas *couldn't* have been turned full on."

127

"Why not?"

"Because you'd have been dead," H.M. said simply. "Let's suppose somebody, in the middle of the night, sneaks in and turns on the gas full-strength. Never mind what time it was. Let's even say it was as late, as impossibly late, as five o'clock in the morning. But there's no person in the world, breathing full-strength gas in an unventilated room, who can breathe it for an hour and still live. So I asked you a question to prove it."

"What question?"

"Oh, my dolly! You could describe every small noise you heard even when you were only half conscious. But you *didn't* hear any noise of a gas fire turned on full, which would have roared like a tornado. That's all."

"Oh!" exclaimed Jenny, caught up with a jolt. "Then . . . ?"

"Yes! Just before you retired to your room, Armand de Senneville—alias Steve Lamoreux—sneaked in and turned on the gas heater a tiny thread—only a tiny thread, not noticeable at all. He went out, leavin' the window wide open for good ventilation.

"You came in and closed the window. Well! What does happen, in very big rooms like that one, with such a tiny leak of gas? You can't hear it, you can't even smell it, for well over an hour. The bed is too far away. And it's caused tragedy before this. Meanwhile, for nearly six hours, the room is very slowly fillin' up with gas. When they found you, you were in just the condition I'd have expected.

"That's pretty much everything, my dolly. Armand de Senneville was lurkin' close outside, of course. You bet he was! He'd calculated his times, as he always does, but he was damned near too late to bust in himself, as he intended.

"He *had* to meet Margot—he couldn't help it. But that gal's a silly kind of wench, so excited she never wondered what he was doin' there. Uncle Fred barely noticed him. Later, it was easy for Aunt Hester to look 'em straight in the eye and tell 'em both they'd been dreaming. She was the only one who knew our Armand by sight. But, as for the 'miracle' of the locked room . . ."

"And that is all?" cried Jenny.

"Sure. What else did you expect?"

"I am disappoint!" suddenly exclaimed Jenny, hammering her fists on her knees. "I think this is a miracle. I think it cannot be solved. And then you show it is easy as eating sweets. Sir H.M., I hate you!"

The subsequent behavior of Sir Henry Merrivale, his martyrdom and his passionate addresses to the ceiling, is best left undescribed.

"So that's all the thanks I get, hey? They come to me and say, 'It's a miracle.' I say, 'It ain't,' and show 'em how it's done. Then they say, 'Oh, is that all? Silly old dummy! Stick him in the dustbin again.' "

It was fully half an hour before they smoothed him down.

"Very well!" he said, with a dark look at Jenny. "I'll not state what I think of some people. I'll just tell you what happened next and upset the whole apple cart. Aunt Hester had to drag a very sick and scared gal all the way to St. Paul's, so that Armand's hired ventriloquist could perform on time.

"But the apple cart was upset with an awful smash. 'Steve Lamoreux,' sittin' in the car just as he said he did, saw you run down the steps of St. Paul's and literally fall into this young feller's arms. When you went into the tea shop—well, Bob's your uncle. You bet he sneaked in and listened behind the partition. What he heard was just what he'd

130

feared. You two were practically fallin' into each others' arms over the tea."

"I feel like this," Jenny confessed.

"I still feel like it," said Tom.

"Shut up," said the great man. "There were several courses open to 'Steve Lamoreux.' He chose the best, which was winnin' Tom Lockwood's confidence and stayin' close to him. So he deliberately sent this gal to me, supremely and conceitedly thinkin' the old goop would never see through *his* scheme.

"After Aunt Hester's row in the tea shop," here H.M. looked at Tom, "he went in and told his story. He more than won your confidence, son. He won your friendship."

"Yes," admitted Tom, and looked down at a closed fist. "He did."

"Of course, he couldn't go with you when you came to my office. He admitted the gal mustn't meet him. What he did is easy to guess. He followed you, and hung about in Horse Guards Avenue. D'ye know, I think I can see his face when we three piled downstairs and out to a police car, and I gave the address of his own hired ventriloquist.

"He got to the house about fifty seconds before we did, probably by waving a fiver in under a taxi-driver's nose. He nipped in by the back door, struck faster than a snake, and nipped out the same way while Johnson's body rolled down the front steps.

"And that tore it. As I said, the whole aspect of the business had changed.

"According to what I could deduce about the gas fire and the whispering gallery, *nobody* was actually trying to kill this gal. Somebody was trying to frighten her so much that she'd take the first plane back to Paris.

"Now who would be interested in doin' that, in conjunction with Aunt Hester? Who? You guess. And what about this odd 'American' or 'Canadian' who kept turning up all over the place without any explanation? Everybody promised to explain him; but nobody did."

H.M. pulled down his spectacles and glowered at Jenny over them.

"You see, my dolly, why I wanted you to go back to your aunt's house that night? You weren't in any real danger. And it wasn't likely somebody would try any games that night. If anything happened at all, it would happen during the expedition to Hampton Court next day—for one thing, Aunt Hester was far too insistent about takin' you there.

"And I could be there to stop it. And yet, burn me, I nearly missed it!"

The somber spectacles were now turned towards Tom.

"Son," observed H.M., "did you see the look on 'Steve Lamoreux's' face when you shouted along the path and asked this gal to marry you? And she said yes?"

"No, but I heard his voice. It was a voice I'd never heard him use before."

"Well! When it turned out you had tons of money and they couldn't accuse you of being a fortune hunter, did you notice him at any time after *that?*"

"Yes! His face was all pinched up and as pale as dough. But I thought—"

"Maybe you did. He had a knife with him, just in case. And that was the time he finally decided you were goin' to die."

Jenny pressed her face in her hands, and turned away.

"Oh, I was the villain!" said H.M. "In my role of guide, I wanted to see how Aunt Hester would act when she met Steve Lamoreux face to face. She behaved pretty well, but she couldn't keep her eyes from slidin' away when she mentioned the gal's *fiancé.*

"It was a silly-ass thing to do. I admit it. 'Cause I'd already made up my mind. That same day, since Armand de Senneville had been attached to the Yanks, I got his record and saw his photograph. To put the tin hat on it, 'Steve Lamoreux' had the star-gazin' cheek to walk into my office and spin his yarn.

"Even if I hadn't known already, the idiot gave himself away. He *would* smoke Yellow cigarettes, and use sulphur matches. Even when he was very excited, he automatically held the match away from him until the sulphur had burned off—"

"Yes," interrupted Tom. "I saw him do that. But what about it?"

"Oh, son! He claimed he'd been in France only six months—"

"Yes, that's what he told me too!"

"And no foreigner on earth, after only six months in France, can get used to those sulphur matches. You always forget and swallow a lungful of sulphur. Only a Frenchman native-born automatically holds the match away for a few seconds. There, in my own office, was a Frenchman speakin' the most exquisite Yank.

"But *you* were the one in real danger, son. If I'd known beforehand you'd spent the night before prowlin' round this gal's windows with Armand de Senneville, I'd have had a fit. I repeat: he struck like a snake and

134

killed poor old Johnson. Why? Just because he didn't want this gal to find out that it was *he* who was scaring her, or he'd lose her.

"Finally, last night at Hampton Court, I still don't know what funny business de Senneville, or Aunt Hester, or both of 'em, had planned. There wasn't time—the fireworks went up with a bang. I tried to keep you from goin' into that maze. Didn't you see me look round? Didn't you notice Lamoreux had slipped away? You dashed into the maze. He must have crawled up on top of it—we didn't see him enter—and followed you. But sometimes, for chivalrous young fools like you, there is mercy. You met the tough egg with his knife, and you knocked him flat. And that was the end."

There was a long silence, until Tom cleared his throat.

"H.M. What will they do to him?"

"Oh, they can't prove yet he killed Johnson. Not yet. In the meantime, he'll do a long stretch on two counts of attempted murder: with gas and with a knife. Then the coppers will snaffle him for killing Johnson. And he'll get what he deserves, son—he'll hang."

Jenny stood up suddenly, trembling. Tom put his arms around her, and held her tightly.

"It's all right!" he insisted. "Jenny, dear, it's all right!"

"Yes," said Jenny, holding him just as tightly, "but that is why you must not leave me, ever. It is all right—*now!*"

For once in his life, Sir Henry Merrivale did not roar out about canoodling in his office. Slowly, somberly, he got up from his chair and wandered over to one of the windows. There, his hands folded behind his back, he stood looking out over the river and the mighty curve of London.

Mom Knows Best

JAMES YAFFE

My MOTHER always wanted me to be a professional man. It didn't matter to her what kind of profession. Any kind would do, as long as it was really "professional," and absolutely not "business."

"Your uncles are in business, your cousins are in business, your Papa was in business, and none of them ever made a cent of money," Mom always said. "Except your Uncle Max, and he don't count, because God forbid you should ever turn out to be such a physical and nervous wreck as your Uncle Max and your Aunt Selma."

And so, even when I was a small boy in the Bronx, Mom saw to it that I got some professional training. She gave me chemistry sets for my birthday; she made me take violin lessons; she even encouraged me to work my childish charms on a distant cousin of ours who was a lawyer. And finally Mom got her wish. Today I am a professional man.

137

But I'm afraid this fact has never given Mom any satisfaction. You see, she didn't exactly expect me to become a policeman.

From the very beginning she raised objections. All sorts of objections, every day a new objection—but most of them were smokescreens. Her antagonism to the life of a policeman really boils down to two points. One: the work is dangerous. "All those gangsters and dope fiends and bookies and hatchet murderers and other such *goniffs* you have to deal with," she says. "Isn't it possible that you could get hurt some day?"

Two: she thinks the job is beneath me. "Always it was my ambition that you should take up something that needs a little intelligence and brainpower," she says. "But this detective work, this figuring out who killed who, and playing cops and robbers like the kiddies in the park, this is no work for a grown-up man. For all the brains it takes, believe me, you might as well be in business with your uncles."

And there is simply no way of talking Mom out of this opinion, of convincing her of the dignity and difficulty of my profession. Even though I've done pretty well for myself, even though I'm in plainclothes now and chief assistant to Inspector Slattery, Mom still makes fun of me. And with justice. Because to tell the truth, this cops and robbers business *is* child's-play—for Mom. Figuring out who killed who *is* an easy job—for Mom. With her ordinary common-sense, and her natural talent for seeing into people's motives and never letting herself be fooled by anybody (this talent comes from her long experience with shifty-eyed butchers and delicatessen store clerks), Mom is usually able to solve over the dinner table crimes that keep the police running around in circles for weeks.

In fact, I might even go so far as to say that my chief value to the Homicide Squad lies not in the strenuous investigating, manhunting, and third-degreeing that I do all week, but in the revealing conversations I have with Mom every Friday night, when she invites my wife and me up to the Bronx for dinner.

Take last Friday night, for instance.

Shirley and I got to Mom's apartment at six. Mom gave us the usual glass of wine, and we sat down to the usual roast chicken dinner (which is really unusual, because who can equal Mom's roast chicken?). For a while, the conversation ran along the usual lines. Mom told us about the ailments and scandals of everybody in the neighborhood. Then she gave Shirley advice on how to shop for groceries. Shirley is a Wellesley graduate with a degree in psychology, so naturally Mom is convinced that she's incapable of understanding the practical affairs of life. Then she lectured me on wrapping up warm in this damp weather. Finally, after bringing in the noodle soup, she asked me: "So how is the work going, Davie?"

"Nothing very interesting, Mom," I said. "Just an ordinary everyday murder case. Three suspects. One of them must be guilty. It's just a question of working on them long enough, till the guilty one cracks."

"And so far he didn't crack yet, the guilty party?"

"Not yet, Mom. But he will, all right. We'll sweat it out of him."

"And out of yourselves, while you're at it!" Mom gave a sigh. "This third degree, it's harder on the policemen than it is on the crooks. If you men only would stop a minute and use your heads, look at all the *tsouris* you'd save. Believe me, there isn't a single one of you that don't need a mother to look after you."

"It's not a question of using our heads, Mom. It's patience, pure patience. I'll tell you about the case, and you can judge for yourself. You see, this girl was killed in a hotel downtown. A sort of high-class low-class hotel, if you know what I mean. Very sporty, expensive crowd. Stage people, gamblers, radio and television people—a pretty flash assortment. And blondes. The place is full of platinum blondes. With no visible means of support. Maybe they call themselves dancers—only they haven't stood on a chorus line for years; maybe they say they're models—only they never get any closer to a magazine cover than a million other readers.

"That's what this dead girl was. A genuine platinum blonde, who used the name Vilma Degrasse. Usual career—quit high school at sixteen to go on the chorus line. Quit the chorus line five years ago—to move into the hotel. Been living there ever since, in two rooms on the fifth floor. Her and a steady stream of admirers. All male—"

"And to make a long story short," Shirley cut in, "last night one of them killed her."

Shirley is always taking it on herself to make my long stories short. This doesn't bother me much—when I married Shirley, I knew I was getting a superior-type woman— but it never fails to get a rise out of Mom.

She rose now. "Well, well, isn't that interesting?" she said, turning to Shirley with a sweet polite smile. "So you're working on the case too, are you, Shirley dear?"

Shirley smiled right back at Mom, just as sweetly and politely. "Not at all, Mother. I'm just trying to help David cure himself of his terrible habit of talking on and on and never getting to the point. It's something he picked up in his childhood, though goodness knows from whom."

"Now here's our three suspects," I interrupted quickly, as I saw a gleam coming into Mom's eye. "At ten o'clock last night the girl was escorted into the lobby by a gentleman—middle-aged banker of this city, named Griswold. Very unhappy about having his name mentioned in the papers. They were seen coming in by the clerk at the desk and by the elevator girl. The clerk is a gray-haired, seedy old man named Bigelow. The grumpy type. When I questioned him this afternoon he complained every two minutes about how he'd been standing on his feet behind that desk for four hours, and how the management don't even allow him to have a radio to help pass the time, and how the Assistant Manager is always poking around to make sure the clerks don't hide any magazines or newspapers under the desk, and so on and so on. And all the time this Bigelow was blowing beer fumes into my face. Unpleasant character, but just the same I think he's telling the truth. No apparent reason to lie.

"The elevator girl is Sadie Delaney, a talkative dark-haired Irish girl. Not married yet, built on the large side, but very cheerful and hearty, always doing special favors for people in the hotel. A good witness, too—cooperative and bright.

"So anyway, Sadie took the Degrasse girl and old Griswold up to the fifth floor, said good night to them, and rode down again. She passed the time with Bigelow about ten minutes, then she got a buzz from the fifth floor. She went up and found old Griswold waiting for the elevator and looking very mad. She took him down and said good night again, but he didn't answer her. He went stamping out of the lobby—"

At this moment there was an interruption as Shirley finished her noodle soup. "Oh, Mother, that soup was delicious," she said. "It's such a pleasure to taste your cooking. You know, that's really what you do *best* in the world."

"Thank you, with kindness, darling," Mom said. "But that's how it was with all the girls in my day, so I can't take any special credit. Even if we was too poor to go to college, we always learned something useful. We didn't fill our heads with a lot of *meshuggene* ideas that are no good to anybody—like so many of the young girls nowadays."

I saw that Shirley was getting ready to answer this, so I took a deep breath and hurried on with my story:

"A minute later, enter Suspect Number Two. This is Tom Monahan, the hotel handyman. He was just going off duty, but he told Sadie that Miss Degrasse had called him earlier that day to fix a leak in her bathtub, and he was afraid she'd be mad if he didn't do it before she went to bed. So Sadie rode him up to the fifth floor and rode down again. No sooner did she get down than she heard another buzz from five. She went up again and found Tom. He said he had knocked on the girl's door, got no answer, so he figured she was asleep already. He'd fix the bathtub tomorrow. Down he went with Sadie, and straight home from there.

"Now Sadie and Bigelow chatted for about twenty minutes in the lobby. They talked about the big prizefight which was on that night, and how brutal it was, and what a beating the champ was taking. Their chat was interrupted by Suspect Number Three.

"This is young Artie Fellows, playboy about town, theatrical angel, and general no-good, who's been showing up to see the Degrasse girl a lot of nights this last month. He was in evening clothes. Just left a party at the home of his young fiancée that he's going to marry in June. Sadie rode him up to the fifth floor and left him there. Five minutes later, the buzzer started ringing loud and long. She rode up again and found Fellows looking green. He told her he'd just entered the girl's apartment with his key—the key she gave him—and found her lying dead on her bed. Well, the house dick was called, and a doctor and the police, and it was finally decided that somebody stunned her with a blow on the back of the head, administered by a bronze candlestick, her own property. And then, when she was stunned, this somebody smothered her to death with a pillow. We found the pillow on the floor next to the body. It was all rumpled up, and there were teeth marks and saliva stains to show what happened."

"Somehow," Shirley said, "I find it hard to feel much sympathy for a cheap unrefined girl like that. Usually such people get what they deserve."

"Not always," Mom said, in a musing voice, as if she were talking to herself. "There's plenty people running around in this world that maybe ought to get themselves smothered. Not enough to kill them maybe—just a little bit smothered, to teach them a lesson." Before Shirley could say a word to this, Mom turned to me very calmly and said, "So go on with the case, please."

"Well, the first thing we did, of course, was to question the three men. Here's what they tell us: Griswold was cagey at first, but finally he came out and admitted that he and the blonde had an argument after they got into her apartment. She told him she was through with him, she'd found another gentleman friend who was younger and richer— young Fellows most likely. Griswold says he was mad when he walked out, but claims he didn't kill her. Says he left her very much alive, turning on her television set to listen to the big prizefight. She was a great sports fan, especially if there was lots of blood. Well, so much for Griswold.

"For a while the handyman Tom Monahan looked like our murderer. We discovered a funny thing. There was absolutely nothing wrong with the bathtub in the Degrasse girl's apartment. So finally Monahan came out with the truth. He and the blonde were carrying on a little flirtation—he's a big husky good-looking fellow, and she wasn't what you'd call particular. Monahan made up that bathtub dodge as an excuse to go up and see her. But he sticks to his story about knocking on the door and getting no answer. Incidentally, we asked him whether he heard the television going inside the room. He says he didn't notice.

"As for Artie Fellows—he still claims he came into the room and found her dead. What's more, he corroborates Griswold's story about the television. The television was on full blast when he came in, he says. In fact, this struck him as an especially gruesome touch, what with that blonde lying dead on the bed.

"So that's the set-up, Mom. It's got to be one of those three. It can't be anybody else who lives in the hotel, because we've checked up on everybody—it's a small hotel, not many tenants, and they've all got alibis. And it can't be anybody from the outside, because the clerk and the elevator girl didn't see anybody else come in or out. In other words, it's strictly a routine job. Griswold, Monahan,

147

or Fellows, take your choice. Eeny-meeny-miney—!"

"You forgot Moe," Mom said.

This remark struck me as slightly senseless, but I gave Mom a sharp look anyway—because her senseless remarks have a way of turning out to contain more sense than you'd expect. "What do you mean by that?"

"Never mind what I mean by that," she said. "Time for the chicken."

I was forced to control my curiosity while Mom served the chicken. When she finally got settled again in her place, I reminded her where we had broken off in our conversation.

"So now you've got those three men in your police station, is that it?" she said. "And you're beating them with rubber hoses?"

"Mom, how many times have I told you, we don't use rubber hoses. Modern police methods—"

"All right, all right, so you're psycho-annihilating them. Whatever it is, I'm positive it don't make no sense. The way you're handling things with this Platonic blonde—"

"*Platinum* blonde, Mother dear," Shirley said.

"So I said it." Mother gave Shirley a sharp look, then turned back to me. "What's hold-

148

ing you up on this case, I'd like to know? Why are you wasting your time with third degrees? A bunch of *schlemiels!* Why don't you arrest the one that killed her?"

"Because we don't *know* the one that killed her! In a few hours—"

"A few hours, phooey! A few years is more like it, the way you're going. So stop using your fists and your lungs, and start using your brains. That's the big trouble with the world today, too many fists and lungs, not enough brains. Listen, I wouldn't be surprised if you never even bothered to ask yourself the four most important questions."

"What questions, Mom! We've asked a million of them."

"Eat your string beans, and I'll tell you. Conversation at the table is fine, but a young man has got to have his daily supply of green vegetables."

I blushed a little, as I always do when Mom treats me like a small boy in front of Shirley, but I obediently started in on my string beans. And Mom started in on her "four most important questions."

"The first question," she said. "This Tom Monahan, the handyman. Has he got a wife?"

"Mom, is that one of your mysterious

questions? Why, that's the first thing we found out. No, he doesn't have a wife. So if you're looking for a jealousy angle, you'd better—"

"String beans!" Mom said, pointing her finger imperiously. "It's my turn now to do the thinking, please. If you don't mind, the second question. How come this Platonic blonde—"

"Platinum, Mother," Shirley said.

"Thank you, thank you," Mom said. "Such an advantage, isn't it, to have a daughter-in-law that speaks such good English and isn't afraid to let the whole world know about it.—So Davie, how come, I was asking, this *Platonic* blonde didn't have any lipstick on when she got killed?"

This question actually amazed me a little. "Mom, how did you know she didn't have any lipstick on? I didn't say anything about—"

"You said that the pillow she was smothered with had marks on it from teeth and saliva. But you didn't mention any lipstick marks. A lady gets a pillow pushed over her face, believe me, she's going to leave lipstick marks as a result from the experience. Unless she didn't have any lipstick on! So how come she didn't?"

"I don't know how, Mom. She was getting ready to go to bed, so I suppose she washed her lipstick off. Is it really important?"

"Only to smart people," Mom said, patting me on the hand with a sweet smile. "The third question. When this playboy found her body, this Artie Fellows, the television was going full blast, is that right? So tell me, please, what program was on the television then?"

"Mom, are you crazy? Who cares what program was on the television? It's a murder we're investigating, not the television schedule—"

"In other words, you don't know what was on the television then?"

"As a matter of fact, I do know. Fellows just happened to say so. A musical program, some concert orchestra playing classical music. He noticed it because the music was very soft and sad, and he says he'll always think of it as Vilma Degrasse's swan song. Very romantic, Mom, but will you tell me what the hell that's got to do—"

"Swearing I don't like," Mom said, quietly but firmly. "Such language you can use in your stationhouse with the other police-

151

men, but in my home you'll talk like a gentleman."

"I'm sorry, Mom," I mumbled, avoiding
Shirley's eye.

"Fourth and last question," Mom said.
"This hotel where she got killed, it's not
located in such a swanky neighborhood, is
it?"

"Mom, what does it matter—?"

"Do you answer me, or don't you?"

"It's a mixed-up neighborhood. The block
that this hotel is on is very swanky and
modern-looking. But right around the corner
is Third Avenue, with all those tenement
houses and dirty little bars where the bums
hang out. All right, Mrs. Sherlock, does that
help you? Is that the significant piece in the
jigsaw puzzle which makes everything else fit
together?"

Mom smiled quietly, unperturbed by my
sarcasm. "If you want to know—yes, it is."

My past experience with Mom was enough
to make me start a little. But at the same
time I just didn't see how she could possibly
have solved the case on the little evidence I
had given her. So I pretended to be
unimpressed. "Well, let me in on it, why
don't you? Which one of those men do you
want me to book?"

"The answer to that," Mom said, with a smile of secret wisdom that infuriated me, "you'll find out in a minute."

"You mean, you really *know*—"

"Why shouldn't I know? I know how people act, don't I? Just because it's a murder case, that don't mean people are all of a sudden going to stop acting like people. A girl like that Platonic blonde—"

"Platinum," Shirley murmured under her breath—evidently just for the principle of the thing, because Mom ignored her elaborately.

". . . a girl who all her life is around men, such a girl is very fussy how she looks when a man drops in. So how come, when you found her dead, she didn't have any lipstick on? When Suspect Number One, this banker, this Mr. Grizzly—"

"Griswold! Just as I suspected!" I cried.

But Mom ignored me and went on, "When he brought her home, she had lipstick on. He took her up to her apartment, she told him she wouldn't go out with him any more, she laughed at him and sent him away—do you think she took her lipstick off before he left? Believe me, it's impossible. When a woman is making a fool out of man, *that's* when she wants to look absolutely at her best! So when Suspect Number One went away, she was still alive—with her lipstick on."

"Well—it sounds reasonable. So it was Suspect Number Two who did it, then. Tom Monahan! I had a feeling—"

"That's a lovely feeling," Mom said. "Too bad it don't have any connection with the truth. This Tom Monahan knocked on the door and asked her if he could come in and see her. A handsome young fellow that she was flirting with—listen, even if she already took her lipstick off for the night, you can bet she never would've let him through the door without putting it right back on again. But she *didn't* put it right back on again. So that means she *didn't* let him through the door. For some reason she didn't hear his knock—maybe because the television was on too loud. Anyway, he couldn't have killed her."

"And that leaves Suspect Number Three," I said. "Artie Fellows. I had a hunch it was him all along. Your lipstick clue won't work for him. He had a key to the apartment. She might've been in bed already, with her lipstick off, when all of a sudden he came barging in with his key."

"Maybe so," Mom said. "But you could

get a big headache trying to prove it. You remember, I asked you that question, what was on the television when Suspect Number Three found the body? Earlier in the evening, when Suspect Number One went away, the girl turned on the big prizefight. But it was an hour later before Suspect Number Three showed up. The fight must be over by then—especially a fight that was so uneven. Like the clerk and the elevator girl said, the champion was taking a terrible beating. So the fight was over, but the television was still on when Suspect Number Three found the body. Why?"

"That's a tough one, Mom. Maybe because she wanted to watch the program that came on after the fight."

"Maybe, maybe not. So what program was she watching? A concert orchestra, playing classical music! Now I ask you, Davie, from everything you know about this girl—a chorus girl that never even finished high school—does she sound like the type that's interested in classical music? Not to me she don't. So why did she still have the television on? Only one answer. Because she was killed while the prizefight was still going, and naturally she couldn't turn off the television after she was dead. So there you are—it couldn't be Sus-

155

pect Number Three, since he got there too late."

"But, Mom, don't you realize what you're saying? It couldn't be any of the three suspects, because you just proved it—and it couldn't be anybody else from outside, because the clerk and the elevator girl were watching the lobby—and we know it couldn't be anybody else in the building, because everyone has an alibi. In other words, it couldn't be anybody!"

"Alibi!" Mom gave a contemptuous little shrug. "Listen, Davie, when you get to be as old as me, you'll find out that the world is full of Alibi Jakes." ("Ikes," Shirley muttered.) "Nothing is easier than tripping up an Alibi Jake. People doing favors for other people, for instance. Take your Aunt Selma's cook—"

"For Pete's sake, Mom, what possible connection could there be between Aunt Selma's cook and—"

"For six whole months, every night, your Aunt Selma's cook sneaked out of the apartment to meet the delivery man from the grocery store. All the time your Aunt Selma's chambermaid knew it—but did she tell your Aunt Selma? Not a word. Every time your Aunt Selma rang for the cook, the chambermaid answered the bell. The cook is busy baking a cake, she said, or the cook has a splitting headache, or the cook is arguing over the phone with the butcher—or some excuse. Davie, you don't know servants like I do. As long as they're not mad at each other, they got a way of sticking together. Especially when it's a question of fooling the boss."

A small glimmer of understanding was beginning to come to me. "Mom, what are you getting at exactly?"

"You don't know yet? What a *nebbish* son I've got!"

"Well, if I'm not mistaken, you could be talking about—Bigelow the clerk and Sadie the elevator girl."

"A genius! A regular Dr. Einstein! Naturally that's who I'm talking about. You told me yourself, how this elevator girl is so obliging and good-natured, and always doing special favors for people. Well, there was twenty minutes *after* Suspect Number Two went away and *before* Suspect Number Three went up in the elevator, and during those twenty minutes this clerk and this elevator girl were supposed to be chatting together about the prizefight on television, how brutal it was and what a beating the champion was getting. But what I'd like to know is—"

I couldn't keep myself from blurting it out. "How did Bigelow know the fight was so brutal if he was standing behind his desk all night—since there's no television or even radio in the lobby? That's what you're getting at, isn't it, Mom? You're saying that after Tom Monahan left and before Artie Fellows arrived, Bigelow came out from behind his desk, took the elevator up to the fifth floor, and killed the Degrasse girl—and while he was killing her, he saw the prizefight on the television in her room! And all this time, Sadie stayed downstairs and watched the desk for him, and covered up for him because she's so good-natured!"

I was extremely pleased with myself for catching on so quickly, and it surprised me when Mom gave an annoyed sigh. "Good-natured," she said. "How good-natured can a person be? Is anybody *so* good-natured that they'd give a man an alibi for a murder? They might be willing to give him an alibi if he slipped away from the desk for *another* reason—but not for a murder."

"But, Mom, you yourself suggested— *What* other reason?"

"You told me the reason yourself," Mom

158

said. "You just don't pay attention, Davie, not even to your own words. You explained to me how you questioned the clerk this afternoon, and how he complained to you every two minutes that he'd been standing behind his desk for four hours, and how he blew beer fumes in your face. So if he'd been standing behind his desk for four hours, and the Assistant Manager was always poking around to see he wasn't hiding anything under it, so where did he get a drink of beer?"

This question stunned me. I couldn't say a word.

"This is why I asked you about the neighborhood," Mom said. "And you told me just what I thought already. Around the corner is Third Avenue. Along Third Avenue is lots of bars. So this is how the clerk got his beer—he sneaked around the corner a few times to one of those bars. Chances are he does it every day—and chances are it's what he did last night, when he and the elevator girl were supposed to be chatting. And she gave him an alibi because she didn't want him to lose his job."

"Very clever deduction, Mother," Shirley said. "But what use is it to David? You know, he can't arrest a man for taking a drink during working hours."

"Oh, thank you very much for the information," Mother said, giving Shirley her most condescending smile. "But who wants to arrest him? David, don't it even pop into your head yet? If the clerk was off in a bar somewhere drinking beer, who's to prove where the elevator girl was?"

"Sadie? Why, she was in the lobby chatting with—" I stopped short, as the truth dawned on me at last. "Of course, of course! That conversation she had with Bigelow about the prizefight! It takes *two* people to make a conversation! The same question I asked for Bigelow also goes for Sadie. How did *she* know that the fight was so brutal and that the champion was taking such a licking? She must've seen it on television—on the blonde's television!"

"Finally you're talking like a slightly intelligent human being," Mom said, beaming with motherly pride, despite her sarcastic words. "While the clerk was away in his bar, this elevator girl went up to the fifth floor, knocked on the blonde's door, then went into the room and killed her. And incidentally, you can see now, why the blonde didn't bother to put her lipstick on when the elevator girl knocked. Because naturally she wouldn't care how she looked in front of an elevator girl."

"But what about the motive, Mom? What was Sadie's motive?"

"Motive? The easiest part. Why do you think I asked you if this handyman, Tom Monahan, was married? A good-looking unmarried Irish boy—a good-natured unmarried Irish girl—and a blonde who's coming between them. Listen, I'd be surprised if such a situation *didn't* end up in murder!"

Well, I spent the next few minutes apologizing to Mom for my skepticism—while Shirley put on a distant, faraway look, as if she were completely indifferent to what was going on, and not the least bit annoyed or jealous at Mom's triumph.

But one little thing still gnawed at me, and finally I came out with it. "Mom, I'm still puzzled about Bigelow, the clerk. He and Sadie both spoke about how brutal the fight was, just as if they'd seen it on television. We know now how Sadie got to see the fight—on the television set in the blonde's room. But how did Bigelow get to see it, Mom?—unless he was up in the blonde's room, too?"

"Davie, Davie, my little baby," Mom said,

with a rather fond smile. "You forgot already where this Bigelow was for twenty minutes. In a bar drinking beer. And these days—though naturally I don't patronize such places myself—I hear that you can't get a beer in any bar without getting, along with it—"

"Television!" I cried. Then I jumped to my feet. "Mom, you're a mastermind! I'll call up headquarters right now, and tell the Inspector!"

But Mom's voice, quiet and firm, made me slink back into my seat. "Such *chutzpah!*" she said. "Nobody's calling up anywhere, or telling anything to anybody, till he finishes his string beans!"

A Bad Influence

HUGH PENTECOST

IT WAS a rare thing for George Crowder to have visitors after dark. His log cabin, where he lived alone with his dog Timmy, was on the outskirts of the town of Lakeview, approachable only by a rough logging road. If you didn't know it well you didn't try to traverse it after dark in a car. And you didn't try making the long uphill climb on foot unless your reasons were urgent.

George Crowder, on this particular summer night, was sitting in the darkness on the deck outside his cabin, listening to the night sounds in the surrounding woods. Timmy, the setter, lying contentedly by his feet suddenly stiffened and growled. Someone was coming up the road. Crowder leaned forward and saw the blink of an approaching flashlight. The dog let out a sharp bark of warning.

A woman's voice came from down the trail. "Timmy—it's me, Timmy."

A wild thumping of the dog's tail on the deck indicated that he knew almost before his master who the visitor was. "Go show her the way, boy," George Crowder said, and Timmy dashed away down the trail.

George went inside the cabin and switched on the inside lights, plus a couple of floods that illuminated the area around the cabin. His sister Esther, who was married to Hector Trimble, the local druggist, was not making a social call at eleven o'clock at night. Only some kind of trouble could be bringing her here. He stepped back out onto the deck. "You okay, Es?" he called out.

Esther came into the circle of light, Timmy bouncing along beside her. She was a handsome woman in her early forties, summer-tanned, her dark hair hanging loosely to her shoulders.

"It's Joey—" she called out to her brother.

George felt his muscles tighten. Joey was Esther's twelve-year-old son. Joey's idol—his role model among men—was his Uncle George. Listen to Joey and Uncle George was the best fisherman, the best hunter, the best man with a dog in the whole world—the wisest and wittiest and most wonderful of men. He talked so much about his Uncle George that the whole town had taken to calling this most wonderful of men Uncle George.

"Is he hurt?" Uncle George asked.

Esther had reached the deck, breathing a little hard from her climb up the trail. "He's been arrested," she said.

"You're kidding!"

"No. He's being held as a youthful offender. Grand larceny, vandalism, and malicious mischief."

Uncle George couldn't believe it. "You and I know he's not guilty of any of those things!"

"How do you know, George?"

"I just know," Uncle George said. "And so should you."

"It's the Hanson mess," Esther told him. "Victor Hanson has a private detective working for him, posing as a gardener. He caught Joey snooping around Hanson's house and grabbed him. Hanson called the State Police and brought charges against Joey."

The Hanson mess had been the talk of the town for the last few days. Victor Hanson was the richest man in Lakeview. He'd bought the old Martin estate some years ago and spent a fortune rebuilding and refurbishing the grounds and garden. He'd contributed generously to local charities, particularly the hospital. He was known around the world as a patron of the arts and a collector of masterpiece paintings. He provided generous help to young people interested in the arts all across the state. He kept a part of his multimillion-dollar collection of paintings in his house at Lakeview. "There's no point in collecting beautiful things if you have to keep them locked up in a bank vault," he'd told a reporter for the local weekly newspaper who questioned the wisdom of having a fortune in paintings in an unprotected setting.

Three nights ago the Hanson house had been invaded by what the police suspected was a gang of kids. A painting of no particular value by a local artist Hanson had been helping had been stolen, and a large black mustache had been painted on a Matisse valued at half a million dollars.

Hanson was properly enraged. The State Police and the local sheriff, Red Egan, had been working around the clock to find the kids responsible. Hanson had obviously called in private help, and Joey had been caught at the scene. "What does Joey say?" Uncle George asked.

Esther looked at her brother steadily. "You and Joey have been reading Sherlock Holmes," she said. "Joey was being a detec-

166

tive." Her smile was tight-lipped. "Hector says he always knew your reading and playing games with Joey would get him into trouble."

"Oh, brother!" Uncle George said.

Hector Trimble was not an Uncle George fan. It would not be uncharitable to say that Hector had no fan club of his own. He was a prissy little man who was said to wash his hands twenty or thirty times a day. He wouldn't allow his son Joey to have a pet on the excuse that animal hairs might get into the prescriptions he was making up for his customers. He was humorless, what Uncle George called "a black-and-white man." There was no middle ground for Hector. Things were either right or wrong. His life was lived by irrevocable time schedules—up at a certain time, meals at a certain time, store hours at a certain time, bed at a certain time. He felt that Uncle George was a bad influence on Joey, with useless time spent on hunting, fishing, training that "damn fool dog," and interesting Joey in worthless reading. But there were two good marks on the public assessment of Hector. He had somehow managed to woo and win the handsome and charming Esther Crowder, and he had fathered a "damned nice kid." Of course,

Uncle George had had a hand in making the boy what he was—or had until tonight.

"Where's Joey now?" Uncle George asked.

"The town lock-up," Esther said.

"Surely they'll release him in your custody?"

"Not tonight. Victor Hanson is throwing his weight around. There'll be a hearing in the morning."

"And Hector?"

"He went to Dave Winship," Esther said. Winship was Hector's lawyer. "Dave says we'll just have to wait till morning. I've decided I'd like to have my own lawyer, George."

It just happened that the best lawyer in Lakeview was not practicing law any more. George Crowder. George Crowder, State's Attorney, headed, everyone said, for the Governor's Mansion or the United States Senate, had convicted a man of murder and seen him go to the gas chamber. Some months later new evidence made it clear that the man had been innocent, the victim of a grave miscarriage of justice. George Crowder resigned his public job, closed his local office, and disappeared from town. No one blamed him. As the state's prosecutor he had acted on evidence supplied by the police.

"George felt he should have sensed the truth, regardless of the evidence," Esther Trimble told her friends. It was rumored he'd taken off on a history-making binge somewhere. One day five years later he reappeared in Lakeview, his dark hair salted with grey, the lines in his handsome face etched deeper than when he'd gone away. He bought a hunting lodge some rich summer resident had built in the woods and settled there to live alone with Timmy and make his contribution to the growing-up process of his hero-worshipping and much beloved nephew.

"Joey deserves the best legal defense he can get," Esther said.

Uncle George hesitated a moment and then put his hand on his sister's shoulder. "Maybe what he needs is the best detective he can get. Come on, Es, I'll drive you home."

Red Egan, Lakeview's sheriff, was an old friend and crony of Uncle George. They had grown up together in the small town. At this stage of their lives the two men shared their free time fishing and hunting and talking about what interested them most, in particular the unpredictable insanities of people.

Uncle George found his lanky carrot topped friend in his office at the Town H even though it was eleven-thirty at night. Red Egan swung his booted feet down off his desk and grinned at his friend. "Been waiting for you, George," he said.

"Oh?"

"I knew when you heard about Joey you'd be on your bicycle."

"I'd like to see him, Red."

The sheriff knocked the tobacco out of his charred black pipe in a metal ashtray on his desk. "Afraid I can't manage that, even for you, George. He's been charged, allowed to see his lawyer, and can't receive any visitors until after the hearing in the morning."

"He's only twelve years old, for God's sake!" Uncle George said.

Red Egan nodded. "But Victor Hanson's on the warpath," he said. "Maybe half a million dollars' worth of damage done at his place, a painting stolen. He's convinced it was kids, and when Joey was caught prowling around he decided they were back for more. He had Joey arrested, brought charges, and we have to go by the book."

"Have you talked to Joey?"

"Yes." Red Egan smiled. "He says he was playing detective. He says he doesn't believe that kids, his friends in the town, could be guilty. He was after the truth, he says."

"And you don't believe him?"

"On the contrary, I do believe him. But Hanson doesn't, and the State Police don't, and the county prosecutor doesn't."

"I'm his lawyer," Uncle George said.

"Hector hired Dave Winship to represent him—he said he knew you'd try to get into the act and we have strict instructions to keep you away from Joey. Hector says you've turned the boy into the irresponsible kid he is."

"Stupid jerk!"

"In spades," Red Egan agreed. "Relax, George—it'll get straightened away after the hearing in the morning. It's set for ten o'clock at the County Courthouse."

"He's not going to spend the night in jail!" Uncle George said.

"You'll have to set fire to the joint to get him out, George."

"Maybe not," Uncle George said. "Why are they so convinced kids robbed Hanson and damaged his property?"

Red Egan shrugged. "The painting that was stolen didn't have any real value. It was a nude painting of a lady, done by Barry Sheldon—young fellow lives up on Mountain Road. He's one of the young artists Hanson was helping out. Hanson bought the painting from him for a couple of hundred bucks when Sheldon needed money. As I understand it, the painting was just a sort of exercise Sheldon did, sketching a nude model. There are a couple of dozen paintings in the house worth a fortune that a professional thief could have taken. Painting a mustache on a half-million-dollar painting by some French painter looks like more kid stuff. A naked lady would attract kids. A professional thief would have gone for the valuable stuff."

"If Joey says he was playing detective, he was."

"I know."

"I'm going to talk to Hanson if I have to drag him out of bed," Uncle George said. He turned for the door.

"Interesting thing about the painting that was stolen," Red Egan said. "The model was a professional girl who posed for students at some art school in New York. She came up here to spend a weekend with Barry Sheldon, whom I guess she knew from the school. That was about a year ago. Sheldon did the painting of her while she was here. She was here for just a weekend and then went back to the city. About a week ago this girl committed suicide—cut her wrists and let herself bleed to death in a hot tub. It was in some of the papers."

"Could there be a connection?"

"The cops asked Sheldon about it. He told them he knew it had happened, said he'd been shocked when he heard about it— she was a nice girl, but he hadn't seen her since the weekend she was here a year ago and he had no way of knowing what had driven her to suicide."

"Bothers you though, Red?"

Red Egan shrugged. "Somebody kicks over a trash barrel, you notice what's lying around," he said.

It was almost midnight when Uncle George drove up the bluestone driveway to Victor Hanson's lovely old Colonial house. Most of Lakeview appeared to be asleep as Uncle George had driven along the main street, but Hanson's home was brightly lighted, both inside and out. A number of parked cars indicated some kind of party was in progress. A variety of license plates suggested an invasion by the media. Victor Hanson and his famous art collection was news to people far beyond the town limits of Lakeview.

A black man wearing a white house jacket answered Uncle George's knock on the front door. The two men weren't strangers to each other. In the days when Uncle George had first started to practice law in Lakeview, Charles Wilson had come to him for help in some minor legal matter and Uncle George had helped him solve his problem.

"Mr. Hanson's been expecting you, Mr. Crowder," Wilson said. "I'll tell him you're here."

"Expecting me?"

"They told him you'd be likely to try to help out your nephew. I guess you should know he's pretty convinced. I'm afraid you won't get very far with him, but he'll talk long enough to speak his piece."

Victor Hanson was a familiar figure in the town of Lakeview—tall, dark, handsome, elegantly dressed for any occasion. Women, Uncle George imagined, found him dangerously appetizing. Men were inclined to think him arrogant and opinionated. "If you aren't that good-looking and that rich, you're liable to resent him," Red Egan once said.

Hanson abandoned his press conference to join Uncle George in the wide entrance hall. He had a deep, almost musical voice, but it was angry now. "I've been expecting you, Crowder," he said. "Before you say anything, let me tell you I will not withdraw my charges against the boy."

"He was trying to help his friends—and you," Uncle George said. "He was trying to find the truth about what happened here."

"A twelve-year-old boy? He's lying, of course."

"Joey isn't a liar," Uncle George said.

"All kids lie when they're in trouble."

"Not this boy."

"Naturally you're prejudiced," Hanson said. "Well, I'm prejudiced too—against today's kids, who take pleasure in the senseless destruction of other people's property. I can understand, maybe even sympathize with, people who steal for money. But senseless destruction? That deserves punishment— and I'm not letting your nephew off on some cock-and-bull story."

"How bad is the damage?" Uncle George asked.

Hanson gave a short mirthless laugh. "Are you thinking of buying him off, Crowder? There's a Matisse, maybe destroyed, worth at least half a million dollars. If it can be saved, it's going to cost me an arm and a leg. I've already talked to an expert in Paris who has restored old masters. He's on his way from Europe and that alone will cost thousands of dollars—God knows what his fee will be."

"I heard there was also a painting stolen," Uncle George said.

"Not of any value," Hanson said, sounding impatient. "An art student's effort, a boy I've been trying to help get a career started."

"Barry Sheldon?"

"Yes. You know him?"

"I've seen him working at landscapes out on the countryside. We've chatted. The boy has big dreams."

"He's talented or I wouldn't be wasting time with him," Hanson said. "He needed money a while back. Rather than make him a loan he'd feel obligated to pay back, or offer him charity, I bought a painting from him for a couple of hundred dollars. It was a painting of a nude model who'd posed at an art school Barry went to in New York for a while."

"Did you know the model?"

"No."

"I thought you might have bought that particular painting because you did know her," Uncle George said. "I understand from Red Egan that she committed suicide a week or ten days ago."

"So I was told. Tragic in a young person."

Hanson frowned. "When I said I didn't know the girl that wasn't quite accurate. She spent a weekend at Barry's cottage about a year ago. I believe that's when he painted her. I happened to drop by one morning while she was posing and was introduced. All in all, five minutes. I didn't *know* her, but I met her that once." Hanson changed the subject abruptly. "Come with me. I'll show you what those little monsters did to my Matisse."

The Matisse, handsomely framed, was hung over the mantel in what appeared to be a study—book-lined, a beautiful old rolltop desk, shelves and shelves of books. It was a painting of a woman in a pale-pink dress, sitting in a garden, surrounded by flowers. What must have been a lovely face had been marred by a grotesque mustache painted on her upper lip. It was a Salvador Dali kind of mustache, curled wildly up at each end so that it spread over her cheeks.

"God knows what it will take to remove that monstrosity without damaging the original," Hanson said.

Uncle George moved close to the painting, studying it. "That's no kid's scrawl," he said. "It's very skillfully painted on. Was the painting that was stolen kept in this room too?"

Hanson laughed. "Lord, no! It wasn't good enough to be kept in the same county with this Matisse. There's a storage room just down the hall where I keep paintings I don't choose to hang."

Uncle George turned away. "You're determined to keep a twelve-year-old boy in jail overnight?"

"You're damned right I'm determined," Hanson said. "It will teach the little creep a lesson."

"I may be back," Uncle George said, and left.

The place where Barry Sheldon lived and worked on Mountain Road had once been a carriage house on one of the big estates. It consisted of one big room with a bath built into one corner of it, a counter-kitchenette in another, with a skylight that had been cut into the roof by Barry himself.

It was well after midnight when Uncle George knocked on the door. There were no lights visible in the windows. After several knocks a sleepy voice asked who was there.

"It's George Crowder, Barry."

"Hold on a minute, Mr. Crowder."

Lights appeared at the windows and presently the door was opened. Barry Sheldon, his blond hair ruffled, was tightening the belt on a pair of jeans.

"Sorry," he said. "Come in, Mr. Crowder."

"It's not a proper time for a social call, Barry," Uncle George apologized, "but this isn't exactly social. You've heard Victor Hanson's brought charges against my nephew, Joey, for stealing your painting from him and messing up a valuable Matisse?"

The young artist's face darkened. "I heard. Hanson must be off his rocker. Joey wouldn't do anything like that."

"He's properly upset," Uncle George said. "He's importing an expert from France to see if the Matisse can be salvaged. It will probably cost him a small fortune."

Sheldon's smile was bitter. "I hope it costs him plenty just to find out that mustache was drawn on with water-soluble paint that can be wiped off with a sponge without harming the original."

"That doesn't sound friendly to a man who's been so helpful to you, Barry."

"In my world you take help where you can get it," Sheldon said.

"You've spent some time in and out of his house."

179

"Lived there for a while before I found this place," Sheldon acknowledged.

"Do you know where the storage room is where he keeps paintings he doesn't choose to hang?"

"Sure—I helped him catalogue what's in there."

Uncle George looked around the room, at the easel and paintbox where Sheldon worked, at the stack of canvasses in a far corner, at the rumpled bed.

"It wouldn't take me long to make some coffee," Sheldon said.

"Thanks, but I haven't got time, Barry," Uncle George said. "I want to get Joey home to his own bed as soon as I can."

"You've persuaded Hanson to withdraw charges against Joey?"

"No, but I will. The painting of yours that was stolen—I understand the girl you used as a model committed suicide a few days ago."

Sheldon's face darkened. "Belinda Marshall. Sweet kid. It shouldn't have happened to her."

"The painting over there with your others?" Uncle George asked, his tone casual.

"What are you talking about?"

"Mind if I look?" Uncle George asked. He started toward the stack of canvasses.

Barry Sheldon blocked his way. Uncle George smiled at him. "Barry, I can take you apart with one arm tied behind me," he said. "I suggest you bring out the painting. It has to be you, you know. You know how to get into Hanson's house without being detected. You know where the unhung paintings are stored. You know that mustache was painted on the Matisse with water-soluble paint. You don't like Hanson, in spite of what he's done for you, so I suspect you wanted to get even with him for something. Was it that girl, Belinda?"

"It was as good as murder, although the law won't see it that way," Sheldon said, turning away.

"Want to tell me?" Uncle George asked.

"*Yes*, it was Belinda," Sheldon said bitterly. He turned back and Uncle George saw tears in his eyes. "She was a sweet girl—dumb, but very sweet. Hanson came here that day I was painting her. She was posing for me, nude. I'd drawn her and painted her dozens of times in art school—in life class. She was a professional model. It didn't bother her when a stranger walked in here. She wouldn't break her pose until I suggested it.

So Hanson just stood in that doorway—"
Sheldon pointed. "He stood there, staring at
Belinda, like a hungry man looking in a
bakery-store window. He excused himself for
barging in. He said he was on his way into
town and thought I might need something.
And he invited Belinda and me for drinks
and a picnic supper at his place that night.
That's when it started."

"Belinda and Hanson?"

Sheldon nodded. He said, "Hanson made
with charm that evening, I guess. He arranged to see Belinda in New York. I had
this place then, had given up going to art
school. Money was tight and I went to
Hanson to ask for a loan. He went through
some high-toned moral hogwash about not
wanting me to feel obligated by a debt, not
wanting me to have to ask for charity. He'd
buy a painting for a couple of hundred bucks.
'Someday when you get famous I might make
a big profit on it,' he said. He looked over
my paintings and chose the life study I'd
done of Belinda. Would you believe it never
occurred to me he'd chosen it for any other
reason than that he thought I'd done it well?"

"I believe it," Uncle George said.

"I sat up here painting the mountains, and
bowls of fruit or whatever when it rained,

182

and Hanson, it turned out, had set Belinda up in an apartment in New York and was buying her clothes and presents."

"And you were jealous when you found out?"

"Hell, no! I didn't have any romantic notions about Belinda. She was a nice kid who'd been part of the art-school world I'd been living in. She was a good model and I enjoyed painting her. But in the end, almost a year after the first time Hanson saw her here, she asked me for help. That's when I heard about the apartment, the gifts, and that she'd been Hanson's mistress for all that time. To him she'd been a sex object; to her he'd been a Prince Charming. She was in love with him and suddenly he'd told her to drop dead. He'd spotted someone he wanted more. She pleaded with me to go to him and ask him to give her another chance."

"And you went?"

Sheldon nodded. "He just laughed at me. 'When you've had enough you've had enough,' he told me. 'There were no promises, no commitments,' he told me. A couple of days later she was dead. She couldn't take it."

"So?"

"There was no way to get at him through

the law," Sheldon said. "He hadn't committed any legal crime. I'm not a macho type. Beating him up wasn't my kind of thing. But I was damned if I was going to let him keep that picture around. So I went and took it. I knew how to get in and out. On the way out I saw the Matisse. I happened to have a marker tube in my pocket and I painted that mustache on it. I hoped it would jolt him a little."

"Would you show me the painting you did of Belinda?" Uncle George asked.

Sheldon crossed the room and brought back a framed painting. Uncle George looked at it for a moment.

"That's damn good, Barry," he said. "It may be worth a hell of a lot more than Hanson paid for it someday."

"So what's the next move?" Sheldon asked, in a dead-sounding voice.

"We go to Hanson, tell him what we know, and get my nephew released."

"And I go to jail," Sheldon said.

"I'd guess the odds are against that," Uncle George said.

Victor Hanson, his face dark with anger, listened to Barry Sheldon's confession.

"You ungrateful bastard!" he said to Barry.

"Barry tells me the Matisse can be restored with a little soap and water," Uncle George said.

"I notice he hasn't brought back my painting," Hanson said. He turned toward the telephone on the table by the door. "Well, now it's a matter for the police and the county attorney."

"Hold it just a minute," Uncle George said. "It seems to me you have two options, Hanson. They both begin with the same action. You call Red Egan in the sheriff's office, tell him you're dropping charges against my nephew and that I'll be over at the county lock-up in fifteen minutes to take him home."

"Of course, since we have the real criminal," Hanson said.

"Now come your choices," Uncle George told him. "You can drop all charges against Sheldon. After all, your Matisse is undamaged," he pointed out.

"Absurd," Hanson said. "You think I'd let a miserable thief and vandal go free?"

"So your second choice is to bring charges against Barry," Uncle George said. "In which case I'll act as his lawyer. I'll defend him the best way I can, which will be, first, to reveal your relationship with Belinda Marshall, which, in the end, drove her to suicide. Sec-

185

ond, I'll have to expose the fact that you bought a painting from my client, under the guise of being a friend, for ten times less what it's actually worth. Since you're an expert you had to know what its real worth was."

"That's blackmail!" Hanson protested.

Uncle George smiled at him.

"I suppose you could call it that," he said. "I'd have to say that your ethics and mine are a little different. Now call Red Egan and tell him I'm on my way."

"Thanks, Mr. Crowder." Barry Sheldon's voice was unsteady.

"My pleasure," Uncle George said.

It was a few minutes before one in the morning when Red Egan brought a smiling Joey Trimble into his office from the jail cell where the boy had been held. Joey's eyes lit up at the sight of his uncle. "I knew you'd get me out, Uncle George!" he said. "I told the lawyer Dad sent that if he'd just see you—"

"I have a piece of advice for you, boy," Uncle George interrupted. "From now on, let me be Sherlock Holmes and you be Dr. Watson. That way you'll probably get into a lot less trouble."

"Amen," Red Egan said.

His Last Bow

SIR ARTHUR CONAN DOYLE

[Sunday, August 2, 1914]

I<small>T</small> <small>WAS</small> nine o'clock at night upon the second of August—the most terrible August in the history of the world. One might have thought already that God's curse hung heavy over a degenerate world, for there was an awesome hush and a feeling of vague expectancy in the sultry and stagnant air. The sun had long set, but one blood-red gash like an open wound lay low in the distant west. Above, the stars were shining brightly; and below, the lights of the shipping glimmered in the bay. The two famous Germans stood beside the stone parapet of the garden walk, with the long, low, heavily gabled house behind them, and they looked down upon the broad sweep of the beach at the foot of the great chalk cliff on which Von Bork, like some wandering eagle, had perched himself four years before. They stood with their heads close together, talking in low, confidential tones. From below the two glowing ends of their cigars might have been the smouldering eyes of some malignant fiend looking down in the darkness.

A remarkable man this Von Bork—a man who could hardly be matched among all the devoted agents of the Kaiser. It was his talents which had first recommended him for the English mission, the most important mission of all, but since he had taken it over, those talents had become more and more manifest to the half-dozen people in the world who were really in touch with the truth. One of these was his present companion, Baron Von Herling, the chief secretary of the legation, whose huge 100-horse-power Benz car was blocking the country lane as it waited to waft its owner back to London.

"So far as I can judge the trend of events, you will probably be back in Berlin within the week," the secretary was saying. "When you get there, my dear Von Bork, I think you will be surprised at the welcome you will receive. I happen to know what is thought in the highest quarters of your work in this country." He was a huge man, the secretary, deep, broad, and tall, with a slow, heavy fashion of speech which had been his main asset in his political career.

Von Bork laughed.

"They are not very hard to deceive," he remarked. "A more docile, simple folk could not be imagined."

"I don't know about that," said the other thoughtfully. "They have strange limits and one must learn to observe them. It is that surface simplicity of theirs which makes a trap for the stranger. One's first impression is that they are entirely soft. Then one comes suddenly upon something very hard and you know that you have reached the limit, and must adapt yourself to the fact. They have, for example, their insular conventions which simply *must* be observed."

"Meaning, 'good form' and that sort of thing?" Von Bork sighed, as one who had suffered much.

"Meaning British prejudice in all its queer manifestations. As an example I may quote one of my own worst blunders—I can afford to talk of my blunders, for you know my work well enough to be aware of my successes. It was on my first arrival. I was invited to a week-end gathering at the country house of a Cabinet Minister. The conversation was amazingly indiscreet."

Von Bork nodded. "I've been there," said he dryly.

"Exactly. Well, I naturally sent a résumé of the information to Berlin. Unfortunately our good Chancellor is a little heavy-handed in these matters, and he transmitted a remark which showed that he was aware of what had been said. This, of course, took the trail straight up to me. You've no idea the harm that it did me. There was nothing soft about our British hosts on that occasion, I can assure you. I was two years living it down. Now you, with this sporting pose of yours."

"No, no, don't call it a pose. A pose is an artificial thing. This is quite natural. I am a born sportsman. I enjoy it."

"Well, that makes it the more effective. You yacht against them, you hunt with them, you play polo, you match them in every game, your four-in-hand takes the prize at Olympia. I have even heard that you go the length of boxing with the young officers. What is the result? Nobody takes you seriously. You are a 'good old sport,' 'quite a decent fellow for a German,' a hard-drinking, night-club, knock-about-town, devil-may-care young fellow. And all the time this quiet country house of yours is the centre of half the mischief in England, and the sporting squire the most astute Secret Service man in Europe. Genius, my dear Von Bork—genius!"

"You flatter me, Baron. But certainly I may claim that my four years in this country have not been unproductive. I've never shown you my little store. Would you mind stepping in for a moment?"

The door of the study opened straight on to the terrace. Von Bork pushed it back, and, leading the way, he clicked the switch of the electric light. He then closed the door behind the bulky form which followed him, and carefully adjusted the heavy curtain over the latticed window. Only when all these precautions had been taken and tested did he turn his sunburned aquiline face to his guest.

"Some of my papers have gone," said he; "when my wife and the household left yesterday for Flushing they took the less important with them. I must, of course, claim the protection of the Embassy for the others."

"Your name has already been filed as one of the personal suite. There will be no difficulties for you or your baggage. Of course, it is just possible that we may not have to go. England may leave France to her fate. We are sure that there is no binding treaty between them."

"And Belgium?"

"Yes, and Belgium, too."

Von Bork shook his head. "I don't see how that could be. There is a definite treaty there. She could never recover from such a humiliation."

"She would at least have peace for the moment."

"But her honour?"

"Tut, my dear sir, we live in a utilitarian age. Honour is a mediaeval conception. Besides England is not ready. It is an inconceivable thing, but even our special war tax of fifty millions, which one would think made our purpose as clear as if we had advertised it on the front page of *The Times*, has not roused these people from their slumbers. Here and there one hears a question. It is my business to find an answer. Here and there also there is an irritation. It is my business to soothe it. But I can assure you that so far as the essentials go—the storage of munitions, the preparation for submarine attack, the arrangements for making high explosives—nothing is prepared. How then can England come in, especially when we have stirred her up such a devil's brew of Irish civil war, window-breaking Furies, and God knows what to keep her thoughts at home?"

"She must think of her future."

"Ah, that is another matter. I fancy that in the future, we have our own very definite plans about England, and that your information will be very vital to us. It is to-day or to-morrow with Mr. John Bull. If he prefers to-day we are perfectly ready. If it is to-morrow we shall be more ready still. I should think they would be wiser to fight with allies than without them, but that is their own affair. This week is their week of destiny. But you were speaking of your papers." He sat in the arm-chair with the light shining upon his broad bald head, while he puffed sedately at his cigar.

The large oak-panelled book-lined room had a curtain hung in the further corner. When this was drawn it disclosed a large brass-bound safe. Von Bork detached a small key from his watch-chain, and after some considerable manipulation of the lock he swung open the heavy door.

"Look!" said he, standing clear, with a wave of his hand.

The light shone vividly into the opened safe, and the secretary of the Embassy gazed with an absorbed interest at the rows of stuffed pigeon-holes with which it was furnished. Each pigeon-hole had its label, and his eyes as he glanced along them read a long series of such titles as "Fords," "Harbour-defences," "Aeroplanes," "Ireland," "Egypt," "Portsmouth forts," "The Channel," "Rosyth,"and a score of others. Each compartment was bristling with papers and plans.

"Colossal!" said the secretary. Putting down his cigar he softly clapped his fat hands.

"And all in four years, Baron. Not such a bad show for the hard-drinking, hard-riding country squire. But the gem of my collection is coming and there is the setting all ready for it." He pointed to a space over which "Naval Signals" was printed.

"But you have a good dossier there already."

"Out of date and waste paper. The Admiralty in some way got the alarm and every code has been changed. It was a blow, Baron—the worst set-back in my whole campaign. But thanks to my cheque-book and the good Altamont all will be well to-night."

The Baron looked at his watch, and gave a guttural exclamation of disappointment.

"Well, I really can wait no longer. You can imagine that things are moving at present in Carlton Terrace and that we have all to be at our posts. I had hoped to be able to bring news of your great coup. Did Altamont name no hour?"

Von Bork pushed over a telegram.

"Will come without fail tonight and bring new sparking plugs.—ALTAMONT."

"Sparking plugs, eh?"

"You see he poses as a motor expert and I keep a full garage. In our code everything likely to come up is named after some spare part. If he talks of a radiator it is a battle-ship, of an oil-pump a cruiser, and so on. Sparking plugs are naval signals."

"From Portsmouth at midday," said the secretary, examining the superscription. "By the way, what do you give him?"

"Five hundred pounds for this particular job. Of course he has a salary as well."

"The greedy rogue. They are useful, these traitors, but I grudge them their blood-money."

"I grudge Altamont nothing. He is a won-derful worker. If I pay him well, at least he delivers the goods, to use his own phrase. Besides he is not a traitor. I assure you that our most pan-Germanic Junker is a sucking dove in his feelings towards England as com-pared with a real bitter Irish-American."

"Oh, an Irish-American?"

"If you heard him talk you would not doubt it. Sometimes I assure you I can hardly understand him. He seems to have declared war on the King's English as well as on the English King. Must you really go? He may be here any moment."

"No. I'm sorry, but I have already over-stayed my time. We shall expect you early to-morrow, and when you get that signal-book through the little door on the Duke of York's steps you can put a triumphant Finis to your record in England. What! Tokay!" He indicated a heavily sealed dust-covered bottle which stood with two high glasses upon a salver.

"May I offer you a glass before your journey?"

"No, thanks. But it looks like revelry."

"Altamont has a nice taste in wines, and he took a fancy to my Tokay. He is a touchy fellow, and needs humouring in small things. I have to study him, I assure you." They had strolled out on to the terrace again, and along it to the further end where at a touch from the Baron's chauffeur the great car shivered and chuckled. "Those are the lights of Harwich, I suppose," said the secretary, pulling on his dust coat. "How still and peaceful

196

it all seems. There may be other lights within the week, and the English coast a less tranquil place! The heavens, too, may not be quite so peaceful if all that the good Zeppelin promises us comes true. By the way, who is that?"

Only one window showed a light behind them; in it there stood a lamp, and beside it, seated at a table, was a dear old ruddy-faced woman in a country cap. She was bending over her knitting and stopping occasionally to stroke a large black cat upon a stool beside her.

"That is Martha, the only servant I have left."

The secretary chuckled.

"She might almost personify Britannia," said he, "with her complete self-absorption and general air of comfortable somnolence. Well, au revoir, Von Bork!"—with a final wave of his hand he sprang into the car, and a moment later the two golden cones from the headlights shot forward through the darkness. The secretary lay back in the cushions of the luxurious limousine, with his thoughts so full of the impending European tragedy that he hardly observed that as his car swung round the village street it nearly passed over a little Ford coming in the opposite direction.

Von Bork walked slowly back to the study when the last gleams of the motor lamps had faded into the distance. As he passed he observed that his old housekeeper had put out her lamp and retired. It was a new experience to him, the silence and darkness of his widespread house, for his family and household had been a large one. It was a relief to him, however, to think that they were all in safety and that, but for that one old woman who had lingered in the kitchen, he had the whole place to himself. There was a good deal of tidying up to do inside his study and he set himself to do it, until his keen, handsome face was flushed with the heat of the burning papers. A leather valise stood beside his table, and into this he began to pack very neatly and systematically the precious contents of his safe. He had hardly got started with the work, however, when his quick ears caught the sound of a distant car. Instantly he gave an exclamation of satisfaction, strapped up the valise, shut the safe, locked it, and hurried out on to the terrace. He was just in time to see the lights of a small car come to a halt at the gate. A passenger sprang out and advanced swiftly towards him, while the chauffeur, a heavily built, elderly man, with a grey moustache, settled down, like one who resigns himself to a long vigil.

"Well?" asked Von Bork eagerly, running forward to meet his visitor.

For answer the man waved a small brown-paper parcel triumphantly above his head.

"You can give me the glad hand to-night, Mister," he cried. "I'm bringing home the bacon at last."

"The signals?"

"Same as I said in my cable. Every last one of them, semaphore, lamp code, Marconi—a copy, mind you, not the original. That was too dangerous. But it's the real goods, and you can lay to that." He slapped the German upon the shoulder with a rough familiarity from which the other winced.

"Come in," he said. "I'm all alone in the house. I was only waiting for this. Of course a copy is better than the original. If an original were missing they would change the whole thing. You think it's all safe about the copy?"

The Irish-American had entered the study and stretched his long limbs from the arm-chair. He was a tall, gaunt man of sixty, with clear-cut features and a small goatee beard which gave him a general resemblance to the caricatures of Uncle Sam. A half-smoked, sodden cigar hung from the corner of his mouth, and as he sat down he struck a match and relit it. "Making ready for a move?" he remarked as he looked round him. "Say, Mister," he added, as his eyes fell upon the safe from which the curtain was now removed, "you don't tell me you keep your papers in that?"

"Why not?"

"Gosh, in a wide-open contraption like that! And they reckon you to be some spy. Why a Yankee crook would be into that with a can-opener. If I'd known that any letter of mine was goin' to lie loose in a thing like that I'd have been a mug to write to you at all."

"It would puzzle any crook to force that safe," Von Bork answered. "You won't cut that metal with any tool."

"But the lock?"

"No, it's a double combination lock. You know what that is?"

"Search me," said the American.

"Well, you need a word as well as a set of figures before you can get the lock to work." He rose and showed a double-radiating disc round the keyhole. "This outer one is for the letters, the inner one for the figures."

"Well, well, that's fine."

"So it's not quite as simple as you thought. It was four years ago that I had it made, and what do you think I chose for the word and figures?"

"It's beyond me."

"Well, I chose August for the word, and 1914 for the figures, and here we are."

The American's face showed his surprise and admiration.

"My, but that was smart! You had it down to a fine thing."

"Yes, a few of us even then could have guessed the date. Here it is, and I'm shutting down to-morrow morning."

"Well, I guess you'll have to fix me up also. I'm not staying in this goldarned country all on my lonesome. In a week or less from what I see, John Bull will be on his hind legs and fair ramping. I'd rather watch him from over the water."

"But you're an American citizen?"

"Well, so was Jack James an American citizen, but he's doing time in Portland all the same. It cuts no ice with a British copper to tell him you're an American citizen. 'It's British law and order over here,' says he. By the way, Mister, talking of Jack James, it seems to me you don't do much to cover your men."

"What do you mean?" Von Bork asked sharply.

"Well, you are their employer, ain't you? It's up to you to see that they don't fall down. But they do fall down, and when did you ever pick them up? There's James——"

"It was James' own fault. You know that yourself. He was too self-willed for the job."

"James was a bonehead—I give you that. Then there was Hollis."

"The man was mad."

"Well, he went a bit woozy towards the end. It's enough to make a man bughouse when he has to play a part from morning to night with a hundred guys all ready to set the coppers wise to him. But now there is Steiner——"

Von Bork started violently, and his ruddy face turned a shade paler.

"What about Steiner?"

"Well, they've got him, that's all. They raided his store last night, and he and his papers are all in Portsmouth gaol. You'll go off and he, poor devil, will have to stand the racket, and lucky if he gets off with his life. That's why I want to get over the water as soon as you do."

Von Bork was a strong, self-contained man, but it was easy to see that the news had shaken him.

"How could they have got on to Steiner?" he muttered. "That's the worst blow yet."

"Well, you nearly had a worse one, for I believe they are not far off me."

"You don't mean that!"

"Sure thing. My landlady down Fratton way had some inquiries, and when I heard of it I guessed it was time for me to hustle. But what I want to know, Mister, is how the coppers know these things? Steiner is the fifth man you've lost since I signed on with you, and I know the name of the sixth if I don't get a move on. How do you explain it, and ain't you ashamed to see your men go down like this?"

Von Bork flushed crimson.

"How dare you speak in such a way!"

"If I didn't dare things, Mister, I wouldn't be in your service. But I'll tell you straight what is in my mind. I've heard that with you German politicians when an agent has done his work you are not sorry to see him put away."

Von Bork sprang to his feet.

"Do you dare to suggest that I have given away my own agents!"

"I don't stand for that, Mister, but there's a stool pigeon or a cross somewhere, and it's up to you to find out where it is. Anyhow I am taking no more chances. It's me for little Holland, and the sooner the better."

Von Bork had mastered his anger.

"We have been allies too long to quarrel now at the very hour of victory," he said. "You've done splendid work and taken risks and I can't forget it. By all means go to Holland, and you can get a boat from Rotterdam to New York. No other line will be safe a week from now. I'll take that book and pack it with the rest."

The American held the small parcel in his hand, but made no motion to give it up.

"What about the dough?" he asked.

"The what?"

"The boodle. The reward. The £500. The gunner turned damned nasty at the last, and I had to square him with an extra hundred dollars or it would have been nitsky for you and me. 'Nothin' doin'!' says he, and he meant it too, but the last hundred did it. It's cost me two hundred pound from first to last, so it isn't likely I'd give it up without gettin' my wad."

Von Bork smiled with some bitterness. "You don't seem to have a very high opinion of my honour," said he, "you want the money before you give up the book."

"Well, Mister, it is a business proposition."

"All right. Have it your way." He sat down at the table and scribbled a cheque, which he tore from the book, but he refrained from handing it to his companion. "After all, since we are to be on such terms, Mr. Altamont," said he, "I don't see why I should trust you any more than you trust me. Do you understand?" he added, looking back over his shoulder at the American. "There's the cheque upon the table. I claim the right to examine that parcel before you pick the money up."

The American passed it over without a word. Von Bork undid a winding of string and two wrappers of paper. Then he sat gazing for a moment in silent amazement at a small blue book which lay before him. Across the cover was printed in golden letters *Practical Handbook of Bee Culture*. Only for one instant did the master spy glare at this strangely irrelevant inscription. The next he was gripped at the back of his neck by a grasp of iron, and a chloroformed sponge was held in front of his writhing face.

"Another glass, Watson!" said Mr. Sherlock Holmes, as he extended the bottle of Imperial Tokay.

The thick-set chauffeur, who had seated himself by the table, pushed forward his glass with some eagerness.

"It is a good wine, Holmes."

"A remarkable wine, Watson. Our friend upon the sofa has assured me that it is from Franz Joseph's special cellar at the Schoenbrunn Palace. Might I trouble you to open the window, for chloroform vapour does not help the palate."

The safe was ajar, and Holmes standing in front of it was removing dossier after dossier, swiftly examining each, and then packing it neatly in Von Bork's valise. The German lay upon the sofa sleeping stertorously with a strap round his upper arms and another round his legs.

"We need not hurry ourselves, Watson. We are safe from interruption. Would you mind touching the bell. There is no one in the house except old Martha, who has played her part to admiration. I got her the situation here when first I took the matter up. Ah, Martha, you will be glad to hear that all is well."

The pleasant old lady had appeared in the

doorway. She curtseyed with a smile to Mr. Holmes, but glanced with some apprehension at the figure upon the sofa.

"It is all right, Martha. He has not been hurt at all."

"I am glad of that, Mr. Holmes. According to his lights he has been a kind master. He wanted me to go with his wife to Germany yesterday, but that would hardly have suited your plans, would it, sir?"

"No, indeed, Martha. So long as you were here I was easy in my mind. We waited some time for your signal to-night."

"It was the secretary, sir."

"I know. His car passed ours."

"I thought he would never go. I knew that it would not suit your plans, sir, to find him here."

"No, indeed. Well, it only meant that we waited half an hour or so until I saw your lamp go out and knew that the coast was clear. You can report to me to-morrow in London, Martha, at Claridge's Hotel."

"Very good, sir."

"I suppose you have everything ready to leave."

"Yes, sir. He posted seven letters to-day. I have the addresses as usual."

"Very good, Martha. I will look into them

to-morrow. Good night. These papers," he continued, as the old lady vanished, "are not of very great importance, for, of course, the information which they represent has been sent off long ago to the German Government. These are the originals which could not safely be got out of the country."

"Then they are of no use."

"I should not go so far as to say that, Watson. They will at least show our people what is known and what is not. I may say that a good many of these papers have come through me, and I need not add are thoroughly untrustworthy. It would brighten my declining years to see a German cruiser navigating the Solent according to the minefield plans which I have furnished. But you, Watson," he stopped his work and took his old friend by the shoulders; "I've hardly seen you in the light yet. How have the years used you? You look the same blithe boy as ever."

"I feel twenty years younger, Holmes. I have seldom felt so happy as when I got your wire asking me to meet you at Harwich with the car. But you, Holmes—you have changed very little—save for that horrible goatee."

"These are the sacrifices one makes for one's country, Watson," said Holmes, pulling at his little tuft. "To-morrow it will be but a dreadful memory. With my hair cut and a few other superficial changes I shall no doubt reappear at Claridge's to-morrow as I was before this American stunt—I beg your pardon, Watson, my well of English seems to be permanently defiled—before this American job came my way."

"But you had retired, Holmes. We heard of you as living the life of a hermit among your bees and your books in a small farm upon the South Downs."

"Exactly, Watson. Here is the fruit of my leisured ease, the *magnum opus* of my latter years!" He picked up the volume from the table and read out the whole title, *Practical Handbook of Bee Culture, with some Observations upon the Segregation of the Queen*. Alone I did it. Behold the fruit of pensive nights and laborious days, when I watched the little working gangs as once I watched the criminal world of London."

"But how did you get to work again?"

"Ah, I have often marvelled at it myself. The Foreign Minister alone I could have withstood, but when the Premier also deigned to visit my humble roof——! The fact is, Watson, that this gentleman upon the sofa was a bit too good for our people. He was in a class by himself. Things were going wrong, and no one could understand why they were going wrong. Agents were suspected or even caught, but there was evidence of some strong and secret central force. It was absolutely necessary to expose it. Strong pressure was brought upon me to look into the matter. It has cost me two years, Watson, but they have not been devoid of excitement. When I say that I started my pilgrimage at Chicago, graduated in an Irish secret society at Buffalo, gave serious trouble to the constabulary at Skibbareen and so eventually caught the eye of a subordinate agent of Von Bork, who recommended me as a likely man, you will realize that the matter was complex. Since then I have been honoured by his confidence, which has not prevented most of his plans going subtly wrong and five of his best agents being in prison. I watched them, Watson, and I picked them as they ripened. Well, sir, I hope that you are none the worse!"

The last remark was addressed to Von Bork himself, who after much gasping and blinking had lain quietly listening to Holmes' statement. He broke out now into a furious stream of German invective, his face convulsed with passion. Holmes continued his swift investigation of documents while his prisoner cursed and swore.

"Though unmusical, German is the most expressive of all languages," he observed, when Von Bork had stopped from pure exhaustion. "Hullo! Hullo!" he added, as he looked hard at the corner of a tracing before putting it in the box. "This should put another bird in the cage. I had no idea that the paymaster was such a rascal, though I have long had an eye upon him. Mister Von Bork, you have a great deal to answer for."

The prisoner had raised himself with some difficulty upon the sofa and was staring with a strange mixture of amazement and hatred at his captor.

"I shall get level with you, Altamont," he said, speaking with slow deliberation, "if it takes me all my life I shall get level with you!"

"The old sweet song," said Holmes. "How often have I heard it in days gone by. It was a favourite ditty of the late lamented Professor Moriarty. Colonel Sebastian Moran has also been known to warble it. And yet I live and keep bees upon the South Downs."

"Curse you, you double traitor!" cried the German, straining against his bonds and glaring murder from his furious eyes.

"No, no, it is not so bad as that," said Holmes, smiling. "As my speech surely shows you, Mr. Altamont of Chicago had no existence in fact. I used him and he is gone."

"Then who are you?"

"It is really immaterial who I am, but since the matter seems to interest you, Mr. Von Bork, I may say that this is not my first acquaintance with the members of your family. I have done a good deal of business in Germany in the past, and my name is probably familiar to you."

"I would wish to know it," said the Prussian grimly.

"It was I who brought about the separation between Irene Adler and the late King of Bohemia when your cousin Heinrich was the Imperial Envoy. It was I also who saved from murder, by the Nihilist Klopman, Count Von und Zu Grafenstein, who was your mother's elder brother. It was I——"

Von Bork sat up in amazement.

"There is only one man," he cried.

"Exactly," said Holmes.

Von Bork groaned and sank back on the sofa. "And most of that information came through you," he cried. "What is it worth? What have I done? It is my ruin for ever!"

"It is certainly a little untrustworthy," said

Holmes. "It will require some checking, and you have little time to check it. Your admiral may find the new guns rather larger than he expects, and the cruisers perhaps a trifle faster."

Von Bork clutched at his own throat in despair.

"There are a good many other points of detail which will, no doubt, come to light in good time. But you have one quality which is very rare in a German, Mr. Von Bork, you are a sportsman and you will bear me no ill-will when you realize that you, who have outwitted so many other people, have at last been outwitted yourself. After all, you have done your best for your country, and I have done my best for mine, and what could be more natural? Besides," he added, not unkindly, as he laid his hand upon the shoulder of the prostrate man, "it is better than to fall before some more ignoble foe. These papers are now ready, Watson. If you will help me with our prisoner, I think that we may get started for London at once."

It was no easy task to move Von Bork, for he was a strong and desperate man. Finally, holding either arm, the two friends walked him very slowly down the garden walk which he had trod with such proud confidence when he received the congratulations of the famous diplomatist only a few hours before. After a short, final struggle he was hoisted, still bound hand and foot, into the spare seat of the little car. His precious valise was wedged in beside him.

"I trust that you are as comfortable as circumstances permit," said Holmes, when the final arrangements were made. "Should I be guilty of a liberty if I lit a cigar and placed it between your lips?"

But all amenities were wasted upon the angry German.

"I suppose you realize, Mr. Sherlock Holmes," said he, "that if your Government bears you out in this treatment it becomes an act of war."

"What about your Government and all this treatment?" said Holmes, tapping the valise.

"You are a private individual. You have no warrant for my arrest. The whole proceeding is absolutely illegal and outrageous."

"Absolutely," said Holmes.

"Kidnapping a German subject."

"And stealing his private papers."

"Well, you realize your position, you and your accomplice here. If I were to shout for help as we pass through the village——"

"My dear sir, if you did anything so fool-

ish you would probably enlarge the too lim-
ited titles of our village inns by giving us
'The Dangling Prussian' as a sign-post. The
Englishman is a patient creature, but at
present his temper is a little inflamed and it
would be as well not to try him too far. No,
Mr. Von Bork, you will go with us in a
quiet, sensible fashion to Scotland Yard,
whence you can send for your friend Baron
Von Herling and see if even now you may
not fill that place which he has reserved for
you in the ambassadorial suite. As to you,
Watson, you are joining us with your old
service, as I understand, so London won't be
out of your way. Stand with me here upon
the terrace, for it may be the last quiet talk
that we shall ever have."

The two friends chatted in intimate con-
verse for a few minutes, recalling once again
the days of the past whilst their prisoner
vainly wriggled to undo the bonds that held
him. As they turned to the car, Holmes
pointed back to the moonlit sea, and shook a
thoughtful head.

"There's an east wind coming, Watson."

"I think not, Holmes. It is very warm."

"Good old Watson! You are the one fixed
point in a changing age. There's an east
wind coming all the same, such a wind as

never blew on England yet. It will be cold and bitter, Watson, and a good many of us may wither before its blast. But it's God's own wind none the less, and a cleaner, better, stronger land will lie in the sunshine when the storm has cleared. Start her up, Watson, for it's time that we were on our way. I have a cheque for five hundred pounds which should be cashed early, for the drawer is quite capable of stopping it, if he can."

Hot Or Cold

ISAAC ASIMOV

JENNINGS SIGHED heavily, and the sound seemed to produce an echo in the cavernous, dim and slightly dusty confines of the library of the Union Club. "I'm getting old," he said. "There's no use denying it anymore. I've just had a birthday and my kids are getting suspiciously kind to me. They did everything but tuck a shawl about my shoulders."

I said unsympathetically, "Do you have arthritis?"

"No, I don't."

"Then you're not old. Old age starts when you become creaky; when it hurts to sit down or stand up and when your joints ache even when you're not doing anything. Except for that, sixty feels like twenty if you're in reasonable shape." I said it all rather smugly. I don't have arthritis and I can do everything the twenty-year-olds can do.—That I want to do, I mean; I don't want to play football.

217

Baranov said, "It isn't arthritis I worry about; it's the gradual decay of mental power. At least you're aware of arthritis when you have it. When your mind begins to decay, you can only tell that you're going mentally downhill by the use of your judgment, which is itself a function of your decaying mind. How many people must be senile and be too senile to tell that they're senile."

Inevitably, our eyes shifted to Griswold, who occupied his usual chair, with his white hair framing his pink and relatively unlined face and his thick white mustache just faintly moist with the last visit of the scotch and soda he had in his hand.

Griswold's eyes remained closed, but he said, "From the talk about senility and the sudden silence, I gather you are all concentrating your feeble minds on me. It won't help you. You may all be admiring my powerful mind, but none of you will ever have one like it for yourself. Of course, we may have immortality someday, or at least potential immortality. In fact, we might already have had it in our own time except that— except that—"

He seemed to be drifting off, but I nudged him gently awake. Actually, what I really did was stamp on his shoe. He said, "Ouch!" and his eyes opened.

"What's this about immortality?" I said.

I cannot vouch [said Griswold] for the story I am about to tell you. If it were something I had personally witnessed and experienced, you could, of course, be sure of its absolute veracity and thorough reliability. The essential parts of this story, however, were told me by a stranger a couple of years ago and I can't be sure about it. He may have been attempting to practice on my credulity, which people often do because they judge from my frank and open countenance that I can be imposed upon. Of course, they learn better quickly.

I met the gentleman I speak of in a bar. I was passing the time in Chicago waiting for a plane that would be taking me to Atlanta on business that has nothing whatever to do with the matter at hand, and sitting on the stool next to me was a fellow who had the subtle appearance of being about to go to seed. His jacket had the beginnings of wrinkles, his jowls the beginnings of stubble, his shoes the beginnings of scuff marks. And he looked sad.

He caught my eye and raised his drink to

me. He had the beginnings of intoxication. Just the beginnings. He was just sufficiently far gone to talk to strangers. He said, "To you, sir. You have a kind face." He sipped a bit, and so did I, and then he said, "I am sorry you will have to grow old and die, and that I will, and that everyone will. I drink to the needlessly aging people the whole world over."

He had the sound of an educated man and the nonsense he was saying made just enough sense to make me curious to hear more. I said, "Will you join me at a table, sir, so that we can discuss the matter privately? And will you permit the next round to be on me?"

"Certainly, sir," he said with alacrity, descending briskly from the stool. "You are a noble fellow."

Well, I am, of course, so I could see that drink had not yet incapacitated his judgment. We sat together at a corner table in a largely empty bar and he began talking at once. He heaved an enormous sigh and said, "I am a chemist. My name is Brooke. Simon Brooke. I received my doctorate from Wisconsin."

"Good afternoon, Dr. Brooke," I said gravely. "I am Griswold."

He said, "I worked with Lucas J. Atterbury. I assume you never heard of him."

"I never did."

"My own feeling is that he was probably the greatest biochemist in the world. He had no formal training in the field and I suspect he never even finished college, but he had a natural flair. Things turned to gold in his fingers as soon as he touched them. Do you know what I mean?"

I knew what he meant.

"You could go to college," said Brooke thoughtfully, "as I did and you would then know all the ways in which a problem could be studied and all the reasons why it couldn't be solved—and Lucas (he wouldn't let anyone call him by anything but his first name) who didn't know all those things would just sit in his chair and think and come up with something that would be just right."

I said, "He must have been worth millions to anyone with problems."

"You'd think so, wouldn't you? Well, that wasn't Lucas's way. He didn't want to solve just any problems that were handed to him, except once in a while just to earn some handsome fees that would keep him in funds and allow him to work on the one problem that interested him."

"Which was?"

"Immortality. He was seventy-seven when I met him and he had been working on that for seventeen years; ever since he was sixty and had decided that he had to do something to keep his life in existence past his normal life expectancy. By the time he was seventy-seven he was in the last stages of annoyance with himself. If he had started when he was fifty, you see, he could have solved the problem in time, but he hadn't felt the approach of old age till it was perhaps too late.

"So, when he was seventy-seven, he was sufficiently desperate to hire an assistant. I was the assistant. It wasn't the sort of job I wanted, but he offered me a decent salary and I thought I could use it as a stepping-stone to something else. I sneered at him as an uneducated tinkerer at first—but he caught me. When he talked to me about his theories, he used all the wrong terminology, but eventually it seemed to make sense.

"He thought that with me doing much of the experimentation, he might still make it before he died, so he kept me working hard. And the whole project became important to me.

"You see—old age is programmed into our genes. There are inevitable changes that

222

go on in the cells, changes that put an end to them finally. The changes clog them, stiffen them, disorder them. If you can find out exactly what the changes are and how to reverse them or, better yet, prevent them, we'd live for as long as we want to and stay young forever."

I said, "If it's built into our cells, then old age and death must have a reason for existence and perhaps shouldn't be tampered with."

"Of course there's a reason for it," said Brooke. "You can't have evolution without the periodic replacement of the old generation by the new. It's just that we don't need that anymore. Science is at the brink of being able to direct evolution.

"In any case, Lucas had discovered what the crucial change was. He had found the chemical basis for old age and he was seeking for a way to reverse it, some chemical or physical treatment that would reverse that change. The treatment, properly administered, would be the fountain of youth."

"How did you know he had discovered it?"

"I have more than a statement. I was with him four years and in that time I had mice that showed the effects. I could inject an old mouse at his instructions, one that was clearly on the point of death from old age, and that mouse would take on the attributes of youth before my eyes."

"Then it was all done."

"Not quite. The mouse would grow young, frolic about in the joy of youth and then, after a day or two, it would die. There were clearly undesirable side effects to the treatment and Lucas had not, at first, managed to do away with them. That was his final task.—But he never gave me any details. I worked under instructions without ever knowing *exactly* what was happening. It was his mania for secrecy. He wanted everything under his control. So when the time came that he had solved the problem, it was too late."

"In what way?"

"On the day he had solved the problem, he was in his eighty-second year and he had a stroke. It was on that very day—the excitement I'm sure. He could barely talk and was clearly dying. When the doctors gave him a moment to himself, he motioned to me feebly. 'I have it,' he whispered with an articulation I could barely make out. 'Carry on. Preparations D-27, D-28. To be mixed but only after held overnight at—at—' His voice grew feebler. 'At forty degrees—'

"I couldn't make out the final mumble, but I knew the only things that could come after 'forty degrees.' I said, 'Fahrenheit or Celsius.' He mumbled again and said, 'Do it today or it won't, won't—' I said again urgently, 'Fahrenheit or Celsius.' There was a pause and then he muttered something that sounded like 'doesn't matter' and lapsed into a coma. He never came out of it and died the next day.

"And there I was. I had two unstable solutions that would not last through the day. If I could mix them properly and inject myself—I was ready for the risk if it meant the chance of immortality—I could then live long enough to rediscover the secret for general use. Or at least *I* could stay young forever. But I didn't know the key point about the preparation—the temperature."

"Is there much difference there?" I asked.

"Certainly. A temperature of forty degrees Celsius is forty degrees above the Celsius freezing point at zero degrees. Every ten Celsius degrees is equal to eighteen Fahrenheit degrees so forty Celsius degrees above freezing is four times eighteen, or seventy-two Fahrenheit degrees above freezing. But the

Fahrenheit freezing point is at thirty-two degrees Fahrenheit, and thirty-two plus seventy-two is one hundred and four. Therefore, forty degrees Celsius is equal to one hundred and four degrees Fahrenheit.

"Now, then, did I use forty degrees Fahrenheit, which is quite cool or forty degrees Celsius, which is quite warm. Hot or cold? I didn't know. I couldn't make up my mind, so the two solutions lost their potency and I lost my chance forever."

I said, "Didn't you know which scale Lucas customarily used?"

"Scientists use Celsius exclusively," said Brooke, "but Lucas wasn't really a trained scientist. He used whichever one appealed to him at the time. One could never be sure."

"What did he mean, 'doesn't matter'?"

"I don't know. He was dying. I assume he felt life slipping away and nothing mattered anymore.—Damn it, why couldn't he have spoken a little more clearly. Imagine! The secret of immortality, and all of it lost in a mumble that didn't clearly distinguish between Fahrenheit and Celsius."

Brooke, who was quite drunk now, didn't realize how bad it was, for of course the dying man's instructions were perfectly clear, as you have probably seen for yourselves.

Griswold adjusted his position in his chair as though to drop off again, but Baranov seized his wrist and said, "Are you trying to tell me you know which temperature scale this Lucas was referring to?"

"Of course," said Griswold, indignantly. "It's obvious. If you say 'forty degrees mumble, mumble' those mumbles don't have to be either 'Fahrenheit' or 'Celsius.' There's a third alternative."

"Which?" I asked.

"He could be saying forty degrees below zero.'"

"Even if he did," said Jennings, "we still wouldn't know if it were Fahrenheit or Celsius."

"Yes we would," said Griswold. "You've heard that forty Celsius degrees is equal to seventy-two Fahrenheit degrees. That means that forty Celsius degrees below zero degrees Celsius, which is the Celsius freezing point, is seventy-two degrees below thirty-two degrees Fahrenheit, which is the Fahrenheit freezing point. But seventy-two degrees below the thirty-two-mark is forty degrees below zero degrees Fahrenheit.

"Therefore, forty degrees below zero Celsius is forty degrees below zero Fahrenheit.

If you say 'forty degrees below zero,' it doesn't matter whether its Celsius or Fahrenheit and that's the *only* temperature where it doesn't matter. That's why Lucas said, 'doesn't matter.'—Well, Brooke never saw that little point and I don't think that he has the brains to rediscover the treatment, or that anyone will in our lifetimes.—So we'll just continue to grow old."

The Hammer of God

G. K. CHESTERTON

THE LITTLE village of Bohun Beacon was perched on a hill so steep that the tall spire of its church seemed only like the peak of a small mountain. At the foot of the church stood a smithy, generally red with fires and always littered with hammers and scraps of iron; opposite to this, over a rude cross of cobbled paths, was "The Blue Boar," the only inn of the place. It was upon this crossway, in the lifting of a leaden and silver daybreak, that two brothers met in the street and spoke; though one was beginning the day and the other finishing it. The Rev. and Hon. Wilfred Bohun was very devout, and was making his way to some austere exercises of prayer or contemplation at dawn. Colonel the Hon. Norman Bohun, his elder brother, was by no means devout, and was sitting in evening dress on the bench outside "The Blue Boar," drinking what the philosophic observer was free to regard either as his last glass on Tuesday or his first on Wednesday. The colonel was not particular.

The Bohuns were one of the very few aristocratic families really dating from the Middle Ages, and their pennon had actually seen Palestine. But it is a great mistake to suppose that such houses stand high in chivalric tradition. Few except the poor preserve traditions. Aristocrats live not in traditions but in fashions. The Bohuns had been Mohocks under Queen Anne and Mashers under Queen Victoria. But like more than one of the really ancient houses, they had rotted in the last two centuries into mere drunkards and dandy degenerates, till there had even come a whisper of insanity. Certainly there was something hardly human about the colonel's wolfish pursuit of pleasure, and his chronic resolution not to go home till morning had a touch of the hideous clarity of insomnia. He was a tall, fine animal, elderly, but with hair still startlingly yellow. He would have looked merely blonde and leonine, but his blue eyes were sunk so deep in his face that they looked black. They were a little too close together. He had very long yellow moustaches; on each side of them a fold or furrow from nostril to jaw, so that a sneer seemed cut into his face. Over his evening clothes he wore a curious pale yellow coat that looked more like a very light dressing gown than an overcoat, and on the back of his head was stuck an extraordinary broad-brimmed hat of a bright green colour, evidently some oriental curiosity caught up at random. He was proud of appearing in such incongruous attires—proud of the fact that he always made them look congruous.

His brother the curate had also the yellow hair and the elegance, but he was buttoned up to the chin in black, and his face was clean-shaven, cultivated, and a little nervous. He seemed to live for nothing but his religion; but there were some who said (notably the blacksmith, who was a Presbyterian) that it was a love of Gothic architecture rather than of God, and that his haunting of the church like a ghost was only another and purer turn of the almost morbid thirst for beauty which sent his brother raging after women and wine. This charge was doubtful, while the man's practical piety was indubitable. Indeed, the charge was mostly an ignorant misunderstanding of the love of solitude and secret prayer, and was founded on his being often found kneeling, not before the altar, but in peculiar places, in the crypts or gallery, or even in the belfry. He was at the moment about to enter the church through the yard of the smithy, but stopped and frowned a little as he saw his brother's cavernous eyes staring in the same direction. On the hypothesis that the colonel was interested in the church he did not waste any speculations. There only remained the blacksmith's shop, and though the blacksmith was a Puritan and none of his people, Wilfred Bohun had heard some scandals about a beautiful and rather celebrated wife. He flung a suspicious look across the shed, and the colonel stood up laughing to speak to him.

"Good morning, Wilfred," he said. "Like a good landlord I am watching sleeplessly over my people. I am going to call on the blacksmith."

Wilfred looked at the ground, and said: "The blacksmith is out. He is over at Greenford."

"I know," answered the other with silent laughter; "that is why I am calling on him."

"Norman," said the cleric, with his eye on a pebble in the road, "are you ever afraid of thunderbolts?"

"What do you mean?" asked the colonel. "Is your hobby meteorology?"

"I mean," said Wilfred, without looking

up, "do you ever think that God might strike you in the street?"

"I beg your pardon," said the colonel; "I see your hobby is folk-lore."

"I know your hobby is blasphemy," retorted the religious man, stung in the one live place of his nature. "But if you do not fear God, you have good reason to fear man."

The elder raised his eyebrows politely. "Fear man?" he said.

"Barnes the blacksmith is the biggest and strongest man for forty miles round," said the clergyman sternly. "I know you are no coward or weakling, but he could throw you over the wall."

This struck home, being true, and the lowering line by mouth and nostril darkened and deepened. For a moment he stood with the heavy sneer on his face. But in an instant Colonel Bohun had recovered his own cruel good humour and laughed, showing two dog-like front teeth under his yellow moustache. "In that case, my dear Wilfred," he said quite carelessly, "it was wise for the last of the Bohuns to come out partially in armour."

And he took off the queer round hat covered with green, showing that it was lined within with steel. Wilfred recognised it indeed as a light Japanese or Chinese helmet torn down from a trophy that hung in the old family hall.

"It was the first hat to hand," explained his brother airily; "always the nearest hat— and the nearest woman."

"The blacksmith is away at Greenford," said Wilfred quietly; "the time of his return is unsettled."

And with that he turned and went into the church with bowed head, crossing himself like one who wishes to be quit of an unclean spirit. He was anxious to forget such grossness in the cool twilight of his tall Gothic cloisters; but on that morning it was fated that his still round of religious exercises should be everywhere arrested by small shocks. As he entered the church, hitherto always empty at that hour, a kneeling figure rose hastily to its feet and came towards the full daylight of the doorway. When the curate saw it he stood still with surprise. For the early worshipper was none other than the village idiot, a nephew of the blacksmith, one who neither would nor could care for the church or for anything else. He was always called "Mad Joe," and seemed to have no other name; he was a dark, strong, slouching lad, with a heavy white face, dark straight hair, and a mouth always open. As he passed the priest, his moon-calf countenance gave no hint of what he had been doing or thinking of. He had never been known to pray before. What sort of prayers was he saying now? Extraordinary prayers surely.

Wilfred Bohun stood rooted to the spot long enough to see the idiot go out into the sunshine, and even to see his dissolute brother hail him with a sort of avuncular jocularity. The last thing he saw was the colonel throwing pennies at the open mouth of Joe, with the serious appearance of trying to hit it.

This ugly sunlight picture of the stupidity and cruelty of the earth sent the ascetic finally to his prayers for purification and new thoughts. He went up to a pew in the gallery, which brought him under a coloured window which he loved and always quieted his spirit; a blue window with an angel carrying lilies. There he began to think less about the half-wit, with his livid face and mouth like a fish. He began to think less of his evil brother, pacing like a lean lion in his horrible hunger. He sank deeper and deeper into those cold and sweet colours of silver blossoms and sapphire sky.

In this place half an hour afterwards he

was found by Gibbs, the village cobbler, who had been sent for him in some haste. He got to his feet with promptitude, for he knew that no small matter would have brought Gibbs into such a place at all. The cobbler was, as in many villages, an atheist, and his appearance in church was a shade more extraordinary than Mad Joe's. It was a morning of theological enigmas.

"What is it?" asked Wilfred Bohun rather stiffly, but putting out a trembling hand for his hat.

The atheist spoke in a tone that, coming from him, was quite startlingly respectful, and even, as it were, huskily sympathetic.

"You must excuse me, sir," he said in a hoarse whisper, "but we didn't think it right not to let you know at once. I'm afraid a rather dreadful thing has happened, sir. I'm afraid your brother——"

Wilfred clenched his frail hands. "What devilry has he done now?" he cried in involuntary passion.

"Why, sir," said the cobbler, coughing, "I'm afraid he's done nothing, and won't do anything. I'm afraid he's done for. You had really better come down, sir."

The curate followed the cobbler down a short winding stair which brought them out at an entrance rather higher than the street. Bohun saw the tragedy in one glance, flat underneath him like a plan. In the yard of the smithy were standing five or six men mostly in black, one in an inspector's uniform. They included the doctor, the Presbyterian minister, and the priest from the Roman Catholic chapel, to which the blacksmith's wife belonged. The latter was speaking to her, indeed, very rapidly, in an undertone, as she, a magnificent woman with red-gold hair, was sobbing blindly on a bench. Between these two groups, and just clear of the main heap of hammers, lay a man in evening dress, spread-eagled and flat on his face. From the height above Wilfred could have sworn to every item of his costume and appearance, down to the Bohun rings upon his fingers; but the skull was only a hideous splash, like a star of blackness and blood.

Wilfred Bohun gave but one glance, and ran down the steps into the yard. The doctor, who was the family physician, saluted him, but he scarcely took any notice. He could only stammer out: "My brother is dead. What does it mean? What is this horrible mystery?" There was an unhappy silence; and then the cobbler, the most outspoken man present, answered: "Plenty of horror, sir," he said; "but not much mystery."

"What do you mean?" asked Wilfred, with a white face.

"It's plain enough," answered Gibbs. "There is only one man for forty miles round that could have struck such a blow as that, and he's the man that had most reason to."

"We must not prejudge anything," put in the doctor, a tall, black-bearded man, rather nervously; "but it is competent for me to corroborate what Mr. Gibbs says about the nature of the blow, sir; it is an incredible blow. Mr. Gibbs says that only one man in this district could have done it. I should have said myself that nobody could have done it."

A shudder of superstition went through the slight figure of the curate. "I can hardly understand," he said.

"Mr. Bohun," said the doctor in a low voice, "metaphors literally fail me. It is inadequate to say that the skull was smashed to bits like an eggshell. Fragments of bone were driven into the body and the ground like bullets into a mud wall. It was the hand of a giant."

He was silent a moment, looking grimly through his glasses; then he added: "The thing has one advantage—that it clears most people of suspicion at one stroke. If you or I or any normally made man in the country were accused of this crime, we should be acquitted as an infant would be acquitted of stealing the Nelson column."

"That's what I say," repeated the cobbler obstinately; "there's only one man that could have done it, and he's the man that would have done it. Where's Simeon Barnes, the blacksmith?"

"He's over at Greenford," faltered the curate.

"More likely over in France," muttered the cobbler.

"No; he is in neither of those places," said a small and colourless voice, which came from the little Roman priest who had joined the group. "As a matter of fact, he is coming up the road at this moment."

The little priest was not an interesting man to look at, having stubbly brown hair and a round and stolid face. But if he had been as splendid as Apollo no one would have looked at him at that moment. Everyone turned round and peered at the pathway which wound across the plain below, along which was indeed walking, at his own huge stride and with a hammer on his shoulder, Simeon the smith. He was a bony and gigantic man, with deep, dark, sinister eyes and a dark chin beard. He was walking and talking quietly with two other men; and though he was never specially cheerful, he seemed quite at his ease.

"My God!" cried the atheistic cobbler, "and there's the hammer he did it with."

"No," said the inspector, a sensible-looking man with a sandy moustache, speaking for the first time. "There's the hammer he did it with over there by the church wall. We have left it and the body exactly as they are."

All glanced round and the short priest went across and looked down in silence at the tool where it lay. It was one of the smallest and the lightest of the hammers, and would not have caught the eye among the rest; but on the iron edge of it were blood and yellow hair.

After a silence the short priest spoke without looking up, and there was a new note in his dull voice. "Mr. Gibbs was hardly right," he said, "in saying that there is no mystery. There is at least the mystery of why so big a man should attempt so big a blow with so little a hammer."

"Oh, never mind that," cried Gibbs, in a

fever. "What are we to do with Simeon Barnes?"

"Leave him alone," said the priest quietly. "He is coming here of himself. I know those two men with him. They are very good fellows from Greenford, and they have come over about the Presbyterian chapel."

Even as he spoke the tall smith swung round the corner of the church, and strode into his own yard. Then he stood there quite still, and the hammer fell from his hand. The inspector, who had preserved impenetrable propriety, immediately went up to him.

"I won't ask you, Mr. Barnes," he said, "whether you know anything about what has happened here. You are not bound to say. I hope you don't know, and that you will be able to prove it. But I must go through the form of arresting you in the King's name for the murder of Colonel Norman Bohun."

"You are not bound to say anything," said the cobbler in officious excitement. "They've got to prove everything. They haven't proved yet that it is Colonel Bohun, with the head all smashed up like that."

"That won't wash," said the doctor aside to the priest. "That's out of the detective stories. I was the colonel's medical man, and I knew his body better than he did. He had very fine hands, but quite peculiar ones. The second and third fingers were the same length. Oh, that's the colonel right enough."

As he glanced at the brained corpse upon the ground the iron eyes of the motionless blacksmith followed them and rested there also.

"Is Colonel Bohun dead?" said the smith quite calmly. "Then he's damned."

"Don't say anything! Oh, don't say anything," cried the atheist cobbler, dancing about in an ecstasy of admiration of the English legal system. For no man is such a legalist as the good Secularist.

The blacksmith turned on him over his shoulder the august face of a fanatic.

"It's well for you infidels to dodge like foxes because the world's law favours you," he said; "but God guards His own in His pocket, as you shall see this day."

Then he pointed to the colonel and said: "When did this dog die in his sins?"

"Moderate your language," said the doctor.

"Moderate the Bible's language, and I'll moderate mine. When did he die?"

"I saw him alive at six o'clock this morning," stammered Wilfred Bohun.

"God is good," said the smith. "Mr. Inspector, I have not the slightest objection to being arrested. It is you who may object to arresting me. I don't mind leaving the court without a stain on my character. You do mind perhaps leaving the court with a bad set-back in your career."

The solid inspector for the first time looked at the blacksmith with a lively eye; as did everybody else, except the short, strange priest, who was still looking down at the little hammer that had dealt the dreadful blow.

"There are two men standing outside this shop," went on the blacksmith with ponderous lucidity, "good tradesmen in Greenford whom you all know, who will swear that they saw me from before midnight till daybreak and long after in the committee-room of our Revival Mission, which sits all night, we save souls so fast. In Greenford itself twenty people could swear to me for all that time. If I were a heathen, Mr. Inspector, I would let you walk on to your downfall. But as a Christian man I feel bound to give you your chance, and ask you whether you will hear my alibi now or in court."

The inspector seemed for the first time disturbed, and said, "Of course I should be glad to clear you altogether now."

The smith walked out of his yard with the same long and easy stride, and returned to his two friends from Greenford, who were indeed friends of nearly everyone present. Each of them said a few words which no one ever thought of disbelieving. When they had spoken, the innocence of Simeon stood up as solid as the great church above them.

One of those silences struck the group which are more strange and insufferable than any speech. Madly, in order to make conversation, the curate said to the Catholic priest:

"You seem very much interested in that hammer, Father Brown."

"Yes, I am," said Father Brown; "why is it such a small hammer?"

The doctor swung round on him.

"By George, that's true," he cried; "who would use a little hammer with ten larger hammers lying about?"

Then he lowered his voice in the curate's ear and said: "Only the kind of person that can't lift a large hammer. It is not a question of force or courage between the sexes. It's a question of lifting power in the shoulders. A bold woman could commit ten murders with a light hammer and never turn a hair. She could not kill a beetle with a heavy one."

Wilfred Bohun was staring at him with a

sort of hypnotised horror, while Father Brown listened with his head a little on one side, really interested and attentive. The doctor went on with more hissing emphasis:

"Why do these idiots always assume that the only person who hates the wife's lover is the wife's husband? Nine times out of ten the person who most hates the wife's lover is the wife. Who knows what insolence or treachery he had shown her—look there?"

He made a momentary gesture towards the red-haired woman on the bench. She had lifted her head at last and the tears were drying on her splendid face. But the eyes were fixed on the corpse with an electric glare that had in it something of idiocy.

The Rev. Wilfred Bohun made a limp gesture as if waving away all desire to know; but Father Brown, dusting off his sleeve some ashes blown from the furnace, spoke in his indifferent way.

"You are like so many doctors," he said; "your mental science is really suggestive. It is your physical science that is utterly impossible. I agree that the woman wants to kill the co-respondent much more than the petitioner does. And I agree that a woman will always pick up a small hammer instead of a big one. But the difficulty is one of physical impossibility. No woman ever born could have smashed a man's skull out flat like that." Then he added reflectively, after a pause: "These people haven't grasped the whole of it. The man was actually wearing an iron helmet, and the blow scattered it like broken glass. Look at that woman. Look at her arms."

Silence held them all up again, and then the doctor said rather sulkily: "Well, I may be wrong; there are objections to everything. But I stick to the main point. No man but an idiot would pick up that little hammer if he could use a big hammer."

With that the lean and quivering hands of Wilfred Bohun went up to his head and seemed to clutch his scanty yellow hair. After an instant they dropped, and he cried: "That was the word I wanted; you have said the word."

Then he continued, mastering his discomposure: "The words you said were, 'No man but an idiot would pick up the small hammer.'"

"Yes," said the doctor. "Well?"

"Well," said the curate, "no man but an idiot did." The rest stared at him with eyes arrested and riveted, and he went on in a febrile and feminine agitation.

"I am a priest," he cried unsteadily, "and a priest should be no shedder of blood. I—I mean that he should bring no one to the gallows. And I thank God that I see the criminal clearly now—because he is a criminal who cannot be brought to the gallows."

"You will not denounce him?" inquired the doctor.

"He would not be hanged if I did denounce him," answered Wilfred with a wild but curiously happy smile. "When I went into the church this morning I found a madman praying there—that poor Joe, who has been wrong all his life. God knows what he prayed; but with such strange folk it is not incredible to suppose that their prayers are all upside down. Very likely a lunatic would pray before killing a man. When I last saw poor Joe he was with my brother. My brother was mocking him."

"By Jove!" cried the doctor, "this is talking at last. But how do you explain——"

The Rev. Wilfred was almost trembling with the excitement of his own glimpse of the truth. "Don't you see; don't you see," he cried feverishly; "that is the only theory that covers both the queer things, that answers both the riddles. The two riddles are the little hammer and the big blow. The smith might have struck the big blow, but would not have chosen the little hammer. His wife would have chosen the little hammer, but she could not have struck the big blow. But the madman might have done both. As for the little hammer—why, he was mad and might have picked up anything. And for the big blow, have you never heard, doctor, that a maniac in his paroxysm may have the strength of ten men?"

The doctor drew a deep breath and then said, "By golly, I believe you've got it."

Father Brown had fixed his eyes on the speaker so long and steadily as to prove that his large grey, ox-like eyes were not quite so insignificant as the rest of his face. When silence had fallen he said with marked respect: "Mr. Bohun, yours is the only theory yet propounded which holds water every way and is essentially unassailable. I think, therefore, that you deserve to be told, on my positive knowledge, that it is not the true one." And with that the old little man walked away and stared again at the hammer.

"That fellow seems to know more than he ought to," whispered the doctor peevishly to Wilfred. "Those popish priests are deucedly sly."

"No, no," said Bohun, with a sort of wild

248

fatigue. "It was the lunatic. It was the lunatic."

The group of the two clerics and the doctor had fallen away from the more official group containing the inspector and the man he had arrested. Now, however, that their own party had broken up, they heard voices from the others. The priest looked up quietly and then looked down again as he heard the blacksmith say in a loud voice:

"I hope I've convinced you, Mr. Inspector. I'm a strong man, as you say, but I couldn't have flung my hammer bang here from Greenford. My hammer hasn't got wings that it should come flying half a mile over hedges and fields."

The inspector laughed amicably and said: "No, I think you can be considered out of it, though it's one of the rummiest coincidences I ever saw. I can only ask you to give us all the assistance you can in finding a man as big and strong as yourself. By George! you might be useful, if only to hold him! I suppose you yourself have no guess at the man?"

"I may have a guess," said the pale smith, "but it is not at a man." Then, seeing the scared eyes turn towards his wife on the bench, he put his huge hand on her shoulder and said: "Nor a woman either."

"What do you mean?" asked the inspector jocularly. "You don't think cows use hammers, do you?"

"I think no thing of flesh held that hammer," said the blacksmith in a stifled voice; "mortally speaking, I think the man died alone."

Wilfred made a sudden forward movement and peered at him with burning eyes.

"Do you mean to say, Barnes," came the sharp voice of the cobbler, "that the hammer jumped up of itself and knocked the man down?"

"Oh, you gentlemen may stare and snigger," cried Simeon; "you clergymen who tell us on Sunday in what a stillness the Lord smote Sennacherib. I believe that One who walks invisible in every house defended the honour of mine, and laid the defiler dead before the door of it. I believe the force in that blow was just the force there is in earthquakes, and no force less."

Wilfred said, with a voice utterly undecribable: "I told Norman myself to beware of the thunderbolt."

"That agent is outside my jurisdiction," said the inspector with a slight smile.

"You are not outside His," answered the

smith; "see you to it," and, turning his broad back, he went into the house.

The shaken Wilfred was led away by Father Brown, who had an easy and friendly way with him. "Let us get out of this horrid place, Mr. Bohun," he said. "May I look inside your church? I hear it's one of the oldest in England. We take some interest, you know," he added with a comical grimace, "in old English churches."

Wilfred Bohun did not smile, for humour was never his strong point. But he nodded rather eagerly, being only too ready to explain the Gothic splendours to someone more likely to be sympathetic than the Presbyterian blacksmith or the atheist cobbler.

"By all means," he said; "let us go in at this side." And he led the way into the high side entrance at the top of the flight of steps. Father Brown was mounting the first step to follow him when he felt a hand on his shoulder, and turned to behold the dark, thin figure of the doctor, his face darker yet with suspicion.

"Sir," said the physician harshly, "you appear to know some secrets in this black business. May I ask if you are going to keep them to yourself?"

"Why, doctor," answered the priest, smil-

251

ing quite pleasantly, "there is one very good reason why a man of my trade should keep things to himself when he is not sure of them, and that is that it is so constantly his duty to keep them to himself when he is sure of them. But if you think I have been discourteously reticent with you or anyone, I will go to the extreme limit of my custom. I will give you two very large hints."

"Well, sir?" said the doctor gloomily.

"First," said Father Brown quietly, "the thing is quite in your own province. It is a matter of physical science. The blacksmith is mistaken, not perhaps in saying that the blow was divine, but certainly in saying that it came by a miracle. It was no miracle, doctor, except in so far as man is himself a miracle, with his strange and wicked and yet half-heroic heart. The force that smashed that skull was a force well known to scientists— one of the most frequently debated of the laws of nature."

The doctor, who was looking at him with frowning intentness, only said: "And the other hint?"

"The other hint is this," said the priest. "Do you remember the blacksmith, though he believes in miracles, talking scornfully of the impossible fairy tale that his hammer had wings and flew half a mile across country?"

"Yes," said the doctor, "I remember that."

"Well," added Father Brown, with a broad smile, "that fairy tale was the nearest thing to the real truth that has been said to-day." And with that he turned his back and stumped up the steps after the curate.

The Reverend Wilfred, who had been waiting for him, pale and impatient, as if this little delay were the last straw for his nerves, led him immediately to his favourite corner of the church, that part of the gallery closest to the carved roof and lit by the wonderful window with the angel. The little Latin priest explored and admired everything exhaustively, talking cheerfully but in a low voice all the time. When in the course of his investigation he found the side exit and the winding stair down which Wilfred had rushed to find his brother dead, Father Brown ran not down but up, with the agility of a monkey, and his clear voice came from an outer platform above.

"Come up here, Mr. Bohun," he called. "The air will do you good."

Bohun followed him, and came out on a kind of stone gallery or balcony outside the building, from which one could see the illimitable plain in which their small hill stood, wooded away to the purple horizon and dotted with villages and farms. Clear and square, but quite small beneath them, was the blacksmith's yard, where the inspector still stood taking notes and the corpse still lay like a smashed fly.

"Might be the map of the world, mightn't it?" said Father Brown.

"Yes," said Bohun very gravely, and nodded his head.

Immediately beneath and about them the lines of the Gothic building plunged outwards into the void with a sickening swiftness akin to suicide. There is that element of Titan energy in the architecture of the Middle Ages that, from whatever aspect it be seen, it always seems to be rushing away, like the strong back of some maddened horse. This church was hewn out of ancient and silent stone, bearded with old fungoids and stained with the nests of birds. And yet, when they saw it from below, it sprang like a fountain at the stars; and when they saw it, as now, from above, it poured like a cataract into a voiceless pit. For these two men on the tower were left alone with the most terrible aspect of the Gothic; the monstrous foreshortening and disproportion, the dizzy perspectives, the glimpses of great things small and small things great; a topsy-turvydom of stone in the mid-air. Details of stone, enormous by their proximity, were relieved against a pattern of fields and farms, pygmy in their distance. A carved bird or beast at a corner seemed like some vast walking or flying dragon wasting the pastures and villages below. The whole atmosphere was dizzy and dangerous, as if men were upheld in air amid the gyrating wings of colossal genii; and the whole of that old church, as tall and rich as a cathedral, seemed to sit upon the sunlit country like a cloud-burst.

"I think there is something rather danger-ous about standing on these high places even to pray," said Father Brown. "Heights were made to be looked at, not to be looked from."

"Do you mean that one may fall over," asked Wilfred.

"I mean that one's soul may fall if one's body doesn't," said the other priest.

"I scarcely understand you," remarked Bohun indistinctly.

"Look at that blacksmith, for instance," went on Father Brown calmly; "a good man, but not a Christian—hard, imperious, unfor-giving. Well, his Scotch religion was made up by men who prayed on hills and high crags, and learnt to look down on the world more than to look up at heaven. Humility is the mother of giants. One sees great things from the valley; only small things from the peak."

"But he—he didn't do it," said Bohun tremulously.

"No," said the other in an odd voice; "we know he didn't do it."

After a moment he resumed, looking tranquilly out over the plain with his pale grey eyes. "I knew a man," he said, "who began by worshipping with others before the altar, but who grew fond of high and lonely places to pray from, corners or niches in the belfry or the spire. And once in one of those dizzy places, where the whole world seemed to turn under him like a wheel, his brain turned also, and he fancied he was God. So that though he was a good man, he committed a great crime."

Wilfred's face was turned away, but his bony hands turned blue and white as they tightened on the parapet of stone.

"He thought it was given to *him* to judge the world and strike down the sinner. He would never have had such a thought if he had been kneeling with other men upon a floor. But he saw all men walking about like insects. He saw one especially strutting just below him, insolent and evident by a bright green hat—a poisonous insect."

Rooks cawed round the corners of the belfry; but there was no other sound till Father Brown went on.

"This also tempted him, that he had in his hand one of the most awful engines of nature; I mean gravitation, that mad and quickening rush by which all earth's creatures fly back to her heart when released. See, the inspector is strutting just below us in the smithy. If I were to toss a pebble over this parapet it would be something like a bullet by the time it struck him. If I were to drop a hammer—even a small hammer——"

Wilfred Bohun threw one leg over the parapet, and Father Brown had him in a minute by the collar.

"Not by that door," he said quite gently; "that door leads to hell."

Bohun staggered back against the wall, and stared at him with frightful eyes.

"How do you know all this?" he cried. "Are you a devil?"

"I am a man," answered Father Brown gravely; "and therefore have all devils in my heart. Listen to me," he said after a short pause. "I know what you did—at least, I can guess the great part of it. When you left your brother you were racked with no unrighteous rage, to the extent even that you snatched up a small hammer, half inclined to kill him with his foulness on his mouth. Recoiling, you thrust it under your unbuttoned coat instead, and rushed into the church. You pray wildly in many places, under the angel window, upon the platform above, and a higher platform still, from which you could see the colonel's Eastern hat like the back of a green beetle crawling about. Then something snapped in your soul, and you let God's thunderbolt fall."

Wilfred put a weak hand to his head, and asked in a low voice: "How did you know that his hat looked like a green beetle?"

"Oh, that," said the other with the shadow of a smile, "that was common sense. But hear me further. I say I know all this; but no one else shall know it. The next step is for you; I shall take no more steps; I will seal this with the seal of confession. If you ask me why, there are many reasons, and only one that concerns you. I leave things to you because you have not yet gone very far wrong, as assassins go. You did not help to fix the crime on the smith when it was easy; or on

258

his wife, when that was easy. You tried to fix it on the imbecile because you knew that he could not suffer. That was one of the gleams that it is my business to find in assassins. And now come down into the village, and go your own way as free as the wind; for I have said my last word."

They went down the winding stairs in utter silence, and came out into the sunlight by the smithy. Wilfred Bohun carefully unlatched the wooden gate of the yard, and going up to the inspector, said: "I wish to give myself up; I have killed my brother."

No Motive

THEODORE MATHIESON

"Murder is like war," said former police inspector McGregor, putting down his wine glass. "The causes are both fundamental and immediate. Fundamental causes may lie dormant, like gunpowder, until a flash touches them off. The flash is the immediate cause. For instance, in the First World War, German imperialism is held to be the fundamental cause; Sarajevo was the flash, or immediate cause."

"You were talking about murder," I reminded my old friend. It was Saturday evening, and in these latter years we usually spent it having dinner.

"Yes, I was," McGregor said. "Let's say a man is jealous of his wife. His jealousy can smolder for years and perhaps never come to anything; yet if he catches his wife *in flagrante delicto* it may trigger not only suicide but multiple murder. The visual impact of infidelity is the immediate cause."

"Seems fairly obvious."

"It isn't always. Take the Reynolds case, for example, which I handled some years ago. Do you recall it?"

"I don't think so."

"Mrs. Reynolds and her husband, who apparently had been happily married for twenty-five years, were simply talking quietly, without emotion, in her greenhouse, where she was pruning a plant. Suddenly, without any warning, Reynolds seized a pair of scissors and plunged it into her throat."

"Was he jealous of her?"

"No. They got on together famously."

"Was he after her money?"

"No."

"Then there was another woman?"

"Yes, there was, but that wasn't the problem, not exactly. Reynolds—Leslie was his first name—had fallen in love with a younger woman and wanted to marry her. Mrs. Reynolds was perfectly willing for him to do so."

"Then why in heaven's name did he kill her?"

"A delicate point, and you have to understand the background of their marriage to appreciate it. Mrs. Reynolds fell desperately in love with Leslie in their undergraduate years at the University. She was the daughter of Hugh McCallen, the multimillionaire who made his money in Pan American Oil, and who died shortly after their marriage, so that she came into a large fortune. Leslie was an artist just marking time at the University, with no goal ahead, when she married him. From all I've heard, it was a warm affair, and the couple hit it off beautifully."

"I think I see," I said. "She made him take up responsibilities in the oil business when he really wanted to paint."

"Not at all. She encouraged him to do exactly as he pleased, and for some years they traveled around the world, he with his box of paints and easel, and she simply doting on him. Then she got pregnant, but the child died stillborn, and she wasn't able to have more. After that her interests began to change. She became more concerned with her status in society, began to subscribe to causes, like the philharmonic, began to give teas for the literati—things of that sort."

"And began to neglect Leslie?"

"Quite the contrary. Her inability to have children made her very maternal towards him. There wasn't anything he wanted he

262

couldn't have. For a while he fanatically collected coins and stamps, then he turned to publishing folios of his own paintings. The publishing never really came to anything, but he had fun, and they lived in perfect domestic harmony."

"Then why on earth did he murder her?"

"We're coming to that. For the last five years before her death Mrs. Reynolds, tiring of social activities, began to take up hobbies—like ceramics, weaving, and the cultivation of bonsai, those Japanese miniature trees, you know. Perhaps *then* her maternal concern over Leslie relaxed a bit—not so you could notice it much, but enough to give Leslie's eyes time to wander. They lit on a young society deb, Patricia Starr. A beauty she was. He was forty-something and she only eighteen, but they fell deeply in love. Then he went to Mrs. Reynolds and told her.

" 'Are you sure this is what you really want?' she asked him.

" 'I've never been surer of anything in my life,' he said.

" 'Very well. I've never denied you anything, as you know. You may have Patricia, but you will have to support her yourself. You won't get a penny from me.'

263

"Well, Reynolds told me later he was over-joyed. He kissed his wife and thanked her, and ran off to tell Patricia the good news. They planned for their marriage and their honeymoon, and then Patricia's parents got wind of his intentions. The parents faced Reynolds with the poser of how he was going to support Patricia in the style to which she was accustomed.

"Well, that stopped Reynolds cold. He'd always had plenty of money, but he didn't have a dime of his own, and the fact he'd have to earn a luxurious living for Patricia just never occurred to him. Mr. Starr, knowing it as a bad deal for his daughter, put his foot down. He sent Patricia off to Europe with her mother, then told Reynolds to return to his wife and settle down.

"But Leslie was determined to marry Patricia. He went back to his wife, found her in the greenhouse, and asked her if she'd give him a settlement so he could get started with Patricia."

"She refused him," I said, "so he killed her."

"Quite wrong. She relented and said she'd give him a hundred thousand."

"Then why in the world—?"

"Wait. Leslie wrote Patricia, who was now

in Paris, about his good fortune. But she wrote back that she had reconsidered, and unless he could support her with money of his *own*, everything was over between them. He was frantic. He flew to Paris, saw her in spite of her mother's attempts to prevent him, but Patricia stuck to her guns. Which left him no hope, you see. What could he do at his age? He wasn't trained for anything practical. He had no business connections. He'd built nothing of his own. So he came back brooding on his misfortune, feeling impotent as a man, feeling humiliated and defeated."

"Now I understand," I said. "He'd built up a murderous resentment against his wife for so smothering him that she'd suppressed his manhood."

"That was the fundamental cause, but the murder needn't have happened, you know. There had to be the immediate cause."

"And what was that?"

"Reynolds only told me much later. 'I was about to walk away and leave my wife alone in the greenhouse,' he said, 'when I saw what she was doing with the little pine tree, cutting away half its roots to keep it small, and suddenly I knew she'd done the same with me, *deliberately*, over the years—had deliberately kept me small, and that I would never grow any more than the bonsai. That's why I killed her.' "

Mrs. Norris Observes

DOROTHY SALISBURY DAVIS

IF THERE was anything in the world Mrs. Norris liked as well as a nice cup of tea, it was to dip now and then into what she called "a comfortable novel." She found it no problem getting one when she and Mr. James Jarvis, for whom she kept house, were in the country. The ladies at the Nyack library both knew and approved her tastes, and while they always lamented that such books were not written any more, nonetheless they always managed to find a new one for her.

But the New York Public Library at Fifth Avenue and Forty-second Street was a house of different entrance. How could a person like Mrs. Norris climb those wide marble steps, pass muster with the uniformed guard, and then ask for her particular kind of book?

She had not yet managed it, but sometimes she got as far as the library steps and thought about it. And if the sun were out long enough to have warmed the stone bench,

267

she sometimes sat a few moments and observed the faces of the people going in and coming out. As her friend Mr. Tully, the detective, said of her, she was a marvelous woman for observing. "And you can take that the way you like, love."

It was a pleasant morning, this one, and having time to spare, Mrs. Norris contemplated the stone bench. She also noticed that one of her shoelaces had come untied; you could not find a plain cotton lace these days, even on a blind man's tray. She locked her purse between her bosom and her arm and began to stoop.

"It's mine! I saw it first!"

A bunioned pump thumped down almost on her toe, and the woman who owned it slyly turned it over on her ankle so that she might retrieve whatever it was she had found. Mrs. Norris was of the distinct opinion that there had been nothing there at all.

"I was only about to tie my shoelace," Mrs. Norris said, pulling as much height as she could out of her dumpy shape.

A wizened, rouged face turned up at her. "Aw," the creature said, "you're a lady. I'll tie the lace for you."

As the woman fumbled at her foot, Mrs. Norris took time to observe the shaggy hair beneath a hat of many summers. Then she cried, "Get up from there! I'm perfectly able to tie my own shoelace."

The woman straightened, and she was no taller than Mrs. Norris. "Did I hear in your voice that you're Irish?"

"You did not! I'm Scots-born." Then remembering Mr. Tully, her detective friend, she added, "But I'm sometimes taken for North of Ireland."

"Isn't it strange, the places people will take you to be from! Where would you say I was born? Sit down for a moment. You're not in a hurry?"

Mrs. Norris thought the woman daft, but she spoke well and softly. "I haven't the faintest notion," she said, and allowed herself to be persuaded by a grubby hand.

"I was born right down there on Thirty-seventh Street, and not nearly as many years ago as you would think. But this town—oh, the things that have happened to it!" She sat a bit too close, and folded her hands over a beaded evening purse. "A friend of mine, an actress, gave this to me." She indicated the purse, having seen Mrs. Norris glance at it. "But there isn't much giving left in this city . . ."

Of course, Mrs. Norris thought. How foolish of her not to have realized what was coming. "What a dreadful noise the buses make," she commented by way of changing the subject.

"And they're all driven by Irishmen," the woman said quite venomously. "They've ruined New York, those people!"

"I have a gentleman friend who is Irish," Mrs. Norris said sharply, and wondered why she didn't get up and out of there.

"Oh, my dear," the woman said, pulling a long face of shock. "The actress of whom I just spoke, you know? She used to be with the Abbey Theatre. She was the first Cathleen Ni Houlihan. Or perhaps it was the second. But she sends me two tickets for every opening night—and something to wear." The woman opened her hand on the beaded purse and stroked it lovingly. "She hasn't had a new play in such a long time."

Mrs. Norris was touched in spite of herself: it was a beautiful gesture. "Were you ever in the theater yourself?" she asked.

The old woman looked her full in the face. Tears came to her eyes. Then she said, "No." She tumbled out a whole series of no's as though to bury the matter. She's protesting too much, Mrs. Norris thought. "But I have done many things in my life," she continued in her easy made-up-as-you-go fashion. "I have a good mind for science. I can tell you the square feet of floor space in a building from counting the windows. On Broadway, that naked waterfall, you know . . ." Mrs. Norris nodded, remembering the display. "I have figured out how many times the same water goes over it every night. Oh-h-h, and I've written books— just lovely stories about the world when it was gracious, and people could talk to each other even if one of them wasn't one of those psychiatrists."

What an extraordinary woman!

"But who would read stories like that nowadays?" She cast a sidelong glance at Mrs. Norris.

"I would!" Mrs. Norris said.

"Bless you, my dear, I knew that the moment I looked into your face!" She cocked her head, as a bird does at a strange sound. "Do you happen to know what time it is?"

Mrs. Norris looked at her wrist watch. The woman leaned close to look also. "A Gruen is a lovely watch," she said. She could see like a mantis.

"It's time I was going," Mrs. Norris said. "It's eleven-thirty."

"Oh, and time for me, too. I've been promised a job today."

"Where?" asked Mrs. Norris, which was quite unlike her, but the word had spurted out in her surprise.

"It would degrade me to tell you," the stranger said, and her eyes fluttered.

Mrs. Norris could feel the flush in her face. She almost toppled her new, flowered hat, fanning herself. "I'm sorry," she said. "It was rude of me to ask."

"Would you like to buy me a little lunch?" the woman asked brazenly.

Mrs. Norris got to her feet. "All right," she said, having been caught fairly at a vulnerable moment. "There's a cafeteria across the street. I often go there myself for a bowl of soup. Come along."

The woman had risen with her, but her face had gone awry. Mrs. Norris supposed that at this point she was always bought off—she was not the most appetizing of sights to share a luncheon table with. But Mrs. Norris led the way down the steps at a good pace. She did not begrudge the meal, but she would begrudge the price of it if it were not spent on a meal.

"Wait, madam. I can't keep up with you," the woman wailed.

272

Mrs. Norris had to stop anyway to tie the blessed shoelace.

Her guest picked at the food, both her taste and her gab dried up in captivity. "It's a bit rich for my stomach," she complained when Mrs. Norris chided her.

Mrs. Norris sipped her tea. Then something strange happened: the cup trembled in her hand. At the same instant there was a clatter of dishes, the crash of glass, the screams of women, and the sense almost, more than the sound, of an explosion. Mrs. Norris's eyes met those of the woman's across from her. They were aglow as a child's with excitement, and she grinned like a quarter moon.

Outside, people began to run across the street toward the library. Mrs. Norris could hear the blast of police whistles, and she stretched her neck, hoping to see better. "Eat up and we'll go," she urged.

"Oh, I couldn't eat now and with all this commotion."

"Then leave it."

Once in the street Mrs. Norris was instantly the prisoner of the crowd, running with it as if she were treading water, frighteningly, unable to turn aside or stem the tide. And lost at once her frail companion, cast apart either by weight or wisdom. Mrs. Norris took in enough breath for a scream which she let go with a piper's force. It made room for her where there had been none before, and from then on she screamed her way to the fore of the crowd.

"Stand back! There's nobody hurt but there will be!" a policeman shouted.

Sirens wailed the approach of police reinforcements. Meanwhile, two or three patrolmen were joined by a few able-bodied passers-by to make a human cordon across the library steps.

"It blew the stone bench fifty feet in the air," Mrs. Norris heard a man say.

"The stone bench?" she cried out. "Why, I was just sitting on it!"

"Then you've got a hard bottom, lady," a policeman growled. He and a companion were trying to hold on to a young man.

Their prisoner gave a twist and came face to face with Mrs. Norris. "That's the woman," he shouted. "That's the one I'm trying to tell you about. Let go of me and ask *her!*"

A policeman looked at her. "This one with the flowers on her hat?"

"That's the one! She looked at her watch,

got up and left the package, then ran down the steps, and the next thing . . ."

"Got up and left what, young man?" Mrs. Norris interrupted.

"The box under the bench," the young man said, but to one of the officers.

"A box under the bench?" Mrs. Norris repeated.

"How come you were watching her?" the officer said.

"I wasn't especially. I was smoking a cigarette . . ."

"Do you work in the library?"

No doubt he answered, but Mrs. Norris's attention was suddenly distracted, and by what seemed like half the police force of New York City.

"I have a friend, Jasper Tully, in the District Attorney's office," she declared sternly.

"That's fine, lady," a big sergeant said. "We'll take a ride down there right now." Then he bellowed at the top of his lungs, "Keep the steps clear till the Bomb Squad gets here."

In Jasper Tully's office, Mrs. Norris tried to tell her interrogators about the strange little woman. But she knew from the start that they were going to pay very little attention to her story. Their long experience with panhandlers had run so true to pattern that they would not admit to any exception.

And yet Mrs. Norris felt sure she had encountered the exception. For example, she had been cleverly diverted by the woman when she might have seen the package. The woman had put her foot down on nothing— Mrs. Norris was sure of that. She remembered having looked down at her shoelace, and she would have seen a coin had there been one at her feet—Mrs. Norris was a woman who knew the color of money. Oh, it was a clever lass, that other one, and there was a fair amount of crazy hate in her. Mrs. Norris was unlikely to forget the venom she had been so ready to spew on the Irish.

She tried to tell them. But nobody had to button Annie Norris's lip twice. It was not long until they wished Jasper Tully a widower's luck with her, and went back themselves to the scene of the blast.

Mr. Tully offered to take her home.

"No, I think I'll walk and cogitate, thank you," she said.

"Jimmie gives you too much time off," Tully muttered. He was on close terms with her employer.

"He gives me the time I take."

"Is he in town now?"

"He is, or will be tonight. He'll be going full dress to the theater. It's an opening night."

"Aren't you going yourself?"

Mrs. Norris gave it a second's thought. "I might," she said.

The detective took a card from his pocket and wrote down a telephone number. "You can reach me through this at all hours," he said. "That's in case your cogitating gets you into any more trouble."

When he had taken her to the office door, Mrs. Norris looked up to his melancholy face. "Who was Cathleen Ni Houlihan?"

Tully rubbed his chin. "She wasn't a saint exactly, but I think she was a living person . . . How the hell would I know? I was born in the Bronx!" A second later he added, "There was a play about her, wasn't there?"

"There was," said Mrs. Norris. "I'm glad to see you're not as ignorant as you make yourself out to be."

"Just be sure you're as smart as you think you are," Tully said, "if you're off to tackle a policeman's job again."

He had no faith in her, Mrs. Norris thought, or he wouldn't let her do it.

All afternoon she went over the morning's

incidents in her mind. As soon as Mr. Jarvis left the apartment for dinner and the theater, she went downtown herself. The evening papers were full of the bombing, calling it the work of a madman. The mechanism had been made up of clock parts, and the detonating device was something as simple as a pin. It was thought possibly to have been a hatpin.

Well!

And there was not a mention of her in any account. The police were obviously ashamed of themselves.

Mrs. Norris took as her place of departure Forty-sixth Street and Seventh Avenue. Turning her back on the waterfall atop the Broadway building, she walked toward Shubert Alley. Anyone who could even guess at the number of times the same water went over the dam must have looked at it at least as often. And Cathleen Ni Houlihan—no stranger to the theater had plucked that name out of the air.

The beggars were out in droves: the blind, the lame, and the halt. And there were those with tin cups who could read the date in a dead man's eye.

Mrs. Norris was early, and a good thing she was. Sightseers were already congesting the sidewalk in front of the theater. New York might be the biggest city in the world, but to lovers of the stage a few square feet of it was world enough on an opening night.

She watched from across the street for five minutes, then ten, with the crowd swelling and her own hopes dwindling. Then down the street from Eighth Avenue, with a sort of unperturbed haste, came the little beggar-woman. She wore the same hat, the same ragged coat and carried the same beaded purse.

And she also carried a box about six inches by six which she carefully set down on the steps of a fire exit.

Mrs. Norris plunged across the street and paused again, watching the beggar, fascinated in spite of herself. Round and round one woman she walked, looking her up and down, and then she scouted another. The women themselves were well-dressed out-of-towners by their looks, who had come to gape at the celebrated first nighters now beginning to arrive. When the little panhandler had made her choice of victims, she said, and distinctly enough for Mrs. Norris to hear:

"That's Mrs. Vanderhoff arriving now. Lovely, isn't she? Oh, dear, that's not her husband with her. Why, that's Johnson

Tree—the oil man! You're not from Texas, are you, dear?"

Mrs. Norris glanced at the arrivals. It was her own Mr. Jarvis and his friend. A Texas oil man indeed! The woman made up her stories to the fit of her victims! She was an artist at it.

Mrs. Norris edged close to the building and bent down to examine the box. She thought she could hear a rhythmic sound. She could, she realized—her own heartbeat.

"Leave that box alone!"

Mrs. Norris obeyed, but not before she had touched, had actually moved, the box. It was empty, or at least as light as a dream, and the woman had not recognized her. She was too busy spinning a tale. Mrs. Norris waited it out. The woman finally asked for money and got it. She actually got paper money! Then she came for the box.

"Remember me?" Mrs. Norris said.

The woman cocked her head and looked at her. "Should I?"

"This morning on the Public Library steps," Mrs. Norris prompted.

The wizened face brightened. "But of course! Oh, and there's something I wanted to talk to you about. I saw you speaking to my young gentleman friend—you know, in all that excitement?"

"Oh, yes," Mrs. Norris said, remembering the young man who had pointed her out to the police.

"Isn't he a lovely young man? And to have had such misfortune."

"Lovely," Mrs. Norris agreed.

"You know, he had a scholarship to study atomic science and *those* people did him out of it."

"*Those* people?"

"All day long you can see them going in and out, in and out, carting books by the armful. Some of them have beards. False, you know. And those thick glasses—I ask you, who would be fooled by them? Spies! Traitors! And *they* can get as many books as they want."

"Oh, *those* people," Mrs. Norris said understandingly.

"And my poor young friend. They won't even give him a library card, and after I wrote him such a nice reference."

"Do you know where he lives?" Mrs. Norris said as casually as she could.

"No. But I know where he works. He fixes watches for a jeweler on Forty-seventh Street. I walked by there once and saw him working in the window. If you wait here for me, I'll walk over and show you the place tonight. He's not there now, of course, but I'm sure he'll be there in the morning. I hope you can help him."

"I'll try," Mrs. Norris said. A watchmaker.

The warning buzzer sounded within the theater. The lights flickered.

"Excuse me for a moment," the woman said, and picked up the box. "I've brought some violets for the leading lady. I want to take them in before curtain. Wouldn't it be nice if she invited us to see the play? I shan't accept unless she invites both of us."

Mrs. Norris followed the woman down the alleyway and then hung back as she handed the box in at the stage door. The woman waited and, observing Mrs. Norris, nodded to her confidently. Mrs. Norris was only reasonably sure the box was empty. She was beset by doubts and fears. Was there such a thing as a featherweight bomb? The doorman returned and put something in the woman's hand. She bowed and scraped and came along, tucking whatever she'd got into her purse.

With Mr. Jarvis in the theater, Mrs. Norris was not going to take any chances. "Wait for me out front," she said. "I want to have a look in there myself."

"Too late, too late," the woman crowed.

Mrs. Norris hurried.

"No one's allowed backstage now, ma'am," the doorman said.

"That box the old woman gave you . . ." It was sitting on a desk almost within her reach. "It could be dangerous."

"Naw. She's harmless, that old fraud. There's nothing in it but tissue paper. She comes round every opening night. 'Flowers for Miss Hayes,' or Miss Tandy or whoever. The company manager gives her a dollar for luck. I'm sorry, ma'am, but you'll have to go now."

Mrs. Norris beat a dignified retreat. The old woman was nowhere to be seen. But a watchmaker on Forty-seventh Street . . . Forty-seventh Street was also the diamond center of New York. What a lovely place for a leisurely walk-through with Mr. Tully!

The Pleasant Assassin

HELEN McCLOY

THE HIGH place had been a grassy knoll a few hundred years ago. It still revealed a view of the countryside beyond the city. Once a watchtower had stood here and beacon fires had been lit when the watchers saw Indians. It was still called Beacon Hill.

From his windows on the twentieth floor Basil Willing looked down on the golden dome of the Bullfinch State House. Beyond, he had a bird's-eye view of huddled roofs and chimneypots. Leafy tree tops traced the paths of old streets winding down to the river. Here and there a church steeple stood, sharp as a needle, against an angry sky.

Black clouds had brought on premature twilight. A hidden sunset touched the lower edge of darkness with flame as if all the fires of hell were banked just beyond human vision.

As indeed they are . . . Basil was remembering the clash between students and police on Boston Common the night before.

He could see the Common now as a mass of tree tops on his left. He could see the river beyond the chimneypots. Little sailboats were tacking to and fro in a cluster, as busily unimportant as a cloud of hovering gnats.

His doorbell buzzed. Twenty floors below someone must have touched his button by mistake. No one in Boston knew he was at this address except his daughter, and she had left him only moments ago. There had been no question of her coming back this evening.

He pushed the button that opened a two-way speaking tube to the vestibule downstairs. "Yes?"

"Dr. Willing?"

It was a man's voice, distorted by the echo-chamber effect of the tube. "My name's Grogan—Aloysius Grogan, Boston Police Department. Inspector Foyle of New York gave me your address. May I come up?"

"Of course."

Basil pressed the other button that opened the door, but he was still puzzled. Foyle had retired to Florida and only came to New York for occasional visits. When, and why, had Foyle been in contact with the Boston Police?

The doorbell rang. On the threshold stood a tall man with a face so young that just seeing it made Basil feel ten years older.

"Frankly I've come to ask your help," Grogan said. "It's sort of off the record."

"It would have to be," said Basil. "Inspector Foyle is not the only person who has retired lately. I'm no longer a medical assistant to the District Attorney of New York County."

"But you're still called in as a psychiatric consultant."

"Only now and then, but I have no official standing in Boston. I'm here because I was asked to deliver a series of lectures at Harvard. I was glad to accept because it gave me a chance to live near my daughter for a while. She's a student at Wheaton."

"I realize all that, but—" The young man sighed. "When I saw Foyle in New York he seemed to think this was your kind of case. Of course I don't want to impose on you. When a man is old enough to retire he wants people to leave him alone."

Old? "Suppose you tell me about this case."

"Thank you, sir."

Basil's lips were dry. He recalled a remark of his father's: *The worst thing is when they start calling you 'sir'* . . .

"You've heard of Professor Jeremiah Pitcairn? Known to students as the Pit Viper?"

"Author of *After the Family: What?*"

"That's our boy. *Brave New World* stuff."

"Stress comes from partial control of environment. Ergo, let's eliminate stress by controlling the environment totally from the moment of birth. Pavlov could never have got those dogs to salivate every time that bell rang if he'd had only partial control of their environment."

Grogan laughed. "You're not in sympathy with Professor Pitcairn's theories?"

"No, but I really cannot see how they could bring him into conflict with the law."

"I'm with Narcotics."

It took a great deal to startle Basil, but this was a great deal. "A full professor! Pitcairn?"

Grogan sighed. "You see? Nobody's going to believe it. That's his strength. But it's not impossible, you know. Small amounts of mood-changing drugs are accessible to experimental psychologists as to doctors."

"I don't believe it, Pitcairn's much too conservative."

"Is he really? Not if you read between the lines. He wants to change things. He wants escape from conflict. Control the environment of children from birth and they'll escape all conflict with environment. I'd say that's pretty revolutionary."

"It would certainly end progress," said Basil. "For progress depends on some people refusing to accept environment as they find it."

"Who wants progress? Not Pitcairn."

"How do drugs come into it?" asked Basil.

"They can be used experimentally to modify reactions to environment. This enables you to command the reaction you want when you want it, for the length of time you want it, so you can study it at your leisure. But suppose you become so interested in drugs that you decide to try some of them on yourself? Like Baudelaire and Gautier, to say nothing of De Quincey and Coleridge. And— just suppose—you get hooked on an expensive illegal drug. Not just marijuana. Something stronger. What happens then?"

"You'd need money. Lots."

"A hundred dollars a day or more. Just

for the drug. You're a full professor, too smart to take to petty crime, like stealing or forgery. So you go into the business of distributing drugs. You become a middleman, recruiting pushers for wholesalers—pushers who are racketeers. That's profitable and you think it will be safe. Who's going to suspect the distinguished author of *After the Family: What?*"

"But you do suspect him. What happened?"

"Stool pigeons. We've had tips—or shall I say, 'information received'? The dope is seaborne. Pitcairn lives down near Buzzard's Bay and comes up to Boston two or three times a week. He always drops in at one place we're watching—The Den of Iniquity."

Basil couldn't help laughing. "Surely with that name the place must be innocent!"

"You can't be sure. We've just arrested a pair of burglars who specialized in rifling summer cottages while they were empty in winter. Those boys sold everything they stole openly, at a roadside antique shop, and their sign read: *Thieves Market.*"

"You think The Den of Iniquity is another double bluff?"

"I'm sure of it, but I can't prove it. We had a tip that Pitcairn was going to be there

289

last Wednesday. He'd been away for three weeks. India. It seemed logical he'd have stuff to give pushers when he got back—at least, logical enough to watch him while he was at The Den. I really thought we had him."

"But you didn't?"

"He never showed. I had The Den staked out—went there myself. Then I had a bit of sheer bad luck. There I was, trying not to look like a policeman, and the first guy I saw, after I walked in, was someone I'd been to school with, who went on to MIT on a scholarship when I joined the police department. He called me by name and asked me how I liked being a policeman. I tried to shut him up, but it was too late. Somebody must have heard him and warned Pitcairn not to come."

"Why are you so sure it was this incident that gave you away?"

"Nobody outside Narcotics knew anything about that stakeout at The Den. It must have been that dear old school chum of mine who blew my cover, damn him! Whoever overheard him must have telephoned Pitcairn."

"Where is The Den?"

"Charles Street. It's just one big room.

290

Used to be a shop. There's a shop window still, with a curtain across the glass to hide the inside from passers-by in the street. There's a beer and coffee bar, a little dais for musicians, some tables and chairs and lavatories and one telephone booth. That's all. Just two outside doors—a front door to the street and a side door to an alley. People kept drifting in all evening, but no one left the joint until it closed. I know because I was in a position to watch both doors leading outside. That's why I'm so sure someone telephoned Pitcairn from inside."

"Were you also able to watch the telephone booth, too?"

"Oh, yes. I was sitting right beside the booth in case a call came through for me from one of the other men in Narcotics. It didn't. There were no incoming calls at all and only two outgoing calls. A girl the others called Anna Warsaw phoned some boy named Sam at Boston University and they had a long silly conversation. No references to drugs or professors. I could hear everything because she left the door of the booth open. It was pretty hot that night."

"My daughter knows an Anna Warsaw. At least she's mentioned the name."

"Students around Boston get to know each

other. Boston is just a big village. The name Warsaw is pretty uncommon, so it's probably the same girl."

"How do you know she was calling Boston University?"

"She asked for Mugar Memorial Library."

"At that hour?"

"It's open until eleven thirty. And she just asked for Sam—no surname. So he probably works there."

"And the other call?"

"A boy made that one. The others called him Gene."

"Was his conversation silly too?"

"There wasn't any. No one answered his call. He waited about a minute, then slammed the receiver back on its hook and came out of the booth. I heard him say to another boy that parents ought to have more sense than to go gadding about at night when they were too old for it, so I assumed that either he was calling his parents or he wanted people to think so."

"And you believe that one of these two calls warned Pitcairn?"

"What else can I think? Pitcairn never showed up, so someone must have got a message to him. No one there left the room or did anything else that could have conveyed a message outside. So someone must have telephoned, but the only two who actually did telephone didn't seem to be passing on a message about drugs or police. So you see, it's impossible!"

"Unless the girl was talking in code, or the boy let the telephone ring a prearranged number of times as a signal. What do you want me to do?"

"Well . . ." The young face got pinker. "We've just had another tip. Jeremiah Pitcairn is expected in Boston again tonight. If he comes it will be the first time since he returned from India."

"And you think he'll visit The Den of Iniquity?"

"He's a regular—always goes there when he's in town. A lot of professors do. Bridging the generation gap, they call it. I can't go myself because I was recognized last time. All the regulars know I'm a cop now. But you've only just come to Boston. No one would recognize you."

"No one would talk to a man my age in a place like that. You need someone who can pass for under twenty-five."

"Students take their parents to places like The Den. It would seem natural if you were there with your daughter and people might talk to you then."

"I think we should leave my daughter out of this." Basil's voice sounded more abrasive than he had intended.

"But she'd give you a good excuse for being there."

"I don't want her involved. The best I can do is to go there alone and look around. I hardly expect anything will come of it, but I might pick up something. How do I find the place?"

"On the west side of Charles Street, half-way between the Common and Cambridge Street. You can't miss it. There's a big neon sign in red that says: *The Den of Iniquity*. I'll give you a couple of hours, then meet you outside. Look for a blue Pontiac without lights or police markings. My own car."

Grogan rose. "A lot of people say that marijuana is no more harmful than alcohol or tobacco. Do you believe that?"

"It might conceivably be true of the crude marijuana we get in this country," said Basil. "I doubt if it's true of the *ganja* and *charas* used in India. They are to pot what brandy is to beer."

"Didn't the strongest form, hashish, give us our word 'assassin'?"

294

"The words 'assassin' and 'hashish' both come from Hashishin, the name of Omar Khayyam's schoolmate who founded a secret society devoted to religious assassination, like Thuggee. Marco Polo assumed that the Assassins committed their crimes because they were under the influence of hashish. Actually they were spurred by religious fanaticism, and hashish was their reward. They didn't know Hashishin was feeding them a drug. They thought they were actually visiting Paradise. They thought Hashishin had solved the riddle of the universe and would tell them the secret when they reached the innermost circle of the society. The few who finally made it were bluntly informed: 'The only secret is that there is no secret.' "

"Didn't someone call marijuana 'The Pleasant Assassin'?"

"That was a botanist, Dr. Norman Taylor. *Cannabis sativa* has taken millions of poor Hindus through famines. Dr. Taylor said that to such it is a 'Pleasant Assassin' that kills only fear and grief. Don't ask me if he's right. I just don't know."

"Neither do I. But one thing I do know: as long as marijuana is illegal it brings young people into contact with the criminal world. The men who distribute to young, newly recruited pushers are professional criminals. They sell worse things than marijuana and they stop at nothing. That's what scares me."

The evening was too warm for an overcoat— it was the mild, moist evening of a New England May.

Basil walked through the archway under the State House, so like the archway under the Institute in Paris. It was like walking through an archway into the past. Gas still burned here in the street lamps. He had left tall buildings and asphalt sidewalks behind him. On Mount Vernon Street there were only low houses, with illumined fanlights above Federal doorways, shining golden through the velvet dusk, and brick pavement that rose in little hillocks over the big roots of the Norwegian maples. As he walked, he crushed maple seeds underfoot.

He passed Louisburg Square, looking like an illustration for a Henry James novel. Wisteria blossoms poured down one house-front, scenting the tepid air with the very smell of spring itself. Cars along the curb, mostly small and foreign, were in jewel colors, polished as lovingly as old silver.

At the foot of the hill he came out on Charles Street opposite the old church that is still called the Meeting House. He could see both sides of the way curving toward Cambridge Street. There was no red neon sign announcing The Den of Iniquity.

Had they moved after Grogan's visit?

He walked on, scanning each housefront. He was halfway to Cambridge Street when he saw, on the other side of Charles, a single low-watt bulb shedding discreet light on a wooden sign. It was decorated with artfully amateurish letters that read: *The Poor Man's Paradise*.

So they hadn't moved. They had merely changed the name, making it less explicit, but still obvious enough to those in the know.

The Sky Flyer, The Giver of Delight, The Soother of Grief, The Heavenly Guide, The Poor Man's Paradise . . . All these graceful phrases were used in India for what the Western mind called by such a short and unattractive word: pot.

There was a curtained shop window, as Grogan had said. Steps led down to a basement door, halfway below street level.

Basil opened the door.

It looked like the usual undergraduate hangout. Coffee and beer were the only drinks in view. Layers of blue and yellow smoke wavered across the room, but they smelled only of tobacco.

The plangent voice of a dulcimer rose and fell, weaving a little silver thread of sound under and over the level mutter of human voices. Some were dancing the still popular monosexual dances in which partners stand a foot or so apart. Most were sitting at tables.

No one looked at Basil. He felt like a ghost until he became aware of a pair of eyes staring at him from the shadows of an unlighted telephone booth, its door ajar.

To give himself countenance he started toward the bar, then came to an abrupt halt. A sudden draft parted the veils of smoke and he saw a face he knew well. Very well indeed.

Ivory-pale, delicate as a cameo, like her mother's face. Dark eyes, luminous in the shadow of fine densely black hair, also like her mother's. A sweet mouth.

Shock held him motionless.

"Why, father, what are you doing here?"

She was sitting at a table with another girl.

"This is Anna Warsaw. She's in my dormitory."

Basil saw a head in shades of bronze and gold, light brown hair, hazel eyes, suntanned

298

skin with a healthy apricot glow under the tan.

"Do sit down, Dr. Willing," said Anna. "I suppose you're wondering how Gisela collected me and Tom after she left you."

"Tom?"

There were only the two girls at the table.

"Tom Piper. He's gone to get us coffee," said Gisela. "I ran into Tom and Anna on Beacon Street just after I left you. They were on their way to this new place, The Poor Man's Paradise, so I came along to see what it was like."

Anna was watching Basil's face. "This isn't New York, you know. Boston is just a village really—you're always running into people you know."

"Not just in Boston," said Basil. "When I lived in Italy I was told that 'Rome is just a village.'"

"You don't like this place," said Gisela.

"I've seen worse." Basil managed a smile.

"It's a do-your-own-thing place," she explained. "The management provides beer and coffee and a record player. People bring their own records, or guitars, or recite their own poetry, and some dance."

Basil looked toward the wriggling couples

on the other side of the smoke veils. "What are they dancing?"

"Father, dances don't have names any more!"

"No names for the steps?"

"There aren't any steps." Her voice reproached him gently for such an archaic idea. "People just get up and make fools of themselves."

Basil's eyes were growing accustomed to the smoke and the dim light. All the boys and girls were in uniform. The new conformity. Pre-Raphaelite girls with long straight hair to their waists. Victorian boys with bushy hair and sideburns or mustaches or beards. Boys in peasant smocks or antique military tunics. Girls in miniskirts or granny skirts that swept the floor. A costume ball without masks.

They didn't need masks. At that age their faces were masks, too bland and unformed to reveal either character or experience. The only clue to their thoughts lay in the pictures on the walls. Antiwar posters that owed something to Goya. Nightmarish fantasies that owed more to Hieronymus Bosch. Caricatures that would have amused Daumier. Nothing new under the sun.

At that thought some of the tension went

out of Basil. How often he had said to his patients, "You must let your children go now. One of the hardest things a baby has to learn is to reverse the grasping reflex—to let go. It's hard for parents, too, but those who cannot let go are emotional misers, hoarders of love, who lose everything in the end."

Through the smoke haze a figure seemed to float toward them like some underwater thing drifting with the current. Orange hair stood out around its head in a great chrysanthemum. The young Paderewski before his hair went white. A sharp narrow face peered out of ambush like a small bird peering from a large untidy nest. He wore a tunic of gold-printed *sari* cloth in shocking pink and tight green slacks. The feet, like all feet that walk city streets in open sandals, were grimy.

"What took you so long?" asked Gisela.

"I stopped to telephone."

"And I bet you forgot the coffee!"

"Gosh, I did! I'll get it now."

"Oh, never mind. Sit down. Father, this is Tom Piper from Chicago. He's a prodigy. He entered Harvard at fifteen."

"And he's been there ever since," put in Anna. "Not a dropout. A dropin."

There were Pipers in Chicago who had

given a Justice to the Supreme Court. Could this be one of that family?

"Hi!" The young man slid into a seat. Now that he was at the table, Basil could see a large button on his chest with a printed legend: *American Students For Mbongu!* Where was Mbongu?

Basil didn't want to reveal his ignorance by asking.

"You're Dr. Basil Willing, aren't you?" said Tom Piper. "I recognized you while I was in the telephone booth and when you walked in. Your picture's on the jacket of your latest book. Must be interesting, being a forensic psychiatrist—at least, you make it sound interesting."

"You mean you're not sure whether I'm a competent psychiatrist or a persuasive writer?"

"Well, writing counts." The boy grinned. "Who would ever have heard of Freud if he hadn't been such a persuasive writer?"

"The sex helped," said Anna.

The crowd was thinning. Afterward Basil was never able to explain the impulse that made him count the number of people left in the room. Perhaps it had something to do with the layers of smoke that blurred their faces. Counting was a reaching out for definition.

"A bad omen. There are just thirteen people in this room now."

Gisela's eyes narrowed against the sting of smoke. "I see only twelve."

"Including me?"

"Including you. Anna, how many people do you see in this room?"

Anna glanced about her. "There are two by the bar. With the bartender that makes three. There are two dancing. There are three at a table. Total: eight. And we four make twelve."

"I must have miscounted," said Basil.

But he knew he hadn't and he was puzzled by the sudden disappearance of Number Thirteen. Where Basil sat he could keep an eye on both outside doors and the two lavatory doors. No one had gone through any of those doors after his count. Was there a fifth door that he and Grogan had missed?

His glance came back to his own part of the room. The little puzzle solved itself as a light came on in the telephone booth nearby. Basil had forgotten the booth—had not seen it when it was dark. Someone must have just stepped inside and hesitated before closing the door that automatically switched on the light.

Now the light was bright inside, a hundred-watt bulb at least. Through the glass panel in the door he could see a boy dialing—the only boy in the room with hair cut short enough to show the shape of his head. Basil couldn't see his face, only his back and the dial of the telephone high on the wall.

The boy didn't look up the number or get it from Information. It was a number he obviously knew by heart. His fingers moved slowly and carefully as he dialed. Basil was close enough to catch the digits: 768-5829.

When the boy finished dialing he half turned, as if he were uncomfortable in the narrow booth. Now Basil could see his intent profile as he stood listening to whatever was coming through the receiver. After a few moments the boy replaced the telephone in its cradle without speaking and came out of the booth.

"Gisela! I didn't know you were here."

"Hello, Gene. This is Eugene Derry—my father, Dr. Willing. You know Anna and Tom, don't you? Do sit down a minute."

"Dr. Basil Willing? I thought I recognized you when I came in."

Basil studied the broad brow, the wide-spaced eyes, the straight nose. Comely, almost Grecian. He wore his hair at almost Byronic length, but he was clean-shaven. His open-necked white shirt suggested Rupert Brooke rather than the Beatles.

He grinned across the table at Tom. "Still working for Mbongu?"

"Damn right," said Tom.

"Where is Mbongu?" ventured Basil.

"Oh, father, Mbongu isn't a place! It's a man—Ariosho Mbongu. He's in jail now, a political prisoner in Mandataland."

"Dare I ask where that is?"

"Before the war it was called East—"

"East Hell," interrupted Eugene. "At least, that's what G.I.'s called it during the war. It was an emerging nation even then. Why can't they emerge and get it over with?"

"You'll have to make allowances for Gene," said Anna to Basil. "His full name is Eugene Debs Derry. When parents give you a name like that you just have to become reactionary."

Eugene smiled at Basil. "Not too reactionary to have enjoyed your books, Dr. Willing. I'm majoring in psychology."

"So am I," said Tom. "One of my professors is Jeremiah Pitcairn."

"The Pit Viper?" Eugene laughed.

"You study under him, too?" asked Basil.

"No, but I've read his books and I've met him. The old fraud!"

"We've all met him," said Anna. "He likes young people."

The innocence of that remark sent a chill down Basil's spine. He turned to Eugene. "Why do you call him a fraud?"

"He's all over you. He tries to make you think he likes you. But it's fake. You can tell after the first five minutes with him."

"Oh, come on!" Tom was impatient. "It's his ideas you don't like. You're living back in the thirties, Gene. The Pit Viper and his kind have gone way beyond you. They're living in the twenty-first century."

"The New Left, I suppose?"

"Hell, no! They're way beyond prescientific ideas like Left and Right. They're in computer country, man."

"Why is he called the Pit Viper?" inquired Basil.

Everybody smiled. It was Anna who answered. "Because he has a temper."

"I hate to break this up, but I really must be going," said Gisela. "Biology at nine A.M."

They all rose.

"I can give you a lift," Anna said to Gisela. "If I haven't been towed away. I'm parked right around the corner. Sorry I haven't room for you, Dr. Willing. It's a Fiat—only holds two."

"Thank you, but I'm living nearby," answered Basil. "Just a walk up the Hill. Good night, Tom. And Eugene."

"Good night, sir."

They left the two boys standing in the smoke haze. The Fiat was still there. Basil watched it drive off with the flat feeling that always comes to those who are left behind.

Slowly he walked back to Charles Street. Across the way from The Poor Man's Paradise a blue Pontiac, without lights, was parked at the curb. Basil stooped to look at the driver's face, opened the door, and sat down beside Grogan.

"Any luck?" asked Grogan.

"Maybe. But it's just a hunch." Basil was looking at the dial of what seemed to be a telephone wired to the dashboard. "Is that a radio-telephone?"

"Yes. My own, not police. Want to call someone?"

"Not at the moment. Do you know anything about a political prisoner in Mandataland named Mbongu?"

"Another case of international injustice. Mbongu was jailed for demanding the sort of

307

rights people take for granted in most Western countries."

"Does the telephone number 768-5829 mean anything to you? I saw someone dial that number."

"If he dialed the digit one first, it's an Essex number. If he didn't it's a Sussex number, closer to Boston so you don't have to dial one first. 768 is the office code for both Essex and Sussex. Both have the same area code as Boston, 617, so neither is a long distance call from here."

"I don't believe he dialed one first, but I'm not sure."

"Let's see what we can find out." Grogan picked up his radio-telephone and dialed. "Grogan speaking. Check the listing of this number, please, and call me back. 768-5829. Either Essex or Sussex, possibly both . . . Who are we waiting for, Doctor Pitcairn?"

"No, I doubt if he'll come here tonight. My daughter was in there with friends. I was addressed by name several times, just as you were. I would hazard a guess that Pitcairn has been warned. Again. Possibly by the same person who warned him last time, and who will now—I hope—lead us back to Pitcairn, and the evidence you need."

"Who is he? The one who phoned, I mean."

"It may be either of two young men. Tom Piper or Eugene Derry. They both knew who I was. Piper was in the telephone booth when I arrived and could have phoned then. Derry tried to telephone after I arrived and got no answer."

"He could be the Gene who telephoned last time and got no answer."

"Anna Warsaw was there again, too—the one who telephoned last time and did get an answer. She was sitting with my daughter when I walked in. She's driving my daughter back to college now."

"Could she have signaled to Piper when she saw you?"

"She didn't have to. He recognized me at once."

"I didn't think so many people there would know you by sight."

"Neither did I, but my picture was on the jacket of my most recent book. They all seem to have read it and they all seem to know Pitcairn. Tom Piper likes him. Eugene Derry doesn't."

"And you got some kind of hunch out of all this?"

"Yes—until I started talking to you. Now I'm beginning to wonder if—"

The radio-telephone buzzed.

"Grogan speaking . . . Thank you." He put down the receiver. "In Essex, 768-5829 is a private house, a new listing for somebody named B. G. Standish. In Sussex it's been the office phone number of a learned society for several years, the League of Spiritual Development. I suppose—"

Grogan's voice died as the door of The Poor Man's Paradise opened.

Three figures climbed up the steps to the street. There was a chorus of goodbyes and two figures turned toward the Common. The third crouched low to crawl into a low-slung Porsche at the curb.

"Can you follow him without his suspecting?"

"Probably not. Are you sure he's going to Pitcairn's?"

"Quite sure now."

"I know some short cuts he may not know and I can go faster than he can without being picked up for speeding. There are still some advantages in being a cop. We'll get to Pitcairn's house first and wait for him there."

Before long they were leaving Taunton and passing the sign that reads: *Cape Cod and the*

Islands. Soon the ancient scent of the sea was salt in their nostrils, waking racial memories almost as old as life itself. They could not see the surf in the darkness, but they could hear its regular breathing.

A large white house stood alone on a spit of land half surrounded by the water of an inlet.

The only light was at a window on an upper floor.

Grogan parked his car in shadow under trees and switched off his lights.

He had hardly done so when a Porsche came around the corner on two wheels. Gravel spurted as it turned too sharply into the driveway.

The boy got out. He didn't knock or ring. He opened the front door without using a key and walked in as if he owned the place.

A French window to the right of the door lit up casting a patch of light on the grass outside.

Basil and Grogan walked across the turf without making a sound, skirting the patch of light from the French window. There were no curtains. They could look directly into the lighted room.

"Amateurs," whispered Basil. "Or they would have had curtains and drawn them."

The scene on the other side of the pane was as clear and bright and silent as something seen on color television with sound turned off.

It was a study, small, elegant, almost feminine. Paneling painted ice-green, molding picked out in silver, French furniture in natural fruitwood, an Aubusson faded to pastel tones on the parquet floor.

Behind the Louis XV writing table sat a bald man with a fringe of gingery hair and a fox face.

"Pitcairn?" whispered Basil.

"Yes."

He was unlocking a drawer in the table, his head bent over it. The boy stood by a fireplace of blond marble looking down at a cold grate filled with maidenhair fern.

Pitcairn took some cellophane packages out of the drawer and put them on the table.

Grogan caught his breath. "Decks. Heroin."

"The not-so-pleasant assassin," said Basil.

The window wasn't locked. Grogan pushed it open. It was the sound of its hinges that arrested the movement of Pitcairn's hand. He looked up—and faced ruin.

"Eugene, you fool!"

It was the cold rage of a viper striking.

"But no one followed me!" cried Eugene Derry.

"You gave the show away somehow or they wouldn't be here!"

"I didn't! I didn't, I tell you! Damn it, how could I?"

At Police Headquarters later, Grogan had some questions to ask Basil.

"I caught on to the League for Spiritual Development. Like 'Lucy in the Sky with Diamonds,' it's slang for LSD. But what put you on to Eugene Derry?"

"The number he dialed, 768-5829. I was hoping I had memorized it correctly. I'd seen him dial it only once, and I hadn't had a chance to write it down. It's not easy to memorize telephone numbers that run to seven digits without letters, yet Derry had dialed it without first referring to a note or to the phone book. I was wondering how he had memorized it so easily when my glance fell on the dial of your radio-telephone. Then I knew."

"Letters that spell pronounceable words with some meaning are far easier to remember than a string of meaningless numbers. On the standard dial each number is associated with three letters. I asked myself: did

313

any of the letters associated on the dial with 768-5829 spell out pronounceable words?

"They did. Derry didn't have to memorize a number to dial the League of Spiritual Development. All he had to do was to dial the letters that spell out the words POT-LUCY—words he could not forget if he were panicky or even stoned.

"The telephone company will give you any number you ask for providing it's not already in use, just as the Motor Vehicle people will give you a vanity number for the license plate on your car. Pitcairn was lucky. No one else in Sussex township already had POT-LUCY—that is, 768-5829."

"Wasn't that risky?"

"Not half as risky as letting Derry and other pushers carry around a written note of that telephone number. Who, watching another person dial, pays the slightest attention to the numbers being dialed, let alone the letters associated with them on the dial?

"There's a commercial firm in Boston that has the same notion. When you want to call them, you just dial the letters that spell the firm's name. Pitcairn may have got the idea from them."

"Why the League for Spiritual Development?"

"So no suspicious calls could ever be traced directly to Pitcairn's own number. Derry made an outgoing call that he knew would not be answered. He let the telephone ring an agreed number of times, then hung up. Whoever was on duty at the League of Spiritual Development would then call Pitcairn and relay the danger signal. So much safer than any kind of conversation in code."

"I didn't suspect Anna Warsaw," said Grogan. "Not after you said you had let your own daughter drive off with her. But I did suspect the other boy. The one you said liked Pitcairn."

"How much more likely that Pitcairn's creature would pretend to hate him! And there's another psychological indication: I can't imagine a dope pusher working for a man like Mbongu."

The Life Of A Big Whale

THOMAS ADCOCK

WHEN I saw Patsy Harmon lying there with
a bullet in his neck I was sadly unsurprised,
and from the expression on his face I would
guess Patsy felt about the same the last time
he could feel anything.

Now he was belly-up on a black-linoleum
floor, his lanky body outlined in white chalk.
Up at the bar where he'd last been leaning
was an ashtray with three Lucky Strike butts
in it, his brand. Next to this was a half
empty lowball glass of Scotch whisky diluted
with milk because of Patsy's ulcers. There
was also a cup of black coffee gone cold, and
since this refreshment was presumed to have
belonged to the unknown person who had
left the encounter alive, one of the forensics
cops was dusting it with fingerprint powder
for whatever benefit it might provide the
host of this gathering, Detective Joseph
Logue of the homicide squad.

It was half past eight in the morning of a

cold, rainy November Sunday. Ordinarily, I would have been home in my warm bed, with my wife Jean up getting dressed and making a lot of noise about it and pestering me about church, which is one of her few faults. Instead, there I was in this illegal saloon and casino in the dank cellar of a nondescript warehouse near the river with my friend Logue, contemplating the dead body of an old hustler acquaintance of mine I'd recently written up for the magazine where I work.

"Sort of ironic, ain't it?" Logue said to me. "Practically nobody in town has the time of day for Patsy since twelve years ago, when he went into the trap the last time, then for all the years since he's been out—"

"Then I go put him in print," I finished his thought, "and the name of Patsy Harmon isn't on the newsstands two weeks before somebody cancels him out. Yeah, Joe, I'd say this is at least ironic."

"So what do you make of it? So far as I know, you're the next-to-last person who talked to Patsy about a serious subject. Which is why I called you exclusive on this story, on account of how you might be able to help me get started."

"I'm flattered as hell you thought enough

of me to drag me out of bed to come shiver alongside you, but this is no scoop for me and you know it. I work on a monthly. Besides which, I'm no detective."

"Let me ask you—you see any signs of struggle anywhere here?"

I scanned the room again and said I didn't. It was a big, rectangular place, with pipes and vents crisscrossing the high ceiling. The bar was set up in the middle and there was a kitchen along one wall. Tables were scattered around for 21, craps, and tonk. And off in a corner was a wire room for horses and the national sports betting line. This was a joint Patsy would have been running himself.

"So you don't need to be a detective to see how this here cancellation was personal business," Logue said. "And you happen to be somebody who was asking the deceased a lot of personal questions not so long ago. So I'm thinking maybe you didn't run all the answers in the magazine."

I thought about how this made sense from Logue's perspective. The only trouble was, I couldn't think of much I'd left out of the article that meant anything in the way of clues.

A couple of the camera boys started taking

pictures of the body from different angles and I looked again at Patsy's face, white from the loss of blood and whiter still in the flashing strobe lights. "To me, it looks like Patsy was lured down here by somebody who had something unpleasant to tell him."

"That's putting it mild."

"And I'd say from the looks of him that poor old Patsy somehow half expected what happened was going to happen—at least when he could see the lights were going to go out on him."

Logue agreed. "Yeah, he don't look at all shocked like most stiffs do when they get it like he did."

"And like you say, Patsy's been out of circulation for years. Maybe you lose your balance after you're out of the game for a while, maybe you can't figure how nasty it can be sometimes."

Logue nodded. "I'll give you that, too. In the rackets, you have to be figuring what awful thing can be done to you that's even worse than some terrible thing you're doing to somebody else. Out of the rackets, you can afford to have a sunnier outlook."

"But, hell, Joe, somebody must have seen something here." This was the dumbest thing I would have to say that entire day, and

319

there it was bright and early out of my mouth—which had yet to taste coffee that morning and that may be the explanation for the lapse in thought.

Logue grinned patiently at me like I was wearing a round haircut and said, "Sometimes it ain't the most efficient thing a cop can do to right away try rounding up witnesses."

And when he said that, a certain part of the Patsy Harmon story I'd written passed through my mind like some old tune whose lyrics I remember for reasons I've forgotten. Joe Logue had telephoned me that morning operating on pure detective instinct, because he knew the chances were good I'd have the quickest answer to the question of the late Patsy Harmon. Because he somehow knew, hours before I did, that the answer was buried somewhere between the lines I'd written.

By the way, I'm Fred Walsh. I work for *Detroit Expression*. And we're quite the unlikely combination.

The magazine is one of those slick, four-color booster jobs you see now in practically any American city bigger than Duluth. The underlying drumbeat of the contents is what a distinct thrill it is to live in the magazine's particular metropolis, even though the vast majority of townfolk spend their nights drinking beer in front of the television set like they do in every other town of any size whatsoever.

I consider myself luckier than most writers for such outfits. Very often in my stories, nobody is what you might call upbeat, though I do like to think my work is uplifting in certain ways. Since I'm considered the office antique by my painfully young colleagues, I'm mostly left alone to pursue what I've been doing for my living since the days when I actually wore a card in my hatband, same as the rest of the street reporters on the *Detroit Times*, now extinct. I wrote about crime and criminals who held a certain moral code, which among other things in those days rendered them too embarrassed to run for public office. And that's what I've been writing about ever since.

I would have happily remained at the *Times* if not for the fact of my being blacklisted in the Fifties, which was a slogan-clogged political era that I wrongly believed would warn us off simpletons and zealots forever. The *Times* gave me the sack because I didn't care to snitch on friends of mine who thought unpopular thoughts. I twisted slowly in the wind until I got the message that I wasn't about to be employed on any of the other respectable papers. So one day, hearing of my jobless plight, the communist *Daily Worker* offered me a job writing about crime and I took it. I didn't think much more of that rag than I think of the place where I'm working today, with the exception that if you allow for inflation the commies paid me better.

Anyway, that's how I continued writing about crime and criminals, all of whom held me in high esteem for my refusal to be a stool-pigeon down in Washington. The by-line still read Fred Walsh all through the *Daily Worker* years, but people took to calling me "Big Red Fred" and most meant it as a slur. The nickname stuck, but the stigma faded over time. I happen to be tall and I've still got some hair on my head the color of carrots.

The *Expression* is a retirement job, for which my wife and I are grateful. Even when you're pensioned off like me, it's important to get out the door every day. So I still work. And the stories I write—like the one just published on Patsy Harmon, a hood in the twilight of his crooked life—keep me on balance. Which I now see can be a major factor accounting for a man's longevity.

You look at his surroundings up in the suburb of Ferndale and you don't right away think, here lives a world-class gambler, pal of mob heavies and overlord of after-hours joints all over Detroit that drew suckers from three states and the province of Ontario. You look at the man's white-frame house with blue shutters and an aluminum storm door on a street full of red maple trees and neat lawns and second-hand cars and you think retired postal clerk.

Patsy Harmon is discreet.

Which is not to say his life has been altogether a quiet affair. He was practically a commuter between Detroit and Amsterdam at one time. He's outlived three wives and twice as many prosecutors. And he's done time, mostly small stretches back during the Depression and the war on various counts of bootlegging and gaming. His longest stretch in the trap was back in the middle of the Fifties when he cooled off a once-friendly rival by the name of Charlie Templeton in Templeton's own joint on Gratiot Avenue out near City Airport. One slug in the chest and Charlie was a dead man. But Patsy's lawyer got him fifteen months in Jackson State Prison on a guilty plea for carrying a concealed weapon.

Then for the next twenty years or so, Patsy was in the headlines all the time. Various raids on his gambling joints or when some of his hired help got busted or grand-jury indictments, that sort of thing. But Patsy always walked, thanks to quality lawyers from the finest schools in the country and to his long-standing custom of making sure every precinct in the city was full of his charity, especially in the station houses.

But one year an auditor from the Internal Revenue Service changed Patsy's life. Among other things, Patsy was sentenced to five years' probation, which is not conducive to Patsy's kind of career. When the Feds give out probation in lieu of stir, a guy like Patsy is automatically assumed by the Feds to be perfectly willing to join up with the frequent-flier program of every airline so he can testify in front of grand juries from coast to coast about the activities of his cronies.

"I ain't no snitch!" Patsy says in the parlor of his little Ferndale house. (He's half-watching the Oprah Winfrey Show and the Sears Roebuck coffee table in front of him is stacked high with newspapers. He's smoking

Chesterfields and drinking milk, which at the stroke of five o'clock he peps up with some Scotch on his personal theory that ulcers are daytime maladies.) "And everybody knew it right up to the time they started flying me all over the place to sing.

"New York, Chicago, Miami, 'Frisco. You name the town, I been in its grand-jury room. Even though I took the Fifth every time, it got so I was spending so much of my life on planes and inside them jury rooms that friends couldn't help imagining I might say something just to break the monotony."

The rumors about Patsy ratting on everybody he knew from his salad days never quite died, despite the fact that to this date nobody in New York or Chicago or Miami or San Francisco or even locally has yet been brought to trial on the basis of one shred of evidence or secret testimony that could possibly be traced back to Harmon. In fact, Patsy so infuriated one Federal grand jury in Detroit twelve years ago—on a day in late July when the air-conditioning blew and the jurors had to sit through a stifling morning and half an afternoon listening to Patsy invoke the Fifth Amendment—that they sent him off to an Illinois penitentiary for eight months on a contempt-of-judicial-process citation. During this last stay in the trap, Patsy slipped and fell on the shower-room floor and broke his left hip.

But at least the government gave up on him as a grand-jury witness.

"There was even this one Assistant D.A.," Patsy says, "who helped me get all the Social Security I had coming to me but I never claimed until ten years after I was eligible."

Which is how Patsy Harmon came up with the downpayment on his little house in Ferndale, where nobody comes visiting or rings him up on the telephone, where he sits and smokes and reads the papers and watches television.

"It's a crime what's been done to me," he says.

By Patsy's lights, maybe it is. He has a good little house, a dependable Chevrolet parked in the side drive, enough money in the mail to take care of his needs, Medicare and so forth, he hasn't been in a grand-jury room in twelve years, he could go fishing any time he wanted to, or own a dog or maybe get married again, but he might as well be in the trap.

"I feel like I'm doing time!" He coughs and uses a remote switch to dial off the news and tune in a rerun of *Gilligan's Island*. "You know, house arrest. You hear the phone ringing anywhere in here? I got five rooms in this dump and five phones—you'd think one of 'em might ring.

"I tell you straight out, back in my playing days I was known to be good for taking ten grand on a number, personal. Now I can't get a jingle outa my phones and the NCAA basketball championship is on and it's six days before the Leonard-Hagler fight in Vegas. Guys used to call me up from all over the friggin' world for odds, or point spreads. Now—zip!

"So get a load of me now and ask yourself, ain't what they done to me a crime? Look at me sitting here in front of the tube, which is like some plug-in narcotic drug, I swear. And nobody calls because they think I'm some kinda big trouble for 'em.

"Oh, I used to have the life. Big broads, lots of dough, a private box at the Hazel Park track, good booze. And the clubs. I always ran a good square club with a little class and plenty of action, especially with the dice, which I personally loved to play myself. Now I'm looking for all the world like some gimpy geek at the senior center—and down at the track they don't want my money no more. Worst of all, the only dice left to me is on Monopoly boards."

When he was a kid and Monopoly was something played on margins on Wall Street trading floors, Harmon used to hang out with a gang on East Jefferson Boulevard in the vicinity of Water Works Park. That's where the better opportunities for mugging and auto theft existed, in the cluster of smart East Side restaurants and nightclubs.

"My formative years," Patsy says.

"Two in the morning every morning like clockwork this Italian guy would come by a place called Curcio's for espresso. He'd come in this big Lincoln with a chauffeur. His name was Fabrizio and he had this club out in Grosse Pointe he thought was too la-de-da for him personally, even though that's where he makes his haul.

"Anyways, he comes by Curcio's every night outa habit—or maybe on business, which don't matter now anyhow since Fabrizio's dead and Curcio's gone and the last time anybody heard an Italian word spoken on East Jefferson was maybe in 'sixty-seven just before the riot.

"I called him Mr. Fab, which he liked so much he used it to rename his club one year to Mr. Fab's. So he takes this shine to me, outa all them guys I hung with.

"One night he calls me over and says to me, 'What are you doing out so late, son?' And I tell him, 'Trying to make a dishonest living.' And Mr. Fab, he laughs so hard I thought he'd lose his teeth. He says to me, 'You want a good-paying job, son, you come to my place and I'll give you work.' So I went out to Mr. Fab's in the suit my daddy bought me for going to church, and they put me to work and taught me."

And what a student Patsy was. He took to the croupier's stick like a baby takes to a rattle. He ingratiated himself with every heavyweight in the national gambling fraternity and he made friends with other young men like himself trying to work up the ranks of wiseguys—including Charlie Templeton.

At Mr. Fab's out in Grosse Pointe, Patsy and Charlie were the prize pupils and the old man's most driven workers. They started out together "on the fence," as Mr. Fab called it—which meant they hung around in the shadows of fences the height of some billboards waiting with their flashlights for the right kind of cars to come by so they could be led to a parking space near the four-story mansion on a cul-de-sac. From there they graduated to the door of the place, where they inspected the membership cards and kept guns in their pockets in case somebody might not understand house rules or objected to being frisked on entry.

And then they were inside, Charlie and Patsy, working the craps tables, card games, and the roulette wheel, and tending to the huge board of race results. They did the smaller tasks, too, such as stocking the bar and hiring show-girl types to run the coat-check rooms and glide around in fishnet stockings under little skirts and low-cut tops that showed off plenty of curves when they leaned forward with their trays of cigars and cigarettes. And, as it sometimes happens in nature, one of the curviest of this bevy eventually came between the two friends.

Her name was Ruby. Patsy was out at Belle Isle Park one steaming July afternoon, all by himself and listening to Dixieland jazz at the bandshell near the fountain with the stone monkeys, when along came Ruby, eighteen and gorgeous and unaccompanied, and young Patsy Harmon went very weak in the knees. Coincidentally, that was exactly what happened to young Charlie Templeton's knees when Patsy first brought Ruby around to Mr. Fab's and dressed her up in a cigarette-girl ensemble.

Inevitably, Ruby had to make a choice—and she picked Charlie. Which didn't sit well with Patsy at all and taught him for the first time how much he disliked losing. Before long, Charlie and Ruby drifted away from their jobs at Mr. Fab's and then they drifted away from everyone they'd known at the place. It was only by accident that Patsy heard about how they'd opened up what is known in the gambling trade as a "sawdust house"—a no-frills, illegal casino with just craps, blackjack, and horses, and a table for holding beer by the pitcher and a couple of runners for Chinese food or cigarettes or scratch sheets. Patsy hadn't been looking for them, but somebody mentioned in passing how Ruby and Charlie had a sweet little operation going for themselves and a curiosity born of residual jealousy is seldom resisted, and one night Patsy found himself in their place.

At the trial, a runner testified that Patsy and Charlie had argued along about three o'clock in the morning when Patsy bulled his way inside, but that Charlie had allowed Patsy to remain on the premises anyway. Which was a bad idea, since Patsy couldn't let Ruby pass without a few choice words for her. And then Charlie walked over to where Patsy was shooting craps right up to the five-hundred-dollar limit and mostly winning and lunged at Patsy and poked him in the chest with what looked like a fist. Then the two old pals took their argument outside to an alley.

After a few minutes in the alley, during which time a shot rang out, Patsy walked back through the open doorway to the casino's back room holding a smoking .45 and was met there by three Detroit cops who claimed they were hanging on their own free time in the interests of "monitoring crime." Patsy told the cops how Charlie had reached into his pocket after a gun and was yelling at him like crazy and cursing his family tree. The alley was almost pitch-black with shadows, Patsy further explained, and he felt he had to defend himself under the law of God.

As it happened, Charlie did have a loaded gun in his pocket. That fact was quickly established by the three public-spirited cops. And so it took a jury only about an hour to decide that Patsy was mostly innocent in the eyes of God, but that he was guilty of carrying a concealed weapon—a crime to which Patsy and his lawyer had already eagerly confessed. Since it seemed that Charlie, too, had been carrying, and paid for this infraction with his life, the jury reasoned that it was only square that Patsy should spend a little time in the slammer and pony up a few thousand dollars' fine besides.

So a little poorer and fifteen months older, Patsy walked out of Jackson State Prison and caught a bus back home to Detroit, where the first piece of news that awaited him was that old Fabrizio was on his deathbed.

Patsy's hand lay on Fabrizio's fevered brow as the old man told him, "Son, you're very big in my will," then slipped away. Patsy felt like a winner, which doesn't usually happen so quickly after better than a year behind bars—even in that short time, even a young man can become an ashen relic from the experience. But according to Fabrizio's will, Patsy was the new owner of the Grosse Pointe property known informally as Mr. Fab's. From a lowly job on the fence, up through the ranks and on through a treacherous love affair and the killing of his onetime best friend, Patsy Harmon now sat in the big chair.

"Out of respect to the old man, we still called it Mr. Fab's," Patsy says. "And out of further respect, we start really making the joint truly fabulous. I mean, it was the best gambling joint between New York illegal and Vegas legal. We had the big whales—what we called the high-rollers good for a minimum fifty-grand credit line—picked up at the airport by some hostesses in the backs of stretch limos and they'd get put up at the old Book-Cadillac in suites that come with whatever they want in the way of comforts, including their choice of sex, quick or slow.

"Then for the big whales, you know, you gotta put out a private floor show, which we did. I ain't going to say the stars we had come in on the hush to do a show because I ain't sure they're all dead and gone, but believe me we had the bigs.

"So you have any idea how much we make back off the tables? Plenty, I can tell you. I got to be a big whale myself, and that's when I started going back and forth to Europe. I'm making so much cash all I can do with it is open up more joints around town, classy places like Mr. Fab's and little sawdust joints for the sailors and the local suckers.

"Oh, they tried busting me all the time. I could understand how somebody figured they could do a Tom Dewey number with a political career, so it didn't bother me so much. I was always pretty careful about balancing out this irritating group of politicians by treating the majority of them like they was big whales even though they weren't. So all my joints were lousy with public servants.

"For twenty-five years nearly, I walk outa every trial they put on me a free man. Nothing they could dream up could stick. And meantime I'm making more and more and more. I don't mind saying it was a little boring sometimes, and I'd just go off on the big-whale circuit and blow my top. Bahamas, Amsterdam, Vegas. Until the day this little creep from the I.R.S. sends around a form letter to my house saying he's set me an appointment to come by and check out my receipts and calendars and every other piece of paper I got laying around for the last three years' worth of taxes. My lawyer, for all the dough he's making off me, says I ain't got no choice about seeing the man.

"So this character in a crummy brown-corduroy suit walks into my life with his adding machine. He's got big glasses and beady eyes and he just sits there with his pencils and his adding machine, measuring up my life. And then he takes me to tax court, where I'm sentenced to this parole officer, who signs me out of town every time one of his government pals calls him up and says they have to fly me someplace to try to get me to snitch on somebody I know from my twenty-five fabulous years.

"But like I said, nobody really believes me from my reputation, which is I ain't a snitch. So I'm out of it, you know? Blacklisted in Vegas. In Amsterdam, they tell me I can buy drinks and watch. And in the Bahamas, the government there has me stop-listed at the airport and I wind up on the turnaround flight to Miami in forty-five minutes flat. The I.R.S. takes over Mr. Fab's for back taxes and one by one they find out where I got sawdust joints and close them up, too, at a public auction. I'm sitting up in my house on Boston Boulevard, this swell Italianate spread, and I just know they're coming after that next, which eventually they do since I'm frozen outa any way of making the fat payments the I.R.S. is gouging me for.

"Which is how come I wind up in this crackerbox in Ferndale, watching the damn tube and waiting for calls that don't come. I can't even go downtown no more since it ain't the downtown I knew.

"So maybe I'll start taking the Scotch straight and do myself in, starting with blowing up my guts on pure booze. I don't know.

Outa respect for the past, when I was just an honest-enough scammer selling a little or a lot of fantasy, depending on a guy's pocketbook, I suppose I ought to stick it out long enough for a merciful God to do it to me natural. But Christamighty, ain't it a bloody crime what's become of me?"

All of this Logue knows from reading my piece in the *Expression* when it hit the newsstands two weeks ago, and from my rehashing the story face-to-face over breakfast at the city's expense—a treat which I did not protest.

Logue and I had removed ourselves from the dank scene of Patsy's untimely end to the warmth of my regular morning establishment, Busy Betty's Cafe on Cass Avenue. It was minus Betty herself that Sunday, but it was nonetheless full of the usual good coffee and ham and eggs I've known since 1945. Like me, Logue drank a beer with his eggs. And I was turning over in my mind the epilogue I would have to start writing, which would contain some answers as to how to tighten up the loose ends in Logue's murder case.

To my question, Logue told me how the call came in about the shooting.

"Just after four this morning, I get this call at home from the desk sergeant out of the Delray precinct station. It seems he's there with a nervous uniform kid who makes a habit out of stopping by this blind-pig establishment of his own free will."

"No doubt he drops by to monitor crime," I said.

"You think anything ever changes?"

I shook my head and Logue went on. "Anyhow, the kid cop is the type we got now who went to college and he's moonlighting as a law-school student, right?"

"Not a bad way to build up a clientele before you get your attorney's shingle," I said. "Everybody you bust may be a customer down the line."

"Also, the kid since he's taking classes knows all about the little matter of misprision, which is especially to be avoided when your day job involves wearing the colors."

"And misprision is?"

"It's when you neglect your civic duty to report a crime when you see one that's just happened—which was the case with the kid. He noticed the blind-pig emptying out at a quick rate of speed and lots earlier than usual, and by the time he got around to the bar where your friend Patsy was having himself

338

a permanent nightcap there's practically nobody around except the body he stumbles over in the dim light.

"So you can see what I mean about the inefficiency of looking up witnesses under the circumstances?"

"You don't have to rub it in."

"Okay. So, anyway, that's how I get the call. Being that it's Patsy Harmon, who I remember from the fog of the past, I decide to get on this. Out of respect, maybe. Patsy was a big guy in this town once, back when the town was big itself."

"How do you figure it played?"

"Like you said, somebody got Patsy down there somehow to tell him something. And Patsy was off-balance enough to take the bait, even if it was an invitation to a blind-pig where he's been eighty-sixed for all these years." Logue belched softly. "You say he had five phones in his house?"

"That's correct."

"You see my point—the guy was begging to be set up for a fall. Somebody's willing to ring, he's willing to jump."

"That makes sense."

"And while the perpetrator's making nice at the bar with him—"

"What kind of gun?"

"Small-bore .25 automatic with blow-back action, it looks like. We got the shell and there ain't any burns on Patsy's neck. The kid cop says he might have been near enough to hear a bigger gun pop, but an automatic's quiet and in a crowd like that it wouldn't be such a trick to squeeze one off with nobody the wiser until they noticed how somebody had fallen on the floor. Which, of course, at four in the morning is likely to happen to quite a few customers even when they don't get neatly shot."

Logue looked at me then like he was thinking the same thing I was and right at the same time.

"Then you're after a killer who's wise to the right kind of tool for the job, a killer who's got entree to a blind-pig and some kind of motive for getting Patsy out of his house arrest up in Ferndale."

We headed up and across town through the grey rain to number 1300 Beaubien Street, headquarters of the Detroit Police Department, which houses a miraculous computerized system of mugshots that enables a person to pick out a photo and rapsheet on known data-search factors as scant as a first name.

Just before noon we walked into the lobby of the Harmony Arms. This is a brick-and-limestome hulk off Grand Circus Park that's sagging and peeling all over—pretty much like the rest of Detroit, except for a cluster of shiny glass-and-steel towers down by Cobo Hall that look like barnyard silos to me but are very big attractions for postal-card photographers and touring convention-site selection committees. Once upon a time not so terribly long ago, you could stroll out from the once gilded lobby and past a doorman who looked like a white-whiskered Prussian general, cross West Adams Street, and find yourself a nice, quiet oak bench in an elegant park right in the heart of the city—a park with gushing fountains full of naked marble ladies holding baskets full of grapes, with grass and flowers and news kiosks, whose attendants sold papers and magazines from all over American and Europe besides.

The fountains sort of dribble and slobber today, the grass and flower beds were asphalted some years back and now sprout pale-green weeds between the cracks, and vandals set fire to most of the benches and made off with all the lovely stone nudes that were hot stuff back before smut had become as American as apple pie and ten times more ubiquitous.

Logue showed the desk clerk a warrant and was given a key to Room 408 on the fourth floor. The elevator was broken, we were informed, so we headed up the stairs.

I hadn't been in the place in a dozen years or better, and despite the fact that it was a weird time for me to be reminiscing I was gently cheered to feel how the house still resonated of palmy times. It was clean and the steam pipes were sound. The desk clerk was apologetic, at least, about the elevator. And the corridors smelled of laundry soap and drugstore talcum like aged, fussed-over hotels should properly smell. Never mind that every last one of the Turkish rugs was frayed, that the plaster moldings were full of chinks, that the floorboards groaned and creaked, that the brocade curtains had grown stringy and brittle—what's important was that the old dump was a real and true home to its now mostly permanent residents.

But one resident was soon to be taken away forever.

Logue knocked on the door of Number 408 and had me stand to the side while he did.

We didn't hear anything by way of response. Logue knocked again and unbuttoned his raincoat and then his suitcoat, in case he had to draw his .38 police special.

Then there was the sound of slippers on a wooden floor. "Yes? Who is it?" The voice was tiny and old and scratched by booze and smoking. And feminine.

"Detective Joseph Logue, Detroit Police Department."

There was a sigh. Then she opened up and stood there in a blue housedress that fit like a light tent over her stocky frame. "Well, you might as well come in," she said.

And, to me, Ruby didn't look any more surprised than Patsy had.

She sat down on the edge of her bed, which was covered over with a thin spread that had little embroidered balls all over it, and motioned us to sit down on the two chairs in the room, a wooden one that was shoved below a little desk by the window overlooking West Adams Street and a green, silk-covered easy chair with fringe on the bottom that looked like it might have come out of an old whorehouse. Logue took the whorehouse chair.

Ruby looked at me like I was guilty of

something. "I seen your picture. You're that writer, Walsh the old lefty, ain't I right?"

I told her she was right.

"You know, Walsh, if it wasn't for you tellin' that story you told, I wouldn't of done it. I didn't want to do it, see. I had to, though."

"Before you say anything else," Logue said, "I have to tell you your rights."

Which he did. And when he'd finished, Ruby said, "Aw, nuts to the damn law, okay? I'll spill right now if you want and then you can haul my old ass away—I don't care no more."

"Go ahead," Logue said. "How come you killed Patsy Harmon?"

"Because the son of a bitch was too lucky, that's how come. Once I thought, okay, he waltzes through a little time at Jackson after he kills my man Charlie. It tears me up, but you know you have certain risks going in—I mean, we're in gambling, after all. But then he comes out and takes over Mr. Fab's— and he's got himself, what, twenty–thirty years of a good old high life while my Charlie's dead and I'm killing myself work-ing sawdust houses and having to sell it on the side besides, just to keep myself going.

"Then I hear on the vine how he's in the

344

clutches of the Treasury boys. Now, finally, I figure the odds are evening out. And besides that, I hear he breaks his hip in stir. Then I don't hear anything more about him and I figure, since he's about that age, he croaked from the broken hip.

"For years, I got my losses cut. I've made peace with my ghosts. Then I pick up this magazine and I read where the guy's up in a house all by himself outside the city and he's feeling sorry for himself because nobody calls him up, the poor sot!

"This infuriates me to no end, so I start thinking how I'm finally going to settle his hash. I claim a couple of I.O.U.s and talk the management of this blind-pig down by the river into letting in this sorrowful old Patsy for one night only, as my guest, and then I call him up and tell him I want to see him for old time's sake, no hard feelings. And the stupe, he buys it."

She pointed a bony finger at a bureau in a corner of the room. "You'll be wanting my gun. It's in the top drawer."

Logue lifted himself up out of the green-silk chair, walked over to the bureau, and pulled open the top drawer. He wrapped up the automatic in an evidentiary plastic bag and slipped it into the side pocket of his suitcoat.

"That's about it, I guess," Ruby said. "I was sitting at the bar with him and not all the way decided on whether I'm going to kill him when he starts blowing off about how me and him could make a good team all over again. I think to myself, this guy's gotta learn what goes up has gotta come down. So with pleasure I give him one pill. Just like he gave my Charlie. Only Patsy, he gets his medicine close up so he's got a couple of seconds to see his luck go to hell at long last."

Later that afternoon I sat down at my type-writer in the little study I made in the attic of my house. And I thought about my epilogue. And the more I thought about it, the more I remembered the sight of Patsy's dead face.

I saw a man who truly saw himself, if only for the trace of a second. He was a guy who had beaten the law most of his life only to be blindsided late in the game. He'd spent the best part of his life on the house side of his favored craps table, and all through those years it had been inconceivable to him that the dice could beat him.

And he realized—so briefly—that all of the things that had gone with the dice and the life of a big whale—the high times, the women, the friends, the booze, the loyalties, the loot—were forgotten or useless or dead.

In the flash-point of Ruby's revenge, Patsy Harmon learned what he should have known all along: ultimately, nobody beats the odds. Not even guys who make them.

Journey for Lady G.

CHARLOTTE MacLEOD

"I'M AFRAID it will have to be Lady Gwendolyn this time," said Miss Henrietta.

Her brother Alexander looked up from his porridge, startled. "But Henrietta, I thought we had agreed to keep Lady Gwendolyn only for the direst emergencies."

"This is an emergency," replied his sister firmly. "The roof is past mending again, you simply must have a few weeks in the sun this winter for your bronchitis, and our bill at Brown's has run on so long I'm ashamed to face them. I hesitate to trouble you about it at breakfast, but we must have cash, a great deal of it, and soon."

"Couldn't the Admiral—"

"You know he wouldn't do. Nobody is going to give us anything for a Kneller these days. No, it will have to be the Romney."

"Very well, if you think it's absolutely necessary." The frail, elderly man touched an exquisitely darned napkin to his lips and rose from the table. "How I always hate seeing them go! You will make the usual arrangements, I suppose. We oughtn't to go through Bumbleby's this time."

"No, I quite agree with you. We must not impose on their good nature again, although they have been of greater service to us in the past than they can ever be aware. I made a discreet inquiry, or two on my last visit to London and obtained the addresses of some other art dealers."

"But they must be reputable," Alexander fussed. "We dare not risk Lady Gwendolyn's getting into the hands of unscrupulous dealers."

"I think," reproved his sister gently, "that you may trust me to show as much care for our family treasures as you yourself would do."

"Of course you will." Her brother beamed at her fondly over his pince-nez. "Better, undoubtedly. Really, your efficiency never ceases to amaze me."

"Considering that we were neither of us brought up to lead useful lives, I think we do fairly well on the whole," said Miss Henrietta with a touch of complacency.

She was right. Their home might not have been maintained quite so impeccably as it had been in their mother's day, but still it remained both comfortable and attractive. Henrietta managed the housework with the occasional help of Mrs. Blount from the village. Alexander had developed all sorts of unexpected talents for mending taps and edging flower beds.

The elegant sufficiency with which their parents had fondly thought to leave them had all but vanished in the bewildering economy of a world they had not been reared to live in. Nevertheless, they stayed warm and well-fed. They wore their clothes an extra few years and darned their linen a little more industriously, but on the whole their standard of living had hardly changed at all.

This would not, of course, have been possible without the pictures. The family had always been fond of paintings and had always until now been able to indulge their tastes. One after another, the Johns and Marys had had their portraits done by the fashionable artists of the day. For generations these had gazed down benignly or, as in the case of the late Admiral, ferociously upon their descendants. Now they were providing a reasonably comfortable income for the last of their line.

It was no wonder Alexander sighed with

mingled affection and regret as he took the lovely Lady Gwendolyn from her place of honour over the drawing-room mantelpiece and wrapped her tenderly in a piece of old army blanket before boxing her up in a wooden packing case, to which he had thoughtfully screwed a carrying handle for his sister's greater convenience.

"I have often wished she were a full-length, but I must say just now I'm grateful she is only a head and shoulders," remarked Miss Henrietta as she juggled the awkward case into a seat on the 12:04 to London.

"You will be careful, won't you?" begged her brother. "And telephone as soon as you have anything to report."

"Don't worry. I shall be an astute bargainer." She waved a small, gloved hand at the slight figure on the platform as the train pulled out.

Alexander was beginning to show his age, she thought with a pang. He must have a new overcoat for his excursion to Antibes. How wonderful it was going to be to have some money again. And how grateful she was to be able to help such a dear, good brother. She gave the wooden case containing Lady Gwendolyn a loving pat and settled back to enjoy the infrequent pleasure of a train ride.

The new art dealer, whose address she had written out and tucked into her glove, was not hard to find. The cab driver was most obliging about helping her inside with the packing case. As she had anticipated, the dealer pronounced the painting a genuine Romney and promptly made her a handsome offer for it.

"You are too kind," she fluttered. "I . . . it is such a tremendous decision. Lady Gwendolyn has been in the family for so long, you see. I must be sure she is going to someone who will really care for her. One has a responsibility, you know."

Knowing how useless it is to argue with sweet little elderly ladies, the dealer pressed his card on her, renewed his offer with a shade more emphasis, replaced Lady Gwendolyn in her traveling case, and handed Miss Henrietta into a cab.

"By all means think it over," he urged, "but I don't think you will find a fairer offer in London."

"I am sure of it," she replied. "Believe me, it is not that. I simply feel I should like to sit down quietly with a cup of tea and think it over. You do understand?"

The dealer assured her that he did, and saw her off with a sigh.

Her driver was surprised at the address of the hotel she gave him. "You sure you've got the right place, ma'am?" His tone was paternal. "Mostly rich Yanks go there, and it costs the earth. Thought you mightn't know, ma'am."

"Yes, I know." Miss Henrietta smoothed down her shabby tweed coat and straightened her sensible felt hat. "It will be a refreshing change to spend a short time among people who have a great deal of money. One was brought up to believe it was vulgar to be preoccupied with such things, but we are all forced to be vulgarians these days, are we not?"

The driver agreed sadly that we were, helped his fare out with Lady Gwendolyn, and forgave the meagerness of her tip.

Miss Henrietta did not go to engage a room. Overcome by her exertions, she collapsed into a chair far more luxuriously padded than her father would have approved, and propped Lady Gwendolyn's case uncomfortably against her knee. A few minutes later, Lady Gwendolyn went tumbling into the path of a passing gentleman.

"Oh I'm sorry. Clumsy of me." The well-dressed man stooped to retrieve the case.

"Do be careful. It's terribly precious," fluttered Miss Henrietta. "Thank you so much. Yes, perhaps it would be better against the chair, but I must confess I don't like letting it out of my sight, even for a moment. Only a short time ago I was offered a great deal of money for it."

"Really?" The indifference in the American's drawl was perhaps a shade overdone. "And what, may I ask, do you have in there?" he asked playfully. "The Crown Jewels?"

"Dear me, no." Miss Henrietta smiled shyly, showing an elderly woman's pleasure at being teased by a younger man. For an American he had rather a decent accent, she thought. She leaned forward with a pretty air of confiding. "As a matter of fact, it's a painting. I do not know if you have heard of an English portrait artist named Romney?"

Her new acquaintance's rather long nose seemed to quiver slightly. "Yes," he replied, "I have heard of Romney. I am, in fact, curator of an art museum."

"Fancy that!" Miss Henrietta smiled and nodded an amiable farewell. The American did not move away.

"About this Romney," he persisted. "You're quite sure it's authentic?"

"Oh yes," she replied. "It has been in my family ever since Mr. Romney painted it. And that gentleman today—let me see, what was his name? Ah, here it is, still in my glove. You see? There would be no point in his declaring it to be authentic if it were not," she added in rather a severe tone.

"Of course not," he half-apologized. "It's only that one doesn't often meet charming ladies in hotel lobbies carrying valuable paintings."

"Leaving them about for other people to trip over, you mean. I do hope you are not bruised."

"I'll tell you what," he said with a gaiety that was somehow out of keeping with his personality, "I'll forgive and forget if you'll come and have a drink with me. Or would you prefer tea?"

"On the contrary, I should enjoy a glass of sherry very much," said Miss Henrietta. "I have had a most exhausting day." She took a firm grip on Lady Gwendolyn's handle and followed her new acquaintance into the bar.

Miss Henrietta had not one but two glasses of sherry. Halfway through the second, her cheeks had become flushed and she was chattering freely to her bosom friend of half an hour about the imponderable difficulties of keeping house on nothing a month.

"And so you see, Mr. Bargraves, I have decided to part with Lady Gwendolyn. What my dear mother would say, I do not know." She drained the last of her sherry with a defiant air. "But I'm going to do it nevertheless. Of course I shall see to it that she gets a good home."

Mr. Bargraves half rose from his chair. "I wonder if you'll excuse me for just a moment, my dear lady. I have an urgent phone call to make. May I order you another glass of sherry while you're waiting?"

"Oh, I shouldn't," Miss Henrietta demurred.

"Nonsense," said the curator jovially. "One more can't hurt you."

"Very well, then. Just a little one."

Mr. Bargraves was back in a few minutes looking very pleased with himself. The art dealer's guarded replies to his cunningly worded questions had been more than satisfactory. He found Miss Henrietta in a state of fuzzy well-being. A few minutes later they were ascending in the lift to his suite, Lady

Gwendolyn's carrying handle clutched possessively in the curator's hand.

"And now let's see this wonderful Romney."

He drew the painting out of its case, studied it for a long time, ran experienced fingertips over the surface, finally took out a jeweler's loupe and studied every inch, both front and back.

"It's a Romney, all right."

His tone was matter-of-fact, but the hand that held the loupe shook slightly. Over Mr. Bargraves's horselike face crept a look his Yankee forefathers would have understood.

"Naow, Miz . . . that is, my dear lady, you've got a nice little property here. Mind you, I'm not saying it's one hundred per cent authentic. That background was done by an apprentice, I'd say, with the finishing touches put in by the master, and of course being just a head and shoulders makes it less desirable than a full-length portrait. If she'd been a well-known historical figure, now—" He shrugged. "Nevertheless, it's a nice little painting."

"I have always been greatly attached to Lady Gwendolyn," said Miss Henrietta somewhat foggily.

"Just so. And I can appreciate your feelings about not wanting her to get into the wrong hands. It wouldn't do for your ancestress to wind up in the ill-gotten collection of some dissolute and lascivious millionaire playboy now, would it?"

"Oh no, that would be too dreadful."

"Well, that's the risk you take when you sell to those art dealers. They don't care who buys what, so long as they get the cash. I hate to say it, but they're a money-hungry lot."

"Alas, so am I just now," sighed Miss Henrietta. "I really do not know which way to turn. I simply must sell Lady Gwendolyn. But oh, if I could only make sure she gets into the right hands!"

A bright green light shone in Mr. Bargraves's eyes. "It so happens," he began cautiously, "that I might be in a position to help you."

"If you only could!" Miss Henrietta's hands in their mended gloves clenched imploringly. "I should be eternally grateful."

Mr. Bargraves cleared his throat. "I should perhaps explain that I am curator of a fine arts museum in that part of the United States which is known as New England." He dwelt on the last word lovingly. "An area, I may say, where we hold our ties with the old mother country very dear. I do wish you could see our museum, dear lady. A magnificent edifice, designed in the finest Graeco-Roman tradition by one of our great modern architects, filled with priceless art treasures from all over the world, visited by throngs of serious-minded art lovers daily from ten to five except Thursdays, and lavishly endowed by—" He checked himself hastily. "Of course it all goes into the building fund. We never have a nickel to spend on paintings. Nevertheless, I think I may take it upon myself to make you an offer for your Lady G."

He pulled out a bulging note case. "What would you say to five thousand pounds, cold cash?"

Miss Henrietta said nothing. She merely stared at the sheaf of notes in his hand.

"Think of it, dear lady. Your beloved ancestress would hang in a place of honour and dignity, viewed only by the worthy and deserving eyes of dedicated students of art and ladies and gentlemen from the best families. And—er—you needn't mention a simple cash transaction like this to the inland revenue man."

"But would you not have to show a bill of sale to Customs when you leave the country?"

"Nonsense! There are ways of getting around these things if you know the ropes. We'll simply dispense with that little formality and nobody will be the wiser."

"Do you mean you simply give me the money and I give you Lady Gwendolyn and . . . and go away?"

"That's the ticket. No names, no pack drill, as you say over here. Come to think of it, you've never told me your name."

"Haven't I?" said Miss Henrietta absently. She was busy doing sums in her head. So much for the roof, so much for Alexander's vacation, so much for a nest egg to tide them over the winter. The figure was ridiculously low compared to what the art dealer had offered, but it was cash in hand and nothing in writing. It would do. She stretched out her small hand.

"Thank you, Mr. Bargraves. Lady Gwendolyn and I are deeply obliged to you."

Mr. Bargraves bowed her out. "It was my pleasure, dear lady." There could be no doubt he meant it.

He was still gloating over his bargain when a firm knock sounded at his door. Assuming it was the chambermaid, Mr. Bargraves opened the door, to find himself face to face with a frail, elderly man who brandished a rolled umbrella in a menacing attitude.

"I believe I am addressing Mr. Lucius Brutus Bargraves?"

"You have the advantage of me, sir."

"Yes," said Alexander, proffering his calling card, "I believe I have. That Romney on your dresser, sir, is mine."

"But I just bought it!"

"You cannot have done, sir, for I have not sold it."

Alexander pulled a sheaf of papers from his pocket. "Please study this inventory of my father's estate. As you see, everything is left to me as his only son, and the portrait of Lady Gwendolyn by Romney is included herein. Here is a photograph of the portrait, and here is its provenance. You yourself certainly have no doubts of my painting's authenticity, or you would not have bothered to steal it."

"I did not steal it. I bought it fair and square."

"Perhaps you can show me a bill of sale, then? Ah no, I thought not. Let me tell you sir, the penalties for theft are severe in this country."

He glared at the dumbfounded curator over his umbrella. "Since Lady Gwendolyn was taken from my home, I have been in touch with London art dealers. When your confederate turned up with her this afternoon and you followed up the visit with a bogus telephone call designed, no doubt, to increase the price they might be willing to pay, the fact was reported to me. I came at once to you, sir, hoping to make you see the error of your ways and avoid criminal prosecution for what I sincerely hope was a rash impulse and not the act of a hardened felon."

Mr. Bargraves wrung his hands. "But I had nothing to do with any theft. I never saw that old bat before in my life. I paid her five thousand pounds in good faith."

"If you paid her such a paltry fraction of the picture's true worth, you hardly did so in good faith," said Alexander severely. "As a self-styled expert in such matters, you must have realized at once that if she was willing to accept such a small figure, there must have been something fishy about the transaction. What was the woman's name?"

"I . . . I don't know."

"Really, Mr. Bargraves," a thin smile flitted across Alexander's lips, "I don't know what effect your taradiddle about an anonymous lady and a five-thousand pound transaction without a bill of sale will have on a jury, but I must say it does not convince me. And quite frankly, I do not care whether you are a thief or merely a receiver of stolen goods. My position is simply this: do I get my painting back *instanter* or do I call Scotland Yard at once?"

"Did you have any trouble with Mr. Bargraves?"

Miss Henrietta and her brother were enjoying a cup of cocoa in front of the drawing-room fire at the end of a trying but rewarding day.

"Not more than usual. He blustered of course, but after all, I had the truth on my side. I must say however, Henrietta, that he referred to you in language most unbecoming a man of his alleged position."

"One can hardly blame him." Miss Henrietta smiled. "The fox hardly expects to be bitten by the goose he is leading to the slaughter. It is curious how all of a pattern these people are, and how extraordinarily easy it is to find one in the right place at the right time."

"The shocking fact of the matter is that there are a great many scoundrels in the world," said Alexander. "Let me see, how many have we met so far? Forty-nine, I believe."

"Fifty," said Miss Henrietta. "Dear me, this is our golden anniversary."

She looked around the pleasant room at the unbroken row of ancestral portraits, safely retrieved one after the other from the hands of the predators. Then she raised her cup of cocoa to Lady Gwendolyn, smiling down again from her place of honour over the mantelpiece. "It seems appropriate to say, many happy returns. And may we all still be together to celebrate our Diamond Jubilee."

Rift in the Loot

STUART PALMER and CRAIG RICE

"I AM in no mood to face it now, whatever it is," said John J. Malone firmly as he came into his office shortly after 11 that morning. "Maggie, have we any aspirin in the place, and if not will you be a good girl and run down to the drug store?"

"No, *twice*," said his long-suffering secretary. "You can sweat out your hangover the hard way. I've got to stay here by the phone, it's been buzzing all morning. First, Joe the Angel called and said that just after you left his bar last night a man came in asking for you. Joe said he could always smell a *wronggo* a block away and maybe you ought to watch yourself."

Malone watched himself in the little wall mirror, wincing slightly. He adjusted his lush Countess Mara tie, already well-dusted with cigar ashes. "So what? In the legal profession one meets all kinds of people."

"Joe the Angel seemed to think that this

365

was one you wouldn't want to meet in a dark alley. And boss, it *may* be coincidence, but it says here in the *Tribune* that Eddie Vance busted his way out of Joliet yesterday."

The little lawyer's face brightened. "Eddie the Actor is loose? This may be good news— maybe he'll get to where he stashed that bank loot and finally pay me my fee!"

"Maybe he'll cut your throat, too," Maggie said darkly from behind her typewriter.

"But *why?* I saved him from the chair, didn't I? Never lost a client yet."

"Yes, you saved him. But he still got a hundred years at hard labor, remember? And before he went to the penitentiary he is reported to have squawked very loud that you double-crossed him and must have made some deal with the D.A.'s office."

Malone grinned. Harbin Hamilton, deputy district attorney for Cook County, had for years been trying to nail Malone's hide to the barn door, and the little lawyer wouldn't give him the correct time. But Malone's grin was feeble. "Yes," he admitted thoughtfully, "Vance may have got stir-happy. I suppose I could leave town until they pick him up."

"I have just seven dollars between me and a life of shame, which they say is nice work if you can get it. You couldn't get to Evanston

366

on seven bucks." Maggie looked at her desk pad. "Also Miss Hildegarde Withers is in town, stopping off en route to New York on a holiday, and she wants to have lunch with you."

"Not that—not *today!*" Malone had three times been involved in murder cases with the irrepressible schoolma'am, always with considerable risk to life and limb and with no appreciable fee; but he still had an inexplicable fondness for her. "Okay, call her back and tell her I'll meet her at Henrici's at 1."

"Since *I* have to put up the money," said Maggie sensibly, "we'll make it Thompson's cafeteria." She reluctantly produced five dollars out of the remainder of her week-before-last's pay check. "And watch yourself, Malone. Eddie the Actor is a very nasty character, and I wouldn't be at all surprised if he's the man with the oily voice who's been calling all morning and trying to find out when you'll be in and refusing to give his name. *Why* we ever took that case—"

"I was appointed by the Court as a public defender," Malone reminded her. "Eddie was supposedly broke, though we all knew that he had some $50,000 of the bank's money hidden somewhere—only he never could get to it and wouldn't or couldn't tell me or anybody just where it was. If he'd talked and turned back the loot, I could maybe have got him off with only fifty years.'"

"Which still is a long time to hang by your thumbs or sit on a red-hot stove, anyway you look at it," Maggie said with a certain tone of veiled sarcasm.

"Not so long when you consider that a bank guard got killed during the caper. We were lucky."

"*We?*" Maggie echoed.

But she relented and went out for the aspirin.

"Exactly why," demanded Miss Hildegarde Withers over their luncheon coffee at Thompson's, "are you looking over your shoulder so often, Malone? Guilty conscience?"

"Maggie believes that I am a marked man," the little lawyer admitted hollowly.

"Another murder case?" cried the schoolteacher, brightening. She wore a hat which could have been put on top of a Dutch chimney for storks to nest in, but her gray-blue eyes were keener than ever. "I could stop over a day or so and help solve it."

He blinked. "This one was solved three years ago—no mystery about it at all."

"Then why are you as jittery as a Mexican jumping bean?"

"Well—I'll fill you in on the story. Eddie Vance, known in underworld circles as Eddie the Actor because he has a wardrobe of uniforms and always manages to look like somebody else when he pulls a bank job, knocked over the Irving Trust, dressed as a window cleaner, with the help of three masked confederates. During the fracas one of them, a cheap hood named Jack Shaw, lost his head and killed a guard. The other two accomplices were shot down by police outside the bank, but Eddie Vance and Shaw escaped in different directions. Eddie himself has never been known to carry a gun, but of course technically he was accessory in a murder. He got away with the loot, some $50,000 in small bills; he was free for just one day but during that time he managed to hide it somewhere. Shaw is still being sought by the police, but since he had no previous criminal record and they have no photographs or fingerprints to work on, it's a tough job. I was appointed to defend Eddie the Actor, and got him off with a hundred years, a minor victory."

"A hundred years is a rather long time," said Miss Withers.

"You took the words right out of Maggie's mouth. But there's still the matter of that cache of dough. Eddie promised me ten grand of it if I saved him from the chair—which I did, with a neat bit of legal sleight of hand, even if I say it myself—but I never saw a red cent of it. Now he's suddenly busted loose and Maggie thinks that maybe he has a grudge because I wasn't able to get him off with a lighter sentence. Maybe she's right, too. Eddie the Actor is a guy who could fight a rattlesnake and give it the first two bites."

"Dear me!" gasped the schoolteacher. "The company you criminal lawyers keep! Malone, it's obvious that you must get out of town for the next few weeks, until the police succeed in re-arresting this unlovely character. You can come along with me to New York; my convertible is having something done to its remission or whatever they call it, but they promised at the garage that it would be ready tomorrow."

Remembering her driving, Malone almost thought that he would rather face Eddie the Actor, but with his usual gallantry he refrained from saying so. "Maybe—"

"Maybe me no maybes. You're coming. I just got a nice bonus on that movie cartoon case I told you about, and I can afford to finance you if necessary, as I presume from past experience that it is. The first thing is to get you packed and out of your hotel before this Eddie character tracks you down. Come on, time is of the essence."

The little lawyer obediently followed her out of the restaurant and they took a taxicab to his hotel. "Maybe you should wait in the lobby?" Malone suggested.

She bridled. "Certainly! Do you think I'm in the habit of going to men's hotel rooms? Besides, the place is probably a shambles."

It was—not to the surprise of John J. Malone when he entered the room, since he had left it so. The only surprise was that a bellboy sat in the one easy chair, reading early editions of the *Herald-American*. On second look he was a rather mature bellboy with a very short haircut and the face of an intelligent weasel. The little lawyer did a double-take. "Eddie Vance!" he cried. He took a deep breath. "Now Eddie-boy, there's no need to get tough about this."

Vance smiled. "You got me entirely wrong, shyster." His hand hovered near his lapel, and it was fairly obvious that if Eddie the Actor had once had an allergy to firearms he had conquered it while in prison. "Siddown, shyster, and listen. I busted out of the pen, see? I came out in a can on the garbage truck—"

"Type casting," murmured Malone under his breath.

"—and I'm going to stay out, understand? I'm going away, to South America or Cuba maybe, but first I've got to get to that dough of mine. You help me get it and I'll see you're taken care of." He made an unpleasant gesture. "If you *don't*—"

Malone sat down very, very carefully on the unmade bed and tried to relight a cigar that was already glowing. "Er—an interesting idea, Eddie. Somewhat startling, and a little out of my line. Where is the stuff?"

"It's safe, in spite of that punk Shaw, the hophead who blew up and blasted the bank guard. He's been trying through the grapevine to get me to spill where I stashed the loot so he can dig it up and get his cut—or more likely, if I know him, to take it all and scram. I figure he's got nothing coming." Malone could see that point of view, and nodded. "Anyway," continued Eddie the Actor, "the place where I hid the stuff I can't go near it, see? On account of right now I'm hotter than a three-dollar pistol and there's always a chance that the law has a stake-out there. So you're going to pick it up for me."

"Have you ever considered that my face is as well-known to the police as yours, if for somewhat different reasons?"

Obviously Eddie hadn't. He thought. "Then you've got to get somebody else to go, somebody you can trust, if you want your fee—and you want to stay alive." The man, Malone thought, was obviously as tense as an E-string. "How about your secretary?" Vance suggested hopefully.

Malone shook his head. "Maggie is strictly on the up and up—she'd have none of it."

"Well then, somebody else—or *else!*" The man was desperate.

At that auspicious moment there came a sharp knock at the door. Malone started to rise, but a pistol popped into Eddie's hand, waving him back. The knock came again, and then a voice from the hallway. "Malone? I know you're there, so open up!"

"It's only—only a client I'm expecting," the little lawyer improvised hastily. "And I've just got the idea that she might be the answer to our problem." He rose and went to the door, to admit Miss Hildegarde Withers.

"Malone, I waited—" she began—and stopped, seeing the ersatz bellboy.

But Malone shook his head at her warningly. "Cut it, Tillie. You don't have to go into your act here. Toledo Tillie, this is Eddie the Actor, a former client of mine, and he wants something done that I think you can do better than anybody—for a reasonable cut, of course. Nothing rough, it just involves picking up some merchandise, and picking up maybe a grand for yourself."

Miss Withers sniffed, sighed resignedly, and sat down on a hard chair. "So what's the caper?" she inquired, in her best approximation of a voice likely to be Toledo Tillie's.

Eddie Vance was staring at her, almost incredulously. Malone said hastily, "I'm defending Tillie when her case comes up next month, charged with conning department stores. She's out on bail now."

"Hiya, Tillie," said Eddie, extending a hand. "You certainly got the front—you look *too* respectable, almost." He turned to Malone. "Can we trust her?"

"I'd trust her as I would my sainted mother," swore the little lawyer shamelessly; his sainted mother had abandoned him on the steps of an orphanage when he was a few days old. "As you can see for yourself, Eddie,

374

she could walk right past any police stake-out without the cops giving her a second look. She could go right into your girl friend's house, maybe peddling books or something—"

"Wait a minute!" cried Eddie the Actor. "How'd you know . . . ?"

"I didn't, until you just told me," Malone admitted. "Though it seemed only natural that you'd have stashed the loot at Ethel Megrim's house somewhere, just as it seems natural the cops would be looking for you to show up there now. Even if they searched the place at the time of your arrest and found nothing. They know how close it was with you and Ethel. Miss—I mean Tillie here can walk into the place and get Ethel to hand over the money. Well, what do you say?"

Eddie Vance scowled, looking at the schoolteacher rather as if she were a used car that he contemplated purchasing. *"Maybe,"* he conceded. "Say something with uptown class in it."

"I *beg* your pardon!" Miss Withers sniffed again. "Beauty is truth, truth beauty; that is all ye know . . . and all ye need to know.' Keats."

"She's got the lingo," admitted Eddie the Actor grudgingly. "I'm not one to trust dames much. I didn't even trust Ethel when the thing happened; I sent her out for a jug that night and stashed the loot while she was gone. She has no idea of where it is, so she can't just hand it over to this old dame or anybody, see? And—" he continued, as Miss Withers seethed inside, "—I don't want Ethel to know about it now, or she'd insist on tagging along with me to Cuba or somewhere and help spend the dough. I'll pick me a señorita down there."

"Very sensible," observed Malone coolly, avoiding Miss Withers's glare.

Eddie the Actor threw away his cigarette and nervously lighted another. "Only how do I know Tillie here doesn't just grab the loot and lam?"

"She wouldn't think of that—" began Malone.

But the schoolteacher interrupted. "Nobody can say that Toledo Tillie is a double-crosser—there are ethics in my profession, Mr. Vance. I only steal from marks. Anyway, I don't need your dough, only I could use a small cut because of this con rap I'm in at the moment."

Vance nodded. "Okay. But remember, even if I'm hot I got connections, and if you did try to get out of town with my money you wouldn't get farther than Gary, Indiana, before you'd feel a shiv in your back. Understand?" He said it almost pleasantly. "Well, then—here's the dope." And he told them where the bank loot was hidden—under the rosebush in Ethel Megrim's backyard.

"How clever!" Miss Withers said admiringly. "It should be a cinch."

"Not unless we get Ethel out of the house while you do the job," Vance insisted. "She's sharp, and she'd catch on if you showed a sudden interest in the garden or anything. There's only one way to work the pickup." And he told them the address and the phone number and the plan—and a rather ingenious plan it was, too. "Take it from there," said Eddie the Actor. "I'll meet you—no, I'll phone Malone here sometime tonight or tomorrow. And no tricks. Understand?"

He went quickly out the door.

"It's much too tricky for me," said Miss Withers to Malone after she had got her breath. "I played along because you obviously wanted me to, but this isn't honest. We should call the police at once. Malone, I'm disappointed in you."

"We haven't much choice," pointed out the little lawyer wryly. "Go ahead, and don't ask too many questions." He picked up a bottle. "I don't suppose you'd care to join me in a highball?"

"There wouldn't be room enough," snapped the schoolteacher, and huffily departed. She had always known that the little lawyer cut corners now and then, but this—even under duress—was violating all sorts of laws about receiving stolen property and harboring a fugitive from justice and heaven knew what else. Well, she had given her word—or Toledo Tillie's word—and was morally or immorally bound to go through with it.

So she sought out a big bookstore on Michigan Boulevard and provided herself with the first volume of an expensive set of encyclopedias; thus armed she set forth for Rogers Park. Argyle Street was mostly lined with apartment houses and stores, but here and there were sandwiched brick bungalows of which Ethel Megrim's was one.

The block in question seemed to be deserted except for a woman with a baby carriage filled with groceries and baby, an empty taxicab, and two small boys who were manfully trying to wreck each other's tricycles. Yet she took no chances, working her way along the street from door to door, peddling her wares. Few people were home at this hour; most of the apartment houses had *No peddlers or agents* signs, or locked entry doors, but somewhat to her surprise she got orders for two sets of the encyclopedia before she finally came to the apartment building across the street from Ethel Megrim's home. It had been too good to last. There was a burly, pink-faced man in the lobby, leaning against the wall and reading a newspaper somewhat too elaborately; from where he stood he had an excellent view of Ethel's doorway. "Oh, my prophetic soul!" murmured Miss Withers. "The Law is already here." But, as she knew from experience, a frontal approach is often the best. So she came boldly up to him. "Excuse me, but do you have the time?"

He looked at her. "Three thirty," he said, unsmiling.

"Oh, dear, only that? And two more hours I've got to spend canvassing for this old encyclopedia before I can take my shoes off and relax." She sighed, and then smiled hopefully. "It's an excellent set—if you don't have one at home would you like to look at the sample volume?" She extended it. "Real buckram."

"No, lady," the man said, with considerable finality. The schoolteacher paid a token call at two apartments in the building, and then went across the street feeling that the man was watching her over his newspaper. Prudently she first tried the house next door to Ethel Megrim's—and walked into an open-armed reception from a wrinkled old lady with incredible, henna-flaming hair, who was obviously dying for someone to talk to. The schoolteacher's pitch for the encyclopedia was almost drowned out by a spate of words; she had to accept a cup of tea and listen to the bright sayings of Mrs. Gardner's grandchildren, admire their snapshots, lend an ear to all the neighborhood gossip, and be regaled by a play-by-play account of a morning soap opera.

Finally in desperation Miss Withers rose to go. "And I'll think about the encyclopedia," Mrs. Gardner conceded. "You drop back tomorrow, and we'll have another chat and another nice cup of tea."

The schoolteacher nodded vaguely. "I must get back to work now, though. How about your neighbor, do you think she might be interested?"

"That Ethel Megrim? I shouldn't think she reads much—she's too busy hanging on that TV set of hers when she isn't carrying on with her boy friend. He's a taxi-driver and if you ask me—"

Finally Miss Withers tore herself away and rang the bell next door. Luckily Ethel Megrim was at home. She turned out to be a rather prettyish woman in her late thirties, carrying a bit of extra weight and somewhat long in the tooth. She was wearing a housecoat that had seen better days; the television set was blaring and she had evidently been enjoying a can or more of beer. She did not feel any desperate desire for a set of encyclopedias, which was no surprise to the schoolteacher; while polite, Ethel was evidently anxious to get back to her beer and her TV program. But as Miss Withers took her departure she managed to distract the younger woman's attention just long enough to press the button which disengaged the Yale-type lock of the front door. Hurdle one was over, anyway. She took the El back downtown and found John J. Malone in his hotel room, alone except for half a bottle of Canadian rye.

"I'm giving you a case of Antabuse for Christmas," she said tartly. But she condescended to report on the recent exploits of Toledo Tillie. Malone sobered up instantly.

"Then all we've got to do now," he announced, "is to figure out a way to lure Ethel out of the house."

"That shouldn't be difficult. Have your precious Eddie Vance call her up and ask her to meet him under the statue in Lincoln Park or somewhere."

"Fine. Only we don't have the faintest idea of where to reach him."

"Too true." Miss Withers tapped her somewhat prominent front teeth with a fingernail. "Wait—I have an inspiration! Ethel Megrim is *mad* for television. Suppose you phone her and pretend to be representing some TV program and if she'll be in the lobby of the Tribune Building at 8 tonight she'll be paged and taken up to the broadcasting studios to appear on a new secret giveaway program with a chance at a truck load of prizes if she can pick the right tune or something?"

Malone stared at her, then raised his glass. "To a brilliant suggestion!"

"And to a brilliant hangover tomorrow morning, if you keep trying to climb into that nasty bottle." But she smiled proudly. "Well, Malone, get on the phone."

It was no sooner said than done, or almost. Ethel Megrim was incredulous at first, but when Malone in his most histrionic manner assured her that her name had been chosen by lot out of the phone book she

382

swallowed the thing hook, line, and sinker. Malone turned to Miss Withers. "We have time for dinner," he said. "Except that the only place I have credit is Joe the Angel's City Hall Bar. . . ." He ruefully surveyed the remains of Maggie's five-dollar bill.

"I insist on treating," the schoolteacher announced. "We'll go to the Empire Room at the Palmer House and fortify ourselves with succulent viands for the nefarious enterprise on which we are embarking."

"You have twisted my arm," Malone told her. "I always like to do my housebreaking on a full stomach."

A couple of hours later they came down Argyle Street in the misty rain, huddled under Miss Withers's umbrella and with Malone's Borsalino pulled well down over his eyes. But there was no sign of the man in the doorway. "Natch," said the little lawyer. "Ethel went out on our fake setup, and the cop tailed her hoping she'd lead him to Eddie the Actor." They went across the street to the narrow brick bungalow. The front door opened easily and they were inside the dark living room, which smelled of cheap perfume, beer, and dust.

"No lights," Malone warned Hildegarde quickly. He cupped his hand over the bulb of his flashlight and they walked through the deserted house which made up in depth for what it lacked in width; it had been built like a New York railroad flat. There was a bedroom and a bath, a dining room, and a long narrow old-fashioned kitchen which Miss Withers thought smelled faintly of mice. They went through a service porch and at last came out into the backyard.

"Holy St. Vitus!" gasped John J. Malone. There were at least *twenty* rosebushes in the narrow place, completely enclosed by a six-foot fence topped with barbed wire. And the only tools available seemed to be a rusty hoe and a trowel. "Where to begin?"

" 'Begin at the beginning; go on until you come to the end and then stop,' " quoted Miss Withers. And so they set to work in the feeble glow of Chicago's moonlight, filtered through the scattering rain clouds, their labors only slightly lightened by the blare of radios from the open windows of the apartment house next door. One was playing a Crime Doesn't Pay program, which the schoolteacher thought especially appropriate under the circumstances. Gloves and fingers were torn on the savage thorns; stubborn roots clung tightly to the sticky clay. They dug and they dug and they still dug, and they still failed to come up with the money.

Suddenly Miss Withers dropped her trowel. "What was that, Malone? Wasn't it a scream?"

"Sure. On the radio programs they always scream. Or maybe a tomcat on one of the fences. Back to work, we've got seventeen more bushes to disinter."

She bent down, and then straightened up again. "Malone, we're wasting time."

"You mean Ethel found the dough? Believe me if she had she'd be halfway across the world by now."

"Not that. But remember, Vance said the money was buried under *the* rosebush, which he then replanted. Wouldn't that indicate—?"

"That when he stashed it she had only one, and later she planted others?"

"You know nothing of roses, except perhaps Four Roses, which I believe is a brand of whiskey. We have only to look for the *oldest* rose—the bush with the thickest stem."

Which they did, and it was there under a foot of muddy earth: a bundle of bills big enough to choke a horse, or at least a pony, wrapped tight and dry in one of the plastic bags ordinarily used to keep vegetables fresh in the refrigerator. Malone reached out his hand, but Miss Withers dusted off the package and placed it firmly in her capacious handbag. "Not so fast," she said firmly. "The disposition of this blood money has to be discussed, and I intend to make one last appeal to your conscience. It isn't rightfully yours, or Eddie Vance's, and—" She stopped short.

From where they were standing, in one corner of the garden, they could see part of the side of the long narrow house. A light had suddenly come on in the windows of the front room!

"She's come home ahead of time!" the little lawyer gulped. They were trapped, just at the moment of victory. He glanced at the fence. "Do you suppose—?"

"No, Malone. I couldn't climb that fence in my prime, which I am definitely not in. Nor could you. We've got to go out as we came in, if at all."

He nodded ruefully. "But *why* would she come back now?"

"I can guess. Suppose that on her way down to the studio Ethel just happened to remember that she had a *private* phone number, known to Eddie Vance but unlisted? So the TV people couldn't have picked her name out of the phone book for their program.

She smelled a rat and came home. Now we're in for it."

"Maybe she'll get tired and go beddy-bye?" Malone suggested hopefully.

"You forget there's no second floor to the place. We have to go through her bedroom, and there's every chance that she'd wake up and grab a pistol and shoot us both for burglars—which in a sense we are." The schoolteacher shook her head. "I don't like any part of this, and besides I think I'm coming down with double pneumonia."

For an eternity of minutes the two conspirators huddled together in the chilly dark. Malone was shivering too, in spite of occasional nips at the trusty fifth in his topcoat pocket. "I'd rather dodge bullets," he whispered through chattering teeth, "than freeze to death. I'm going to reconnoiter. You wait here."

He tiptoed toward the back steps, but Miss Withers tiptoed right behind him.

"Where you go, I go," she told him firmly. "Up to a point, that is." They moved silently across the service porch, into the kitchen which was as dark as the bottom shaft of a coal mine, though somewhat warmer. Malone felt his way forward and into the dining room, with Miss Withers sticking closer than a sand-burr. His cupped flashlight cast a faint glow ahead.

Through the bedroom they crept, toward the faint crack of light under the door. Malone waved Hildegarde back, and cautiously squatted in front of the keyhole.

"What do you see?" the schoolteacher whispered.

"Nothing but a piece of wall," he muttered. "Hildegarde, it's *too* silent in there!"

"Maybe she's gone out again?" Miss Withers suggested hopefully.

He turned the knob, a fraction of an inch at a time, and then softly pulled the door toward him. As it swung open, the bright lights of the living room half blinded them—and then they saw it. Miss Withers bit her knuckles to keep from crying out.

Ethel Megrim lay sprawled in the center of the rug, her limbs every which way—like a puppet loosed of its string. There was red seeping through the bleached honey-color of her hair, and blood on her face. As the two intruders bent over her, she raised herself a little and moaned something through bruised and battered lips. Then they heard her say, "He—he hurt me—I didn't *know*, I *didn't*—" Her body gave a convulsive shiver, and she fell back again.

"Do something, Malone! Get an ambulance!"

He shook his head, and surreptitiously crossed himself. "There's nothing for us to do now but make tracks out of here—and quick!"

Malone was mistaken about that. They weren't going anywhere, according to a pink-faced, burly man who stood in the door of the front hallway, hands in the pockets of his gray topcoat. To Miss Withers he looked at least half again as tall and as broad as he had looked that afternoon, pretending to read his newspaper in the lobby across the street.

"Officer, we can explain *everything!*" she cried quickly. "We were out in the back-yard, and we heard a scream. . . ."

He came slowly forward, tense and frightening. "I heard a scream too," he said. His hand went into his pocket, and they caught the flash of metal. "Kelleher, Fourth Precinct. Get back against the wall, both of you." He looked down at the dead woman, almost incuriously. "Pistol-whipped her, eh?"

"But we don't even have a gun!" Malone put in. "You can search us! The person who did this must have got out through the front door—"

"And if you were watching the house from

389

across the street you must have seen him go out!" finished the schoolteacher triumphantly. "You did, didn't you?"

"I'll ask the questions," the big man said. "First, who are you and what in hell were you doing in the backyard at this time of night?" He looked at them. "Making mud pies?"

"See my lawyer," said Miss Withers, nodding at Malone.

Malone gulped. "Look, officer—I'm John J. Malone, the attorney. Call Captain Daniel von Flanagan at Twelfth Street, he'll vouch for me. I hope!" the little lawyer added under his breath.

"Shut up. So you're Malone, eh? The criminal attorney who defended Eddie Vance—and now you're caught red-handed over the corpse of his former girl friend! This is bigger than I thought. What did you come here for, Malone? And where is it?" The big man took a .45 automatic out of his pocket. "I said, *where is it?*"

He had backed Malone against the wall and was deftly frisking him. Then he stood back. "Okay, take off your clothes and throw 'em over here to me!"

"*Please!*" gasped Miss Hildegarde Withers in horror, stumbling swiftly into the bed-

390

room and closing the door firmly behind her. There were sounds of fervent protestations from Malone, which suddenly ended. There was no arguing with a detective who packed a .45, Miss Withers conceded. Again she thought longingly of that back fence—if somehow she could hoist herself over it . . . And then a better idea came to her.

But ten minutes later, when the door was flung open, she was standing in the bedroom, looking as innocent as a newborn babe is supposed to look—by anyone who has never seen a newborn babe.

"*Your* turn, sister!" announced Kelleher.

"Over my dead body!" the schoolteacher snapped. "You have no right even to suggest such a thing! When you call Headquarters to report this you can ask them to send a matron, but until then—" She raised her omnipresent umbrella menacingly.

"That's the law," put in Malone, "as you know very well, officer."

The man hesitated uncertainly, and then compromised by patting her exterior somewhat gingerly. Next he reached for her handbag. "Give, sister."

"Has a lady no privacy?"

"Not when it's homicide, she hasn't." He snatched the bag from her fingers and unceremoniously dumped the contents on the floor. It was Malone's turn to gasp—there was everything in that magpie's nest *except* Eddie the Actor's loot! The little lawyer stared at her in wonder.

"Blast it!" their captor swore, with trimmings. He hesitated for a moment, then made up his mind. He snatched the tie which Malone was at the moment replacing around his neck and tossed it to Miss Withers. "Tie his hands behind him—behind the back of that chair!" The gun waved menacingly, and the schoolteacher obeyed. The belt was whipped from Malone's waist, and she had to strap it around his ankles. Then, horror of horrors, she was herself tied up in the same fashion with curtains ripped from the windows. "There, I guess *you'll* stay put," said the man with the gun. And he disappeared into the back of the house, whence echoed sounds of a frantic search.

Miss Withers looked from Malone to the stiffening corpse on the floor and back again. "For a policeman, he has very unorthodox methods," she said calmly.

"He's no cop," Malone agreed. "He didn't phone in, and cops in Chicago carry .38 pistols, not .45 automatics. He's obviously after that dough. Where'd you hide it?"

"Never you mind! We've got to get out of here, now!"

"Now, *how?*" the little lawyer asked reasonably.

"I tied you with a granny knot, naturally. It'll slip if you work at it."

"No!" But she had and it finally did, and they went into what was undoubtedly the fastest disappearing act in recent history. It was not until they were half a dozen blocks away that Malone slackened his pace and entered a drug store to telephone, emerging almost immediately. "That was quick," the schoolteacher remarked. "What did von Flanagan say?"

"I didn't talk to him. I just told the cop at the switchboard that I was a neighbor of Ethel Megrim's and that I'd heard a scream there . . ."

"But we ought to go back and be around when the police arrive!"

"You mean be around when that thug comes out shooting! And Hildegarde, he's a cinch to have found that money by now, wherever you hid it."

She shook her head, smiling a Mona Lisa smile. "No, Malone."

"Well, where is it?"

Another shake. "No, Malone."

"You don't trust me," the little lawyer said sadly.

"Of course I do—just the way I'd trust my poodle with a piece of T-bone. And now, if you don't mind, it's late and I'm wet and muddy and I've just had about all an old-maid schoolteacher can take for one day. Good night, Malone—phone me in the morning." And she popped into a waiting taxi and was off and away. Malone stared after her with some bitterness, and then noticed the lights of a Bar and Grill across the street, gleaming a welcome through the mist.

"With my luck it'll be a mirage," he muttered gloomily. But at this point even the mirage of a saloon would be better than nothing.

In the cold gray light of the early morning something awakened John J. Malone. He sat up in his own bed and gingerly shook his head to see if it would fall off, which it almost did but not quite. It was amazing that a man could get a hangover like this on one bottle and two bucks to spend in a bar; somebody must have liked the way he sang *By Killarney's Lakes and Dells* and set up the rest of the drinks.

Then the knock at the door came again,

more insistently. He fumbled his way into a robe and shot the bolt. "Come in, Eddie," he said.

But it wasn't Eddie Vance, it was six feet of policeman in the shape of his ancient adversary, Captain Daniel von Flanagan, who almost trod on Malone's toes as he pushed his way into the room. He was smiling, but you could have refrigerated Death Valley in July with that smile. He folded his arms. "I should have known better," said that worthy if thumb-fingered policeman with some bitterness, "than to trust a lawyer any time, anywhere."

"Wha-a—huh?" muttered Malone brilliantly. "Look, Captain, I haven't even had breakfast—"

"Well, pour yourself three fingers of breakfast and then talk. See if you can talk yourself out of having your meals behind bars for the next dozen or so years. Let's start with Ethel Megrim, huh?" He plumped himself down in a chair.

"Oh, *her.*" Malone drank, choked, and drank again.

"Yes, her. She up and got herself murdered last night, as if you didn't know."

The raw whiskey hit Malone's stomach with a comforting warm thud, and rose slowly to dispel some of the fog in his brain. "And just *why* should I know?"

Von Flanagan snorted. "Because you yourself called Twelfth Street before the poor woman was cold, and reported it without giving your name. Only the man at the switchboard happened to recognize your golden tenor voice." Malone said nothing, and the other pressed on. "There's them downtown that think you yourself killed her."

"Me? Why?"

"Maybe because she came home unexpectedly and found you burglarizing her place, looking for that loot of Eddie Vance's. Maybe it was you who was digging up her backyard?"

Malone's mind was dashing about like a bird-dog in a thicket. "How can you say such a thing, Captain?" Von Flanagan made no answer, but he was staring significantly at the heap of muddy clothing flung on the radiator last night. The little lawyer winced, and decided to retire to previously prepared positions. "All right," he said resignedly, "I'll tell you. It was the fake cop who did it. When Miss Withers and I—"

"Not *her* again?" cried Von Flanagan. "This is too much!"

"I was saying that when Miss Withers and I came in out of the backyard we took him for a cop attracted by the scream—he was in the doorway, only he must have been just *leaving* instead of just coming *in*. Only he hadn't got what he came for, and went along with the gag when he saw us, thinking that maybe we had it . . ."

"The dough—Vance's loot! And you did have it? Where is it, Malone? Did he get it?" The questions came thick and fast.

Malone shrugged. "I'll swear by all the saints in heaven, I'll swear by the memory of my blessed mother, God rest her soul, that I have no idea of where on earth that loot is, unless it's still somewhere in Ethel's house."

"Phooey! My men tore up every inch of the backyard, they ripped up floors and knocked out walls, and I'll swear that there isn't even so much as a postage stamp that they missed! But go on talking."

Malone talked as he dressed. He told the whole story, with some cautious emendations—all about the talkative woman next door who had told Miss Withers about Ethel's new boy friend who was a chauffeur or taxi-driver or something, about the fake summons from the TV studio that was supposed to keep Ethel safely out of the way, about the cop who wasn't a cop at all and who had tied them up while he went on searching the house . . . He told everything except about the money; at the moment that wasn't his secret anyway. "So there's your murder case, Captain," he concluded, "tied up in a bag. With Eddie Vance safe in prison, this guy started to cultivate the ex-girl friend, because he must have figured that she knew where the money was. Eddie's prison break forced his hand—he watched the house figuring Eddie might come there to pick up the cash. When Ethel left the house last night he tailed her, figuring maybe she was going to meet Eddie somewhere. She got wise, turned around, and came home, and he followed her in and tried to beat her into telling him where the loot was. But she couldn't tell him because she didn't know, and he lost his head and hit her too hard—just like he blew his top and killed that bank guard three years ago."

"*Shaw!*" cried von Flanagan triumphantly, as if it had been his own discovery.

"Who else? All you have to do is pick him up—"

"Phooey! If we couldn't pick up Shaw for that other killing after three years of trying, how do you expect us to pick him up for this one?" The policeman shook his head. "Get the rest of your clothes on, we're going down and see the D.A. This is one time you've overreached yourself, Malone."

The little lawyer thought fast. "And just what do you think Deputy District Attorney Harbin Hamilton will say when he finds out about a certain phone conversation we had yesterday?"

It didn't stop von Flanagan, but it slowed him down a little, and Malone worked fast on his temporary advantage. "I've got an idea," he said. "We're all in this pretty deep, but I see a way out. You want Eddie the Actor for prison break, you want the loot, and you want Shaw for two killings, right?" He went back to the selection of a tie, almost too casually. "What do you think of this one with the hand-painted flamingoes?"

"I wouldn't wear it to a dog fight. Yes, we want Vance and Shaw and the dough. But you've fixed it so all three slipped through our fingers . . ."

"Well, then," said Malone—and in a few well-chosen words he stuck his neck out farther than ever before in his checkered existence. It took some fast talking, but he was used to bedazzling twelve jurors and a judge, and von Flanagan was only one man and not too bright at that.

"It better work, before 7 o'clock tonight when I go off duty!" warned the detective from the doorway. "Or I know somebody who'll get disbarred but fast." He went out, slamming the door. Malone sighed, and knotted the tie with the pink flamingoes, but his heart wasn't in it. And what to tell Hildegarde when he called her? He decided to fortify himself first with another drop, but had barely lifted the bottle when there came a knock at the door.

"Western Union for Mr. Malone."

Wearily he opened the door, "Come in, Eddie." This time it *was* Eddie Vance, shaking the drops from his uniform cap. He kicked the door shut behind him.

"Well, shyster? What luck?"

"Plenty," Malone said quickly. "Sit down and have a drink. I have every reason to believe that Miss—I mean Toledo Tillie— was successful, but it's a ticklish situation and I haven't got in contact with her yet. You see, Ethel Megrim got killed last night—"

"I heard," Eddie said. "Poor Ethel. But what about my dough?"

"Tillie is under wraps because of the murder, but she'll find a way to get in touch with me. Only we've got to be careful—von Flanagan was just here."

"I saw him in the lobby," said Eddie the Actor. "And if you're thinking of making a deal with him—" He patted his pocket with an evil grin. "I want my dough and I want it today, see?"

"You name the place and we'll be there, or at least she will. How about Field's basement at closing time, or the IC station at Randolph when the commuters are all going home? Or the south lion in front of the Art Institute?"

Eddie hesitated. "I like to work in the open. I guess the Art Institute is best. Six o'clock, okay?"

"Okay. You can take the dough, hand over my fee and Tillie's cut, and lose yourself in the crowd."

"Check. But tell her to be there on the dot. And don't foul this up, Malone, or you'll both be using a marble slab for a mattress, see?" He went out, slamming the door. Malone took a deep breath and a deeper drink, then called up Miss Withers. The schoolteacher was in a somewhat better mood than last night, and agreed to buy him a cup of coffee in fifteen minutes. He went out of the hotel through the rear service entrance, just in case von Flanagan wasn't trusting him, and shortly thereafter he was seated in the Palmer House coffee shop opposite his partner in crime. Her guilty conscience was not preventing her from attacking a copious repast of oatmeal and bacon and eggs, all of which made Malone feel slightly green.

They were both slightly green when he told her what he had promised von Flanagan to get rid of him. Miss Withers dropped her spoon. "No!" she cried.

"Yes," he said. "Look, you know where the dough is, so that takes care of Point One. We can deliver Eddie Vance, who's so crazy-mad for his loot that he'll walk into the trap—I'll phone von Flanagan to have his men at the Art Institute at six. Then all we've got to do is to get ourselves off the murder rap by locating Jack Shaw—unless he found where you stashed the money and is far away by now."

She shook her head. "I'm positive he didn't, or the police either. Let me think, Malone. We know Shaw is a cab-driver. If we checked all the taxi companies—"

"It would take days, and undoubtedly he's using a phony name. It isn't as if we had a picture of him," the little lawyer objected. They sat for a while in glum silence. Then the schoolteacher's long and faintly equine face lighted up like a lamp.

"But I *have* a picture of him, indelibly imprinted on my mind! Don't you see? The man has gone scot-free so far because he had no police record, no photos or fingerprints on file, and he wore a mask on the bank job. But now it's different. Now two people know what he looks like! Malone, do you know any friendly newspaper reporters?"

"I know all of them," he said with some pride. "And they're all friendly."

"Well, one of them is going to have a story for the early afternoon editions. Because it will help if while we're looking for Mr. Shaw *he* is looking for *us!* We'll spill the news that there are two eye-witnesses to the Megrim murder who can positively identify him!"

"A trap—with you and me as the cheese? Look, Hildegarde, isn't it enough to have Vance and the police on our tail without bringing Shaw into the act too? I'm too young and too wicked to die just yet." But Miss Withers prevailed, as she had a way of doing, and Malone went ahead and phoned one Ned McKeon at the *Herald-American*. "He says he'll squeeze it on page one somehow," the little lawyer reported. " 'Two unidentified witnesses, names withheld, at scene of the Megrim murder . . .' Only Shaw can identify *us* all right."

"And so perhaps can your friend Captain von Flanagan?"

Malone said that he wasn't sure von Flanagan could read, and that if he could, and did see the story, he'd probably keep his promise to hold off long enough to give them rope to hang themselves. They could only wait, and hope. The waiting, they decided, should be in or around Malone's office; his name and address were in the book and if Shaw came sniffing after the bait he would presumably come there first.

It was Miss Withers who brought up the moot question of what, if anything, they could do with or to Mr. Shaw if he did come. Malone thought. *"Maggie!"* he said.

"I have the greatest admiration for your secretary, but—"

"Maggie has a brother, and the brother has friends," Malone explained.

So it was that some hours later—about the time the *Herald-American* hit the stands— Miss Withers found herself staked out in the vacant suite across the hall from Malone's office, in the company of the little lawyer and two very tough-looking characters indeed, who had mumbled, "Pleasetameecha," and then settled down to a fast game of pinochle.

"Gangsters?" she whispered.

"Worse," Malone came back. "From the circulation department of the *Gazette*—to them murder and mayhem are jolly pastimes."

"Are they armed?"

"Tire irons and a length of heavy chain, I gather," he said.

So they waited and waited—and still waited. The hands of the old-fashioned watch pinned to the schoolteacher's old-fashioned blouse crawled around and around. There was no sound anywhere but the snap of the cards and the occasional tinkle of small change. Nothing happened, and nothing kept on happening. " 'The watched pot—' " quoted Miss Withers.

And then the phone rang suddenly in Malone's office across the hall, whose door had been left invitingly open. Malone leaped eagerly to answer it, since Maggie for obvious reasons had been given the afternoon off and sent out of the combat area. "Hello?" he cried breathlessly, Miss Withers leaning over his shoulder. "Hello? John J. Malone's office—hello?" He put down the phone in disgust. "They hung up on me!"

"You mean *Shaw* hung up on you! Obviously he was making sure you were here. Malone, it's working!" She almost did a little dance.

"It had better work, before 7 o'clock!" he came back grimly. "Von Flanagan is a man of his word and if we don't make that deadline . . ." He shuddered, and they went back across the hall, eyes glued to the crack in the door, ears keyed to the sound of approaching footsteps . . .

Five o'clock—then 5:15. "I can almost hear the clang of that cell door right now," Malone murmured sadly.

"Well," the schoolteacher said sensibly, "why not get out of town? My car ought to be fixed by now—we could be halfway to New York by morning."

"And von Flanagan could have Wanted flyers out for us before that. We'd be hauled back in handcuffs." They waited some more. It became 5:30, then 5:45. "That's that," said Malone. "We've just got time to get to the Art Institute and keep the date with Eddie Vance. Let's go." He borrowed a ten from Miss Withers and slipped it to their troops, who departed in some disappointment.

"Von Flanagan should certainly settle for two-thirds of what you promised," the schoolteacher said. "Getting Eddie the Actor—and the money—"

"Maybe," said Malone, without much hope. "He is a reasonable man, but not very." They hurried out of the building. There was a taxi at the head of the line, the driver a shortish stocky man deep in a racing form, a battered uniform cap over his eyes.

They hustled inside. "The Art Institute, and hurry," Malone ordered. He leaned back in the seat, and refreshed himself from the remains of his bottle. It was the hour of densest traffic, and Miss Withers felt that they could have made better time by walking. Once or twice their driver cut through alleys with the dexterity of long practice, but always sooner or later they found themselves hemmed in with traffic again.

"Malone, isn't the Art Institute east of us, on the lake front?"

He barely opened his eyes. "Yes, Hildegarde."

"Well, our driver is going west."

"Probably making a circle to avoid the jam in the Loop."

She was silent for a block or so. "Malone!" she whispered. "Notice the door handles?"

He looked, then gaped—there weren't any! "Driver!" cried Malone, and tapped on the glass partition. The driver half turned, suddenly sitting up straight so that his bulk showed. He also showed an automatic pistol in his left hand, and his face was the face they had seen last in Ethel Megrim's living room over her dead body.

"*Shaw!*" gulped Malone.

Miss Withers was frantically pounding on the door window with her umbrella handle, and waving pleadingly at passers-by. One or two of them waved back at her, but that was all. She tried to scream . . .

Shaw rolled down the partition and waved the gun in their general direction. "Cut it out," he spat at them. "Or you'll get it here and now."

They cut it out. The man was driving like a madman, but evidently that was the way taxi-drivers were expected to drive. They beat red lights and raced past boulevard stops, heading west and south, with the driver keeping one eye on the rearview mirror. Miss Withers moved a little closer to Malone, as if for comfort, but he caught her lips moving almost soundlessly. "Next stop—the one, two, three." He nodded a quarter of an inch . . .

There was a moving van at the next light, waiting for a left turn, and the taxi had to screech to a stop. Miss Withers kicked Malone sharply on the shin, and then her trusty umbrella came up like a striking snake, the crook of its handle around Shaw's neck, and she jerked with all her strength. The gun went off through the top of the cab and John J. Malone lovingly brought down his whiskey bottle on the man's head to finish the job. "Bull's-eye," said Miss Withers placidly.

It took only seconds for the little lawyer to climb over into the front seat, shove the unconscious Mr. Shaw to one side, and take the wheel. It had all happened so fast that they had rounded the corner and were a block or so north again before he remembered to pick up the uniform cap and put it on his own head.

"It's only ten after 6!" announced the schoolteacher. "Perhaps we can still make the Art Institute in time!"

Malone's only answer was to put his foot on the accelerator and his hand on the horn. A traffic cop or two whistled shrilly after them, but as luck would have it they met no minions of the Law on wheels, and soon they were rocketing up the Boul Mich, now heading north. They roared up before the Art Institute at last, to find the area practically deserted. There was no sign of Eddie Vance, no sign of von Flanagan and his men. Two husky street cleaners were sweeping the gutters nearby and putting refuse into a Department of Sanitation truck—but both were too tall and brawny to be Eddie Vance. The only other figure in the vicinity was an art student with owlish glasses and a smock who was painting a portrait of one of the benign stone lions against a background of lighted skyscrapers. He was obviously not Vance either.

"You'd better get out and look around and let yourself be seen," advised Malone. "I'll stay here and sit on Shaw—maybe you'd better give me your scarf so I can tie him up."

Hildegarde left the cab, strolled up the sidewalk for half a block, and then back again. It was almost six thirty, and she had a deep presentiment that they had missed the boat. Back at the steps of the Institute again, she paused to pat the north lion, paused again to admire the painting of the solitary artist . . .

There were two sharp beeps from a cab which had just pulled up in front of Malone's. "Taxi, Tillie?" It was a voice she recognized, though it now wore a mustache.

She leaped a foot in the air, and then started down the steps, her knees trembling like jello. Her eyes flashed this way and that in a desperate appeal for help—but there seemed no help in sight. Malone was either bent over his bottle or his prisoner, or both. There was nothing to do but to get into that second taxi—and what Eddie the Actor would say and do when he found she had doublecrossed him . . .

Eddie leaned back to open the door for her and she stumbled inside. The taxi moved ahead.

And then suddenly the truck from the Department of Sanitation pulled out squarely in their way. One of the street cleaners produced a riot-gun, the other a pistol. Wonder of wonders, the artist on the Art Institute portico ripped off his glasses, kicked aside his easel, picture and all, and turned out to be Captain von Flanagan. Miss Hildegarde Withers flung herself to the floor of the cab, both hands over her ears—and then it was all over, without a shot being fired. Eddie the Actor came out into the street, both

411

hands held as high as he possibly could. When frisked, his pockets produced only a water pistol.

"Take him away," said Captain von Flanagan to the two street cleaners, who turned out to be crack detectives from Fifty-fifth Street. "And him too," he ordered, when Malone opened the other cab door and Mr. Shaw rolled out into the gutter.

Miss Withers took Malone's arm, and they stood there, waiting for von Flanagan's applause. But the Captain squirmed out of his smock, hurled it to the ground, and faced them belligerently.

"I'll never hear the last of this down at Twelfth Street," he growled. "And say, you—where's that loot you were supposed to deliver?"

Malone shrugged, and looked at Miss Withers. "I could tell you," she said, "but I'd rather show you—if you don't mind a trip to Ethel Megrim's house."

"We searched that place with a fine-tooth comb!" von Flanagan roared. "I'll eat my hat—or your hat or *anybody's* hat—if there's so much as a dime there!"

"Did you ever read *The Purloined Letter* by the late Edgar Allan Poe?" she inquired sweetly. Von Flanagan snorted, but it was nothing to the snort he snorted when, after a fast ride uptown in a squad car, she led them to Ethel's refrigerator and took from the vegetable compartment a plastic bag containing lettuce. Inside the lettuce was a wad of currency large enough to choke a horse, or a small pony. "The loot, Captain," she beamed. "As Poe definitely would not have said, 'Look for the lettuce in the lettuce.' I put it there while Shaw was searching Malone's clothing for it, since at the time I trusted neither Shaw nor Malone."

There was a long silence. "Hildegarde, you wrong me," said the little lawyer sadly. "I was always going to turn it in, wasn't I, Captain? Didn't I phone you when all this started and promise to deliver it if you'd keep hands off for a day or so?"

The policeman nodded.

"Well, then," said Miss Withers. "I owe you an apology, Malone. I thought you were after the money, or a large slice of it. But virtue, this time, is its own reward."

Malone smiled. "There are *other* rewards. This is bank loot, remember—and banks have surety companies. We should not do too badly. Now let's get out of here before Captain von Flanagan keeps his promise and eats your hat!"

The House of a Hundred Birds

EDWARD D. HOCH

MY WIFE Shelly had just learned I was going off again on a trip with Simon Ark, and we were having our usual quarrel. "Where is it this time?" she asked. "India? North Africa?"

"London, actually. We've been there before a couple of times."

"I remember. The first time was right after our marriage."

"Look, Shelly," I pleaded, "why not come along with us? You could shop and see the sights while I'm involved with Simon."

She shook her graying blonde head and I knew it was hopeless. "I can't get away this week. The committee dinner is on Thursday and mother's coming for a visit on the weekend."

"I'll bring you a gift from London," I said.

"The last time it was a bottle of perfume from the airport gift shop."

"I'll do better this time," I promised.

Her face relaxed into a tired smile. "I suppose it could be worse. You could be running off with another woman instead of Simon."

"That would never happen," I assured her. "Not unless she looked just like you."

That evening Simon and I were on the plane to London.

The trip began badly for me. At Heathrow Airport a mousy little man bumped into me and stole my wallet. Luckily my traveler's checks and credit cards were in another pocket, but I still resented the loss. In the cab to London I grumbled all the way. "If you're such a great detective, Simon, why can't you catch the guy who stole my wallet?"

"My friend, a pickpocket is hardly the kind of challenge I seek."

He seemed about to drift into his philosophical ramblings about pursuing Satan for nearly two thousand years, and I was in no mood for it just then. I changed the subject. "Would you mind telling me just what it is that brought us to London? On the plane all you would say was that it involved Chauncey Rideout."

Rideout was a friend of Simon's whom I'd

met once or twice in New York. He ran a large London travel agency, and was a garrulous man who seemed to fascinate Simon with his endless stories of faraway places.

"We're seeing Chauncey this afternoon. Perhaps it's better if he tells us himself. He did mention some intriguing aspects on the transatlantic phone, though. A murder, for one thing, and a house of a hundred birds."

"A house of—"

But Simon motioned toward the taxi driver's back and would say no more. I settled down and contented myself with the passing scene. Rideout had arranged for our airline tickets and hotel through his travel agency, and he'd booked us into a luxurious Park Lane place we could ill afford. Happily he was paying the expenses.

Chauncey Rideout was never overlooked when he entered a room. His large stomach, always covered by a bright red vest, announced his presence even before his booming voice. Seeing him later that day in his fancy London office I found him more subdued than I remembered, but still wearing the red vest.

"There were two sisters," he began after the usual preliminaries about our trip. "Anna and Gertrude Stigner. Retired civil servants, both in their sixties, never married. Lived in a big old family house in the north of London. I got to know them through the travel agency. Booked them on a two-week tour every spring, regular as clockwork. They liked the Mediterranean—the Greek islands and such—and I sort of took them under my wing."

"You speak of them in the past tense," I observed.

Chauncey Rideout nodded. "Gertrude was killed four days ago—last Friday night. Stabbed to death by an intruder in her own kitchen. About six months back they asked my advice about taking in a boarder. I suggested they advertise for one, and next thing I knew they'd rented to a chap named Irving. Now Anna fears he might be involved in the murder. She's scared stiff and I can't console her. I couldn't begin to tell her if this mysterious boarder might have killed her sister."

Simon Ark smiled slightly. "So you telephoned me across the ocean."

"You were the only one I knew who might be able to help," Chauncey said. "And you didn't seem very interested until I mentioned the birds."

"Yes, tell us about the birds," I urged.

417

They seemed to be the key to Simon's interest in the affair, and I wanted to learn more.

"There's not much to tell, really. The sisters kept a great many caged birds in the big house. Canaries, doves, songbirds of various sorts. In every room. Anna told me once there were a hundred all together."

"A hundred birds!" I glanced over at Simon. "Is there any significance in one hundred caged birds?"

"Not in the number. But their presence suggests—"

We were interrupted by Rideout's secretary who entered the office with the afternoon's correspondence requiring his signature. She was a comely brunette named Thelma Bok and she flashed me a broad smile as we were introduced. "We were just talking about the birds out at the Stigner house," Rideout told her.

Thelma nodded. "I went there once last year to deliver their plane tickets for a tour. You wouldn't believe that many birds!"

"Are they quite noisy?" Simon asked.

"Noisy enough! Though she did cover their cages when they got too bad."

"She? Gertrude or Anna?"

"Gertrude—the one who died." She lowered her voice on the final word, as if in respect. "The birds were hers, really, though I think Anna cared for them too."

"I see." Simon turned back to Chauncey as his secretary left with the signed letters. "Would it be possible for us to meet Anna Stigner?"

"Certainly. Today was the funeral, so maybe tomorrow morning might be best. I'm sure she'll tell you whatever she knows."

"This boarder—have you ever met him?"

"I caught a glimpse of him the other day when I went out there. Young chap, with a beard and long hair. Don't know why they rented the space to that type in the first place. I suppose they needed the money, but they have some valuable pieces of furniture downstairs."

"One other question," Simon said as he stood up. "Did the hundred birds come before or after this boarder?"

"Oh, before. They've had the birds as long as I've known them, and Irving has only been there about six months. Since around the time they both retired. Douglas Irving—that's his name. He's a baker, which is supposed to explain why he's out all night and home during the day."

"I'll look forward to meeting him," Simon said. "In the morning."

A misty drizzle was falling the next day as we drove out to a residential section in the north of London. It was an area of big old houses, many of them now cut up into apartments for young working people. But even in such surroundings the Stigner house stood out. It was a rambling three-story monster, with little porches and gables everywhere. I suppose it was the perfect place to house a hundred birds.

Chauncey Rideout led the way up the steps to the porch, where dusty rockers creaked in the breeze just beyond the reach of the rain. He let the heavy knocker fall three times and presently the door was opened by a pale woman in black. She had once been beautiful, I thought, though age had played its usual unkind tricks. "This is Anna Stigner," Chauncey said, introducing us.

"Please come in." Her voice was soft and cultured.

She led us through a dim hallway into a pleasant sitting room at the front of the house, and I saw at once what all the bird fuss was about. There were cages everywhere—hanging from the ceiling in the outer hall, on standards in the sitting room, even resting on a table in an adjoining room. Some cages held a single bird, but many had pairs of doves or lovebirds. Their chirping, soft but constant, seemed to fill the house.

"I see you are a lover of birds," Simon remarked to the woman as he seated himself by the fireplace. I took a chair on the other side, grateful for the warmth after the chill drizzle outdoors.

"They were really Gertrude's," Anna Stigner explained, "but I may keep most of them. I couldn't imagine living here without them."

Chauncey shifted uneasily in his chair. "Tell them about Gertrude's death, Anna, and about your boarder."

Her thin hands moved on her lap as she spoke. "I hope you can help me, Mr. Ark. I just don't know what to do now. Gertrude was older and she always made the decisions for both of us. It was her thought that we should get a boarder for the downstairs after we both retired and our income dropped off. Douglas Irving seemed a nice enough chap at first."

"At first?" Simon questioned.

"Well, he simply appeared at our door one morning about the room, before we'd even had a chance to run an advertisement. He's a baker and works from two a.m. till ten in

421

the morning. He baked cakes and pies for us, and even built a special table in the kitchen for mixing his dough. But he began having strange visitors a few months back. They'd drive up at night in fancy cars. Always men—he never had women visitors. My sister was bothered by it."

Simon Ark nodded. "Tell me about last Friday."

"It was late in the evening, a little before midnight. I hadn't been feeling well and I'd gone to bed early. I was awakened by a sound. It might have been Gertrude screaming for help. I called to her and there was no response." She hung her head, as if in silent prayer. "I put on my robe and slippers and went downstairs—and found her stabbed to death on the kitchen floor. Stabbed with one of our own knives."

"Was there any sign of forced entry?"

"No. I called the police at once, of course, but they could find no signs either. Gertrude and I each had keys, and of course Mr. Irving has one too. The police believe the intruder entered with a duplicate key."

"Did Douglas Irving have an alibi for the time of the murder?"

"He claims he'd stopped at a pub before work. The bartender remembers seeing him just before they closed, which was eleven o'clock. Of course the killing wasn't till a bit later than that, but the police don't seem to consider him a serious suspect."

"You do, though."

She looked away. "He just acts strange. If Gertrude surprised him doing something bad he might have killed her."

"Had she ever surprised him at anything in the past?"

"Once she told me she came downstairs around midnight and he was in the kitchen with some men. They had flour spread out on the table and Douglas said they were making dough for bread."

Simon Ark asked, "Could we see this kitchen where your sister was stabbed?"

She led us through a dim back hall and a large pantry, with caged songbirds hanging overhead. Pausing at one of the cages she covered it with a fancy satin drape. "Time you were sleeping now!" she told the birds. But I noticed she did not cover all the cages.

The kitchen itself was large and roomy, with a big double-door refrigerator and modern sink and stove. But Simon's attention was drawn to a large square table with closed sides, closed from table top to floor, standing against one wall. It seemed almost like an altar to some ancient kitchen god. Simon ran his hand over the smooth knotted wood surface and commented, "Very good workmanship. Is this the table Irving built for his baking?"

"Yes. He said we could have it if he ever moved out."

"I think Douglas Irving is a man worth meeting."

"He should be home from work very soon."

"While we wait, Miss Stigner, suppose you tell me the real reason for all these birds."

She shot a glance at Chauncey Rideout, as if suspecting he had told us some secret. "I don't know what you mean. My sister liked—"

"You covered only some of the cages," Simon Ark said. "I'll venture a guess you have so many birds so that some may be left uncovered in each room day and night. It is believed in certain parts of the world that caged birds keep ghosts and evil spirits away from a house that may be haunted."

"I don't—"

"Isn't that what you really fear, Miss Stigner? That your sister was killed by a ghost?"

Anna Stigner had steadied herself against the table, her face suddenly white as chalk. She might have been seeing one of those ghosts herself in that moment. Rideout went quickly to her side and turned to scowl at Simon. "I asked you to help the poor woman, not frighten her!"

"If I am to help I need to know the truth. I believe she wishes to blame her boarder for the crime to free herself from the terror of the unknown, from the possibility of evil spirits lurking in this house she loves so much."

"I do love it," Anna Stigner gasped.

"Of course you do, or you would have moved long ago rather than fill the place with birds to keep away the spirits." Simon's voice turned unusually gentle. "Now tell me why you think a ghost may have killed your sister."

"Could I have a glass of water, please?"

Rideout ran the cold water and brought her a glassful. She drank it down and then straightened to face us, hands gripping the edge of the table behind her. "I didn't tell the whole truth about Friday. Gertrude had always been afraid the house was haunted. Our mother had told us years back of seeing ghosts here. That was the reason for the birds, and it was the reason we took in a male boarder. We believed it would give us some sort of protection. We traveled frequently when we could, just to be away from here, but it is a lovely house and we couldn't bear to sell it. So we put up with the creaks and crashes in the night—"

"The wind," Chauncey Rideout insisted. "Nothing more."

"—and we brought in all the birds, because they seemed to offer some protection. Then we took in Douglas Irving, to have a man on the premises. For a time it was good, despite his odd hours and strange companions. But then came last Friday. I was ill, as I've said, and had retired early. But about half-past eleven Gertrude came and awakened me. She said she heard a noise downstairs, though we both knew Irving had not returned. His car was not in the driveway."

She paused and Simon had to urge her on. "What happened next?"

"Gertrude went downstairs while I waited in my bedroom. I heard her say something unintelligible and then she screamed. It was the most terrible sound I've ever heard in my life! I hurried downstairs and found her stabbed to death here on the kitchen floor."

"And the ghost?"

"Mr. Ark, I will swear that I heard not a sound after Gertrude screamed. There were no running footsteps, there was no slamming door. The killer never left, and yet there was no one here!"

"There are many explanations," Rideout insisted, trying to calm her. "A thief may have been in his stocking feet to avoid making noise. He could have slipped out unnoticed as you came downstairs."

"No," she insisted. "I'd have seen him."

Then we heard the front door open and footsteps approaching. We all turned toward the doorway as a slim young man entered. He must have been in his mid-twenties, with hair just over his ears and a dark fringe of beard across his chin. He seemed surprised to find us all gathered in the kitchen. "What's this?" he asked Anna Stigner. "More police?"

"This is my boarder, Douglas Irving," Anna said, and introduced Simon and me. Apparently Rideout had met him at the funeral.

"If you're not police, who are you?" the young man asked.

Simon answered for us. "I am an investigator of unusual phenomena. It's possible the death of Miss Stigner's sister was not caused by a human agency."

"Not caused—? You gotta be kidding, mate! I don't believe in ghosts!"

His arrival had set the kitchen birds to chirping and Anna Stigner covered their cages. Chauncey Rideout cleared his throat. "It's not a matter of believing in ghosts, Mr. Irving. But there was a crime committed here and the police seem unable to get to the bottom of it. If my old friend Simon Ark can shed some light on the matter, I believe we should listen to him."

"Sure, sure," Doug Irving agreed. "So long as you don't try and pin this thing on me. I was down at the Cross and Anchor and I got witnesses to prove it."

"The Cross and Anchor closes at eleven o'clock," Rideout pointed out. "The police checked on it."

"The bartender let me stay later, in the back room. We were drinking till past midnight. I couldn't have been here killing anybody."

"We'll see about that," Chauncey Rideout turned to us. "I have to get back to the office now. Can I drop you anywhere?"

"Our hotel, I think," Simon decided. "Goodbye for now, Miss Stigner, Mr. Irving. We'll be talking to you again."

As we were leaving the house Simon saw

the rubbish men removing the Stigners' week's trash. Something in one of the cans attracted him and he walked over to examine it. The trash collector looked annoyed as Simon pulled out a large folded sheet of thin clear plastic and held it up.

"What's that?" Rideout asked, turning up his coat collar. The morning's drizzle had stopped but there was still a chill in the air.

"A plastic sheet," Simon remarked, stating the obvious. "There seems to be a small hole near the center." He put his finger through it.

"About the size of a knife blade," I suggested. "But wouldn't the police have found it?"

Chauncey Rideout was excited. "You mean the killer stabbed her through this to keep the blood off his clothes?"

"Such things have happened," Simon agreed. He tucked the folded plastic under his arm as the trash man went away grumbling.

Simon would say no more about his find, and when Rideout dropped us at the hotel I asked what we were going to do next. "I want to get this analyzed at a private lab," Simon said, patting the sheet.

"For traces of blood?"

"For whatever is to be found."

"How did you happen to notice it in the trash?"

"It seemed an odd thing for Miss Stigner to have—and odder still to be discarding, since it's still as good as new."

"Except for the hole."

"Except for the hole," he agreed. "While I'm doing that, I wish you would go to this pub, the Cross and Anchor, and speak with the bartender. It's increasingly important that we verify Irving's alibi for the night of the killing."

"Then you don't believe in ghosts?"

"Not unless I see one."

The Cross and Anchor was a typical London pub, located on the corner of a well-traveled street a few blocks from the Stigner house. The bar area had a number of afternoon drinkers, and I had to edge between them to order a pint of bitter. When the barman served me I asked, "Know a fellow named Doug Irving? He's a baker."

The barman, a burly fellow with muscular arms, wiped some moisture from the bar. "Oh, sure—Doug's in here evenings, before he goes to work."

"Was he in here last Friday evening?" I took a sip of my beer.

The barman turned away. "I already talked about last Friday to the police. You more of them, or are you a reporter?"

"Neither one. I'm just looking for information." I slipped a pound note across the bar.

"What do you want to know?"

"Were you on duty last Friday night?"

"Sure, I was on. I'm on most of the time. My brother and I own the place. I'm Ike Dalton."

"Glad to know you, Ike." I shook his hand. "You know Irving pretty well, then?"

"Sure, I know him. Known him for years."

"Where'd he used to live before he moved in with the Stigner sisters?"

"Oh, he had an apartment over on Buckley Terrace. But he said his girl friend told him about the Stigner place and he took it. Said it was cheaper rent and closer to the bakery where he works."

"What about Friday night? He said he was drinking with you after the place closed."

Ike Dalton eyed me suspiciously. "You're not checking my hours, are you? I don't want no trouble on that."

"No, I just want to know about Doug Irving."

"Yeah, we were drinking in back. I told the police that, off the record. Nothing wrong with it. The drinks were on the house. Just a sociable thing."

"Till midnight?"

"Somew'at past, I'd say."

"He kept drinking till it was nearly time to go to work?"

"Hell, he don't work on Fridays! The other baker comes in then."

"You sure of that?"

"Pretty sure. I know he wasn't working last Friday. He was going back to his place to meet some people."

I slipped him another pound. "You've been a great help. Do you know the names of any of these people he hung around with?"

"No, he usually comes in here alone. I don't know much about his friends, except what he tells me."

"Thanks, Mr. Dalton. You've been a big help."

"Come again. And call me Ike. Everybody does."

I finished my pint of bitter and started for the door. I hadn't even noticed the woman

432

in the booth until she spoke. "Buy me a pint, honey?" she asked.

I glanced down at her, ready to walk on, and then stopped dead. It wasn't her voice, with its accent verging on Cockney, that stunned me. It was her face.

It was the face of Shelly, my wife.

For just an instant I thought it might really be Shelly, following me across the Atlantic to surprise me like this; but then I realized the face was not quite right. It was a younger Shelly for one thing, looking the way I remembered her from a decade earlier. And even then the nose was not exactly hers. But the resemblance was still remarkable.

I sat down in the booth opposite her. "You look exactly like my wife."

She gave a bit of a chuckle. "Now that's a new line, mister."

"No, no, it's absolutely true! I simply can't believe it."

"Maybe I'm her sister."

"No, she's back in America."

"Does that win me a pint?"

"I think so." I stepped back to the bar and ordered two pints. Ike Dalton grinned a bit but said nothing. He'd seen it all before.

When I returned to the booth the woman

introduced herself. "Mine's Milly Yeats. What's yours?"

I told her my name, still half stunned by the resemblance to Shelly. "Do you come here often?" I asked.

"This is my first time. I'm in West Kensington. Don't get up this way very often."

"What brought you here today?"

She smiled coolly. "Maybe I was following you."

"Oh, come now!" But I felt an uneasiness at the thought. I remembered the birds at Anna Stigner's house and wondered if ghosts ever walked by daylight, in English pubs.

"Why did you come to London?" Milly Yeats asked.

"I'm here with a friend."

"Girl friend?"

"Hardly! I told you I was married."

"Handsome chap like you can still have a girl friend."

We talked on like that for some time, and I wanted to get away but I couldn't. We had more beers, and presently the pub closed for its three-hour afternoon break. I was having trouble standing by then, and someone helped me outside. I'd never felt that way on beer before.

Presently I remember I was in the back seat of someone's car, and Milly Yeats was leaning over me and asking, "Why did you come here? What are you after?"

I answered something, hardly able to concentrate on my words.

"Who is Simon Ark?" someone else asked me.

Presently I remembered nothing except the car starting. We drove for a long time and I heard more voices. I opened my eyes and saw it was dark.

"We'd better finish the job," a man said quietly.

Then Milly's voice seemed to swim at me out of the darkness. "No, you don't! I didn't agree to anything like that! Dump him out if you want, but you're not killing him!"

"He could tell the police—"

"He won't remember a thing! Dump him out!"

The car slowed and I closed my eyes, trying not to move. The rear door opened and rough hands grabbed me under the shoulders, yanking me out. I tensed as I hit the ground, still not certain which of them had won the argument. But after a moment the doors slammed and the car drove away.

I started to get up but then fell back onto

the roadway. That was the last I knew for some time . . .

When I came to I was in a hospital and Simon Ark was standing by my bed with Chauncey Rideout. "Can you talk? What happened, my friend?"

I struggled to sit up in bed. "It was Shelly—"

"Shelly?"

"A woman who looked like Shelly. I think she drugged me. They were going to kill me but she wouldn't let them."

Simon took a deep breath. "Try to tell us everything that happened."

I did that, repeating what the bartender, Ike Dalton, had said. Then I went on to my meeting with Milly Yeats. When I'd finished, Rideout could only shake his head. "You're lucky to be alive."

"Indeed," Simon agreed. "Do you think this bartender, Dalton, put them on you because you were asking questions?"

"Maybe. But the girl—she looked so much like Shelly!"

"This is some sort of gang," Rideout said, "but what are they up to? And why did they kill Gertrude Stigner?"

"Do not jump to hasty conclusions,"

436

Simon Ark told him. "If this so-called gang had committed one murder, they'd hardly have stopped at a second." He turned to me. "The doctors say you can be released after the drug wears off. How are you feeling?"

"Better every minute. Let's get out of here."

I tried to stand but was still wobbly. Simon helped to steady me. "You say they were questioning you. I suspect this woman slipped a knockout drug into your beer and then they injected you with one of the truth drugs like amobarbital or thiopental."

"Why? What were they after?"

"Information. They're worried we might have discovered something."

Finally I was feeling steadier, and as I slipped into my clothes Rideout phoned his secretary at the office. "Thelma, I'm at Charing Cross Hospital. I'll be in shortly. Are there any messages?"

If his secretary was in the office it had to be morning. I realized for the first time that I'd been unconscious all night. I pulled open the drapes and squinted against the morning sun. "What time is it?" I asked Simon.

"Just after nine. The hospital found your room key and called the hotel. I contacted Chauncey and we came right over."

Rideout hung up the phone. "I'm glad I called Thelma. She says that Anna Stigner phoned first thing this morning, very agitated. She wants to see us as soon as possible."

Simon rested an arm on my shoulder. "Are you up to it? Can you manage it?"

"Of course!"

But on the drive to the Stigner house I was still bothered by what had happened to me. "Put it out of your mind for the present," Simon advised.

"She looked just like Shelly—the way Shelly looked ten years ago. Even her hair was the way Shelly wore it! How is that possible, Simon?" And when he said nothing I asked, "You do believe me, don't you?"

"All in good time, my friend."

We arrived at the house to find a distraught Anna waiting to greet us at the door. "What in heaven's name is it?" Rideout asked.

"My birds! Three of them are dead!"

The news didn't seem to surprise Simon Ark. "Kitchen birds?" he asked.

"Yes, they were some of the ones I kept in the kitchen."

"And I imagine you let them fly around

438

the room occasionally while you clean their cages?"

"Yes, but—"

"I should have warned you," he said, almost to himself.

"Was it the ghost? Did the ghost kill them? There's something evil in the kitchen, isn't there?"

"Yes, but it is not a ghost."

We followed her into the kitchen and she showed us the dead birds. But Simon was more interested in the rest of the room. It didn't seem to have changed from our visit the day before, although he obviously had spotted something. He got down on his knees very gingerly and inspected the floor near the table at close range.

"What is it, Simon?" I asked.

"Nothing that I didn't expect to find." He got to his feet and I put out a hand to help him. "Miss Stigner, I need to ask a favor. I want you to tell your boarder when he comes in from work this morning that the past week's events have upset you so much you're going away for a few days' rest. Tell him you're going up to Harrogate to relax at one of the resort hotels."

"How long will I really have to be away?"

"Only a few hours if we're lucky.

Chauncey, could she stay at your house, just for this evening?"

"Certainly!"

"But not a word of this to anyone! We're very close to finding the killer now, and getting to the bottom of this entire business."

"I hope so," I said. "Where will we be going, Simon?"

He smiled. "We'll be staying right here. I don't want anyone who's watching the house to see us enter later in the day."

"You mean—"

"I mean we'll be here tonight to see what happens in Miss Stigner's absence."

We hid ourselves in an upstairs bedroom as soon as Douglas Irving made his appearance. It was a long afternoon and once Anna Stigner had departed, the big house seemed strangely desolate. The constantly chirping birds did nothing to dispel the feeling, at least for me.

"We're to remain here until evening?" I asked Simon quietly, munching on a sandwich Anna had left for us.

"Correct. Irving must be convinced he's perfectly safe and alone in the house."

"Then you believe him to be the killer?"

"I didn't say that. I believe him to be in

charge of the strange happenings in the kitchen."

"What are they—ghosts, devil worship? That table he built could be an altar." I took another bite of the thin sandwich. "And what killed the birds?"

"Freedom, in a sense."

"Stop talking in riddles, Simon! If I'm going to be stuck here all day you can at least give me a few facts."

"Very well," he agreed with a sigh. "What do you want to know?"

"That woman, Milly Yeats—the one who looks like Shelly. How was it possible that one of the gang—if there is a gang—could so resemble my wife?"

Simon leaned back in his chair. "Nothing supernatural about that. Many men carry a picture of their wives in their wallet."

"My wallet!" I started to reach for it and then remembered it was gone. "You mean the man who stole my wallet at the airport was—"

"Part of this so-called gang? Yes, I think so. You said her appearance and hair style were the way Shelly looked years ago. The way she looked in the photo you carried in the wallet—correct?"

"My God, Simon, I never thought of that!"

"They stole your wallet to find out who you were, what you were doing here. But the wallet contained no incriminating identification—only a picture of your wife. By chance they knew someone who resembled her, and with some makeup and a change in hair styling they made her look like the picture of Shelly. It was enough to grab your attention so this Milly could drug you and they could question you further. I suspect Milly will prove to be a prostitute or some sort of shady character."

"I think she saved my life, Simon. They wanted to kill me but she wouldn't let them."

There was a creaking on the stairs and Simon motioned me to silence. We waited, barely breathing, as we heard doors opening down the hall. "He's checking the rooms," Simon whispered. "Quickly, into the closet."

We huddled in the darkness, up against some musty coats, as our bedroom door opened and then closed again. After a time we heard steps going back downstairs. "He's not taking any chances," I whispered.

"We may not have much longer to wait."

About an hour later the doorbell rang and we heard low voices in the downstairs hall. Then there was silence again, for nearly another hour. It was almost evening when a car

442

pulled up across the street and we saw three shadowy figures emerge. They came quickly toward the house and the doorbell sounded again.

"This is it," Simon said. "Come on—but very quietly!"

We left our hiding place and crept out to the top of the stairs. As the evening shadows lengthened in the house, the birds had quieted down. In the upper hall Simon covered their cages so our presence wouldn't stir them up again. The downstairs seemed almost dark now, though there was a glow of light from the hallway leading to the kitchen.

We moved slowly down the stairs, well aware of their tendency to creak. I tested each tread lightly and stepped over the worst of them, helping Simon to do likewise. Finally we were at the bottom, and made our way down the hall to the kitchen.

I'd expected some devilish rites, or a sinister meeting at the very least. But what we saw was prosaic in the extreme—four men in bakers' whites standing around the kitchen table. A sheet of clear plastic had been spread across the table, and several small mounds of flour emptied on it. I might have been standing in the back room of the corner bakery.

It was Irving who whirled around and saw

us. For just an instant there was a trace of panic on his face. Then he relaxed and said, "Simon Ark, isn't it? And your friend. What are you doing here? I thought the house was empty."

"We came to watch," Simon explained simply. "And to solve a murder."

The other three men were older than Irving, and one of them was a mousy little fellow who looked familiar. "Simon," I said, suddenly remembering, "he looks like the fellow who bumped into me at the airport when my wallet was stolen!"

"I never—" the man began, but Simon cut him short.

"I'm sure it's the same person. They needed to know what we'd come for. They must have suspected we were drug-enforcement agents of some sort."

"Drugs?"

"Of course. Did you suppose merely because they are dressed like bakers that is flour on the table? It is pure cocaine, waiting to be cut and no doubt distributed through Irving's bakery."

That was when the mousy little man drew a pistol from beneath his white jacket. "We should have killed them earlier," he said. "This time I'll do it myself."

Simon Ark held up his hands, as if to deflect the bullets. "It would be unwise to shoot us until you hear what I have to say. It should be very important to you."

I was dumfounded by the turn of events. "How did you know it was cocaine, Simon?"

"There were traces of it on that plastic sheet I had analyzed, and the death of the birds confirmed my belief it was being cut here in the kitchen. Out of their cages, the birds found bits of the drug on the floor, ate the bits, and died. You'll remember Anna told us her sister surprised these men once with flour on the table. Only it wasn't flour that time either."

"So she found them again Friday night and they killed her," I suggested.

The mousy man cursed and raised his gun. "We've had enough talk."

"If you kill us," Simon said, speaking quickly, "the police will be certain you killed Gertrude Stigner as well. Put down your gun and I'll tell you who really killed her."

The man hesitated and Irving said, "He's trying to trick us, Harry."

Simon pressed his advantage, like an elderly schoolmaster making his point to an unruly class. "Listen to me, Harry. You're being cheated. Mr. Irving here has very cleverly connived to steal some of your cocaine."

"Don't listen to him!" Irving shouted, in full panic now. "He's crazy! He's a cop!"

But one of the men with Harry ordered, "Let him talk."

Simon strode carefully past the pointed gun and pushed aside the pile of cocaine from the center of the big wooden table. "Let me tell you a story—about bakers in Fourteenth Century London. Not many people know this story, but I imagine it's well known to London bakers like Douglas Irving here. It seems there was a baker named John Brid who often invited neighbors and others to bake their bread in his oven. They would come with their flour and put it on his table. But in the top of this special table was a small hole which could be opened from below—perhaps about the size of one of these knots in the wood. John Brid had a servant hidden beneath the table, to open the hole and steal the flour, little by little. It was said he and other London bakers stole a large quantity of flour from their neighbors in this manner."

The man named Harry peered more closely at the table top. "You mean he's been stealing my pure cocaine through a hole in the table?"

"If you need any more evidence, here's a tear in the plastic sheet, just over this knot. When the hole was opened the sheet had to be cut from below to get at the cocaine."

Harry swung the pistol on Doug Irving. "You dirty crook. I'll—"

"And," Simon hurried on, "that was what caused Gertrude Stigner's death. She didn't come upon you mixing your so-called dough. After all, that had happened before without her realizing the truth. No, this time she came downstairs to discover Irving's confederate crawling into position beneath the table. And for that she was killed."

The wooden panel hiding the end of the table suddenly swung open, and a black-clad figure tried to scamper to freedom. But Simon grabbed at it and I helped, catching a leg and holding firm. "Let me introduce Irving's accomplice, and the killer of Gertrude Stigner," Simon Ark said.

It was Chauncey Rideout's secretary, Thelma Bok.

Then a great many things happened at once. Irving dove for Harry's gun and wrestled him to the floor while Simon and I clung to our captive. The other two men decided to run, and they were at the front door when we heard the sound of police whistles. In a few moments it was all over. There were police and detectives everywhere, and in their midst was Chauncey Rideout looking aghast at his secretary. "Thelma, what in hell are you doing here?"

"I'm sorry, Chauncey," Simon informed him. "She killed Gertrude Stigner."

"I can't believe it! Did you know this all the time?"

"I had a strong suspicion," Simon admitted. "My friend's pocket was picked on our arrival at the London airport, by this man Harry who was seeking more information about us. He later had my friend drugged for the same purpose. But who knew we were arriving in London? Only you, Chauncey, because you made our reservations. Only you, and of course your secretary who always handles the actual arrangements.

"We heard from Anna Stigner that Doug Irving came looking for a room before she'd even had a chance to advertise for a boarder. Again, only you—and Thelma here—knew of the Stigner sisters' intentions.

"The bartender at the Cross and Anchor informed my friend that Irving's girl friend told Irving about the Stigner house. Who could the girl friend be, other than our Thelma here? There was confirmation in the fact that Anna told us Irving never had women visitors. Why should his girl friend stay away after suggesting Irving move here, unless it was because she was known to the Stigner sisters and didn't want to be connected with Irving?"

"That told you she was his girl, but what about the murder?" I asked.

"Remember the hole in that plastic sheet I found yesterday? That plus the look of the table Irving built suggested to me that he might be familiar with John Brid's old baker's trick. Of course the scheme called for an accomplice hidden under the table to steal the flour—or cocaine in this case. Irving's girl seemed the likely person. She would enter the house with a duplicate key before Irving arrived with the rest of the gang to cut the cocaine. They probably worked the scheme several times before Gertrude caught Thelma sneaking into the kitchen.

"Thelma stabbed her with a kitchen knife and hid under the table when Anna came to investigate. That's why Anna didn't hear anyone leaving the house. Then Thelma no doubt sneaked out while Anna was on the phone to the police. You see? Thelma was Irving's likely girl friend, and supplied the information about our arrival. The girl friend was most likely Irving's accomplice in the cocaine stealing. And the accomplice was the most likely killer, because Irving had an alibi and the accomplice knew a natural place to hide after the killing when Anna heard no one. Therefore, Thelma Bok is the most likely killer."

"But you weren't sure until she came out from under that table."

Simon Ark smiled. "No, I wasn't sure," he admitted.

One of the Scotland Yard men came in from outside, leading Milly Yeats by the arm. "I found this one waiting in a car down the street," he announced.

Simon stared at the face that was so much like Shelly's. "Is she the one who drugged you?" he asked.

I looked into Milly's eyes. "She's the one," I said quietly. And then to the detectives, "Go easy on her. She wouldn't let them kill me."

Milly stood for a moment staring at me. "I swear I didn't know what was going on. Harry just hired me to do a job. I was waiting to get paid now." Her voice softened a bit. "You got some lucky wife, fella. I envy her. You know, you and I could have had some great times together."

The birds were still chattering as Simon and I left the house. Maybe they were keeping the ghosts away.

Index of Titles and Authors

Acknowledgments

The editors gratefully acknowledge permission to reproduce the copyright material included in this volume. In the event of any error or omission, they will be pleased to make the necessary correction in future editions of this book.

"The Case of the Perfect Maid" by Agatha Christie, Copyright © 1942 by Agatha Christie. Copyright renewed © 1969 by Agatha Christie Mallowan. Reprinted by permission of (Putnam) and Harold Ober Associates Incorporated.

"Never Shake a Family Tree" by Donald E. Westlake. Copyright © 1961 by Donald E. Westlake. Reprinted by permission of Knox Burger Associates Ltd.

"The Man Who Explained Miracles" by Carter Dickson (John Dickson Carr). Copyright © 1956 by John Dickson Carr. Re-

The publishers hope that this
Large Print Book has brought
you pleasurable reading.
Each title is designed to make
the text as easy to see as possible.
G.K. Hall Large Print Books
are available from your library and
your local bookstore. Or, you can
receive information by mail on
upcoming and current Large Print Books
and order directly from the publishers.
Just send your name and address to:

G.K. Hall & Co.
70 Lincoln Street
Boston, Mass. 02111

or call, toll-free:

1-800-343-2806

A note on the text
Large print edition designed by
Kipling West.
Composed in 18 pt Plantin
on a Xyvision 300/Linotron 202N
by Tara Mc Sherry Casey
of G.K. Hall & Co.